DISCARD

CASH MONEY CONTENT

Fly Betty

Treasure Blue

A HARLEM GIRL LOST NOVEL

Fly Betty

Cash Money Content™ and all associated logos are trademarks of
Cash Money Content LLC.

First Trade Paperback Edition: February 2013

Book Layout: Peng Olaguera/ISPN

Cover Design: Emily Mahon

Front Cover Image: Getty Images .

Back Cover Images: Shutterstock

For further information log onto www.CashMoneyContent.com

Library of Congress Control Number: 2012953421

ISBN: 978-1-936-39931-4 pbk

ISBN: 978-1-936-39932-1 ebook

10 9 8 7 6 5 4 3 2 1

Printed in the United States

To Mrs. Dolly Sellers
You showed me a mother's love
when I had forgotten.
Rest In Peace.

Fly Betty

"God gave man the strength to conquer the world, but God gave woman a vagina to conquer man."

—TREASURE BLUE

Prologue

First off, let's get one thing straight. If you are a hater, a broke broad, or simply a girl who believes that a woman's place is supposedly in the kitchen, barefoot and pregnant, this book is NOT for you, so I suggest you put it down, find one of those Dr. Seuss books, and continue living in la-la land, or go wash your feet or something.

Now, for those who live in reality that are still reading I'll assume that you are none of the above, so we can move on and you might learn a thing or two.

Let me start by telling you a little something about myself. My name is Betty Blaise—that's pronounced *"BLAZE"*—I'm twenty-two, and I'm in my last year at Columbia as a psychology major. I got my own three-bedroom condo in Harlem, a 2013 X5 BMW (paid for, mind you), and all the designer clothes that'll make Kim Kardashian envious.

I'm saying all this to say that a girl got these things all

by her lonesome. Well, not everything, I did have some help but I'll tell you about that later. But if you want to know the sweetest thing about it all, I'm still single and don't need a man to justify my cause because I get it how I get it, and that's all that matters to me right now.

I know what some of you are thinking, and let me clear this up right now—I'm not a stripper, dancer, or anything else these broads call it that requires them to undress and shake that ass for a dollar. I'm not knocking their hustle, but that's not what I do. And no, I'm not a prostitute, nor do I open up my legs or sleep with men to pay my bills.

If you are still with me and want to learn more, kick back and let me share with you some of the secrets I've learned about men.

I'm what you may call a working student practicing the art of making love without taking off your clothes. Yes, fuck men, but I do it mentally, filling the void that many, many women choose not to do, and I make much more by doing it that way than I would lying on my back. If you think about it, it makes perfectly good sense. See, all you got to do is be aware of the mind of men and to understand that you not only have to stimulate men's loins, but you must also equally stimulate their intellect as well, and that's where I come in. If I could get a nickel for every time a brother tells me that's what they are missing from his wife or girlfriend in their relationship I'd be one rich bitch.

Now here's the second secret: a woman must learn to think like a man. Yeah, I know Steve Harvey put out a book with the same premise, but trust me, I was living this shit since he was hosting *Showtime at the Apollo,* so I'm hardly impressed. Let's be real. What could a nice, happily married man who's been out of the game for years tell women who are in the game, living and breathing this shit, how to play their position? Steve is telling you what he hears. That's called ear hustling, and like I said, I'm knee-deep in this shit. I could sum up in ten seconds what it took him in one book to say:

BETTY'S FIVE RULES TO ANY RELATIONSHIP:

1. *Never love a man who doesn't love you back.*
2. *Never give a man who won't give back.*
3. *Never try to keep a man who doesn't want to stay.*
4. *Never cry over a man who won't cry over you.*
5. *<u>And the most important.</u> Every man GOT to know, from the very beginning, that if they should ever disrespect or violate you for ANY reason, they MUST know you would not hesitate to leave them without looking back.*

That's all you need to know if you are just looking to have a fruitful relationship. Period!

I don't make claims to be the prettiest girl in the world, don't have natural hair flowing down to my ass, nor am I light skinned with hazel eyes, and I damn sure don't have Indian in my family like all these dumb bitches be claiming.

I'm five feet ten, brown skinned, have brown eyes, and

wear many different weaves. Just say I keep my shit tight. You can call me what you want, but when it comes to styling, I'm the black Erica Kane for real.

So, I know you must be wondering where I got all my game from. Well, I got it from my mother, talking to and observing the nature of men, but more importantly, studying the human mind. My mom in her day was the best that ever did it, and she passed all her knowledge down to me. She gave me her diaries, *The Blaise Diaries,* sort of like a family inheritance. Back in her day they called her Black Betty. I really don't know why they called her Betty because it's not even her name, so I don't know where she got that from.

Unfortunately, like all playettes in the game, somewhere down the line she fucked up and paid for it by breaking the very rules she taught me. But, trust me, that will never be me. My plan is to get my doctorate degree and never have to rely on no man ever.

My mother's downfall was that she let her heart dictate to her, instead of her head. Yes, she made a living stripping and occasionally selling her body, but my mom came from nothing and had to do what she had to do to survive. Without giving up too many details, I'm going to take you into my world and show you how it's done and hopefully you can learn something from it. But I warn you, you must take caution when you use these secrets because things aren't always what they seem and you'll see what I mean.

FLY BETTY: A girl or woman, as knowledgeable in the streets as she is intelligent, and has that look and attitude that every woman wants.

BOOK 1

The Second Betty

Chapter 1

Betty Blaise agilely maneuvered her slender, almost perfectly proportioned lean body through Columbia University's crowded hallway, taking unnaturally elongated strides, accentuating her long, stunning legs. Betty had just received her final grades in Ethics, and she was livid. Outfitted in a spectacular short red dress, expensive matching silken high-heel shoes that clacked loudly with each determined step, she made students and staff members part ways, reminiscent of the cinematic biblical scene when Moses parted the Red Sea.

With a fierce, determined face, Betty rounded the corner, reached in her Coach bag that dangled precariously over her shoulder, and pulled out a transcript before she reached the professor's door. Betty entered the office in a blind anger, in total disregard of the PLEASE KNOCK BEFORE ENTERING sign that was displayed in bold letters on the door.

When she entered his office, Betty took three quick and

deliberate steps and was already at the front of his desk in the small, cramped, paper-clustered office. "Professor Dvorkin, may I have a word with you?" she huffed, trying her best to control her anger.

Professor Dvorkin wore a fuzzy, well-worn tweed jacket, a white, cheap, collared shirt, a striped tie, and pleated blue trousers from Old Navy that saw better days, and brown loafers. His entire attire looked if he'd simply woke up, dressed, and was out the door bypassing any form of a once-over in a mirror. Professor Dvorkin's round, salt-and-pepper bearded face peeked out from under the *Wall Street Journal* he'd been reading.

"Ms. Blaise, as usual, you show clear disregard for policies by overlooking the sign on my office door. Now what is it that you want, Ms. Blaise?"

Betty wasn't in the mood for hearing his normal self-righteous syllogisms and was far too riled up for formalities. She spewed her displeasure by slamming the transcript down on his desk and demanded, "I want to know why you gave me a B in your class, Professor."

The arrogant professor knew quite well why Betty was in his office and was fully prepared for confrontational meetings, as had happened with many of his students at the end of the semester when they received their final grades. He knew why his prized student, the one he was mystified by, who gave him more erections during class than any female student in his entire tenure of teaching had given him, was there. Betty knew in an instant he was feigning ignorance by the way he smirked as he examined the final grade on the transcript.

With a shrug of his husky shoulders, he said, "Yes, I gave you a B. Congratulations; you passed my course, and now have a great day."

"But, Professor Dvorkin, I don't deserve the B you gave me. I got all *A*s on every one of your tests, and I didn't miss one single day of your classes, so why would you give me a B?"

"Yes, it's true you aced every one of your tests and never missed any one of my classes, but—"

"See?" Betty quickly interjected, feeling she'd proven her point.

"—But," Mr. Dvorkin repeated, "class participation is twenty percent of your grade as well and you sat duly content in the rear of the class, never once raising your hand or participating in classroom discussions."

Betty couldn't believe her ears that something that simple had ruined her 4.0 average. He handed her a sheet of paper, and she took it. "That, my dear, is your syllabus that all the students sign at the beginning of the semester. It clearly states my requirements for my students, and class participation is one of them."

Betty stared dumbly at the paper as if it was a snake. "But . . ."

"But, Miss Blaise," he mockingly repeated, "that *is* your signature, correct?"

Betty felt her pleas grow dire as her shoulders fell in defeat and grew desperate and did something she never did—beg. "Mr. Dvorkin, please, this is very important to me. I won't graduate cum laude without a perfect 4.0 average, and if you give me a B, it would ruin my dream." Betty strived and worked harder than any student in his class, but she knew she wouldn't have a chance in hell of graduating cum laude without an A. She worked too hard and too long for anything less than perfection for four straight years and refused to let something like class participation be the determining factor, so she decided to use what got her over her whole life—her beauty and charm.

Columbia University was an Ivy League college, with some of the greatest minds from all over America vying one day to graduate summa cum laude—the best of the best—with the greatest honors. For a girl who was literally born in the gutter to a mother who was a drug addict, who later went insane, this accomplishment would be validation—redemption of her mother's sullied past.

She softened her eyes for the professor with a pouting and glossy-lipsticked mouth and cooed with all the vocal range of an innocent little girl. "Professor Dvorkin, I agree with what you're telling me, I really do, but do you think you can reconsider and discuss this further over some coffee? I know a great French bistro not far from here."

Professor Dvorkin grew an instant hard-on under his trousers. He secretly lusted over black women, mainly his students—had fantasized about them for many, many years.

He had many lewd and lascivious thoughts, and he would never risk his career or his marriage, but Betty was his most prized possession in his sordid mind.

Betty recalled how at the beginning of the semester he would compliment her by saying she reminded him of the black model Naomi Campbell. She could tell by the way she caught him staring at her during class he was probably a pervert who fantasized jerking off thousands of times to his wife's *Victoria Secret* magazine. Betty couldn't deny the fact that she and Naomi could've been twins. She'd been told that thousands of times since the age of fifteen because of her high cheeks, robust, full lips, sharp, piecing eyes, and smooth, dark caramel skin that illuminated in light.

She was the reason he arrived at his class earlier than usual, just to get a glimpse of her, front and back view, to take to memory so he could pleasure himself off that lewd fantasy. The professor was lost for words, but recovered quickly and couldn't wait for her to leave his office so he could potentially give himself the greatest climax yet.

"Ms. Blaise, save yourself from embarrassing yourself any further. The answer is no. It will be no today, no tomorrow, and no chance in hell."

Betty burned with rage within and could do nothing but stare grim-faced at him. "Accept the grade you received and move on. So, if there's nothing else, I have other students to see, thank you, Miss Blaise, and have a great day. He coldly turned back to his *Wall Street Journal,* and swiveled his chair around exposing the back of his huge head.

Betty winced from his coldness. She wanted to slap him sideways, but instead, she turned on her heels and fumed out of the office.

Betty was even more upset than when she arrived, and when she exited the campus she could hardly think straight. She wanted to cry so badly but refused to accept defeat, something she never got used to. She had to think her way out of it; better yet, scheme her way out of it, she thought, and the one way to clear her head was to go home, take a bath, and get some rest before she hit the club that night since it was Friday. But first, she had to run a few errands and had some shopping to do.

Betty jumped into her 2013 BMW X5 black-on-black Jeep in haste, slamming the door, still feeling the sting of the professor's words. She turned on the ignition, and the soulful sound of Keyshia Cole's "Love" blared through her custom-built Bose speakers. The angst that she had just seconds earlier experienced instantly subsided, and she snuggled back into her comfortable, plush seats, closing her eyes, and sang at the top of her lungs until she was purged of any anguish. Suddenly her cellphone began to vibrate. She looked at the number and decided to take it. It was Fabian.

She and Fabian had become fast friends about five years ago, and it was he who turned her on to the secret society of the entertainment world; he was a drama queen from day one, and she liked his eye for fashion, and liked him for his honesty, directness, and ability to make her laugh. Fabian was small in stature. He had honey-hued, flawless skin that any woman would die for and was an impeccable dresser. Though he was two years Betty's senior, he looked as if he was still in his teens.

They met at a listening party for a top rapper when Betty was denied access because she wasn't on the party list. Fabian took notice of her because she was carrying a five thousand dollar Hermès bag. He was curious to know how such a young girl could have one, so he talked to the bouncer who he knew very well and got her in. He was very well-connected. They'd been the closest friends ever since. He worked as a sales associate at an exclusive high-end women's clothing store on Fifth Avenue in Manhattan.

This was perfect timing because that's where she was going anyway, and she needed the hookup at the cash register. They did this for years, and it worked out sweet for the both of them. Betty would pick out five to ten outfits that she liked; the most expensive, of course, and match them with the same number of the most inexpensive pieces. Because of Fabian's eye for fashion, he would just ring up the least expensive pieces and place the expensive pieces in the bag. They made off like bandits for years, and Betty would give him a nice sum for his services in return.

"Hello," answered Betty.

"Cunt, where you at?" he questioned. "They just got a new line of Marc Jacobs and Chanel in and those shits are fierce."

"Girl, I'm on my way; I'm in my car in front of the school."

"Well, bitch, you better get it moving cause these white ladies are already waiting for them to rack, and they will be gone by the end of the day."

"All right, I'm coming. Bye."

"Bye, bitch," Fabian ended with a chuckle.

Betty never paid Fabian any mind when he cursed her because she knew he would take the shirt off his back and give it to her. She decided to take the eastside of Manhattan toward the highway, and when she approached 59th Street, she suddenly heard a lopping sound coming from her tires and pulled to the curb. She got out, checked her tires, and then cursed when she saw her front right tire was as flat as a pancake. The timing couldn't have been worse, she thought. Betty looked around in frustration but was relieved when she saw directly across the street an auto repair station. She couldn't believe her luck. She quickly scurried across the street and entered the shop as if she owned it and approached a Spanish guy who appeared to be working on the engine of a car.

"Excuse me, sir."

The man, thinly built in his mid-fifties, raised his head from under the hood and was instantly taken by the beautiful young girl standing before him. He smiled and grabbed a towel to wipe the grease off his hands and answered in a thick accent, "Yes, Mami, how can I be of service to you?"

"My car just caught a flat, and I need it fixed in a hurry."

"My name is José. Where is your car at?"

"Betty," she answered as she pointed. "My car is right there across the street."

He smiled. "I'm at your disposal, beautiful Betty, just lead the way."

Betty smiled back and was very happy that he dropped what he was doing to take care of her problem. She was used to men doing that for her since she was fifteen and knew how to handle it. He looked at the flat tire and told her to drive it into the shop. When he put the truck up on the lift and removed the tire, he had bad news for her.

"Mami, this tire cannot be repaired. You need a new one."

He spun the tire around to show Betty the large hole that was in it.

Betty closed her eyes and let out a weak sigh and asked, "Well, do you have another tire that I can buy?"

"No, this is a special type by BMW; you need to purchase a new one at the factory. But don't worry, you must have a spare one in the back."

Betty winced, and said, "No, this one is my spare from the last flat. I left the old one in my storage room. I didn't think I'd get a flat so quickly."

"Oh, Mami, you got to always keep a spare with you."

Betty knew he was right and wanted to punch herself. "Where is the factory at?" she inquired.

"On 11th Avenue by the Westside Highway."

Betty looked at her watch and cursed.

"If you got somewhere to be, I can get the tire for you and you can come back when it's ready, but you got to give me the money first."

Betty wanted to kiss him because she didn't want to lose out on the items at Macy's. "How much?" she quickly asked.

He wiped his brow with the sleeve of his uniform shirt. "I know it's over one hundred dollars so give one fifty just in case and you'll be OK."

Small price to pay, thought Betty and reached in her purse and gave him three hundred. He looked at the money and frowned.

"No, Mami, that's way too much—"

Betty waved him off. "Don't worry about it. You're doing me a favor, so I'm not taking no for an answer."

Still uneasy, he gave her a raised brow and asked with uncertainty, "Are you sure?"

Betty nodded. "I'm sure, José." She left her cell number and asked him to call her when he finished. He happily said he would. She smiled and hailed a cab and knew she just saved well over three hours time and was on her way to Fabian's boutique to do a shopping explosion. She decided to put the professor situation behind her—for now. She was sure she could make the good professor an offer he could not refuse.

Chapter 2

KNOW THE RULES . . .

There are rules to this shit and a woman will fare much better if she only knows the rules to the game—the man game. The way I see it, the more men you talk to, the more you learn. They are not that hard to figure out. See, once a man realizes that you're not a typical hoochie mama, he begins to respect you. They will no longer look at you as a mere piece of ass and become protective and begin treating you like black diamonds, and you know, nobody ever leaves their expensive diamonds just lying around like house keys. No, they guard them with their lives, and when that happens—jackpot!

After that, he will give you whatever you want just to keep you, as well as give you straight knowledge—the game, which, in my opinion, is equally as important as money—most times. With wealthy or rich men, and I'm not talking about men with old money, I'm talking about the men who became rich because of their talents, their gifts, such as athletes, or people in the music industry—they are a special pedigree altogether, and it's no longer about working harder; it's now about working smarter.

An hour and a half later, Betty walked out of the store with over five thousand dollars worth of clothing, but her sales receipt said only nine hundred and seventy-five dollars. Betty would give Fabian his cut later that night when they met up at Club Vertigo that was having an exclusive *by invitation only* birthday party for an NBA player. Betty was about to hail a cab when her phone rang—it was José. *Perfect timing,* she thought. José told her that her car was ready and she could pick it up whenever she wanted. When she got outside, however, six bags in hand, she cursed as it began to drizzle. All she thought about was not getting her hair wet as she looked around for a cab.

Betty ran to the curb as the rain began to fall harder and waved for a Yellow Cab, in a futile effort. All the cabs had occupants so she quickly gave up, opting for the train station opposed to getting her hair wet any further. Betty hadn't ridden the train since high school, and it seemed like a foreign experience. She didn't even remember how much the fare was or how to work the metro card machine, so she just waited in the long line at the Sixth Avenue line token booth. She purchased a metro card and entered the subway to the F and D line to 59th Street.

When Betty got on the northbound D train, she took the first empty seat she saw, struggling with all the bags in tow.

Relieved, she patted her hair, happy that not much damaged was done, then scanned the contents of her bags, praying the rain hadn't ruined her fine, expensive clothing. Probing through the bags, she noticed a grim, unkempt-looking man whose face was obscured by the black hooded sweater he wore standing directly in front her by the door. She could tell he was wearing headphones listening to music from the sounds that blared from under the hood. He was staring intently at her bags when their eyes suddenly locked. Never in her life had she seen eyes like his that bore straight through her— almost deathly she thought. Across from him also sat a homeless man slouched in the seat with a matted-looking jacket covering his head as he slept.

For the first time she noticed how empty the train was and cursed herself silently for forgetting how dangerous the New York City Transit System was, especially during the holiday season. She decided the best thing to do was to show no fear and match the man's stare to leave no doubt in his mind she was far from weak and damn sure wasn't a tourist. The man finally turned away and continued bobbing his head to the music he was listening to, allowing her to breathe again.

Never the fool, she lifted her purse flap and removed her keys out of her purse that had a three-inch flip knife attached to it and opened it, just in case. Betty learned from her Uncle Chubby to always stand your ground and fight to the death if she had to, but there was something about the man's presence that sent chills through her spine. When the train finally pulled into 42nd Street station, the once-empty train filled quickly with commuters scattering in total disregard of discretion in a desperate search to secure a seat.

Betty tucked her bags between her legs to give the occupants some room to pass when a loud group of teenage boys ambled in just as the train doors were about to close. They were unruly and rambunctious as they walked toward the rear of the train and passed a cluster of nervous passengers. Soon, the passengers began distancing themselves from the group and headed toward the other end of the train and into another train car, sensing they would be trouble. Seeing their fear made them grow even tougher and bolder by the second. When they finally settled in the rear of the car, one of them noticed the lone girl with all the packages—Betty.

"Hey, baby," said one of the boys, "look like you spent some crazy loot with all those expensive-looking bags you got. What you got in them?" He approached her and attempted to grab one of the bags.

"Touch my bags, motherfucker, and I'll cut your throat." She exposed the knife, letting them know she was no easy mark.

The teen paused in his tracks, unsure of what to do next until his friends began egging him on with taunts. "Oh shit, this nigga is scared of a bitch with a butter knife."

It infuriated the boy and forced him to maintain his already bruised ego. He turned and leered at Betty. "Bitch, I will take that li'l-ass knife from you and take all yo' shit!"

Betty stood up. "Then try it, motherfucker. I'm right here."

The boy stared into the determined girl's fiery eyes and

was sure she meant it and laughed it off. "You lucky you're a bitch and not a nigga or else I would take that Mickey Mouse knife and cut that pretty face of yours to leave you something to remind you of me for life, bitch, word to mother."

Betty's heart raced with adrenaline and fear, but she refused to show it and challenged his threat with her own. "Yeah, and I'll send you back to that bitch of a mother of yours in a casket. Now try me, motherfucker! Come get some."

His cohorts' laughter grew louder, infuriating the young boy even further. He feigned a smile, but Betty knew her words cut through him. He waved her off and turned to walk away, when suddenly, and without warning, he unleashed a vicious brutal punch to Betty's mouth, causing her to fall backward into her seat.

"Now, you bitch, talk that shit now."

Betty's head was spinning; she was dazed, but fear made her regain her equilibrium. Gripping the knife tighter she gritted her jaw and went on the attack and raised the knife high in the air when suddenly the young boy was snatched off his feet. The eerie man wearing the black hooded sweater became the assaulter. He began beating the teen like a rabid animal, digging hungrily into its prey with brutal and bone-breaking rains of punches on his young victim. The man grabbed the boy by his neck with a vile grip and lifted him to his feet and pulled him closer to his face. The young boy didn't know what hit him, off balance, beaten to a stupor when his assailant spoke eerily through gritted teeth.

"So you want to hit girls, motherfucker?"

The helpless boy's friends attempted to intervene by surrounding and threatening him. "Yo, let my nigga go or we fuckin' you up, man."

The man removed his hood from over his head, exposing a huge, hideous razor scar on the side of his face and scowled at them all. He didn't look human; he looked almost like a wild animal with small beady eyes that favored a great white shark. He tossed the boy he had in his grip to the side as if he were a rag doll, but, at the same time, maintained a tight, secure grip on his collar. He was not quite finished with him. "Li'l nigga, don't talk about it; be about it. Step to me and come get some."

"It's five of us and one of you, and I'm holding." The boy who spoke up first reached in his waistband and coolly gripped a small caliber pistol in front of him. He just knew the man in front of him would falter and run away as he'd watched so many men and boys before in his short lifetime whenever he pulled his piece. The man tossed the dazed teen to the floor like a piece of rubbish. To the teen's utter surprise, the man flashed a sinister, almost sadist smile and said, "Squeeze that shit." He approached the one with the weapon.

The man stared into the young boy's eyes who was totally transfixed. He was studying those young eyes, never batting an eyelid. At once, the teen was lost and unsure what to do next and turned his head toward his friends for answers. When he received none, he realized he had made a fatal miscalculation of judgment.

Whether it was pride, stupidity, or both, the boy chuckled

and said, "Motherfucker, I ain't gonna shoot you, my nigga, because a bum like you ain't worth doing life over, but me and my niggas are gonna stomp yo' punk ass out for putting your hands on my man."

The teen stuffed his weapon back in his waistline as his three friends surrounded him from all sides and smiled. "Four on one, my nigga. Fuck are you gonna do now?"

The man was still unfazed, looking from one boy to another that surrounded him and all of them ready to pounce, and said, "Oh, I didn't introduce you to my man?"

The young leader looked around the now-empty train and saw no one that posed a threat. "Yeah, where they at?" the boy responded with confidence.

The man simply pointed to the man slouched down sleeping in the seat. All the boys chuckled, when another said, "What, that bum is your help? It's only two of y'all and four of us."

They readily stepped toward the man when he answered, "That's where you wrong, my dude. It's me, my man right there, and 3-5-7."

The slouching man revealed a huge .357 Magnum from under his coat, making them all stop in their tracks. They scattered, leaving their fallen friend and fleeing into the adjoining train cars. Betty, still in a daze, was even surprised by the size of the weapon and the man holding it, who was now very alert. He was dark, real dark, with wild, bloodshot eyes that looked like they hadn't seen sleep in weeks.

The man then turned his attention back to the boy on the ground and wrapped his gargantuan hands around his collar and whispered chillingly in his ear, "Time to pay the piper, motherfucker."

He ordered the teen to stand to his feet. "So, you want to slap women, huh, my dude?"

The young boy could not answer as he eyed the floor like a child.

"So, you said she's a bitch, right, my man? I want you to spell *bitch* for me."

The boy finally looked into his face to see if he was serious and asked, "What?"

"Motherfucker!" the man snapped. "Don't make me have to ask you again. Spell *bitch*."

The man who was slouching finally stood to his feet. He was equally intimidating at first stare, with wild, tired eyes that looked as if he hadn't slept in weeks either, nappy dreaded hair, and dark black skin.

As the boy stared back at the weapon, almost losing his bowels, he quickly turned toward his captor and answered, "B—"

Before the boy could call out the next letter, the shark-faced man slapped him viciously across his face.

The boy cringed in pain, but was ordered to remain standing up straight.

"Finish spelling!" he ordered.

"I—"

Once again, the man unleashed another slap to his face until the boy finished spelling the word. The man looked at Betty and simply asked, "Hey, Ma, you want a piece of this?"

Betty slowly walked up to her attacker and stared him in

his eyes and unleashed a vicious knee to the boy's groin area. He instantly fell to the ground in pain, but Betty wasn't finished with him as she kicked him in his face and ribs. Betty was breathing rapidly when she finished with him and hadn't noticed that the train had pulled into the station. She was oblivious to all the people who were watching and applauding her. She turned to look for the man who had saved her, but he was nowhere around. Betty quickly scooped up her bags and exited the train. She couldn't help but think about the man that saved her and how mysterious the encounter had been, but in her mind she thanked him.

When Betty finally arrived back at the auto repair station, she was met by José with a smile. He was taken aback by the blood on her mouth and inquired, "Mami, what happened to you?"

Betty shook her head, and José pointed to his mouth. "Your lip is swollen and has blood on it."

Betty touched her mouth, not knowing she was bleeding. "Oh, I was almost mugged on the train, but I'm alright."

José shook his head. "Oh, Mami, I'm sorry to hear that. This is why I don't like this city anymore; we didn't have local crime back in Cuba. The government was our only enemy."

"Is that where you're from?"

"Yes, I came to New York in the early eighties. I was part of that whole Cuban 'crime wave' as your country called it."

"You mean the Mariel boatlift?" Betty inquired.

"Yes, Mami, you smart; you know your history," José said with a cunning smile. "But, don't believe everything you read, or American movies like *Scarface*. Not all the Cuban people were criminals; the majority is good, hardworking people. Back then, most of us were imprisoned for speaking out against about our conditions and the Cuban government. We revolted against them by fighting back, so whoever Castro suspected being against him was thrown in jail or executed. So, we formed, how you say, a community interest group and waged our own war against them just to stay alive."

He shrugged and finished, "But, America has been good to me and my family when we got to New York and here I am." José frowned and went to retrieve a tissue for Betty.

"In Cuba, where I'm from, the community dealt with criminals by ourselves," he said with disgust. "We didn't need the police to handle our crimes."

"So, how did you deal with the criminals?" Betty asked out of curiosity, always in thirst for knowledge.

"It was swift justice. I myself was a specialist." He saw Betty's questioning eyes. He cautiously looked over both shoulders and whispered, "Let's just say when I worked on their vehicles that once they got in they didn't get out."

José was thirteen years old when he joined the resistance and was trained to rig cars to explode when they turned on the ignition.

Betty was familiar with Cuba and Castro's history, especially their civil revolt and knew exactly what he meant. A smile returned back to his face, and then he shrugged. "But that was long time ago. I'm an old man now."

Betty nodded and thanked him as he helped her load her bags into her truck. When she got into the car, she immediately checked her lip in the rearview mirror and cursed at the sight of her wound. She sighed loudly, immediately debating whether she should risk going out in public with a bloated lip. Then suddenly, as if she had an epiphany, her eyes lowered to a slant and smiled almost wickedly.

She thanked him one last time, and he added, "If you ever have a criminal you can't handle, look me up and I'll come out of retirement only for you," he joked.

Betty waved him good-bye and peeled away from the curb.

Chapter 3

RULE #1

Be bold. A man's ultimate woman has always been the consummate "Freak in the sheets, but lady in the streets." Think about Lil' Kim, and you can call her what you want, but she made some of the hardest niggas blush when she took the microphone and told them what she wanted them to do to her sexually as opposed to what she could do to them. She flipped the game on them and played on men's weakness—pussy!

She made men think she had the world's gushiest pussy and the best head in the Western Hemisphere and all she did was cut out all that middle shit, the good girl image, and spoke her mind and told them, "Lil' Kim got the ill deep throat and how she make a Sprite bottle disappear in her mouth." She is rendering niggas silly because they never heard shit like that, and they won't have a comeback. Sounds like some shit a man would say, huh? Again, she's thinking like a man. If you think about it, a woman is not that much different from a man when it comes to thinking. For example, women scheme to get the paper, men scheme to get the pussy. What's the difference?

CLUB VERTIGO 11:45 P.M.

"Oh, look at her, Betty. Isn't that the same outfit she had on two weekends ago? Now you know that bitch is crafty," said Fabian as he and Betty sat in the lounge area of Vertigo, an upscale nightclub located on the eastside of Manhattan on Twenty-first Street. Betty nodded. After Fabian fussed over Betty's attack and her swollen lip, he started back gossiping about the regular attendees.

The nightclub hosted many industry parties and brought out some of the richest and most notable celebrities and athletes the city had to offer. On the flipside, it also attracted some of the hungriest gold-digging women the city had to offer. This is where Betty met most of her clients, and there were many to choose from in spite of the stiff competition.

There is a circle of women that are sort of a fraternity, unknown to the vast majority of people outside the industry, whose sole purpose and ultimate dream is to one day get impregnated by a famous and rich athlete or entertainer. This is their version of hitting the million-dollar lottery. They plan to be set for life by simply having a love child from one of them. There are, however, certain prerequisites and requirements to even be part of such an illustrious circle.

The vast majority of these young women are between the ages of nineteen to twenty-eight years old, whose faces and bodies are nearly flawless—in other words, they are drop-dead gorgeous and they know it. Most of these women learned about this society by default, through meeting one such wealthy suitor by happenstance at a big city exclusive party, restaurant, or an industry connection and became addicted to the money, glamour, and lifestyle. And once they had a taste of that inner sanctum, they couldn't see themselves living any other way and would do ANYTHING to maintain or achieve it, by ANY means necessary.

But, great looks and a super fine body are only a mere fraction of what it takes to snag these wealthy and highly sought-after men. Luck, timing, and persistence are also determining factors, but, hands-down, the single most prerequisite is how well they can manipulate and lie—and great acting skills don't hurt. That may sound cold and callous to some, but that is the only way to have equal footing with these kinds of men. Most of these young millionaires are arrogant and used to having thousands of women, not excluding men, cater to their every whim and beck and call. The only thing they like more than pussy is more pussy, and they don't trust nobody but their mamas, so it would take a very special woman to ever be respected by them.

Traditionally, these women aren't always friendly among the competition. They are sometimes divided into cliques, so they are downright mean and catty in the circle of women who they see throughout the party circle, time after time because it is a business for them. Still, they have to be cordial at best and maintain a high classy image and reputation and *never* act ghetto.

Betty was no such woman. She didn't need any cliques or validation because she believed she was in a class by herself, so their tradition and rules did not apply to her—her mother had ensured her of that. She made her own rules, and that's why all the other girls silently hated her.

There was another class or group of women that had few morals and even fewer values, but still had big ambition—and they were called jump-offs. These women did unspeakable sex acts and nothing—absolutely nothing—was forbidden, which made them too nasty to ever consider marrying, yet much needed because the wealthy elite couldn't get satisfied like that anywhere else, not even their real girlfriends or wives. These women knew their positions and were fine with it, so long as they got paid for their services. They were despised most next to groupies by the other upper echelon society of women who felt they were not only ghetto, but they were fucking up the game for the rest of them by settling for less—much less. The inside joke about them was that if the athletes treated them to Red Lobster, gave them a bootleg Coach bag and enough money for some Ugg boots, these women were in ghetto heaven.

If these jump-offs got involved with a NBA or NFL player, who happened to be the easiest targets, they stood to gain millions if they became their jump-offs, which was a woman who had elusive rights of sex for money whenever they were in town. They didn't care about the men having a wife or girlfriends; they knew their position and played it well. Many of these jump-offs could hit the jackpot if they came up pregnant by one of the athletes, and if that happened, they had the courts behind them. From then on, they could live very comfortably for the rest of their lives on Easy Street.

Some of these women knew their man used condoms when having sex with them, but what these scandalous women would do was try everything in their power to convince them it was safe to have sex with them because they were on the pill. If all else failed, they would prick small holes in the condoms and pray that they would come up pregnant that way. In extreme circumstances, some women would go as far as to retrieve the used condom and use a turkey baster to suction out the sperm and inject it into their vaginas, hoping to come up pregnant that way. If that didn't work, and as a last resort, they took matters into their own hands and blackmailed the men by saving the sperm for the right moment and framing them by saying they were raped and threaten to go to the police if they didn't post millions of dollars into their bank account. The person was likely married and the publicity would kill him, so a couple million was a small price to pay to keep their reputation intact.

RULE #2
After a man romances you, takes you on fabulous trips, and spends a gang of money on you, and you are still not feeling him, don't drag out the relationship. Never get greedy—just end it. No matter how close the two of you get, you got to end the relationship in a timely fashion or it will blow up in your face.

Because, despite how protective he may feel about you and how he believes you are his friend, his very nature is to feel that he still can hit that so he will never give up trying. Two things will happen after that if you don't break it off: either he will become obsessed with you and you'll end up with a stalker, or he will grow cruel and get fatal attraction on your ass.

Either way, you are fucked. To offset this, you will have to give him what I call the ninety-day rule. Three months is ample enough time to gain his confidence and a hefty sum to help out with, say, your mortgage, car note, and tuition, get it? On the flip side, it's just enough time to make a break without him catching feelings behind it.

Chapter 4

NINETY DAYZ . . .

When they arrived at the party, they were immediately given access and escorted to The Platinum VIP area. This part of the night was fun for Betty and Fabian as they watched all the desperate girls flaunt callously, vying for the men's attention.

"Great day in the morning, Betty, look at Sherri play herself out," said Fabian, as they watched one of their acquaintances follow behind an A-list rapper around the club like a puppy.

"Yeah, I see. The girl doesn't know when to stop. She should have gotten the hint when he stopped taking her calls," said Betty with a chuckle. "These chicks just don't get it. Acting like that will only make him distance himself from her."

"Oh, Lord," said Fabian, "look like the security gonna get a free blow job tonight. He's letting them in the VIP."

"Please, bitch. I see you waiting for Main Man right now, and it's way past your so-called ninety-day rule."

"Don't even try to play me like I'm a chicken. I keep my shit tight, and it's only been eighty-one days, and I'm cutting him off tonight."

Fabian turned his lip up. "Well, if you don't want him, slide him my way because I think he's on the down low anyway. I see how he look at me."

Betty simply laughed him off and responded, "Why do you think everybody is on the D.L., Fabian?"

"'Cause I know my people. Trust me, Main Man is down with the program. You may be getting a degree in psychology, bitch, but I already got a Ph.D. in common sense, from the University of Spotting Niggas on the Down Low, and Main Man graduated first in his class."

Betty couldn't help but laugh out loud. "Fabian, you were the first one complaining he doesn't like you. What makes you think he would ever want to get with you?"

Fabian quickly responded, "And those be the main ones who want to get with. Trust me, I been in the life for a long time and seen the hardest thugs you ever want to see when they in the public, but behind closed doors . . ." Fabian rolled his eyes, pursed his lips, and said, "Girl, they turn into a little fairy lifting up their tutu while bending over for you to do them."

Betty frowned. "You are so crazy."

"I'll be crazy, but if I tell you a duck can pull a damn truck, you need to shut the fuck up."

Betty chuckled loudly as Fabian continued. "But, what you need to do is direct him over to my fine ass and let a bitch like me rock his world and I'll have him quacking like a dead duck, and then he won't have to worry about your conceited ass."

Betty just waved him off. "Fabian, you are full of it."

"Anyway," Fabian remembered "where's my eight hundred dollars you owe me from today?"

Betty reached inside her purse and pulled out an envelope and gave it to him. Fabian was so excited he began bouncing up and down in his seat.

"Did I tell you we got a shipment of Chanel handbags coming in next week?"

"I'll see you then," Betty laughed. They sat back and chatted about everyone in the club when suddenly their rivals took a seat behind them chatting loudly. Betty and Fabian knew nearly every one of them, but there was always one who would simply be over the top and spiteful for no other reason but jealousy. That one was a girl named Sherri. She was young and drop-dead gorgeous. She was a regular in the music video circuit, but was renowned for even more famous oral skills and the ability to never say no. But her ghettoish, childish, and petty behavior made nearly everyone detest being around her—and she hated Betty, especially because she knew that her ex, Main Man, was with her.

"I remember when I was fucking Main Man . . ." Sherri said loud enough for Betty and Fabian to hear, trying to draw a reaction. "His dick was so big I refused to fuck him anymore. I just let him eat my pussy. He called me last night and said he wanted to fuck this gushy sweet shit, but I told him I couldn't because I just got my pussy back in shape from last time."

Betty and Fabian couldn't help but laugh at her stupidity and couldn't help from showing it. They laughed so hard that she grew vexed and said under her breath, "Black bitch," then she walked away in a huff with her friends.

Main Man was a dashingly handsome and popular rapper from Queens. He was only twenty-five years old and already had been in the entertainment business for nearly eight years with many hit records under his belt. He was known to have dated many beautiful women, mainly industry groupies or predatorial women that actively sought out wealthy public figures. He had a reputation for beefing with many rappers, and then putting out diss records. He remained in the news and in magazines, which is the reason he stayed so fresh and relevant.

Betty first saw him over a year ago at his listening party for the release of his first single on his fourth album. Tons of pretentious women were flocking Main Man that evening and literally threw themselves at him—everyone except Betty who Main Man first noticed.

He had seen her many times after that at various functions and after-parties, and she always held a high degree of class about her he thought, and he became curious that night.

Main Man sent one of his boys over to her to ask if she wanted to come over to meet and have a drink with him. Betty turned to look at who the man was talking about. She saw who it was and saw that he was surrounded by a host of scantily dressed and beautiful women. She smiled at the man and asked politely, "So, what is he drinking?"

The man smiled knowingly and answered, "We drinking Dom, baby. What do you know about that?"

Betty was not impressed. "Tell him I said no thanks," she said politely. "I only drink the top of the line champagne."

The man took offense and said, "What the fuck you know about the top of the line shit? That shit is five hundred dollars a bottle! You can stay right here sipping on that cheap-ass drink you drinking with your broke ass!"

He walked off in a huff and told Main Man what had happened and went about his business. Moments later, a bar runner came over to Main Man's lounge area with a bottle of champagne standing in an ice bucket. Main Man immediately waved at the employee and informed her, "Lady, I didn't tell you to order me any more champagne."

He examined the bottle closer and continued. "Especially that red label shit."

The employee continued placing napkins and glasses around the table. "This is already paid for."

He immediately asked, "By whom?" The bar runner gestured with her head over her shoulder. "The lady over there wearing all white."

RULE #3

Wealthy men will always remember how women treated them when they were poor and broke, versus how they are treated now that they have money—a huge difference, and they will definitely know you are only interested in them and are out for their loot, so they don't trust anybody but their mama. They are very guarded when they are dealing with women and will almost always look at you as a ho before a housewife. But, no worry, they are still a man, and they have needs.

My job is to exploit that fact and do the very opposite of what they are normally used to and what other women would do. For instance: Say you're in a club and a guy taps you on your shoulder and asks you your name. What you do is do the very opposite and ask him for his name. If he tells you some shit like, "My name is Sincere" or "E" or whatever street name they fancied back on the block, ask him what his mother calls him, and go by that. Then if you are really feeling him, he will ask to buy you a drink. Once again, flip that shit on him and offer to buy him a drink instead. This will be like speaking a foreign language to him; he won't understand it, and you just separated yourself from the hundreds of women he is used to dealing with.

Now this is important. When it comes to the number exchange, never give out your number, never; only take his. If he is really feeling you, which he is, he will be waiting for your call and that's when everything will fall into place.

Their eyes immediately honed in on Betty, and Main Man looked at his cohort he sent over to talk to her. "How much did she pay for the bottle?"

The bar runner looked at the bill receipt. "Seven hundred and fifty dollars even. That's the most expensive champagne we have in the house. Dom Pérignon Rose."

Main Man was speechless as he stared at Betty with even more interest. He quickly reached inside his pocket and pulled out a wad of money and peeled off eight one hundred dollar bills and handed it to her. "Give this back to her and keep the change." She took the money, nodded, and walked off.

He was baffled. Nothing like that ever happened to him before, and it bruised his superstar ego. He instantly wanted to possess or conquer the strange and eccentric woman in white. Learning from his first mistake, he went over to her shortly after and introduced himself to her formally. He was immediately smitten by her natural beauty, grace, and especially—her mind, and was strung ever since. The more they dated, he soon learned that Betty wasn't the typical woman he was used to being out with and treated her with nothing but the utmost respect.

What intrigued him the most was that she seemingly did not want or need anything from him. He saw how she lived, what she drove, and the career that she had and that rendered him defenseless because he had never met a woman like her who carried herself that way.

Betty began to show him how to manage his money better and how to carry himself better in the public and changed him into a totally different person in a matter of months. It wasn't long before he began to give her anything she wanted without her even asking. Betty knew he was sprung when he gave her her own American Express Black Card that had an unlimited spending limit. Main Man would have given her anything, she knew, but being true to the game and knowing the nature of the young, rich, and famous, it was best if she ended the relationship, the sooner the better.

When Main Man finally made his way over, Fabian whispered in Betty's ear, "All right, girl, your soon-to-be ex just entered the club. Make sure you don't leave me. I need a ride home."

Betty nodded. Fabian stood up and said, "Time for me to go on the prowl. I might wind up getting lucky and find one of those super-homo thugs up in here."

The extravagant huge club was filled with a mixture of celebrity entertainment figures and high-profile athletes, and everyone wanted to meet Main Man. It took Main Man thirty minutes just to make it over to the plush VIP room where Betty was because everyone wanted to talk to him or shake his hand. Main Man was a popular rapper that was on the come up and projected to be the next huge rap sensation, maybe even bigger than Lil Wayne one day. Though he had a platinum-selling album out and millions of fans, Betty knew that he still had a lot of growing up to do because he was a typical kid from the ghetto that wasn't used to new-found money and blew through it like it was going out of style before he met her. She taught him how to manage his money better.

Main Man greeted Betty with a kiss on the cheek and a hug and huddled close to her.

"So, how you been, baby?" he asked. Then he pulled back and took off his shades, and asked in surprise, "What happened to your face?"

Betty had totally forgotten about her injury, which she'd

tried to cover with makeup. Obviously, her makeup didn't work. She quickly lied. "Oh this? I woke up in the middle of the night and bumped right into a wall before I could reach the light switch, but I'm OK. What about you? How did the show go in Amsterdam?"

"Oh shit, that shit was the bomb! We wrecked it. And the weed out there, that shit is legal! I'm talking about weed bars and everything. We stayed fucked up."

Betty put her head down and wondered why that was the only thing he did in all of Amsterdam when he could have visited such places as the Anne Frank house, the canals' seven bridges, or the Rembrandt house. It perturbed her that he didn't capitalize on these once-in-a-lifetime things, yet all he talked about was the weed bars. She couldn't wait to get everything over with tonight because he always worked her nerves with all his shallow and banal conversations.

"You should have came with me like I asked you to," Main Man told her.

"Thanks, but you know I got school and finals were going on."

"Oh, yeah, how did you do this semester?"

Betty was surprised he asked because all the time they were together, he only talked about himself. But Betty didn't mind; she wanted it that way; less said is more in a male-female relationship.

"I got all *A*s in my classes, except one of them. I got a *B* in it."

"Damn. A *B* and you're worried about that. I'd be happy if I got just one *B* and all *A*s."

Betty didn't have the strength to tell him that it just brought down her average from a 4.0 to a 3.8. She knew that Main Man would never understand and chose to let the conversation die and changed the subject.

"So, um, listen, I got something to discuss with you," Betty said seriously.

"So let's get out of here and go to a hotel so we can talk," he said with a sly smile.

Betty knew what he was driving at because he had been trying to sleep with her since they met. She always broke off a relationship in public just in case they flipped out or something, "No, Jeffrey, I'm serious."

Main Man chuckled, because Betty was the one rare person outside his immediate family, or when he went to court, that still called him by his given name.

"OK, what's on your mind?"

Betty took him by the hand. "I think it's time for us to move on from each other."

Main Man pulled back.

"With my classes coming to an end I really can't handle juggling a relationship and school at the same time. It wouldn't be fair for me or you." She could tell that he was stunned by the way he looked at her. He was the one who was used to cutting women off by the dozen, and now that the shoe was on the other foot, he didn't know how to respond.

"So . . . what you saying? Are you cutting me off?"

"I don't want to put it like that, but, I know I have to move on."

His stare suddenly turned icy as he removed his hand from

hers. "You selfish, ungrateful bitch! You played me. I took care of your ass, buying you shit and paying for your classes and damn near paid your entire car note and mortgage to show you I was real and wanted to be with you, and you do a nigga like this?"

Betty wasn't totally surprised by his response; she was used to it. She found out the best way was to be calm and not react to his words and just patronize him. "Jeffrey, I know you're upset, but would you rather me just turn my back on you and leave without saying anything?"

"Fuck you and all that bullshit you talking. I got a good mind to crack your fuckin' forehead, but I would be doing your stink ass a favor. You'd probably sue me and get millions."

Betty just remained silent because she did milk him for over fifty thousand dollars in jewelry, clothing, and money, so she just chilled.

"So, you been playing me from the very beginning, weren't you?"

"I don't know what you're talking about. I never asked you to do any of those things for me. You did that on your own."

"Yeah, but I didn't hear you saying no." Main Man stood up and wiped some invisible lint off his clothing, then stared down at her in disgust and threatened, "That's all right. Somebody gonna come along and knock you off that high horse of yours, and I'm gonna be there to watch you, stink-ass bitch. I got plenty of bitches who look way better than you any damn way."

He lumbered off in a huff and in an instant a group of

girls had surrounded him vying for his attention. He looked back at Betty and smirked as he walked off with two girls on his arms. Her job was done, and now she was scanning the club for Fabian to leave.

Betty could hardly sleep that night thinking about the grade that her professor gave her and decided that she would not take it lying down without a fight. She knew her chances of graduating Columbia summa cum laude, with the highest GPA, was all but history if she didn't get the *A*.

RULE #4

This rule is perhaps the most overlooked one. Ladies, if you pump out a baby or two, that stretch mark-free, tight body is almost nonexistent. One thing your man is never going to tell you is that that little bubble gut and cellulite ass is not attractive.

Invest in a local gym and work that ass out, if not for him, for yourself, because chicks like me will come along and make you look bad.

Chapter 5

She arrived at Professor Dvorkin's office early the next morning, wearing an outfit that she would normally never be caught dead in. She knocked on the office door and heard his voice telling her to enter. She opened the door and walked in. He was busy reading a copy of the *New York Times* newspaper and lifted his head from behind it and gave her a knowing smile and asked smugly, "What is it I can do for you now, Ms. Blaise?"

Betty folded her arms, despising his arrogant smile. "I want to discuss my grade again."

"Ms. Blaise, I already told you yesterday the reason for your grade, so that should be the end of it. All grades are final so that's all, now have a good day." Professor Dvorkin continued with his article by burying his head back into the newspaper. Betty simply stood there. After a few moments, the professor peeked his head out from behind the newspaper again and stated, "I said that will be all, Ms. Blaise."

Betty was unmoved and remained silent. The professor sighed and was about to speak when Betty said, "Professor Dvorkin, it would be in your best interest if you would listen to what I have to say and change my grade to the *A* that I earned and deserve."

The professor was amused and chuckled. "Excuse me?"

Betty nodded and replied, "You heard me."

He put down the newspaper and removed his glasses and said seriously, "I am doing neither. So, please leave my office now before I call security."

Betty only smirked and suggested, "You do just that, but in the meantime, let me tell you a story. It's a story about a young, impressionable student and a dashingly, mature older professor."

The professor sat back in his chair to listen to where she was going with this as Betty continued. "Earlier in the semester, this professor would compliment the young student on how well she was doing in his class and soon after, he began to compliment her on how she looked. This went on for months, and each time the professor would get bolder with his advances until one day the student had enough and threatened to report the incident if it persisted. Well, it was safe to say that the advances by the professor ceased, and the two never exchanged words after that incident. That was, until the day the student received her final grade in his class and decided to confront the professor because she felt the grade was unfair."

The professor had enough. "Ms. Blaise, I have never, and will never conform to idle threats or coercion. You are already facing expulsion by even attempting to do that—especially with me. I have an impeccable record in my seventeen-year tenure with this university, and I refuse to back down to a person of the likes of you."

He grabbed the phone on his desk and warned, "Now, I will be calling security, so I would suggest you wait here and deal with them now rather than later."

Betty slowly removed the bag off her shoulder and smiled wickedly at the professor. "I guess you have to do what you got to do, but believe me, I think you want to hear the ending." Betty began running her fingers through her normally immaculately coiffured hair until it was frizzy and in disarray.

The professor was still unmoved and dialed the operator. "Yes, this is Professor Dvorkin in room 601. Place me to security please."

Betty simply continued. "The young student continued resisting his advances and that's when he grabbed her and began ripping away her clothing." She began to rip the worn shirt she was wearing, exposing her bra. Professor Dvorkin could not believe what he was seeing and stared at her with utter confusion as she stared directly back into his bulging eyes as she continued telling the believable tale.

"The young student desperately tried to run and thwart his advances, but he was much too powerful and threw her on his desk." Betty began swiping off all his books and papers that were on his desk onto the floor.

The professor was frozen in despair; still in too much

shock to even speak as he watched the normally reserved girl in front of him, who never even so much as uttered a single word in his class, turn into a demonized lioness. Betty refused to relent.

"The professor tried to force her into submission, but she fought and begged, pleading with him to stop, but the sexual frenzied professor only grew angrier and that's when he began using brute force and began beating her."

Betty began punching herself viciously with a closed fist to her mouth, the same area of the wound that she received from the train incident, causing it to reopen and spew fresh blood in her mouth. The educator could only stare back at her with disdain and sheer horror. Betty smiled wickedly, exposing her once-sparkling white teeth that had now turned crimson red from her blood.

"Then imagine the police putting those icy steel handcuffs on behind your back, walking through the school with all the students staring, your former colleagues gaping at you, whispering among themselves, 'I always thought he was a pervert.' But, that's not the worst part."

A grim, sadistic smile overcame her as she continued. "After you are booked and fingerprinted, imagine being locked down in a piss-and-rat-infested cell at Central Bookings, with all those murderers, rapists, and drug dealers while you—or IF you—wait to get bailed out. Even if you do, do you really think this school is going to want you back here working with students again?"

With a depraved, cunning leer, Betty shook her head. "Now, Professor, you do have an option. If you're as smart as

I think you are, you can simply go to your computer and hit a button and change the *B* to an *A,* or you can risk throwing away your entire career, go to jail, and become somebody's butt boy."

There was a deafening moment of silence as the faint tone from the phone receiver could be heard.

"Campus police, how can we assist you?"

The tense silence was broken when Betty interjected, "Your call, Professor Butt Boy."

The professor was still in too much shock to respond to his student and to the campus police that could be heard still saying, "Hello, campus police, how can we assist you?"

Finally, the professor managed to regain his composure and answered, "Sorry, I dialed the wrong number." The professor hung up the phone and sat down in his chair and looked back at Betty in a sheepish daze. He slowly turn toward his computer and began typing.

RULE #5

Be original and don't follow trends or fads. Men, especially men with money, think nothing of women that wear the trending fashion that is worn in Every Ghetto, USA. It doesn't even have to be expensive, just something that's original to separate you from the masses.

Chapter 6

THREE MONTHS LATER . . .

The summer arrived and the nightlife was ablaze with activity within the club circuit, and Betty hadn't been out on the scene in months because of her heavy class schedule. She knew she would have to get back out soon because she had to fulfill some financial obligations that had been mounting. She was down to less than twenty thousand dollars in her bank account, so she had to find a temporary male suitor to solve her problem, but she wasn't in a rush; she had some time. Betty decided to concentrate solely on her studies, and it paid off, because she finally received her formal acceptance letter into the Ph.D. program as she continued at Columbia University and would be attending that fall. Since Betty had doubled her classes since her freshman year, she would graduate in three years instead of four, and was only shy of four credits to graduate.

She only needed to complete an internship class, because she completed all her curriculum classes. This was one required class she was dreading to take because it was a community advocate position and she would either have to spend time and sponsor some children or the elderly—Betty had no patience for either, which was the reason she never took it, and it was now holding her up from getting her diploma, so she was forced to take it during the summer. Betty was still apprehensive which group she'd work with, but knew she had to make a decision soon.

On Wednesday, Fabian had an evening off and spent a full day with Betty. They simply stayed home and watched television. Betty rarely watched television, but when she did, her favorites were reality shows like *The Basketball Wives, Love & Hip Hop,* and *The Housewives of Atlanta,* which she watched religiously, DVR segments, of course. She and Fabian got a big kick out of watching the women, many of whom they knew before they got on television, and cracked up when they fought and such.

"See," chuckled Betty, "that bitch is playing herself now. She looks stupid. What makes her think that if her man don't want her now, he's going to want her after seeing her fighting over some trivial, petty shit, exposing her breasts and ass for the world to see on television? I would never let a nigga play me like that. I wouldn't put myself in that position."

Fabian pursed his lips and concurred. "Seriously, them

bitches is damn sure looking stupid. And what do them dudes see in them trifling hoes anyway? Half of them look like fleas or a moose." Fabian sighed and threw up his hands. "Anyway, I'm going to make some green tea. You want a cup?"

Betty thought about it and shook her head. "Naw, I'm good."

Fabian nodded and proceeded down the hall and into the kitchen. Bored, Betty picked up the remote and started changing stations when she happened upon a corresponding Entertaining News report.

> "This is Sherry Landon, Entertainment News reporter. History was made yesterday in the hip-hop world. The reckless and bad boy of the rap industry, Rapper Scar the Hyena, was signed to the single biggest contract ever."

A picture of the rapper flashed on the screen during a performance that caused Betty to suddenly sit up erect. She perched forward and adjusted her eyes, then yelled, "Fabian, Fabian! Come here, quick."

In a panic, expecting the worst, Fabian rushed in with a cutting knife brandished in his hand. "Betty . . . What's wrong . . . What's wrong?"

Betty didn't even turn his way as she pointed frantically at the television. "That's him, that's him!" she shouted, more excited than he ever remembered.

Looking at the television, Fabian watched a segment of a man with the coldest, deadest eyes he ever saw on a human exiting a courthouse, angrily cursing and spitting on news reporters that were taking his picture and got too close. Fabian frowned and inquired, "Him . . . Him who?"

Still excited, Betty explained, "Remember I told you a few months ago about the incident I got into on the train?"

Fabian did remember. "Is that that motherfucker who put his hands on you and tried to take your shit?"

"No, he was the one who stopped them and protected me from them and whipped the guy's ass."

"*He* was the one?" Fabian asked, more curious now.

Betty gestured with her hand for silence and honed in on the reporter.

"Our reliable sources have said that Scar, who *Rolling Stone* magazine dubbed, 'The Most Dangerous Rapper Alive,' signed a lucrative multi-album, five-million-dollar contract—the biggest contract of its kind for a new artist without even a single record or album on the airwaves. Here's a clip when they caught up with Scar right after he inked hip-hop's groundbreaking deal."

"Scar, can you tell the people how you feel about signing such a huge deal and making history?"

With a toothpick in his mouth and black hood over his head, Scar looked as if he was unfazed by the deal and all the attention and said, without even addressing the camera, "It's a'ight. I could've did better, but I understand that I have to crawl before I walk, pay my dues. But I ain't going to be happy until I get that Baby and Slim money—that Cash Money money! Until then . . ." Scar looked directly into the camera, and his black, beady eyes went cold and hard and warned, ". . . I'm putting all you fake-ass rappers on notice that I'm eatin' any motherfucker standing in my way, so watch what come out of your mouth!" and walked off.

Both Betty and Fabian turned toward each other in awe-struck surprise.

"Scar's career started on the New York City hip-hop underground circuit with several top-selling mixtapes under his belt. He made headlines last year, after being arrested for breaking the jaw of a top music producer. The case was dismissed when the producer failed to appear in court to testify against him.

"Scar and his entourage were also banned from virtually every major hotel chain in the tri-state for his erratic behavior, and he has several paternity suits pending from an assortment of women. This all comes just days after being released from Riker's Island on another assault and weapons charge from a club bouncer at a popular midtown club. Reporting from 125th Street in East Harlem, this is Sherry Landon, Entertainment News at 6."

Betty was speechless. Fabian rubbed his chin. "I heard his name before. He's from Wagner Projects on Second Avenue, but I never knew who he was. But I did hear that he was no fucking joke and that all those other rappers are scared to death of him." Fabian chuckled. "I can see why. He looks exactly like his name, a hyena with those dead eyes."

Fabian shuddered in fear again just thinking about them. He looked at Betty who seemed to still be in awe and asked, "Now, I *know* you ain't thinking what I think you thinking."

Betty, still stuck in thought, suddenly jumped up off the couch and ran to her laptop. Fabian followed close behind her and chided, "Yeah, bitch, I know *exactly* what you thinking. You thinking about going after him, aren't you?"

Betty couldn't even hear him at that point and quickly entered his name into Google and, *bingo*. She smiled. Scar's name appeared everywhere, and she began reading every article about him.

Harlem rap artist, accused of wounding eight people in a shooting in downtown Manhattan early Friday turned himself in to authorities hours later.

Calvin McGriff aka Scar the Hyena, 25, is charged with aggravated assault with a deadly weapon. He is being held on bail for $1 million. Another suspect is also being sought.

Betty and Fabian sat for what seemed like hours as they read one violent incident after another, and Fabian began to grow very weary.

"Betty, I don't know about this. They saying he is really crazy. I hope you're not thinking about hooking up with that sick individual," Fabian protested, forever the cynic.

Betty was drawn to his picture on the screen, remaining silent, which angered Fabian further.

"Betty, are you listening to me? Don't take a risk messing with a person like him who couldn't care less about himself, much less somebody else. Just look at him, Betty! Look at his beady, fuckin'-looking eyes. Look at that big-ass scar on his face. That nigga look like he would kill his own mother—if he didn't do it already."

Fabian grew angrier by the second from the lack of response and yelled, "Betty!"

Betty finally snapped out of her deep thoughts and looked at Fabian and shook her head. "No, I'm not thinking about getting with him. He just got me curious about him. That's all."

Fabian knew Betty far too well. "Yeah, that's what your mouth say, but your mind is telling you something else. Something like *cha-ching*—five million dollars worth. You can lie to yourself all you want, Betty. But you ain't going to lie to me."

Betty knew she could not win with Fabian and simply confessed. "Fuck that! Why not, if I get the opportunity to fix his life up and in the process get something out of it? Shit, that's a win-win if you ask me."

"Betty, please. You sound like you some kind of life coach or something."

Betty smiled and thought about what he said and nodded, "Yeah, that's about right. I'll be his life coach."

"Betty, I'm fucking serious. This dude ain't like all those other guys you were messing with. He's from the gutter; an orphan raised by his grandmother in wild-ass Wagner Projects. Look . . ." Fabian said, pointing to the computer screen, ". . . it says he was in juvenile detention and jail for half his life, and it says he's only twenty-five. So, that means this nigga been locked up since he was eleven or twelve years old for God knows what."

Fabian paused to see if that hit home and grew angrier by Betty's lack of response. "All right, Betty, I'm letting you know right now I'm not supporting you on this one here." Not only was Fabian Betty's connection on her expensive clothes and access to the VIP in the clubs, he was also her connection when she needed information on each and every target she went after. Betty always did thorough research on her potential victim, more so to gain the upper hand to find out their strengths and weaknesses. Pertinent information about their parents, siblings, how and where they were raised plays a huge factor in a person's life, and Betty had mastered the human mind, their perception, cognition, attention, emotions, motivation, brain functions, their personality, behaviors, interpersonal relations as a human, but most importantly, what makes them the happiest and their greatest fear.

All her life, Betty knew exactly what buttons to push in anyone to get what she wanted, especially when it came to men. But Betty knew her next mission would not be easy, and she knew she needed all the help she could get, and it started with Fabian. "Fabian . . ." Betty said in a soothing voice, "I hear what you are saying, and you are right."

Fabian quickly turned his attention back to Betty, happy that he could change her mind so quickly. "You not lying to me, are you, Betty?"

Betty stood up and assured him, "Fabian, you are my best and only friend who knows me better than anyone, and I know you are only looking out for my safety, but I'm not going to lie to you. I do want to meet him, to at least thank him for having my back that day."

With his arms folded and still skeptical, Fabian tried to read her, but all he saw was sincerity in her eyes and submitted. "OK, Betty, I'll help you, but just promise me that you won't get involved with him. I just got a bad feeling about him. He is *not* for you." Betty smiled and gave him a loving hug. He hugged her back.

When they pulled away, Fabian assured her, "I'll have my people do a background check on him and have it back to you soon." Betty thanked him as she walked him to the door. Fabian stopped short and turned around with excitement gleaming in his eyes and said, "Oh shit, I forgot, my homegirl Pebbles lived in Wagner her whole life and knows everybody and everything. Maybe she'll know something, or know someone that knows about him." Fabian sucked his teeth. "Damn, I forgot she just got locked back up recently and is on Riker's Island on skid bid." He shook his head in disappointment and assured her, "But don't worry. I still know a few people in Wagner, so I'm gonna talk to them."

Betty thanked him and led him to the door. She could see he wanted to make one last plea by the concerned expression on his face, but he dismissed it and told her good-bye. She closed the door gently and ran back to her laptop to do more research on her next subject.

RULE #6
The women who ask for nothing will eventually gain everything.

Chapter 7

Over the next few days Betty seemed to be on a mission, and for the life of her, she thought, she didn't know why she found this rapper so different from the many men she dealt with in the past. Normally, she found the alpha male type to be the easiest targets, because their huge ego wouldn't allow them to think a woman was smarter than them, and because of that fact, they never saw it coming until Betty already got everything she needed out of them, but by then it would be much too late—blindsided. Through Fabian's connection, they were surprised by how much information they found about him. The public education record on him was when he attended P.S. 92, when he was in the fifth grade, and seemingly no other record followed. All of his juvenile criminal records had been sealed because of his age and the law. They did, however, have access to all of his crimes as an adult, and it read like a seasoned criminal twice his age.

He was a downright sociopath, she determined. But, the best tidbit of information that she received came from Fabian's contact that lived in Wagner Projects, his homegirl Sean.

From what Fabian gathered from her is that nobody really knew him back in the day because everyone was too scared of him even back then, and he was also known to stick up low-level crack dealers in the projects. Scar stayed with his grandmother who happens to still live in the same apartment for over thirty years. Everyone in the neighborhood knew Ms. Clara Mae and loved her. She was a volunteer, played bingo, and socialized five days a week at the Senior Citizens Center during the week and went to church on Sundays. That was her routine. That's when it hit Betty, and she immediately put it into action to knock out two birds with one stone. She decided right then and there where she wanted to spend her summer internship. Perfect!

Betty showed up at the Wagner Housing Project Community Center early two days later with two dozen donuts and one gallon of coffee from Dunkin Donuts. She wore a simple blue Donna Karan pantsuit number, with librarian glasses and her hair in a bun. As conservative as it gets, she hoped. Though it was only 8:30 in the morning, it was already thriving with idle chatter and a festive mood. Betty's presence was immediately noticed by everyone. A woman approached with a gleaming, bright smile to offer her a hand and asked, "Is this for us?"

Betty smiled back and answered, "Yes, yes, it is, ma'am."

The woman called out to tall, older man. "Mr. Davis." That was all she had to say, and he scampered over to lighten their burden of goods from the two of them. She said, "Thank you, Mr. Davis. You can clear off one of those tables over there and place them on it." As an afterthought, she continued, "And, Mr. Davis, could you also go in the kitchen and bring out the Styrofoam cups and napkins and set them out." He happily complied.

The other members, full of glee, approached Betty and thanked her for the kind gesture. Betty hugged each and every one of them. Then she turned her attention back to the woman before her and formally introduced herself. "Yes, ma'am, my name is Betty, Betty Blaise, and I'm from the university. I'm here to meet with the person in charge, Mrs. Cathi Miller." Betty had done her homework. She knew that Mrs. Miller was a tall, butter-brown skinned, middle-aged woman and was the only paid employee there as a social worker. She was originally from Memphis, Tennessee. Betty already knew from the time she walked in who Mrs. Miller was by how she stood and gave orders. Betty knew flattery gets you everywhere so she threw in the term "in charge" to inflate the woman's ego, while also letting her know that she knew she was the boss.

Betty used this tactic throughout her life when needed. She learned that most people who are in charge, supervisors, managers, bosses, etc., are most threatened when one of their subordinates lacks respect for them or if one has the potential of taking their position. In any of those instances, they are a threat to their livelihood, and they must get rid of them at all costs. But, when you convince them you do respect them and lack the smarts to ever be a threat to them, you have mastered the art of deception, rendering them powerless without them even suspecting a thing, and once again, it is too late.

"Yes," the older woman said, wearing a huge smile. "I'm Mrs. Miller, and I'm so glad you are here. Let me show you around." Mrs. Miller took her by her arm and introduced her to everyone, who showered Betty with plenty of welcomes and hugs. She was in.

An hour later, a small, elderly woman with noticeably shiny white hair ambled in and greeted everyone with a soft smile and nod as she passed them. Mrs. Miller, still in the midst of showing Betty the ins and outs, spotted the regal woman and said, "Betty, there's someone I'd like you to meet."

Betty followed closely behind her like an obedient servant. "Betty, I'd like you to meet one of our most senior and devoted members, Ms. Clara Mae."

At that moment, Betty felt as if she just found a buried treasure. It might as well have been, she thought, because the way to any bad boy's heart is through their Nana, and Scar would be no exception. Betty put on the most loving and humblest smile she could conjure and gently hugged the small, frail woman before her.

As they pulled away, Ms. Clara Mae marveled at Betty through her thick bifocals. "Wow, if you ain't one of the prettiest interns we ever had here. You look like you could be a model." She turned toward a table where four elderly men sat and whispered to Betty, "Just, watch out for ole Mr. Johnson. He still thinks he is in his twenties and is frisky as an alley cat."

The three of them laughed. "OK," said Ms. Miller as she checked her watch, "I have a meeting with the City Pantry for more donations to our center. If you need anything else, Betty, Ms. Clara Mae is in charge and will see you through it. I'll see you both next week." They watched her race out of the center at record speed.

"OK, my dear, looks like it's me and you for the summer," said Clara Mae with a smile. She took Betty by her arm and once again, showed her around and explained how the center functioned on a weekly basis.

The community center relied on small government grants and stipends, but thrived mostly from donations around the city such as food banks and pantries. The senior citizens received a free lunch five days a week, and twice a week they were given canned goods, fresh produce, and dry products from the community. Betty was truly amazed and hadn't a clue about how much of an impact the small center had done for the community. She made a mental note to ensure that the next time she got her hands on a substantial amount of money, the center was the first in line to benefit. Betty went as far as to purchase brand-new board games, cards, a Bingo set, etc., and the members loved her for it. She brought new life into the center, for both the men and women, and even found time to give the ladies makeup makeovers. They were all thrilled. She was setting the stage for the day she would ultimately meet her target—the infamous Scar.

RULE #7

The only thing men like more than pussy is more pussy, so keep on believing that your pussy is the be-all and end-all. You can't fault a man for wanting to fuck other women. They can't help themselves. It's like asking women why they like to shop, or get their hair and nails done—it comes naturally. Put it like this. If you're young and your man isn't fucking somebody else, then there's something wrong with him. Now a man who attracts other women has it going on, so just be happy that you got a keeper.

The women who can deal with their men's nominal indiscretions of cheating every now and then are the ones who have the most lasting relationships. Trust me, ladies—you're mastering the art of wifeyhood. Just be smart and make him pay to play and get your groove on the down low, if that's how you get down. There's a saying that women are about ten years mentally older than men anyway, so, say you are twenty-five and your man is twenty-six, it basically means you are dealing with a sixteen-year-old, so allow him time to play catch-up.

Chapter 8

By the end of the week, Betty and Clara Mae were fast becoming closer than she ever expected. Betty saw in the woman a caring and endearing mother figure she never had—her own mother being institutionalized ever since she could remember. It was a new world for her. Betty had been taught her entire life to keep up her guard and vigilance when she was around people, no matter who they were or their circumstances. But, whenever she was around Ms. Anna Mae, it was as if she had no worries, fears, or distrusts. Though Betty was scheduled to sign out at three P.M. each day, she opted to stay the extra two hours daily to assist Clara Mae in cleaning and organizing the center for the next day.

It was Friday evening, the end of the week, and Ms. Clara Mae, refusing to let good food go to waste, would drop the food off to one of the many homeless shelters throughout the city. Betty offered to drive her there, but Clara Mae said she had done enough and she could handle it. Betty, however, wouldn't take no for an answer and walked her to her vehicle. Clara Mae was surprised at the size and luxury of the vehicle and joked, "I might need a stepladder just to get into it."

They finally made it back two hours later to Wagner Projects where Clara Mae lived, and Betty insisted she walk her to her door to ensure her safety. As soon as they entered the elevator, Betty was hit by the familiar, yet acrid smell of human urine burning her nostrils. She looked at Clara Mae, who appeared oblivious to the smell, and continued her idle conversation while she searched through her purse for her keys. Betty was relieved that she only had to withstand just three floors when the elevator opened and she could breathe again. Clara Mae's apartment door was the first door as they turned right off the elevator, and they went inside.

Clara Mae welcomed her into her modest, well-kept home and offered her a seat in the living room while she put on some tea. Betty smiled and looked around at all the plastic slip coverings on every piece of furniture in the living room. It reminded her of a place and time she once knew in her past. She noticed portraits that hung on the wall and stood up for a closer look.

The first picture she came across was a wedding photo, in what appeared to be Ms. Clara Mae, in her early twenties. Betty was in awe of how young and beautiful she was. She had long, shimmering, flowing black hair, wearing a pristine white-laced wedding dress, standing next to a tall, handsome man about the same age, who wore a regal black tuxedo. They seemed the perfect couple, Betty thought.

Next to it were two pictures in frames. Betty could immediately tell it was Scar in his younger years, around five or six years of age. Betty marveled at the two pictures of him and how innocent and cute he once was—nothing like the person he portrayed today. Betty continued from one picture to another, when she noticed a huge figure appear from the corner of her eye. She turned and gasped when she saw Ms. Clara Mae's grandson staring menacingly down upon her.

"Who the fuck are you, and what are you doing here?" he demanded chillingly, while pointing a huge, black weapon directly at her. Betty lost her breath, too shocked to respond, so she pointed toward the kitchen.

"Did you say something, dear?" said Clara Mae, as she appeared with a silver tray of hot water, cups, and teabags. "Oh, dear, I didn't hear you come in," Ms. Clara Mae said to her grandson, smiling from ear to ear.

Scar quickly hid the weapon behind his waistband, changing his demeanor from a savage wolf to a gentle lamb. "Hey, Nana . . ." He bent over and gave his grandmother a gentle kiss on the cheek. Clara Mae set the tray down on the glass end table and said proudly, "You're right on time too; I want you to meet a good friend of mine." She grabbed him by his bulging arm and proceeded toward Betty.

"Betty, this here is my grandson . . ."

"Grandma . . . !" Scar snapped loudly, cutting her off. He immediately apologized for his rudeness to his grandmother. "I'm sorry, Granny, but what did I tell you about strangers?" Scar gave her a long hard stare and said without bothering to look at Betty, "Calvin. My name is Calvin." Clara Mae studied her grandson and realized her infraction.

She turned toward Betty and explained. "I'm sorry, Betty, but my grandson doesn't like me meddling in his business with people, but this is my grandson . . ." She paused and looked at her grandson uneasily and said, "Calvin, this here is my good friend and coworker, Betty."

Both were too uncomfortable with how to greet each other until Scar forced a smile and extended his rugged hand and said, "Sup."

Betty finally snapped out of her momentary shock and obliged him. "Nice to meet you also, Calvin."

Ms. Clara Mae beamed proudly. "Ain't she the prettiest thing ya ever seen?"

Still uncomfortable, they simply smiled and eyed the floor. "Not only is she cute," Ms. Clara Mae added, "but she nearly finished college and is going on to be a doctor," she said proudly.

She looked at Betty and said, "My grandson is into that music mess. I tell him all the time that he should get out of that and go get a real job."

As if he heard it a million times before, Scar sighed and said, "It is a real job, Grandma." Clara Mae still dismissed him and chided, "Anyway, you take off that hat and sit down. I got some of your favorite in the freezer that I'm going to heat up. In the meanwhile, you keep my guest company, boy." Scar was about to protest, but he stopped short because he knew better and took off his hat. When his grandmother walked back to the kitchen, his eyes again turned cold and darted toward Betty. He said, "I hope you ain't here to gas my grandmother's head up just so you can get close to me. That's been done before so I suggest you get your ass up out of here now if that's what you came for."

Betty stared at him with displeasure and said with attitude, "First of all, what type of disrespectful nigga are you to pull a fucking gun on a female inside your grandmother's house, then turn around and play that shit off when she enters the room and suddenly turn into the good son? Second, what type of woman in her right mind would want a disrespectful, scary-looking motherfucker like you?"

Scar was unmoved by her words and gave her a pretentious smirk. "C'mon, Ma, you really expect me to believe that you don't know who I am or never saw me before?" There was a momentary pause and that's when Betty decided to work her game and flip it on him. "No, the question should be, do you really believe you don't know who *I* am?"

For the first time, the man looked into her eyes and began to study her. Betty watched his eyes grow inquisitive, then it hit him. "You that chick on the train that day with all them bags." Betty lowered her head and smiled with relief, then nodded. For the first time, the menacing man seemed to drop his guard and gave her a rare smile, exposing a set of sparkling white teeth. He almost looked like two different people she thought. There was a long pause until Betty admitted goofily, "I never got a chance to thank you for helping me, so, never a good time like the present. Thank you for helping me."

Before the man got a chance to respond, Clara Mae walked in smiling widely. "I see you two are hitting it off. Betty, I know it's late, but it would bring such joy to my heart to see my two favorites eat a hearty dinner."

Ms. Clara Mae and Calvin aka Scar the Hyena looked toward Betty for a response. She finally smiled. "I would love to stay."

RULE #8

Some of the richest, most powerful men in America think a certain way. All have defining characteristics and an image of themselves above everything else that will always put them light-years ahead of their competition. That one thought, that one image, that one thing is they all believe they have the world's biggest dicks.

You might be laughing or think it's funny, but it's the God's honest truth. In hood terms, this is what you may know as swag. Think about it. Even the most powerful and visible black women in America think they have big dicks—metaphorically speaking, of course, but it holds the same principles and that's the only way they made it to the top in a male-dominated world.

Tyra thinks she got a big dick, so does Beyoncé—she got a huge dick and Oprah thinks she got the biggest dick of them all—this is the REAL reason it's called thinking like a man. We know we aren't men or have a dick, but it's all about attitude and self-image of who you think you are—"I think, therefore, I am." How you see and depict yourself will be the exact way people will treat you—period! Think you're worth millions, people will treat you like millions; think pennies, you'll get pennies; think dollars, you'll get dollars. Once you master that, the rest is easy because a woman has another weapon more powerful than a nuclear bomb—it's called a vagina.

Chapter 9

After dinner, Betty wanted to help Clara Mae with the dishes, but the elderly woman insisted that she was a guest and that she should relax in the living room with her grandson. She whispered, "He needs to be around more people of your kind instead of what he's running around with now. It's just plain disgusting." Clara Mae peered over her shoulder to ensure he wasn't around and continued, "He don't think I don't know who he be bringing in here late at night when he think I'm sleep, but these walls are thin, and I hear everything."

She shook her head. "He doesn't like me talking his business, but God knows it ain't right. But a good, clean girl like you can change him; I can feel it. Calvin got some bad ways about him, but he has a good heart. He doesn't let anyone close to him in to see that. He's been like that his whole life, and now he's into this music stuff and people are pulling at him, offering him things he doesn't need." Clara Mae closed her eyes and took a deep breath. She opened them and said sadly, "I don't think I can go on if something ever happens to him; he is all I have."

Curious, Betty asked, "I saw the picture in the living room. Doesn't he have a brother?" The discussion was interrupted when Scar walked in the kitchen and inquired, "What are y'all talking about?" He was towering over them with a half smile on his face. Betty noticed that he had an uncanny way of appearing without making a sound.

Clara Mae chuckled, "Oh, she was just thanking me for a fine dinner." Betty looked at her watch. "Ms. Clara, thank you so much again, but I best be getting on my way."

As Betty was gathering her things, Clara Mae offered, "It gets dangerous around here at night. Why don't you let my grandson see that you get home safely?"

Scar rolled his eyes and said, "Grandma, I ain't no bodyguard. Besides, word is ole girl can handle herself. She is pretty good with the knife and fist," Scar joked. Betty and Scar shared a smile together for the first time.

"Nah, no problem. I got you," Scar said. Clara Mae smiled with glee and saw them both to the door.

When they got to the elevator, Betty frowned and asked Scar, "You think we can take the stairs down?" Understanding, he opened the stairway door, and they walked down the three flights together.

Outside, a group of young men were playing music and smoking blunts directly in front of the building. Betty noticed as soon as they saw Scar they immediately parted for them to get by. The music came to a cease, and each man greeted him with a nod or "What's good, Scar?" Scar returned pleasantries with a nod. Betty whirled around at the group of men and saw them staring long and hard at them, more in awe, she thought, because she was good at determining body language. There was nothing threatening about them, at least at that moment. Every few feet or so, it seemed, Betty watched as they greeted him with nothing but love and respect for one of their own, one who clearly was known as a millionaire, but he was still right there in the very hood that raised him, and he seemed to take it all in with a certain nobility, a certain air about himself, in spite of it being in the most dangerous public housing complex on the eastside of Harlem–Wagner Projects.

Betty knew many rich celebrities and knew even more about the inner-city mentality and politics, and knew they didn't mix.

History has proven that when a local makes it big and becomes a public figure—a professional ball player, actor, or entertainer—the vile elements of jealousy and envy would rear their ugly head, and they become targets of robberies. They could have been well-respected drug dealers, even predators when they were on the streets, but as soon as they achieve a certain level of fame and fortune, the tide turns and they find themselves as the mark, the target of robberies by the very people they grew up with. They suddenly realize they lost their ghetto privileges. Those privileges were revoked, and they could no longer step foot in the hood, especially alone.

But not Scar; he was a different pedigree that seemed to

dare a motherfucker step to him. Betty knew he had a gun on him, but so did every other youngster in the projects; yet, she felt safe. It was as if he hadn't a worry in the world. Scar finally spoke. "Yo, listen, I'm sorry about the things I said and did upstairs, but that's my grandma, and she ain't had an outside guest in the apartment in years, so . . ."

Betty spared him the apology. "I understand. I would have done the same, too. But, honestly, you scared the mess out of me."

He smiled and put his head down. Betty said, "But, really, she never mentioned you to me, that she had a grandson who lived with her before."

Scar shrugged and confessed, "I don't live with her. I just come by from time to time to check on her. Keep up appearances to let these motherfuckers around here know I'm still close, and not to fuck with her. Besides, I tell her not to mention anything about me to anyone."

Betty noticed that Scar rarely looked her in the eye when he talked to her. The only time he ever looked at her was when he seemed to be threatening her or someone, like he did to her in the apartment with his gun. Through her studies, she learned that people who do this hold a very poor or low feeling of self-esteem about themselves, brought on most likely because of guilt or shame of their past.

There was a loud silence until Scar asked, "So, you saying she never mentioned me to you before and you seriously don't know who I am?"

Betty stared blankly at him for a moment and lied. "No. Should I know who you are?" He stared at her deeply, as if he was searching her face to determine if she was lying. He relented with a nod of approval. Betty stopped short of asking him another question when she noticed a large group of boys, about twenty or so, walking briskly toward them as they crossed the street on Second Avenue.

It suddenly occurred to her that she was walking with what the papers dubbed as "The Most Dangerous Rapper Alive" and began to believe she may have made a grave miscalculation in her judgment, and Fabian's words suddenly came back to haunt her. She looked up toward Scar who seemed to not have changed a bit. She was sure he could see the mass of bodies. She held her breath expecting the worst.

They were no more than twenty feet in front of the mob, when out of nowhere, a huge, dark figure appeared behind them. She watched the man walk beside him and whisper in Scar's ear, and it was then her heart stopped when she noticed the man dangling a huge gun behind his back. Betty wanted to run for her life, but the Harlem in her knew that she should remain calm and show no fear. From the corner of her eye, and for the second time that night, she saw Scar's eyes and face grow cold.

They were within five feet of each other when they stopped and a boy, no older than fifteen but one who had a look in his eyes as if he saw too much death in his short lifetime, spoke first.

"Yo, you Scar?" the young boy asked in a thick Brooklyn accent. Scar scanned the boy up and down. He wore enough platinum jewelry around his neck and wrists to feed an entire project for a month. Scar knew by his swag and by the way the young gun spoke that he could only be from Brooklyn. He also knew that Brooklyn cats' main hustle was sticking up and extorting weak entertainers or rappers, so he gripped the pistol he had stuffed in his hood sweater and shrugged.

"So, what's up? You know me from somewhere, shorty?" Scar brazenly took a step forward. "You steppin' to me or something?"

"Nah, fam, it ain't like that . . ." the young boy answered rather calmly and explained. "But you and my brother were locked up together up north, and he told me I should come holla at you." His response didn't satisfy Scar, so he pressed. "Fuck all that, my nigga, I want to know who the fuck gave you a pass to roll up into my block twenty-deep?"

"My bad, and no disrespect either, but that's just how me and my niggas get down anywhere we go. I wouldn't be rolling through ya hood without an invite. That's why we supposed to meet a friendly in front of building 2370. He said you were his people and he was going to do the intro." Scar studied the short little man-child, and demanded, "Who the fuck is ya brother?"

"Big Felony from Brooklyn, homie . . . they call me Li'l Felony, and these are my niggas."

Scar studied the young boys behind Li'l Felony who looked like a pack of wolves ready to eat anything in front of them. The moment grew tenser when Betty looked over her shoulder and saw what looked like the entire Wagner Project lumbering toward them.

Leading the infantry of young black and Hispanic boys was Weeg, a chubby, bowlegged man in his early twenties that wore a permanent and menacing scowl riddled across his face. He was draped in red on red everything, from his red Yankee hat, red tee shirt, and red Uptown sneakers.

He stood directly next to Scar, mean-mugging, never losing eye contact with the unfamiliar faces before him, and gave Scar an intricate handshake, obvious to Betty. Weeg scanned the group and as if it was intuitive, he determined that the short teen wearing heavy jewelry was the leader and the one to address first. He demanded to know, "Yo, you Felony peoples?" Weeg tapped the waist of his tee shirt exposing a large bulge that was obvious to anyone it was a weapon, daring him to give a wrong answer.

Unnerved, Li'l Felony answered, "Yeah, that's my big brother. You Weeg?"

Weeg threw up what appeared to Betty as a gang sign. In an instant, Li'l Felony flashed the same gang sign back to Weeg and smiled and extended his hand and both shared the same intricate hand maneuver and a warm embrace. Li'l Felony lifted his hand and without a word, one of the boys behind him placed a long elegant shiny chain with a cross in his hand.

"Out of respect and on some grown-man shit, we brought you a gift." Li'l Felony extended the chain out to Scar who accepted it. As Scar examined the shiny piece he instantly felt the weight of it.

"That's platinum, my dude, and the cross is diamond-encrusted, brand-new, never around a nigga's neck. From the Diamond District, worth over twenty stacks. Our gift to you."

Scar's demon-like cold black eyes continued to study the

piece in silence, and then he looked up at the purveyor who was looking proud. Li'l Felony added, "I'm not on no punk smooth shit, so I tossed the box and bag it came in because I know you a real nigga."

Scar nodded. Everyone's mood changed from that point on, and they stuffed their weapons back on their person. Scar affirmed to Li'l Felony, "Yeah, yo' brother is a thorough nigga. We held shit down and represented up top."

Li'l Felony agreed with a nod and got straight to business. "Yeah, those crackers gave my brother life without parole, plus three hundred years, but I'm going to hold him down as long as I'm breathing. He told me I should get up with you and Weeg and let y'all know that if you should need anything from me and my niggas, and I mean *anything* . . ." Li'l Felony emphasized and gestured by him pulling a trigger of an imaginary weapon, "You got crazy Brooklyn hotheads to represent you in state or out of state to do whatever, whatever for you, my dude." Li'l Felony flashed a demented smile and parted his thin black jacket exposing a compact automatic submachine gun with a long clip that was concealed and strapped tightly to his small body to ensure Scar knew it wasn't just in the talk. He smirked proudly, "And so do the rest of my niggas."

In unison, the young boys behind him pulled out their weapons collectively. Li'l Felony's grim deathly stare returned. "And we are all ready to put in work in case any of these niggas try to front you. All you got to do is say who, and we gonna have that bitch of a mother of these out shopping for a casket."

The young teen's words sent chills down her spine. Betty

saw in Li'l Felony's eyes that he was a baby-faced killer that could stand by his words. Scar nodded. "All right, all right. But, listen, let me take my peoples to where she got to go. Y'all chill here for a minute, and then we'll chop it up from there."

Scar tossed the thick chain to Weeg, who caught it. "I ain't on that bling shit. That's not my style. I let my niggas shine."

For the first time, a huge smile overcame Weeg's face as he examined the expensive chain in his hand and placed it over his head and tried it on. His crew behind him gave Weeg a pound and ensured that, in fact, it wore well on him.

"My nigga Weeg will take care of y'all with whatever y'all need."

Weeg nodded. Li'l Felony crossed his arms and rubbed his bare chin and inquired, "I heard y'all Harlem cats be having some of that wavy Sour shit." Weeg's dark, sullen eyes sparkled and again, displayed a rare smile, and he reached deep inside his pants and between his legs and pulled out a huge plastic bag and said, "Like you said, my dude, 'Harlem niggas got that wavy shit,'" and tossed him the bloated bag of cannabis.

Li'l Felony smelled the exotic weed and was highly impressed and asked, "All this is sour?"

Weeg nodded and assured his newfound brethren, "That's yours, my dude, and I have five more bags just like that coming to you before the night's out."

Betty watched Scar gesture to the man who first walked toward him with his gun only minutes earlier and whispered in his ear, and he took off. Scar then turned his attention back to Li'l Felony and said, "My man went to the liquor store to cop two cases of Henny."

A smile came over Li'l Felony's face for the first time, and he nodded excitedly. "A'ight, man, we'll be here." The two groups of men and boys all converged on each other with the secret handshake and slight hugs and walked to the benches to roll up blunts.

Scar then looked at Betty and gestured with his head it was time to go. He turned around back at the group of men and boys, what now appeared nothing more than a sea of red, then stared at Betty who seemed unfazed by it all so he asked, "Yo, you held shit down back there. You didn't even blink despite all the guns that were being waved around. What's up with that?"

Betty only smiled coyly and answered, "Well, you know what they say about Harlem girls, 'You don't have a future if you never had a past.'" Betty knew she could impress him more by being mysterious, only giving him short, vague answers. She was cautious not to ask his kind any questions, because she already gathered he was the guarded type. Guys like him detest people prying into their business. Betty knew the more he talked the better off she'd be. She knew it would be only a matter of time and he would be spilling his guts, all his deep, dark secrets, and when that happens, she would be in a class all by herself.

"So, what you saying? Are you a bad girl trying to be good?" he inquired.

"Maybe, but I look at myself more as a girl who survived on her own for a long time, doing it on her own without needing nothing from anyone." They walked in silence a few more feet until Scar posed another question. "So, what are you studying to become anyway?"

"I'm going to become a doctor."

Scar stopped short, truly impressed, and repeated, "A doctor? Are you serious?" Betty nodded casually.

"You must be really smart to even think about becoming one in the first place." Scar added, "What kind of doctor you studying to become anyway?"

"I'm studying to be a psychiatrist."

Scar tilted sideways and asked, "Oh, so you going to fuck with people's minds. Be messing with them crazy-ass people."

"No, I won't be messing with people's minds. It would be quite the opposite, and I would be helping them straighten out past mental issues that may have stemmed from their childhood. You'd be surprised how many people, black people especially, who are walking around as ticking time bombs because they bottled up all those issues such as being mentally, physically, or sexually abused as children. The only reason they don't talk about is because they're ashamed of what happened to them or were taught to suck it up and just accept it and grow up, never realizing that keeping all that toxic pain and shame in them makes things worse. Then one day, could be five years or fifty years later, all those built-up suppressed secrets, pain, and guilt come out and they explode and pray to God they survive because of no fault of their own."

Scar stared at her in silence, realizing how deep and serious a person she really was about her goal and ethics and was dumbfounded. Betty realized that she may have given up more information than she liked and changed the subject with a bright smile.

"Enough about me. I noticed a little gangster boy back there call you Scar. What's that about? Is that your street name or something?"

Scar smirked and simply answered, "Something like that."

"Well, your grandmother called you Calvin, so, that's good enough for me. But, from what I know about you since I met you, that name surely fits because you damn sure remind me of Tony Montana." Scar only smiled and admitted, "Well, that's also my professional name."

"Professional name?"

"Yeah, I'm in the entertainment business."

"What are you, one of those bad boys trying to turn good?" inquired Betty.

Scar chuckled and answered, "A brother got to follow his dreams, just like you."

They stared at each other until Betty smiled and nodded, "You're right, everyone's got to have a dream."

"Anything else you like to know about me?" asked Scar.

They finally arrived on Second Avenue, and Betty asked flatly. "That guy who came up behind you. Wasn't that the same man who was with you on the train that day?"

Scar nodded reluctantly. "Damn, you don't miss shit, do you? Yeah, that's my man Diesel. He's like my manager." Scar changed the subject and looked around and asked, "Anyway, since you getting close to my grandmother, I think it's only right I get to know you too. You think I can get your number or something, and take you out . . ." he shrugged his broad shoulders, "you know, so we can get to know each other better?"

Betty peered down toward the ground, "I don't think so, Calvin," she said, shaking her head with reluctance. "You seem like trouble. I don't even know anything about you besides you have a loving, sweet grandmother and you like pulling guns on people." They both laughed.

Scar offered, "Okay, fair enough. I tell you what. Look me up and make up your mind then."

Betty studied him before she responded. "Look you up? Who are you?"

He smiled briefly and said, "I told you, I'm an entertainer. You a smart girl. You know how to use the Internet."

Betty didn't want to appease his ego, so she showed little interest. "OK, whatever, Calvin," and continued on her way.

"Yo, you want me to hail you a cab or what?" he asked.

Betty didn't respond, so he was about to call her again, unsure if she heard him when suddenly he heard *bleep* . . . *bleep,* then watched the headlights and roaring of a beautiful white BMW truck engine come to life. Betty jumped in her truck and rolled down the window, smiled, and said to a flabbergasted Scar, "No, that won't be necessary. I'm straight."

Scar walked slowly toward her and looked at the shiny and expensive truck from front to rear and said, "Damn, I didn't know they paid interns that well." He looked at the jeep again. "Either that, or your man must be taking good care of you, huh?"

"Like I told you before, I don't need a man to take care of me. I make everything happen on my own."

"Then your parents are spoiling you." He gave her a know-ing smirk and nodded, "Women always have it easy. An ugly nigga like me ain't never had shit . . . nobody ever gave me nothing. That's why I had to take mines." He smirked smugly and said, "Some people have it easy like that."

Betty looked at Scar who never looked her in her eyes. Normally she would not lose her cool in front of anyone when she was on the hunt, but he hit a nerve like no other man had been before. "First of all, I grew up my entire life without a mother or father to guide me, so in that time I learned, just like you, there's not many people in this big ole world you can rely on, so I learned to rely only on myself. So, don't get it twisted. Everything I got I worked hard to get it on my own by using this . . ." she pointed toward her head.

There was a brief pause until Scar smiled and said, "I feel you, Ma, but, damn, I ain't never heard of a sixty thousand dollar car note and insurance being paid for off of a pretty face and smarts, with no job, that is, unless . . ." Betty knew he was testing her and cursed herself under her breath for underestimating his trust issues. He was insinuating she was getting money from men, but recovered quickly. "Well, I do have my own little personal business."

"And what is that?"

"I'm a life coach."

"A what?" asked Scar, ignorant of the terminology.

"A life coach is when you mentor, consult, and counsel certain people, in my case, mostly professionals, and address specific personal issues they may have in their life, personal or professional, by examining what is going on right now, discovering what their obstacles or challenges might be, and help them choose a course of action to make their life be what they want it to be."

Scar nodded his approval and joked, "By seeing how you roll, you must really be good at what you do."

"I do all right," was her reply.

He nodded again and asked, "So, after you look me up, maybe we can talk about me being one of your clients over dinner sometime?"

Betty tossed him a sly smile and simply said, "Maybe."

"Maybe . . .? What, my money ain't green enough for you?"

"Life isn't always about money, Calvin, it's about coming to terms with yourself . . . to liberate your mind."

Scar frowned and asked "Liber-*what*?"

Betty looked up at him and explained. "It means being free."

He nodded and asked again. Scar was growing bored with all the technical stuff and spoke on a subject that he knew best and asked, "So, we gonna hook up, or are you one of the pretty girls that don't like being seen with ugly niggas in public?"

"Calvin, stop saying that. You are not ugly, and I'm not vain enough to judge a person other than by their character. I'm not that shallow." Betty saw the confused look on his face again. He hadn't understood what she meant. She made a mental note on word usage around him so that he wouldn't feel inferior, so she simply smiled and said, "But to answer your question, I'm not into dating right now, nor am I into bad boys. I'll see you, Calvin."

Betty peeled away from the curb while looking through her rearview mirror and watched Scar the Hyena standing poised, but baffled, as she drove down Second Avenue—perfect!

RULE #9

If men think pimpin' ain't easy, let them try being a woman. Early in any relationship it is the most important thing, I mean critical. The minute he sees you differently from the time you met him, things will go downhill steadily after that. Take, for instance, the relationship is still fairly new and you are not fully committed yet, but stay with him overnight or away somewhere knocking boots all weekend. He will see how you really look in the morning, and, ladies, you know what I mean. Once he sees the real version of you, your stock has declined drastically in his eyes, so I suggest either never spending the night with him or leave before he wakes up.

During your courtship, never, ever let him see you wear the same outfit twice. It's your job to maintain character and poise at all times and never let him catch you slipping. It's a hard job, but the payoffs are incredible.

Chapter 10

It was 7:35 a.m, Saturday morning, and Betty dressed slowly and meticulously, as she did on a daily basis most of her life. But, this was the last Saturday of the month, visiting day, a day she looked forward to, yet dreaded, so she was even slower with her actions. Every month for the past twenty years, Betty was doing her duties of the good daughter, the daughter of Ms. Annabelle Blaise, to her mother at the New York State Mental Institution for the Criminally Insane.

Betty had been making the trip on her own since she turned eighteen years old and hadn't missed a single visit in four years. But, no matter how many times she visited, she still had the same fluster within the pit of her stomach each and every time. She loved her mother more than life itself, but she simply never came to grips with seeing her mother withering away in an insane asylum.

Annabelle Blaise, better known on the streets as Black Betty, made national news headlines after she was arrested and convicted of killing and mutilating her pimp by stabbing him over three hundred times, cutting off his penis, and slicing his face beyond recognition. The case was so grim and macabre, she was facing a guaranteed life sentence, but luckily for Annabelle, she had a fairly wealthy cousin named Chubby, who had the best criminal lawyer money could buy, his longtime attorney Mr. Greenberg, who engineered and convinced the jury that she was insane at the time of the crime. So instead of being sent to a state prison, she was committed to a state mental institution for the criminally insane for the past twnty-one years.

Deep down, Betty knew her mother wasn't as insane as the papers and state deemed her, because she never displayed any form of insanity all the while she was visiting her growing up—she was normal. Her mother was her biggest motivator through the years, as were her legal guardians, her Aunt Vonda and Uncle Chubby who raised her.

Whenever things got tough from the pressure of school and life, Betty visited her mother. As far back as Betty could remember her mother had been telling her how important it was to get her education, to stay in the books, to be the best at everything she did so she could never fall victim to the streets like she had. But when Betty began to grow into a young woman, preadolescent age eleven or twelve, everything changed and her mother grew more intense, more serious. She knew, even back then, that her daughter had exceptional beauty and was afraid for her because of the evil that men do, and what would happen to her if she was not prepared for them.

Black Betty's history, right on down to her own mother, was that men used them up, sucked them dry, and were their ultimate downfall—they were their family curse—and she knew it and refused to let it happen to her daughter if she could help it. So Black Betty began to literally spend every waking hour studying the sociology and psychology books to teach her only daughter about the human mind and social behaviors, combined with her own street knowledge and experiences. On every visit, since the age of eleven, Black Betty would give detailed lessons to her daughter about the "Game" which was basically the games men and boys played when they want to get women in bed or use them. She developed what would come to be known as "The Blaise Diaries."

Her mother indoctrinated these principles so deeply in her daughter's mind that over those years, Betty developed a deep sense of distrust for boys when she was growing up so she never even had a boyfriend, or friends, for that matter, and concentrated solely on her education. She became guarded and vigilant at all times—she lived and died by them and would not compromise them for anything. One thing always stood out and resonated in her mind when her mother would remind her each time right before she was about to leave from their visit: "Betty, always remember, *'If ever you become a fool for love, be prepared to become a fool for pain.'*"

This visit at least had some special significance, because, not only was it her mother's birthday, but also she didn't have to make the visit alone and she was relieved about that fact.

Today she would be making the trip with her Aunt Vonda and Uncle Chubby. Though they were actually her mother's first cousins, Betty grew up calling them both aunt and uncle when the two of them stepped into her life when her mother first went away.

"Hello?" asked Betty through her cellphone. "Hey, Auntie Vonda. Oh, y'all downstairs right now? Yes, I'm ready. I'm coming down right now." Betty gave herself a quick once-over in her huge bathroom vanity mirror, grabbed her Coach bag, and she was out the door.

By the time she stepped off the elevator, her Auntie Vonda was already in the lobby to greet her. Even though they lived within three blocks from each other and spoke to each other at least twice a week, they hadn't seen each other in well over three months because of either their heavy work or school schedule.

Vonda was the regional director of a drug treatment facility called Visions. She was also an active board member for a battered women's shelter right in Harlem, so they rarely had time to see each other, but when they did, they made a day of it.

"Hey, li'l girl," said Vonda as she gave her niece a warm embrace. Betty smiled widely and closed her eyes as she felt the warmth of family in her arms.

As they pulled apart, Vonda gazed loving upon her niece with pure admiration, so proud of what she had become. "Baby girl, look at you!" Vonda shook her head, "You are looking more and more like your mother every time I see you. You're beautiful."

Betty blushed and thanked her. "What about you, Auntie? When are you going to look your age? Looking like a young Tyra Banks. How do you manage a career, bring home the bacon, and still manage to have a flawless body?" Betty joked seriously.

Vonda simply said, "Well, you know what they say, 'Pimpin ain't easy.'" They both laughed.

They held hands as the walked toward the lobby door. Vonda asked her, "So, how does it feel to be a college graduate?"

"Well, I haven't graduated quite yet. I've still got this summer internship to complete."

Vonda chuckled, "Summer intern? Oh, child, please. All you have to do is show up, smile, and put in your three hours and say, 'Have a nice day.' If that's your problem, you have none." Betty agreed. "So, where you choose to do your internship at anyway?"

"At a senior citizen center over in Wagner."

Vonda paused and questioned, "Wagner . . . Wagner Projects on the eastside?" Betty nodded and asked, "Yeah, why you surprised?"

Vonda gave her niece Betty a knowing look and said, "C'mon, Betty, who you think you talking to? I'm a college graduate myself, and even back then, everybody wanted crème internship jobs, like the mayor's office, major law firms, hospitals, or corporations, to look good on their résumé, so don't even try to play me, little girl. I know you, so what's your angle?"

Betty knew her Aunt Vonda wasn't only book smart, but

she was also street-smart and knew she couldn't get anything past her, so she fessed up and admitted, "Well, there's this guy—"

Vonda cut her off quickly, "Betty, have you fallen and bumped you head or something? Since when have you become tender tit for some dick?"

Betty twisted her lip and assured her, "Auntie, now, you should know me better than that. Let's just say, I'm working on a project right now that may prove to be advantageous to my livelihood."

"So, is this one an athlete, entertainer, or businessman?"

"He's an entertainer . . . a rapper," Betty freely admitted.

Vonda rolled her eyes and cracked, "I sure hope it's not that same dumb ass you was telling me about, what's his name . . . Mail Man or something."

Betty laughed and corrected her. "His name is Main Man, but, no, I cut him off a while ago."

"I thought you told me you hated dating rappers and wasn't going to mess with them anymore."

Betty sighed, "Yeah, you right, but there's something about this one that intrigues me. I don't know. But I work with his grandmother at the senior citizen center at Wagner, and she is so sweet. Plus this dude is about to become filthy. He just signed a big-ass contract . . . They say it's the biggest ever given to a rapper before."

Vonda simply chuckled and shook her head. "You got the mind of your mother, I swear. She always aimed for the top." Vonda got serious and warned, "I want you to be careful though, Betty. Your mother was the same way all her life growing up, always had to be the best and have the best, and you see how things turned out for her."

Betty put her head down. It wasn't Vonda's intention to make her feel bad, but the opposite. She loved her niece enough to tell her the truth, even if it hurt. Vonda lifted Betty's chin and looked her straight in the eyes and said, "I'm not telling you this to hurt you in any way, but just to let you know there's two sides to everything. Now, a pretty and smart girl like you can fool most of these men most of the time, but you can't fool them all, all the time. It only takes one."

Vonda put her hand gently on her niece's shoulder and softly said, "And that is what happened to your mother. She met that one, and I don't want that to happen to you. You understand?"

Betty nodded. "I understand, Auntie."

Vonda smiled but warned, "Listen, don't tell your Uncle Chubby about any of this. You know how he feels about you. He still thinks you that li'l girl who used to ride around on his shoulders."

Betty laughed and nodded her head in compliance. "Now, you know I don't tell Uncle Chubby nothing. He's the reason I never had a boyfriend growing up, because they knew he was my uncle and got scared."

They both laughed.

"Oh . . ." remembered Vonda, "Chubby got some money for you. Don't turn him down this time like you did before; he was upset about that last time and got suspicious. You don't want him all up in your business."

Betty agreed.

As soon as they exited the building, Betty spotted her Uncle Chubby's SUV parked right in front. Suddenly, the vehicle jerked violently to one side as she watched a huge figure exit from the driver's-side door. She smiled instantly.

"Come here, girl," he bellowed loudly from the curb.

Though Betty was a full-fledged woman, she reverted back to a child's heart and ran to her uncle's awaiting open arms. Chubby snatched his niece off her feet like a rag doll and swung her around like he hadn't seen her in years.

Chubby finally released her and took a step backward to get a full view of his precious, yet stylish niece. "Little girl, look at you . . ." he raved. "You are really grown now." Betty could only blush like a child. As an afterthought, Chubby's proud smile suddenly turned into a frown. "For real, for real, Tootie . . ." Chubby never called her by her given name because Betty happened to be her mother's nickname, so he always called her Tootie Too. "I'm gonna have to dust off my shotgun and keep more of an eye on you, I see."

Though Betty continued to smile, she knew her uncle and only real father figure she'd ever known in her life was deadly serious.

"You still doing what you supposed to do in college, right?"

"Yes, Uncle Chubby. I actually finished college earlier than scheduled and just have this internship to do which is over this summer, and then I enter my Ph.D. program."

Chubby's serious demeanor faded, and he smiled again and praised her. "I knew you could do it, Tootie Too." He shook his head. "Ya mama is real proud of you—you know that, right?"

There was an uncomfortable silence, and Vonda picked up on it and said, "Well, that's exactly why your uncle got a li'l something for you." Chubby was excited about the news and was still staring at his niece with admiration when his sister gave him a light jab to his side and reiterated, "Which is why your uncle brought you something."

Chubby finally picked up on the hint. "Oh, Tootie Too . . ." he lumbered back to his vehicle and in his hand was a brown shopping bag. He handed it to her. "This is just a little something-something for you from your Aunt Vonda and me; you know, something to help you with school and shit like that."

Betty gazed uncomfortably at her aunt who gave her a slight nod of assurance, and then she accepted the bag graciously and thanked her uncle with another hug. "Thank you, Uncle Chubby, Auntie Vonda."

Chubby beamed like a proud father and quickly said, "You deserve it, Tootie Too. We family, and we got to look out fo' one another 'cause we all we got." Vonda agreed with a nod.

"That's twenty stacks in that bag, so take that back up to your apartment and stash it. We'll be down here waitin' for you to go see your mother."

Betty complied and turned on her heels back toward her building as ordered.

Sister and brother watched their niece enter the apartment building. Chubby rubbed his chin and questioned, "Did you see how she didn't even flinch when I told her that was twenty Gs in the bag?" Vonda eyed the sidewalk and remained silent. Chubby shook his head and continued, "When she came out of the building I swore I was looking at Annabelle . . ." It was rare that Chubby got emotional because Betty was to him his pride and joy, not having any kids himself. He turned toward his big sister and admitted, "And that's what scares me, yo."

Vonda understood and gave her baby brother hope. "Come on, Chubby, you got to let that shit go and stop thinking like that. It's not your fault what happened to Annabelle, and you can't save everyone."

Chubby knew she was right, but he knew if he wasn't in prison and on the streets things would definitely have turned out differently. He inhaled deeply, turned away from his sister so she wouldn't notice the water forming in his eyes. They stood silent, entranced in individual thoughts of their cousin . . . Black Betty.

BOOK 2

The Original Black Betty:
The Story of Annabelle Blaise

Chapter 11

1990 . . .

The sun was just setting over the city of New York as the amber hue illuminated the sky in a biblical fashion. It was early for most women of the night to be on the strip, but this night was an exception. Not only was it the beginning of the month when everyone received their monthly government check, it was also Friday, when most of their potential clients got paid, so this day was considered a promising one. This day also brought out the best the underworld had to offer—the pimps, the pushers, the thieves, and yes, the women of the evening—and they all wanted to get a jump on the soon-to-be competition.

Hunts Point, a low-income neighborhood located on a peninsula in the South Bronx, was the spot choice for many local and out-of-town whores to peddle carnal knowledge—sex for sale. Though competition was thick in this cutthroat profession, most of the whores got along because they all had a common interest at stake and formed a common thread of friendship based on survival. Most girls didn't have a pimp for protection, so it was only smart for them to look out for each other by writing down the license plate when any girl jumped into a car or take note of any identifying features of any trick and commit them to memory just in case a girl came up missing, which happened often. But there would always be one, one who did not go along with the program. One who needed no pimp or any of the other girls for protection. One who went by her own rules and did not care about what others thought of her because she could stand alone—and stand alone she did.

Annabelle Blaise, her birth name, was barely nineteen. On the streets everyone called her Black Betty. Though they called her Black, it was in no way a reference to her complexion. She was a mulatto, with golden glowing skin that rivaled any *Cover Girl*'s. She was called Black Betty because of her heart—she was as cold as they came to be so young. She stood a perfect five foot seven, nearly six foot in heels, and had a swagger and sureness that made her seem even taller, with deep, penetrating eyes that burned through you. She took pride in everything she did, stemming from a complex she attained growing up poor as a child and being maliciously teased. Though she was only nineteen, she'd seen more drama than she should have, growing up with an alcoholic mother who cared more about her liquor and men than she ever did her daughter. She learned at an early age how to fend for herself.

First, it was stealing ice cream or candy from the local store, and then later on, in her pre-teens as she developed early, the power and control she had over men and boys. Her earliest recollection of her powers to earn money was when she was nine years old, and her mother's male friends would come over to their apartment. She learned how some of the men were extra friendly when she gave them a hug, or whenever she let their hands roam in her sweet spots. She loved the attention, because she never received any before that, and in no time, she figured out that in addition to that, she could even get a little change or even a dollar or two if she worked it right by running up to them as they picked her up and she wrapped her small legs around them, or bounced up and down real hard when she sat on their laps. She noticed that if they got real hard "down there," they'd always reach inside their pockets and give her a dollar, sometimes even two, for her services.

Black Betty was then on a mission soon after perfecting her skill and even started doing it to all her neighbors just so she could earn enough money to buy some clothes so she wouldn't have to get teased at school any longer. By the time she turned eleven, she'd take local boys from the neighborhood to a rooftop and charge them to see her privates and let them hump her. Never in her short lifetime did she give any thought about having sex with a boy or man for free. It always came with a fee. By the time Betty turned thirteen, she was totally on her own and basically knew everything she ever needed to know about men and boys, and used them dearly for whatever she needed—and sex was now her weapon of choice and she was ready to make them pay real money from that point on.

Usually, Black Betty and the other younger girls would be working at the strip club just up the block, The Kitty Kat Club, but today was special, and they stood to quadruple their money by hooking up with patrons after they finished stripping without needing to give the house a cut, though it was policy not to do so, though it was never enforced. Because of Betty's youthful looks, her petite, perfect body, and exceptionally pretty face, she was always the center of attraction wherever she worked. When she danced, she exploited her body like a true pro. She would end each set with her placing both her ankles behind her head, exposing her entire love box for all to see.

After she danced, a rush of men would flock around her hoping to get a bit of her time by buying her the "sucker's special," watered-down alcohol for twenty dollars a pop—ten dollars of that going in her pocket—and she had at least forty takers a night. She also worked the lap dance which brought her an additional five hundred dollars a night. The word around the club was that she was definitely worth the time because of her sexual favors, but she didn't come cheap at all. For the lucky soul who had the right money at the end of the night, she charged a minimum of five hundred dollars to sleep with her, earning her nearly two thousand dollars on a good night. The other dancers despised her because she was antisocial as well as taking the choice customers, so they left her alone.

Though she made good money in the club, it was nothing compared to the money she could make this night by working the strip—the ho stroll. Betty didn't do it often, maybe once a month, if that, but the money she could make with just one white trick, as much as two thousand dollars, was irresistible. Betty knew most white men that prowled that area were in deep search to fulfill their sexual fantasy; they wanted a black girl—the younger the better.

Though Betty was young, she knew they wanted taboo young, and she could still pass for fourteen or fifteen years old easily. They paid her dearly for the opportunity to hit it. But, Betty knew working in the club and on the streets were two different animals. She was protected by security staff if things got out of hand in the club, but working the streets was much more dangerous because you never knew who the trick really was or their true intention no matter how nice they appeared. But Betty grew up in the streets and navigated through some of the toughest sections of Harlem including Grant, Manhattanville, Drew Hamilton, St. Nick, Wagner, and Douglass projects. She had been a part of many beefs with girls and boys alike simply because of jealously and envy for her looks, coupled with her stuck-up behavior. She always came out unscathed. But, like all neighborhoods, people were always watching, waiting to expose your weaknesses, and the one weakness of Black Betty had always been and always would be the almighty dollar—she had to have it.

Today was one of those days that Betty smelled money looming in the air; she could sense it and decided that this day was a good day to go on the prowl. Betty opted to knock off early from stripping that morning, around 11 P.M., so she could still catch some action on the ho strip.

Since it was only a short distance from The Kitty Kat Club, Betty decided to walk the five blocks rather than wait for a cab. Just as she predicted, cars by the droves honked at her, all vying for her attention, but Betty ignored all of them until she reached a more populated area, so if she did get in one of their cars, they'd know that someone had seen her get in their vehicle, giving the trick something as leverage in the event that he wanted to do something wrong, maximizing her chance of survival. Black Betty was far from stupid. She always had an equalizer just in case. She was quick to pack weapons, and even quicker to use them, a knife, a pistol, or both, if she felt threatened in any way, and she surely would use them.

When Betty turned the corner on Taylor Avenue, the main strip in the industrial area of Hunts Point, which consisted of shamefully and provocatively dressed hookers that paraded around with next to nothing on their bodies—oftentimes flashing their goods to show potential Johns or tricks a prelude to what they could get. Whores were already scattered and stretched strategically throughout the street, with their pimps positioned in their nearby cars, overseeing their interests.

The pimps came alive at the sight of Betty's arrival; all knowing full well she never gave them the time of day. Betty was an independent, which was a whore that worked alone without protection—a pimp, and that was even more of a reason to pitch woo each time they saw a young potential money maker like her that would make them a future if they could only control her.

Three scantily dressed young women were all huddled together when one of them spotted Betty walking in their direction and gave her friends the heads-up.

"Oh no, y'all, don't look now, but that Black Betty bitch is back."

The two other girls turned and looked in her direction and immediately began to grimace and grumble. Though they all were in their late twenties or early thirties, they knew they might as well have been in their sixties whenever Betty— Black Betty which is what they called her—or any other young girl, for that matter, was out on the scene. Their once cheerful mood turned uncertain as their hopes and dreams of a big evening slowly began to dissipate before their eyes. Betty had more than her share of conflicts on the strip when she first arrived on the scene, but none more than with these three girls that always seemed threatened by her presence.

"If this bitch say one thing I'm gonna have to fuck her up," growled one girl under her breath low enough only for the other two to hear.

As Betty got closer, the women changed the subject and continued on with idle conversation. Betty was no fool; she saw the evil stares from way down the block and was already prepared for them if things should jump off. She squeezed her purse for assurance. As she passed them, the taller one let out a chuckle and said, "I wonder if she had her Similac before she starts lying down on her back tonight."

Betty knew it was coming and was ready for them and

refused to let anybody punk her. She turned on her heels and snarled, "I'd rather have Similac than a bottle of Geritol, you dried-up pussy old bitches."

The three girls' heads immediately pulled back as if they were hit in the face with bricks. The smallest one reacted first.

"Who the fuck are you talkin' to, bitch? Don't make me have to get ugly out here."

Betty smiled and countered, "Ho, by the way you look, your mother made sure of that a long time ago so don't blame your ugliness on me, trick."

The girl's eyes lit up even wider. "Oh, hell, no, this bitch doesn't know who she's fuckin' with." She bent over and began removing the cheap high heels she had on. All the while, the two other girls were instigating her as they coached her on and collected her shoes.

"That's right, girl, don't let that yellow bitch front on you," said the taller one who started it all. Betty smiled and reached in her purse and pulled out a switchblade and waited for her to get closer. She dangled the blade near her side, out of sight, yet open enough to let them know she had something and was ready. The rambunctious girl caught a glint of the knife's blade and had the good sense to pause, unsure of what to do next. It was a standoff until the shorter girl defiantly spewed, "Why the fuck you got to pull a knife? Give me a one-on-one, and I'll show you what's up, bitch."

Betty smirked and dangled the knife callously without a care in the world. "Bitch, what the fuck I look like fighting when I could cut you a new asshole much quicker?" Betty dropped the bag she was carrying to the ground to let them know she was deadly serious and said, "Now come get some." Her coldness paralyzed the girl instantly from going forth with her threat, unsure of what to do next.

Suddenly, a slim, well-dressed man exited from out of a white Lincoln Town Car that was parked directly across the street. He gingerly ensured that his clothing was in top order, wiping off invisible lint before he proceeded in their direction.

Rico was his name, and pimping was his game, and those were his whores.

There were commonly two kinds of pimps in the streets. One such was the gorilla pimp, who controlled his women with fear and intimidation by keeping them in line with shear brute force. Nothing was off limits when they wanted to control their whore. They used their fist, Pimp Sticks (well wrapped iron hangers), belts, and extension cords, even two by fours, and would beat them into submission, instilling deep fear in their brains.

The second was the Pretty Pimps or Sugar Dicks, which they are sometimes called. They are the ones who had the gift of gab, a silver tongue that could keep his whores in line by controlling their mind and body with mental verbosity and emotional needs. Rico was one such, and he was both pretty and sugar dick. He originally was called El Rico DeBarge as a teen because he looked like a cross between brothers El and Chico DeBarge, singers of the group DeBarge that was popular at that time because they were both rail thin and had smooth amber-hued fair skin, rich straight and curly black hair with female features, sharp defining eyes, high cheekbones and full, robust lips. He was born to a black father and a Puerto Rican mother in Flatbush, Brooklyn.

His mother, Sedona, was a prostitute since she was thirteen years old, and had him at seventeen, and it's been her and her son ever since. Rico was born Tristan Franchese and was extremely close to his mother who didn't shy him away of who she was. She fed him the reality of life and how to survive and knew that the best gift to give her only son was to master the oldest craft in the world—prostitution. The neighborhood boys would tease him and call his mother a whore and gave him the nickname "Whoreson" when he was just eight years old.

Rico never cared; in fact, he wore that title like a badge of honor because he had the finest of everything and knew they were only envious of him. By age nine, little girls would swoon over him and giggle whenever they saw him in class. They were magnetized by his presence, which his mother already told him would happen, and she prepared him for how to react and how to take advantage of it. By ten, he began charging little girls a dollar just to feel his hair, and two dollars for him to give them a kiss on the cheek.

But, by the sixth grade, he stepped up his game and income, and sweet-talked the older more developed seventh- and eighth-grade girls to work the school yard, staircases, and boys' bathroom for him by creating a menu of services to offer his male classmates: $2 for a kiss on their lips, $5 to touch their breasts, and $10 for the girls to show their audience their bare breasts or pull down their pants to show their privates to sixth-grade boys. He kept ninety percent of the take from each girl, which the girls thought was unfair, but he simply pacified them by telling each girl in private that she was his main girl, and he was holding the rest of the money to build them a future so they could one day get married and live together forever and ever. With a deep, sincere look in their eyes, a soft, gentle touch, and a sensual kiss on the cheek, they would never question him again, and would work even harder for him.

At thirteen, after his mother saw her son was an earner, she knew it was time that she laid the sex game down to her son and recruited a girl she knew from her profession, a seventeen-year-old black prostitute named Candy who had an unusually pretty face and legs that were long and slender for such a petite body. His mother was adamant about picking only the best quality for his first sexual experience which would set the stage for picking and choosing only the finest class of girls and women to be in his life. Since his mother mastered the art of how to please a man, she gave strict and detailed instructions to Candy for what to do for her son and sent them both in the room.

Almost eight hours later, the bedroom door finally opened and Candy exited from the room walking awkward and frazzled. His mother, already anxious to find out the results of her son's first sexual encounter, asked, "What's wrong, Mami? What happened?"

The young girl's eyes looked as if she was in an altered state, and she quickly said, "Ms. Sedona, I got to explain to you when I get back. I got to go to McDonald's and get

Tristan something to eat because he's hungry. He got me on a time limit, so I got to be back quickly."

"Slow down, Candy; what are you talking about a time limit? Just tell me how it went!"

Candy paused as if she was trying to catch her breath, and asked, "Ms. Vera, you didn't tell me how big Tristan was. He ripped me up down there, and I'm sore, and he said he still wasn't finished with me." She took another breath.

"I thought you said he was a virgin and *I* was supposed to show him."

His mother was proud and offered, "Don't worry, Mami, I'll pay you extra and I'll talk to him—"

Candy quickly cut her off. "No! Sorry, Ms. Sedona, but he won't like that," said the distraught young girl. "I'm OK. I can't take your money anymore; in fact, I gave him the money you gave me because . . ." Candy put her head down and then admitted, "I just choose your son's property now, and I work for him. I'm his bottom bitch."

His mother was stunned, but not surprised. Candy quickly pleaded, "I got to hurry, Ms. Sedona . . . I got to go get his food."

She then ran out the door like a bat out of hell. Mother Sedona then turned around when she heard his door open. Her son was bare-chested with a blue towel wrapped around his waist. He ambled into the kitchen without a word being spoken. He opened up the refrigerator and while looking inside he cavalierly informed her, "Oh, Ma, Candy is going to be living with us from now on. You don't have to worry about paying the rent anymore." He peered inside once more and asked, "Ma, we have anymore orange juice?"

But, one tactic above them all that most pimps used to keep their stable of whores controlled was heroin, which was more powerful than any heavy hand could ever deliver. They would start them off sniffing a little of "Girl"—cocaine which was a euphoric stimulant to keep them selling sex day and night. They'd then mix the heroin in the cocaine unbeknownst to them. It would only be a matter of time before their bodies began to crave the drug, and they'd get painfully sick if they didn't receive it on a daily basis thereafter.

Rico wasn't built for violence; it wasn't in his nature. He would slap his girls around just to maintain his presence. But he was as heartless and cunning as they come—a rattlesnake, and would outsource and hire a gun in a second if there was something he couldn't handle. To Rico, it was mandatory to string every one of his whores out, and if he felt any of his whores wanted to leave him, he would give them a "hotshot" heroin laced with battery acid—pure rattlesnake!

Rico's presence seemed to give the three whores confidence as their voices rose to a crescendo with each step he took.

"Yeah, bitch," screamed one of the girls, "what's up now? What's up now?" she repeated as she edged forward.

"Ladies, ladies," the man said with an earnest smile stepping between them, "you girls are way too fine to be out here fighting." He turned and flashed his golden smile on Betty, who he had his eyes on since the day he first saw her over a year ago and asked, "Now, what is that seems to be the problem you're having with my ladies, beautiful Betty?" He strategically wanted Betty to know that he was their pimp.

Betty didn't even acknowledge him and just remained silent and continued to give the three girls the death stare. Betty already knew that he was their pimp and wasn't about to plead her case to him. She was above him and bigger than that. She also knew from past experience that he wanted her in his stable and would often drop subtle hints to her in passing, but she didn't pay him or any other pimps, for that matter, any mind. Betty could never, ever comprehend why a woman would have use for a pimp anyway since they beat their ass half the time and took most of the money. The way she figured it, she could do badly all by herself, and she damn sure wasn't letting any man put his hands on her. Betty watched her own mother get beaten and abused by so-called boyfriends all during her childhood up until she died a slow, miserable death all alone. She was sure of one thing when she got older, that she would never let it happen to her. Betty swore on everything she loved, and that wasn't much, she'd kill the first man that ever tried.

The short girl grew louder and cockier. "This bitch always be acting stuck up like she better than somebody. She a ho just like the rest . . ." Her pimp turned, and his smile turned into a scowl.

His voice laced with his displeasure. "Bitch, was I talking to you?" He stared her down until she submitted like an obedient child and eyed the ground. He turned his attention back to Betty with an instant smile and put his hand on her shoulders. "You see, baby, you ain't got nothing to worry about as long as I'm around."

Betty looked at his hand on her shoulder, then square in his eyes and said in a sharp, cold tone, "Nigga, if you don't get your filthy, fucking hands off my shoulder, you coming back with nubs."

He was caught off guard from her iciness and watched her raise the knife he had yet to see. He quickly pulled his hand back and stared at her as if she was out of her mind.

"Damn, baby . . . why you so cold? I was only trying to help you out."

Betty didn't miss a beat and said, "You can help me out by getting the fuck out of my face, you simple-ass mother-fucker." The pimp's face turned flush. Betty was more than prepared and assumed battle position and gripped the knife tighter, causing him to rethink his earlier intention.

"All right, bitch, if that's how you want it." He turned toward the three girls and barked, "Trina, Cocoa, Diamond . . ." They snapped to attention like robots. "Two hundred dollars to anybody that'll fuck this bitch up here and now!" He peeled off two bills, both one hundred dollar bills, and threw them to the ground. The girls didn't know if it was a joke or not, because they had never seen their pimp so liberal with money and didn't react at first. He seemed to read their minds and repeated, "Bitches, I said *two hundred dollars to whoever fucks her up right now!*" Each girl reacted by reaching into their purse for their own blade or razor and kicking off their heels. Betty stood her ground unfazed, then reached inside her own handbag and pulled out an equalizer—a .38 revolver and rang a shot in the air to let them fully know she wasn't playing games and wasn't afraid to bust a cap in their ass, then pointed it at them, causing the three of them to stop in their tracks. They were completely caught off guard, and it suddenly occurred to them all why she was known as BLACK BETTY. They had made a fatal mistake.

"Now, who want it first?"

The three girls didn't wait around to answer and took off running barefoot for dear life as far away from Betty as possible.

The loud scene caught the attention of neighboring pimps and whores, who lived for the drama to break the monotony, to have something to chatter about, especially to see how a pimp handles his business.

The pimp stood his ground and watched his girls' backs turn the corner. Rico's pride and reputation was on the line and would not allow him to show any weakness, especially among the other pimps who were now lounging back waiting to see how the pimp named Rico handled his business.

To any pimp, their reputation on the streets and how they handled their whores are their résumés. The only way other pimps and whores could measure them was by how cold-blooded they could be, and if they were ever disrespected, especially by a whore, it would be career suicide, giving other pimps an open invitation to go after their whores or worse— so, how Rico handled this situation was going to make him or break him. Rico saw all eyes on him and decided to play it smooth and smiled. "So that's why they call you Black Betty."

Betty squared the gun directly at him and answered, "What you think?"

He shook his head and smiled. "Damn, I like your style. I may have misjudged you, baby. I was just trying to give you a shot at the big time, that's all, but I see you're too young to recognize your ticket."

Betty laughed in his face. "Big time? Negro, please! If that twenty-three-year-old Lincoln you drive and that forty dollar-tired suit you got on is your idea of big time, then you better go back to the seventies and take those busted crackhead broads of yours with you."

The open disrespect and slight caused open snickers from pimps and whores alike that stood by watching and hearing everything. Rico had to act and assured her so all in earshot could hear, "All right, bitch, I see you really don't know exactly who you are fucking with, but just remember, bitch, what goes around comes around."

Betty was unnerved by his open, yet vague threat and said, "Yeah, whatever, nigga. Tell that bullshit you talking to someone who cares."

Rico's pride was so wounded he bit down on his tongue till it bled. This was the one and only time in his life he had no control over a girl and was blinded by hatred toward her to the point where he just wanted to throw up, but refused to let her see just how bad he felt. Speechless, Rico decided to not further embarrass himself and deal with her later. He crouched down to collect his two hundred dollars off the ground. Betty knew she could have let it go, but her adrenaline was flowing so rapidly she wanted to make him suffer for calling her a bitch and decided to humiliate him some more.

"Don't even think about it. Leave the money where it is."

Rico couldn't believe what he was hearing, but looked at the gun pointed at him and paused. "So it's like that? You just gonna take my shit, huh?"

Betty smiled wickedly and said, "Just like that!"

Rico's ego was bruised beyond measure, but he stood tall and surveyed all the onlookers that were staring and waiting for his next move. He simply smiled and brushed invisible lint off his sports jacket and responded, "You know, girl, one day you not gonna be on that high horse of yours." He pulled off his shades and looked her straight in the eyes with a sinister glare, "and I'm gonna be right there to watch you fall off, that's for damn sure." He shrugged his shoulders, turned on his heels, and walked away. Betty watched him retreat back toward his car and was finally able to breathe again. She was safe for now and wasn't too worried about his idle threats because she assured herself she wouldn't have to deal with the streets much longer and had enough money to live off for years. But she refused to be anyone's fool and made a mental note to herself to watch her back for just a little while longer, and then it would be all over.

Chapter 12

The music blared loudly and wafted through the speakers as a barrage of half-nude strippers danced to "Baby Got Back" by Sir Mix-A-Lot. Men vied for their attention by waving and tossing dollar bills like confetti for the girls to come over so they could slide some bills into their skimpy outfits, or if they were lucky, got a slight touch of their privates. Betty let the other girls service the men with the singles bills. She didn't accept them. She was waiting on the real men who would wave twenties or better to get her attention, so she stayed back popping her hips melodically to the beat while the other girls played themselves out.

She knew men held a higher standard for strippers that weren't easily swayed by simply waving a couple of dollar bills. Betty also knew by spending time with them and just talking, they would spend more money for a stimulating and intellectual conversation, with hopes of a blooming romance—not just sex. So she would just dance in the background and let her body do the talking until a man invited her over to have a drink with him or a lap dance. She let them know her time was money, and they would sit and talk for hours, buying twenty-dollar watered down drinks to boot.

Black Betty was amazed how men would tell her their deep dark secrets, or how unhappy they were with their wives or girlfriends. For the most part, she never ever had to utter a word, but simply listened earnestly and agreed with them with a nod every now and then, and in the end, she made much more money this way. It was then that she first thought she was a natural and considered when she moved to go back to school that maybe she would become a counselor or something. That's how she met Marvin.

Marvin was a simple postal worker only three years her senior, twenty-two, who patronized the club every Friday and Saturday. He befriended Betty on the basis of conversation, and Betty really liked his style because he was low key and never played himself by acting a fool with the other girls. Each time he came to the club, he sat in the same corner of the room and sipped on orange juice and gin and took in the scene. When the girls came up to him and asked if he wanted to spend time with them, he kindly declined and gave them a dollar or two for their trouble. He was a handsome man, but the only fault the girls could see in him was that he was rather short for the average man, five-foot-five.

Curiosity piqued Betty because he never even once seemed to notice her. She watched him for weeks before she finally approached him. She was more inquisitive than anything, because he turned every girl away, and she wanted a challenge to see if she could make him feel different about her. Betty was still stigmatized about not feeling worthy and had low self-esteem issues stemming from her childhood. But as a teen, she began to develop and men and boys suddenly began to notice her and the attention seemed to empower her. Betty learned the power of her worth and beauty, and slowly learned that she was good enough, if not better, than the average girl and sought a challenge whenever possible.

After a set one evening she decided it was time to cross paths with the mysterious stranger and didn't accept any money nor did she give any man a lap dance that night. Betty walked over to him and sat down next to him without saying one word. Betty studied men and learned that silence is more powerful than any words and waited for him to make the first move. After nearly twenty minutes, a waitress came over to refill his drink. He whispered in her ear, and then she approached Betty with an attitude and asked, "What do you want to drink?" The girl popped gum loudly, waiting for Betty to respond. The waitress rolled her eyes and said, "It's on him," and pointed her thumb toward the man sitting next to her.

Betty acknowledged him with a nod and answered, "The same thing he's having." And the rest was history.

Within three months of courting and getting to know each other, Betty moved from her small kitchenette room, and in with Marvin in his much-larger one-bedroom apartment in Harlem.

Before Betty had her own place, she was living with her

mother's sister's family after her own mother finally succumbed to cirrhosis of the liver from drinking too much alcohol three years prior. She loved staying with her older cousins, especially Chubby and Vonda, and for the first time in her young life she felt like she was loved and was part of a real family. Black Betty changed her old ways and found out she was actually an excellent student when she applied herself. Her cousin Chubby, who was heavy in the streets, treated her like his little sister and bought her any and everything she ever needed. He was the brother she never had. But that all changed when cousin Vonda got arrested, and Chubby not long after, and she found herself, once again, alone, and slipped back into old behaviors in order to survive when she found herself on her own at age seventeen.

But before she moved in with Marvin, Betty had to ensure that he could handle her profession, because most men, once they catch feelings for a stripper, what they originally agreed to before they got with them suddenly goes out the window when the heart is involved. What man, other than a pimp and a real secure man, could handle seeing his woman get pawed, groped, and gyrated on night in and night out, she thought. So to be sure, she put him through all sorts of tests.

One night she would have little contact with men, and the next night she would give more than thirty lap dances, as nasty as she could give them. She would overly flirt with men right in front of him, and then right after, she would sit next to him silently to see if he caught any feelings. He passed each test with flying colors. But one thing he did mention, even though she didn't do it that often, was that she didn't have to sleep with them for money and how it wasn't safe. Marvin offered to give her anything that she needed not to do it. She understood, but that was part of the business, part of her ultimate plan for the future to earn as much as she could in the shortest period of time, and then move to a place where no one knew her and leave New York behind to start anew and live normally. Though she had huge feelings for Marvin, it wasn't enough to make her deviate from her dream—she was on a mission to turn it into fruition in a matter of months.

She even asked him if he wanted to move down with her, but he was reluctant because New York was all he knew, and he wasn't too convinced she loved him the same way he loved her, because she never told him. In moments like that, Black Betty would tell him she couldn't say it back to him because she didn't know what love was, but she assured him that she would not lead that life for long and had plans to go to school and settle down soon, and to just give her some time. Though he had no choice but to accept it, he didn't like the idea and didn't stress her. He loved Betty so much and was genuinely concerned about her safety that he left well enough alone.

Betty liked him because he was a compassionate man, unlike her father who she hated for the bad memories of him beating on her mother mercilessly. She still couldn't get those memories out of her mind. When he was murdered in the streets, it seemed her mother died also from a broken heart and tried to drown her pain in alcohol and men who trampled over her throughout the years. That became Black Betty's greatest fear, and she vowed to never, ever love a man more than she loved herself. Betty saw it far too many times to allow herself to give a man her heart, only to be hurt and rejected. No, before she allowed that, she told herself she would remain single for the rest of her life if need be. Betty really loved Marvin, but all the painful memories of the men in her mother's life still haunted her.

Since Marvin worked for the federal government, he put in and got a transfer to Atlanta and they would be moving within seven months, which he thought couldn't come soon enough. When he broke the news that he had landed a spot in Atlanta, Black Betty was so excited she would not have to do it alone. In the midst of the grand news, Marvin surprised her by getting on his knees, and pulled out a ring, and asked Betty to marry him. In a million years, Betty never thought or imagined that someone would genuinely want her to be their wife, and when he put the ring on her finger, a flood of emotions that she never knew she had were suddenly awakened and she burst into tears. Emotional beyond words, she rapidly nodded her head and managed to say, "Yes, I'll marry you."

Marvin excitedly jumped to his feet to kiss her and said, "I love you, Betty."

Betty looked him in his teary eyes and at that moment some of the last words her mother told her before she died flooded her mind, *If ever you become a fool for love, be prepared to become a fool for pain.*

For reasons she simply could not explain, she just could not lower the impenetrable wall she built within her that protected her from being hurt, so she answered the only thing she could, "I know."

Chapter 13

Two Months Later . . .

Sunday through Wednesday were Betty's days off. These were the days that she and Marvin loved the most, because he was off on Sunday and Monday also. On these days, they totally dedicated time to each other, and they did all the things normal couples do, like go to the movies, stroll through the park, or just stay home and cuddle up under the covers on the couch. It was times like these that assured Betty that she was doing the right thing by settling down with a man and starting a new life and felt she was making the right decision. But the moment that she dreaded most was slowly coming to fruition. Marvin now wanted things to change with her since he committed his life to her, and this would be the time when the arguments would arise.

"Why can't you stop doing what you're doing now, Betty? I have enough money saved to keep you off the streets until we move, baby."

"Because," said Betty.

"Because what?" snapped Marvin.

Growing desperate by the minute, Betty had no feasible answer that would satisfy him and continued to eat her cereal slowly, hoping he'd give up like he'd done so many times in the past, but he would not relent today.

"Tell me why," he pressed.

She dropped her spoon and searched for the right words to speak. "Marvin, baby," Betty cooed, "we ain't got nothing but five months to go. Don't ruin it now, baby. Please," she pleaded earnestly. "Remember, you knew who I was when you met me." He remained silent, because he knew she was right.

Betty stared at him with her caring brown eyes and gently grasped his hands in hers. "I know it's hard on you, and we gonna be fine, but you just got to be patient. I'm doing this for both our future, so you don't have to struggle by yourself when we get to Atlanta."

He put his head down and eyed the floor like a child. This is what Betty loved most about him, his childlike qualities, and she adored him for it. She lifted his chin to ensure he could see her sincerity.

"Do you trust me?"

He stared at her eyes before he answered and lowered his head again before speaking. "Yes, but do you trust me?" he countered.

She nodded her head and said, "You know I do, boo."

He grasped both her shoulders and said excitedly, "Wait here." He scurried down the hall and into the bedroom and came back shortly after. He extended out his hand and told her to take it. In his hand was a bank statement book which she took. He smiled proudly and said to her, "Go ahead, open it." She looked at him curiously with a smile and obliged. She scanned the bank book and was surprised by the amount he had saved. She nodded, as if she was impressed. Marvin basked proudly and said, "That's twenty-one thousand dollars. I been saving that for four years." He waited for a reaction, but she surprisingly remained subdued so he explained.

"See, baby, I told you don't have to work no more." She looked him in the eyes, and then finally answered.

"Baby, I got something to show you too." Confused by her lack of enthusiasm, he watched her back as she retreated to the bedroom. When she came out, she carried one of her many shoe boxes and held it out to him.

Marvin stared at the box and asked, "What is that, baby?"

Betty coyly answered, "Open it and you'll see."

He chuckled and shrugged. "OK." When he opened it his smile dissipated and his face deadened as he stared into a shoe box filled with stacks of money. Betty wore a smile from ear to ear and awaited his response, but there came none.

"Well, say something."

He still couldn't find the words, then finally responded, "How, how much is this?"

Betty said, "Well, there's about twenty-five thousand in that box . . ."

He looked up from the money exasperated and asked, "You mean you got more?"

She nodded slowly and guffawed, "Yeah," she blushed. "I got another one with about the same amount in the closet." She suddenly saw distress written on his face and instantly realized she made the wrong decision by showing him the money.

"What's wrong, Marvin?" Betty asked.

He was still speechless but managed to utter, "Are you telling me you made all that stripping . . . ?" Betty put her head down in shame. She knew Marvin wasn't a fool, and that he knew that she also made money on the side by sleeping with some of her clients, but she refused to feel sorry for herself and defiantly answered, "Mostly, yes." Marvin lowered his head even more. She walked closer to him and reminded him, "You knew what I was doing long before I met you so why are you so surprised now, Marvin?"

He remained silent. Betty relented and attempted to walk away, but he stopped her by grabbing her hand. "I'm sorry, Betty. It's just that I didn't expect you to have so much money, that's all." He pulled her closer and wrapped his arms around her. She hugged him back as he continued. "I . . . I just wanted to be the one who takes care of you, that's all."

"You do take care of me, Marvin," she reminded him quickly. "You provide me with a home; you feed me and keep me safe." She looked him in his eyes softly. "Now it's time for us to take care of each other, OK?"

He stared deeply into her eyes and nodded, then asked, "Do you love me, Betty?"

She paused briefly, and before she knew it herself she nodded her head and said, "Yes, Marvin." A huge smile came over Marvin's face, and he picked her up and swung her round and round.

Putting her back on her feet Marvin joyously repeated, "I love you too, Betty, just promise me one thing." She stared into his watery eyes, not used to anyone giving her demands when he asked, "Just promise me you won't sleep with anyone anymore."

She thought about it for a moment and realized that with his money and hers, they had enough money and she didn't have to anymore. She made a good living just stripping, and besides, a few more months she thought and she'd be home free living the life that she dreamed since she was a child—a normal one. She nodded and answered, "Yes." They embraced and kissed softly as she unbuckled his pants and made love right there on the kitchen floor.

Chapter 14

THREE WEEKS LATER . . .

Everything was going fine for Betty. She'd saved up nearly fifty thousand dollars for her and Marvin's new life in Atlanta, but Betty wasn't satisfied with that uneven amount and swore when she made ten thousand more she would leave all the madness behind her forever. The only thing she knew she would miss were her cousins Vonda and Chubby, who both were still doing their bids in state prison. She was sure of that. But, she made sure she did the right thing and stopped by her auntie's house on a weekly basis and left money with her to fill both their commissaries so they didn't need for anything. Betty hadn't the heart to go visit them because she knew they both could read right through her, and she respected them too much to lie. They both knew her past and what she did to earn money to survive. The one thing Betty promised them when she did speak to them and at their request was that she would finish high school, but she never did and felt so much guilt for breaking that one and only promise. Unfortunately, after both her cousins Vonda and Chubby went to prison and getting kicked out by her aunt, Betty had no one to take care of her and had to do what she had to do to make money and school took a backseat for survival.

Betty knew early on that she would have to rely on herself and herself only if she wanted to get ahead in this world and knew nothing was given to her—she had to take it, and that's when she learned about the stripping game at the tender age of sixteen.

It was a beautiful spring night when Betty arrived at the club at ten o'clock. When she got there, she passed the three girls and pimp she had an altercation with some months earlier. They were traveling whores that worked in various cities like Atlantic City, Kansas City, Atlanta, and Las Vegas. Betty matched their angry stares by leering back at them and gave them a salty grin but remained silent. She knew not to press them too much because she didn't have her gun on her tonight. Still, Betty didn't want to look away and show any weaknesses either because they would surly try her again. She wasn't too worried at that point; it was their pimp Rico she was more worried about.

Rico was known not as a gorilla pimp, who handled his girls with an iron fist; he was the sneaky, master of mental manipulation and played on women's weaknesses. He was known to have a huge ego and was as cold and devious as they come. His reputation was on the line, and the streets were always watching.

Betty bluffed by clutching her purse closer to her body so they could all think she was still carrying her weapon and simply smiled at them and kept it moving. This infuriated Rico, who said to his girls, "Don't none of you bitches get it twisted and think I forgot about that bitch because I got something for ole girl, and she don't even know it yet." His frown turned into a sadistic smile as he walked off to the nearest pay phone and fished in his pocket for a quarter. Whenever he made "the call," the men or women who betrayed him in the past were never seen again. The three girls were sure of one thing at that moment—it was all over for the girl who everyone knew as Black Betty.

Three hours into the night it was very slow for Betty and the rest of the girls so Betty decided to knock off early. As she headed to a pay phone to call Marvin to let him know her plans and to pick her up, someone grabbed her arm from behind. Sheer reaction made her pull away from the assaulter and instantly turned to confront the individual when she realized it was one of the bar runners.

The girl saw the anger in Betty's eyes and quickly apologized. "Sorry, Betty, but this dude . . ." the girl pointed in the direction where a man was sitting, ". . . he gave me this to give to you to come over and talk to him." A hundred dollar bill was on her serving tray. Excited, she continued, "And he gave me a fifty just to deliver it to you, Betty." The girl tried her best to hide her greed.

Betty could not see him from that distance and questioned, "You ever saw him before?"

"No, but that brother is paid . . . he pulled out a fat-ass knot from his pocket, and it looked like nothing but hundreds and fifties because he fanned it out when he tipped me."

Betty strained her eyes to get a better look at him when the waitress added, "And he sounds like a foreigner—African, I think." The girl once again gave Black Betty a sly, greed-filled stare, both knowing that foreigners were the most gullible ones and easiest to take advantage of. Betty knew from experience in their country they watched American movies and television shows all their lives, and when they came to America they were looking to fulfill some of their sexual fantasies.

If he was tossing around money like he was doing now, Betty thought, she could easily smooth talk him out of at least a thousand dollars in one sitting. Betty thanked the waitress and slowly sauntered over in her scantily bikini-like outfit to where the man sat, hoping to build his anticipation. As Betty got closer, the man stood up immediately. He was tall, handsome, and very well-dressed in an expensive dark suit. He was so dark that in the dimly lit club all you could see was the white of his eyes and teeth as he smiled. He extended his midnight hand to offer a seat next to him. He seemed overly excited and immediately offered to buy her a drink—

she accepted and said she'd have a cognac and coke, which was actually plain soda and no alcohol so the profit could go into Betty's pocket. He raised his hand for the bar maid who quickly scurried over and took his order.

After a few uncomfortable moments, Betty broke the ice and asked him, "So, where are you from?"

"I'm from West Africa." Between the loud music and his accent Betty barely understood him so she just nodded.

In return, he asked her name. "So what is your name?"

"Betty," she replied lacking enthusiasm, "and yours?"

"Sebastian," he smiled. "Just call me Sebastian," he said in a thick native accent. Betty nodded again.

After a half hour of touch-and-go conversation, Betty found out that he was in America on business and that he was only in town for three days. After ten more minutes of chatting Betty asked if he wanted a lap dance. He appeared confused. Betty had to point to another girl across the room to show him what it was. He quickly waved his hand and said, "No, you are too beautiful to do that."

Betty stood up and put her hand on her hip and sassed, "Well, baby, I don't sit here with you for my health. My time is money; we got to do something." He began to smile and extended his hand for her to sit once again.

"Sit, please, maybe we can figure something out."

Betty knew what he meant, but she really wasn't in the mood to sleep with anyone; besides, she promised Marvin not to, but her hustler mentality told her to hear him out. "So, talk," she said.

"I don't want to seem crass, but I know your time is

important. I would like to spend time with you outside the club. I so long dreamed of spending time with a beautiful American woman."

Black Betty appreciated his candor; she hadn't time to sit and chat all night and would rather get it over with as soon as possible. "So how much are you talking?"

Sebastian paused, then said, "Let's say, two thousand American dollars." Betty couldn't believe her luck, yet sat as if she was unfazed by the amount and remained silent.

"Is that satisfactory to you?"

"It's OK, but that's only for an hour, and you must wear a condom." Sebastian agreed with a huge smile, hardly able to contain his excitement and nodded quickly. "Agreed?" Betty wasted no time and stood up and said, "OK, I have to change clothing, I'll be right back." He followed suit and rose to his feet as Betty made her way to the dressing room. She stopped at a pay phone and dialed home.

"Hey, babe, it's me. Listen, you don't have to pick me up tonight because I'm knocking off early; it's slow, so I'll just take a cab."

"It ain't no problem, babe, save your money. I'm not doing nothing. I can scoop you up in like fifteen minutes."

Betty quickly lied and stammered, "Oh, no, that's OK. Me and Rena are going stop off at her house so I can buy these boots she got from a bolster that don't fit her. So, I'll just meet you at the house." There was a brief pause, and Betty bit down on her bottom lip, hoping she'd convinced him.

"OK, I'll be here waiting for you. Do you want me to cook?"

"No," Betty answered, "I'll bring home some Chinese."

"All right, that sounds good. Oh, and Betty . . ."

"Yes, Marvin . . ."

"I love you."

Betty instantly felt worse than she already did and closed her eyes when her mother's words began to echo once again. *If ever you become a fool for love, be prepared to become a fool for pain.*

"Betty, did you hear me?" he asked.

"Yes, Marvin, I heard you."

Twenty minutes later, Sebastian and Betty pulled into the Bronxwood Inn parking lot, a low-budget motel that was close to the Bronx Zoo. Betty knew she could have convinced him to drive to a more expensive hotel, but preferred to stay in a more familiar setting that she was used to. Besides, many of her clients preferred such an obscure location when they were doing wrong and figured he was no different, so that was the last of it, she thought.

Betty sat in his car until he paid for the room. She could tell he was new to the game and naïve because he left his keys inside the ignition. Even though she knew the car was rented by the strip on the keys that stated Budget Rent-A-Car, she knew many girls would've taken the car to a chop shop that the Bronx had many of and earned thousands with no questions asked.

When they got into the room, it was business as usual. Betty requested payment up front, which he gladly gave her.

She watched the African peel off hundred after hundred from the huge bankroll, standing poker-faced, trying her best to remain unflustered. He handed her the wad of money, which she placed without delay in her purse and proceeded to the bathroom. "I'm going inside the bathroom to freshen up so time will start when I come out. You may as well get undressed now."

He agreed and added, "I forgot something in the car. I'll be right back."

Moments later, when Betty exited the bathroom, she was taken aback and disturbed by the lights being off and the room now being illuminated by an assortment of candles lit all over the room. "What the hell is this?" Betty questioned angrily.

Sebastian threw up his hands and pleaded, "Oh, don't be alarmed, please . . . I studied your culture, and it said that American woman like to be romanced." From behind his back, he pulled out a bouquet of fresh roses and explained, "I didn't have time to place the rose petals for your path, but tried my best to surprise you." She followed his hand as he pointed toward a bottle of what appeared to be champagne and two glasses that sat upon the nightstand. She stared at the bottle, and then at him, to see if he was really that naïve or just plain stupid. When she looked in his wide childlike eyes, she realized it was a combination of both and chuckled.

He flashed a smile, revealing a perfect set of white teeth, and offered, "Shall we have some champagne?" Betty smiled as she shook her head in disbelief.

"Sweetheart, you do understand that you're being charged

by the hour and time started ten minutes ago, so if you want me to sit here and have a glass of champagne with you, it's all the same time."

He quickly answered seriously, "No worry, I don't care about the time or the money. In my country, a beautiful woman like you should be treated as delicate as the flowers in my hand." He then handed Betty the bouquet of roses. Before Betty knew it, she found herself blushing like a child, truly flattered. He walked over to the nightstand and picked up the champagne, turned his back, and poured her and him a glass and handed her one and gingerly asked, "Shall we sit?"

Betty shrugged her shoulders, and thought, *Why not? Less time for me,* and sat on the adjacent double bed. He raised his glass to toast to the joyous occasion. Betty followed suit and raised her glass and tapped it, and they took a sip.

After a few moments of idle conversation Betty asked, "So what is it that you do in your country?"

He took another sip from his glass and answered, "I'm in the medical field."

Betty then inquired, "What are you, a doctor or something?"

He pondered before he answered, "Something like that."

"Baby, it's not that hard. Either you is or either you ain't. Do you help sick people?"

"Uh, in that case, yes. In my country it's different from yours, because here you require licenses and degrees, but in my country, you simply need education. So the formalities are not that stringent because of the lack of professionals needed in rural villages and tribes."

Betty pulled back and asked more jokingly than serious, "What are you, some type of witch doctor?"

He laughed but admitted, "In many parts of my country it is called that, but for many of my people back home that is all they know. You must remember, most tribal members have never even seen a television, have electricity, or running water. They are very primitive and live very meager lives."

Betty simply nodded and stared at his face and couldn't help but ask because of her inquisitive nature, "So, what's with all those scars on your face?"

Sebastian chuckled. "These are not scars; they are ceremonial markings which are tradition in parts of my country that identify you as part of a particular tribe or even give your status. For many warriors, the more markings displayed on one's body, the more heroism they achieved in a lifetime, such as battles won and even slaying a lion. They provide the potential to become chiefs and village elders, no different from your military and ranking system. It's a practice that has been around for thousands of years, but not very familiar to the Western part of the world, such as your country."

Still curious, Betty asked, "Do the women in your country have scars . . . I mean, markings on their bodies too for status?"

Sebastian smiled and said, "You are very perceptive. Yes, women in my country do receive markings, but mainly for only two reasons."

He paused, making Betty even more curious. "So, what are the two reasons?"

He pondered deeply and answered very carefully. "One

reason would be the same as many markings that identify what tribe you come from, but the other would be a marking of a woman who disgraced her tribe." He was reluctant to elaborate, but he looked in Betty's eager eyes and simply told her the truth. "A woman who committed an indiscretion toward her husband with another tribe member or a woman who was a harlot, a person who sold their body for money."

Betty tried to show no reaction, but she did feel a slight sting. She cursed herself for being too friendly, something she'd never done before, and blamed it on the alcohol making her feel overly relaxed. Sebastian had no intention of making her feel awkward and changed the subject quickly and asked, "More champagne?"

Betty glanced at her watch and saw that forty-five minutes had already passed and decided there was no harm to try to milk him for another two thousand for the next hour. She wiped her brow and answered, "Sure, but let me go to the bathroom. The champagne is making me so light-headed."

He answered, "Of course." He stood up.

When Betty entered the bathroom, she tossed some cold water over her face and neck and suddenly felt a strong urge to sit down on the toilet seat, and that would be the last thing she remembered before passing out on the bathroom floor.

Betty drifted in and out of a drug-induced, soothing, womb-warmed foggy haze. As if she was outside of herself, but still within, floating images and muted sounds of her suitor named Sebastian dangled in front of her. Betty lay immobile, but she now had sufficient clarity to watch Sebastian, who was totally nude with the exception of a white smock he was wearing, the type similar to the ones a local butcher wore at a meat market, walk around. She watched him draw a clear liquid from a small bottle and intravenously inject it into a drip bag solution that hung precariously by wired hangers and a standing coat rack next to her bed in the filthy motel room. From there, it flowed into her left arm. When it all began to process in her mind, Betty's first reaction was to yell, to jump up and run, but she was helpless, she simply could not move—she was completely paralyzed.

Sebastian noticed that she had awakened and smiled blasphemously—so happy he could hardly hide his contentment. He went about his business, with methodical precision, as if he hadn't a care in the world, the very way in which he met her. He disappeared for a moment, but came back into her line of vision, but this time he held a large black suitcase and laid it on the neighboring bed. She heard the snapping of the suitcase latch and the clanking of what sounded like metal as he rummaged through it. He once again appeared, but this time his facial expression deadened as she watched him shake and put on beige latex surgical gloves.

Betty slowly processed that he looked like a doctor who was about to perform some kind of surgery and recalled that he did say that he was some sort of doctor in his homeland in Africa, but nothing at that point could register in her mind because of the soothing romance of the drug that ravaged within her body.

Sebastian reappeared, but this time he held in his enormous hands sleek, shiny objects that glinted from the flickering flame of the candlelit room as he moved—they were flesh-cutting tools—scalpels. He was no mere doctor she thought, he was a surgeon who was about to perform an operation on a patient—her!

Sebastian neatly lined up all the sharpened tools perfectly on a fresh white towel. He backed away and grinned as if he was studying a prized catch and reached under his smock and began to massage himself. He spoke in a language she couldn't decipher, possibly his native tongue she thought. He sat down beside her and perched forward till he was within centimeters of her face and grabbed her by the jaw and stuck his tongue in her mouth and kissed her forcefully. He kissed her hard and long until he built himself up into a rabid frenzy, and did not stop until gobs of spit and saliva thickened her mouth and face. Then he stood up, lifting the smock up, quickly pulling out his hardened and thick penis and began jacking and jerking it violently.

Betty caught a glimpse of him despite her hazed state, watched his lean and muscular charcoal-black body glisten with sweat under the ominous flickering of the candle flames. His lust-filled moans and growls reached a sexual crescendo as his eyes rolled to the back of his skull, contorting into a craze and demented scowl as he leaked profusely from sweat. As he neared his climax, his body began to tremble and jerk ferociously. He ambled toward her, grabbing her by her hair violently until her face was touched his freakishly huge penis. With fast successions of rapid strokes, he howled at the top of his lungs like a stuck pig from the release.

Betty's view was suddenly partially obscured by what she believed to be sperm that shot into her eye. Breathing heavily, Sebastian turned slowly and picked up one of the shiny carving tools and laid his long, sweaty body on top of hers and began to stuff his thick, blood-gorged penis inside of her, barely getting it all in because of its length and girth. He brutally pounded and stabbed her with his penis and hips, ripping her insides to shreds, but she could do nothing but lie paralyzed on the bed like a log. She felt nothing but the blobs of sweat plop down into her eyes and the tugging and pinching on her lips from him gnawing and chewing at them until they bled profusely.

Hours seemed to pass; Betty watched him raise his body off of her and walked slow and weakly toward the front of the makeshift drip bag to give her another high dose of the liquid. He wiped his body free of sweat with a bathroom towel, then walked back to where he had his cutting tools stationed, picked one up, and examined it. Satisfied, he walked toward the front of the bed and parted her nonresponsive legs open—wide.

The drug took immediate effect, and Betty could only watch him explore between her legs again and again, each time feeling a sight tugging and pinching, but this time it was at her vagina. She watched him stand up holding something between his fingertips, but was unclear what it was. To Betty's horror, she watched him slither it into his mouth like a shelled oyster and chew it heartily. He continued to busy himself between her legs. Betty felt the drugs forming heavy on her eyes and heard the gushing sound of her flesh being sliced until everything suddenly went dark again.

Betty awoke in a stupor almost twenty-three hours later in a groggy, sedated state after hearing voices. She tried to adjust her eyes to the blinding light but only saw shadowy silhouettes of figures that stood before her.

"Miss, can you talk? What is your name?" Betty, still dazed and confused, finally adjusted her eyes and saw a white face in front of her. "What is your name, miss?" she heard him repeat. "Do you know where you are?"

Betty tried to respond, but her face felt as if it were on fire each time she tried to move her mouth. As each face poked within her view she caught a glimpse of paramedics and uniformed police officers swarming around the room. She heard some footsteps and inaudible chatter around her grow to a crescendo and began to panic. She tried to sit up. In an instant, an explosion coursed through her body and she was overcome by excruciating pain.

"Ahaaaaah!" Betty shrilled in agonizing and absolute pain. It was so loud and terrifying that her screams echoed off the walls. The pain was too unbearable for her to handle as emergency personnel immediately tried to settle her back down. She fought frantically as her heart raced off pure adrenaline and fear. She really panicked when she gazed down at the lower portion of her body and saw the sheets saturated with thick, dried blood.

"Lay her back down and stabilize her!" screamed emergency personnel. The pain and fear had become far too great for her to handle. Her body convulsed and shut down from shock from her sinister and morbid wounds.

"She went into shock. She lost too much blood, and her vital signs and blood pressure are dropping. We've got to get her out now!" yelled one EMT member.

They rushed Betty toward the awaiting ambulance; onlookers stretched their necks to get a glance at all the commotion and the occupant on the stretcher.

The sight was so grim and ghastly, another ambulance was needed to take the motel's housekeeper, who found Betty, to the hospital as well. She had passed out and needed resuscitation from the gory sight.

Chapter 15

MOUNT SINAI HOSPITAL . . .

Eight days later, the Jane Doe awoke in the intensive care unit at Mount Sinai Hospital from the drug-induced coma doctors administrated to her to offset sure death by shock and gruesome pain. Over the course of the first three days, Betty was on the operating table four times for internal and external injuries and trauma. Dozens of staff members came by simply to witness the woman who'd suffered horribly at the hands of some sadistic pervert and apparently survived, one of the most horrific crimes every seen done to a human being in recent history. The tragedy was too unbelievable to fathom.

Once again, Betty would awaken to unfamiliar faces and bright lights in her eyes. She wasn't sure if she was in heaven or hell, but she caught a whiff of the concentrated smell of disinfectant and saw garbed professionals draped in white or blue uniforms confirming that she was in neither, but, in fact, in a hospital. But that brief good news would soon be short-lived when she began to feel a culmination of pain and ghastly memories of a dimly lit motel room that began to surface, where Sebastian hacked away at her flesh. All at once she began to panic, praying that it was only a demented dream, but the intense burning sensation throughout her body convinced her otherwise and she emitted an ear-piercing scream.

"Give her 7 ccs of morphine," said Dr. Marc Jessup, Betty's attending physician who treated her since her arrival. Mere minutes after receiving the high dose of painkilling medicine, the fire of pain was lessened and she slipped back into a soothing calm bliss.

This was their first and best opportunity to get much-needed information from the unknown patient. Betty's purse and all her identification had been taken, and the hospital staff had yet to determine who she was or her closest contact. Normally, a crime such as this would've been top news, but since the motel staff informed the police and detectives that she was a known prostitute, priority wasn't given to the case, not so much as a single sound bite or write up in the news occurred.

The mayor and police commissioner simply didn't want to provide the city with another black eye and felt a hacked up black prostitute wasn't worthy enough to commence an expensive dragnet and many man hours on this particular case, so they kept everything hushed from reporters.

In a calm, soothing voice, the seasoned doctor smiled and

asked, "Ma'am, my name is Dr. Jessup, and you are in Mount Sinai Hospital in the Bronx. Can you tell us your name?"

For the first time, Betty noticed some bulky material from her peripheral vision that was wrapped around her face. She closed her eyes and flashing moments of her captor Sebastian appeared, painting on her face with a sharp, silver instrument. Her horrid thoughts were interrupted by the same voice she heard seconds ago.

"Ma'am, can you tell us your name?"

She opened her eyes and began to mumble inaudibly, giving the detective who stood in the background hope. They'd been coming back and forth to the hospital for days, hoping to get some needed information to proceed with the case.

"We need your name. Tell us your name," the doctor repeated. Each time Betty tried to speak, the louder she became until finally, she said, "Annabelle Blaise . . . 212-555-7360 . . ." The detective vigorously annotated the information down in his notepad and exited the room to contact her closest kin.

A few hours later, Betty was stable enough to give the two detectives a statement to proceed with starting their case. Just as they finished, Betty's boyfriend Marvin came rushing into the room catching the detectives and doctors by surprise.

"Whoa . . ." one detective said while stopping him, "who are you?"

Marvin tried to explain, but when he caught a glimpse of

his precious Betty's small, helpless body wrapped in bandages with mountains of coils of intravenous tubes hanging by the bedside and attached to her body, he cringed and began to break down and cry for his woman. Marvin lost the ability to stand and collapsed to his knees, and cried, "Betty . . . Betty . . ." over and over again. The detectives helped him to his feet and gave him some encouraging words of support to be strong for his girlfriend.

After getting over the initial shock, he regained his composure and wiped the tears from his eyes. Seconds later, he slowly approached her. When each made eye contact, it took every fiber in his body to prevent himself from breaking down again. He forced a smile and wanted to rub her hand. But the intravenous tubes appeared to be everywhere. Marvin cautiously gave her a gentle kiss on her lips and whispered that he loved her and was there for her. For the first time, Betty had no reservations and repeated, "I love you too."

Later, Marvin spoke to both the detectives and doctors and filled in the blanks. Though she was in such terrible condition, Marvin was thankful that she was alive because he hasn't heard from her in over a week and thought the worst. The detectives and hospital personnel were careful not to disclose all the details to Marvin because of confidentiality, but they did tell him she was a victim of a horrific crime and the detectives gave him their card and told him they would be back to question him more. Since Betty was still highly sedated, she slipped in and out of consciousness throughout the night and Marvin stayed right by her side.

Days later, Betty was more alert than ever, but the pain

still hadn't fully subsided. She was more concerned at that moment, however, to know what her condition was, which was still unknown to her. Marvin was concerned also; he still didn't know what had happened to Betty. Who could have possibly done that much damage to her to require round-the-clock monitoring, to be fed through a feeding tube, and to need to wear a plastic bag for her urine and feces? But nothing was worse than seeing her swollen face wrapped in white bandages and thick gauze.

Dr. Jessup and the staff arrived midafternoon to Betty's room. A total of four specialists were with him to give them their prognosis and determinations to better assist Dr. Jessup in explaining future surgeries and aftercare that would surely be needed. The specialists consisted of a urologist, a plastic surgeon, a gynecologist, and the resident chaplain. All four specialists and the attending nurse who had been watching her around the clock stood nearby in the wing while Dr. Jessup took the lead and greeted Marvin, who stood immediately, nodded, and gave him a brisk handshake. Then he turned his attention toward Betty. With a jovial smile he greeted her.

"Good afternoon, Ms. Blaise. I hope you are feeling better today." Dr. Jessup didn't wait for a response and quickly buried his nose inside her medical chart and began to review it. Once finished, he got straight down to business and asked, "Ms. Blaise, we will be discussing with you this morning our findings, so will you be comfortable with Mr. Riley present?" Betty squeezed Marvin's hand and knew this was the moment she had dreaded the last twenty-four hours, but she simply had to know if her injuries, particularly her face, would have a permanent and everlasting effect. She wanted to know now rather than later. Besides, she was so anxious to know the extent of damage that was done to her face that nothing else mattered at that point. She simply nodded.

As if on cue, the two detectives showed up and entered the room with caution when they saw the group of doctors. Everyone did a half turn at their presence. Dr. Jessup, safe that no breach of confidentiality would be an issue by them being present, continued on beat.

"OK . . ." said Dr. Jessup. He removed his glasses and eyed the chart in a brief search bore he bared the news. "Miss Blaise, there's no easy way of telling you this, but your kidnapper caused some great trauma to your body." Betty and Marvin gripped each other's hands and looked at each other. Seeing the fear in Betty's eyes, Marvin took the lead and inquired, "What kind of trauma, Doctor?"

"Well, severe trauma. Let me start with the one we are concerned with the most." Dr. Jessup inhaled and exhaled deeply and explained.

"Apparently your assailant harvested one of your kidneys."

Both Betty and Marvin stared in horror at the doctor, unsure if they processed correctly what he had said. Marvin shook his head and frowned, "What . . . what do you mean 'harvest' one of her kidneys?"

Dr. Jessup tried to answer as sympathetically as he could, but there was no other way to put it.

"One of her kidneys was removed from her body and stolen." Betty stared blankly at the doctor as his harrowing words resonated through her head, not wanting to believe what she just heard. Marvin stood baffled and strained for an answer.

"Why would someone take her kidney?"

Dr. Jessup grasped his hand and explained, "Over the last decade or so, there have been many documented cases in our medical journals of victims being drugged and having their kidneys surgically removed to be sold on the black market for large sums of money. These cases all used to take place overseas and in poorer countries, but the demand has become so high that it seems to have made its way into the United States, as we believe was the case with Ms. Blaise because we found high doses of morphine and anti-infection drugs in her blood."

Neither Marvin nor Betty could believe what they had just heard. They were totally at a loss for words. Seeing the shock on their faces, Dr. Jessup attempted to soften the blow by adding, "The good part is that you can live a normal, healthy life with just one kidney. When one kidney does not function properly or has been removed, as in your case, more nephrons and tubules, which are the basic components of kidneys, open up in the functioning one to assume the work of the nonfunctioning or missing kidney. With regular visits to your primary doctor and medicine, your body should adjust to this loss." He gave them both a moment to process the news, but knew he wasn't nearly finished with the disturbing results of their findings.

"Dr. Levi," Dr. Jessup waved his hand in the doctor's direction, who nodded, "is our urologist specialist that will be treating you while you are here and can explain and answer any questions you may have." He cleared his throat and continued by asking, "Do you need some time before we proceed with the rest of our findings?" Both Betty and Marvin were still in too much shock to even respond and squeezed hands, bracing themselves for the rest. Dr. Jessup took their silence as a no, and continued.

"It's also been determined that your assailant performed a form of a mutilation ritual on your face and body."

Hearing that confirmed Betty's fears and took her breath away. She began to hyperventilate. Her greatest pride had always been her looks, and her body had been her greatest asset, what paid her bills—how she survived all her life since she was thirteen. It took Marvin and the nurse several minutes to calm Betty down and through her tears she gritted her teeth and demanded, "I want to see my face!"

Dr. Jessup turned toward Dr. Shafer, the unit plastic surgeon, for an answer. Dr. Shafer nodded and stepped forward and introduced himself formally to Betty.

"Hi, Ms. Blaise, I'm Dr. Shafer, and I've been treating your facial wounds since your arrival—"

Betty was at her wit's end and didn't want to hear any more formalities, cutting him off in haste, and spewed, "Just show me my face and tell me how many stitches I have!" Dr. Shafer looked at Dr. Jessup who nodded his approval, and then whispered to the nurse what to retrieve.

"OK, we have to clean the wound and put fresh bandages on anyway," he said. The nurse returned moments later with a mirror, scissors, fresh bandages, cotton gauze, and iodine solutions, all on a portable cart, and rolled it next to Betty's bed. Slowly, the doctor began to cut and unravel the bandages and gauze. When he got down to the last layer, he informed her, "Now, I want to warn you, because of the bruising, swelling, and redness, it will look much worse than it really is."

He removed the last layer very slowly and carefully, then handed her the mirror. Betty took one look in the mirror and dropped it wayside to the floor. Her body jerked violently, and she placed her hand over her eyes and sobbed so hard no sound came out. Marvin gasped and stood paralyzed; his eyes filled with utter horror staring gravely at the destruction done to Betty's beautiful face. The entire right side of her face was marred to a red, bloodied pulp with hideous lineage markings with the word "WHORE" engraved on it.

Dr. Jessup gave them a few moments to process it all, but knew he had to deliver them the rest of the bad news. He nodded toward the chaplain who came closer toward Betty's bed and displayed a genuine soft concern as he placed one hand on her shoulder and held the Bible near his heart with the other. He closed his eyes and began to mumble what sounded like a silent prayer.

"In addition to the mutilation of your face . . ." In the twenty-three years of his career as a medical physician being the bearer of bad news to patients, Dr. Jessup still found it to be the toughest part of his profession. There was never any right way to give a patient bad news so he just came out and said it, "disfigurements were also done to your vagina."

There was an eerie silence. It was such a sad and poignant moment each staff member, even the detectives, couldn't bear to watch her any longer and lowered their heads and eyed the floor.

"It appears that you were given what is called a 'female circumcision,' where layers of your clitoris have been removed." Marvin stood glassy eyed and grew light-headed.

Dr. Jessup cleared his throat and stared at the chart in front of him. "It appears that your assailant also practiced cannibalism, because the investigators found pieces of your flesh chewed and disposed of on the floor."

Marvin could no longer take it and fell backwards and collapsed into the chair. Betty sat in paralysis, her heart stuck in her throat. She was unable to process what she had just heard; she couldn't think straight—she couldn't think at all. It was as if she was outside of herself, but within herself at the same time—dreaming, living a nightmare, but Dr. Jessup wasn't finished and delivered the final blow.

"And after thorough and conclusive testing, it was also revealed that you are two weeks pregnant . . ." The curt, cold news was far worse than she'd ever imagined, each word resonating in her mind repeatedly, over and over, *two weeks pregnant, two weeks pregnant . . .*

Chapter 16

The news proved to be too overwhelming for Betty, and she found living in a drugged, induced state of morphine drips was easier than living in reality, so she slept most of the day and night in a foggy haze. Still, Marvin stayed unyieldingly by her side and hadn't once questioned Betty about her actions or whereabouts leading up to the crime, though it heavily burdened his mind. He put his feelings aside for the moment, for the sake of Betty's present mental state of mind which was very delicate. He only focused on getting her better.

When conscious, Betty and Marvin sat in silence, him gazing out the window, her lying back in her bed pondering their ominous future most of the time and what lay ahead for them. Betty knew it was impossible to keep the truth from Marvin, and just as she was about to purge a confession, Detectives Foye and Torres entered the room. They greeted both Betty and Marvin with general pleasantries, then got straight down to business.

"Ms. Blaise, we completed our initial investigation," said Detective Foye as he consulted his notes. "In the investigation, we contacted your employer, Mr. Nero, owner of The Kitty Kat Strip Club, and were told that you worked in the capacity as a . . ." Foye took a gander at his notes again and said, "dancer?" She nodded.

"Other than dancing, do you provide any other services in or outside the club?"

Betty didn't feel comfortable where this was leading and shook her head.

"You stated in our report that you stopped work at around 6:30 P.M. Correct?" Once again, Betty nodded.

"Did you leave with anyone other than a fellow employee? Say, a patron or such?"

Betty realized where he was going with this and looked at Marvin who was hanging on to every word. She knew this moment would eventually come, and there was no way to circumvent the truth and keep Marvin from knowing, and so she answered honestly.

"Yes."

Foye looked at his partner and then inquired, "Do you know the race and gender of the person you left with?"

Betty stared at the detective with malice, knowing he knew full well she went over this with him already. "Yes, he was an African male."

"Did he tell you his name?"

"Sebastian. He said his name was Sebastian," she quickly admitted.

"Was this the same person who assaulted you at the

Bronxwood Motel?" he said, showing her a photo. Reluctantly, Betty nodded yes.

On cue, his partner, Detective Torres, handed him a thin beige folder and Foye opened it and produced a white piece of paper and asked, "This is the rules and regulations from your employer that you signed upon employment. Could you read the part where it is highlighted in yellow?"

Betty was growing defiant and said, "No, I can't see too well at the moment."

The detective apologized. "Sorry. But, do you mind if I read it?" Betty simply remained silent, giving him a knowing look by slanting her eyes in displeasure. He lifted the single sheet of paper and began reading.

"No employees will fraternize with any patrons or guests of the establishment, other than the scope of their duties, not limited to private dance sessions inside or outside the club. Carnal knowledge is illegal and will be grounds for dismissal." After he read it he asked, "Ms. Blaise, did you leave the club willingly with your assailant for the purpose of prostitution?"

Betty refused to answer and couldn't bear to look at Marvin because she knew she lied to him that night after she promised not to sell her body anymore. Hearing no answer, the officer threatened, "Ms. Blaise, we lost a huge amount of time already, and it would be in your best interest to give us everything you know so we can catch the person who did this to you."

"Yes," Betty finally admitted. She slipped back on her pillow and closed her eyes and once again wished that this was all just a demented dream.

Over the next couple of weeks, it was routine touch and go as Betty saw doctor after doctor who wanted to run more tests and poked and probed her body, ensuring she was stable enough to finally be released. Her wounds all healed well, the swelling on her face subsided, but the markings were still highly visible and a vivid contrast on her light skin. She developed an immediate complex because the scars were so hideous, so she wore her hair on the right side over her eyes as a shield to protect her from scrutiny.

Betty felt Marvin was becoming more and more distant as the days and weeks went by. His hospital visits became less frequent, and she became incredibly helpless whenever she was alone without him. She knew, being the person Marvin was, he would be able to get past her indiscretion because he knew it was only business, but her being pregnant by her assaulter—her rapist—was a totally different subject altogether. The thought of having a child in her, especially under the present circumstances, made her have conflicting feelings. She had every right to abort that child. She even was presented with the option by the hospital staff of that right, but each night she lay in bed, she thought of the growing child in her and thought about its innocence through no fault of its own and grew wary of a rash decision. Betty needed to be assured of Marvin's commitment and state of mind before she could move forward in life, so she made up her mind to have their first heart-to-heart talk to see where their future was going to go.

Early the next morning when Marvin arrived, he was in his normal, subdued, unreadable mood. Betty was happy to see him because she hadn't seen him in the past two days and had great news for him—she would be released after almost two months in the hospital.

Marvin gave her a kiss and a warm embrace, then apologized for not showing up the past two days. He explained that he worked a double shift at the post office and needed some rest. She told him she understood. Betty then gave him the great news.

"Baby, guess what?" she said with a sparkle in her eye. "They said I can be released as early as Thursday, in two days, just as long as I have someone to pick me up." Marvin appeared equally excited, but Betty knew that it was just the beginning and she needed to talk to him further.

Betty didn't hold anything back and explained how she felt and that she wanted him very much in her future. Marvin listened earnestly but with disdain in his eyes and knew he still had some questions that needed to be answered. She felt it was time to speak about these matters and told him the honest truth.

"Marvin . . ." She bowed her head and spoke in a lower octave, "you stood by me from the very beginning, and I honestly believe without you being there for me, I honestly believe I wouldn't have made it, and I love you so much for that." Marvin gazed in her eyes and was sincerely moved by her words.

"From the day I met you, you never judged me for what I did, and I fell in love with you for that." Betty bowed her head and admitted, "Ever since I was young, I've been used by boys and men. They never looked at me as a person; they only looked at me with lust—for what was between my legs." Betty laughed a mechanical laugh, swiping the hair away that fell in her eyes as she reminisced. She shook her head. "And they got what they wanted too." She chuckled. "I realized now that my mother was using me, even back then to get what she wanted from the men and to keep them coming back or to stay with her. Whenever she knew they were coming by, she'd go into the dresser drawer and pull out the special panties, the small ones that were so tight that they showed a li'l camel toe and expose my li'l fucking ass cheeks."

Betty shrugged and admitted, "I could never understand why she did that shit. I'm only like six years old at the time. What could I know?

She spoke sullenly, "She told me that as soon as they entered the apartment, I should jump in their arms and kiss them on the cheek. They always brought a brown bag of some cheap wine or liquor with them whenever they came over, and they'd sit in the kitchen or living room and get drunk. She'd tell me to prance back and forth all night in that skimpy li'l underwear until she'd give me this signal with her eyes, then I'd jump in their lap and start bouncing up and down or grind in the center of their pants until something poked me.

"That's when I started to notice that every time they get swollen and poke me, they would reach in their pockets and give me money, and then I could go bed. As soon as I got in bed, they would go to my mother's bedroom and that's when the bed started shaking and a whole lot of grunting was going on. No more than ten minutes later I heard the front door slam and my mother would walk in my room smiling, waving a whole lot of bills around and give me some of the money." Betty chuckled. "I guess she was teaching me how to be a ho even back then."

Betty got more serious and said, "That shit worked for my mother for years, up until I was about ten or eleven and she had this regular boyfriend who used to stay overnight all the time." Betty's voice stiffened, and her head was totally still. "One night, he and my moms were drinking as they always did, and she must have passed out. I woke up to something heavy on top of me. It was so dark in the room I couldn't see who it was. All I remember was hot breathe that smell like whisky and then . . ."

Betty dropped her head and with a deep moan, placed her hand over her face and could no longer continue. It was now obvious to Marvin that was the first time she ever told someone her past. He understood now why she was so guarded and cold at times. She wiped the tears that fell from her eyes and composed herself quickly. Betty was facing her demons. She looked at Marvin for the first time since she started revealing her painful, horrid past, and continued, "I told my mother about it the next day when she woke up and can you believe she didn't believe? Her own fucking daughter!" Betty searched Marvin's eyes for an answer, but received none. "She didn't so much as question his ass and still let him into the house like nothing happened. Do you know how that shit made me feel? I was only a child!" Betty screamed. "I felt so alone and so nasty after that."

Marvin took her hands into his to show her some support.

Betty wiped the remaining tears from her eyes. "That's when I stopped trusting people and grew angry and cold against the world. The only good thing about my childhood was when I went over to stay with my cousins Vonda and Chubby at their apartment. They let me stay over at their place the whole summer, every summer. They were the only two I ever trusted my entire life, and wouldn't you know God seems to not want to give me a break and take the only two people who ever cared about me and put them in jail?" Betty shook her head.

"After they were gone, I turned fifteen, and I was on my own ever since and did what I had to survive and started using the very thing everybody else used me for—my body— to make money." Betty looked deep into Marvin's eyes. "Marvin, that was the reason I never would tell you I loved you, because I had trust issues and in my mind I expected everyone I get close to, to leave me eventually. I built up walls to protect me from being hurt, but the bad thing about those walls is it also prevents love from getting in. You are the only man I ever trusted, other than my cousin Chubby, but you were the one who showed me what real love is."

Tears began to trickle down Marvin's face. Other than sex, this was the first time she made him feel loved emotionally, and he now understood why. Betty continued, "I made you a promise not to be with any more men, and I betrayed your trust, but it was for greed. I was just thinking about our future together in Atlanta and did it for us, but I fucked up and let this happen to me." Betty inhaled deeply and admitted, "Marvin, I think I'm going to keep the baby." She waited for a reaction, but he didn't show any. He simply sat stoic.

After a few moments in total silence, Betty said in a soft voice, "Marvin, say something to me."

Marvin stood up and walked toward the window and gazed out at the waning light of the day over the city's horizon.

"Marvin, this wasn't an easy decision; in fact, it is the hardest decision I've had to make in my life. The chaplain and I spoke every day about this, and it didn't come easy. Despite what happened to me and how bad the circumstances of how this came about, it doesn't outweigh the fact that my child is innocent in this matter and shouldn't die through no fault of its own."

After he gathered his thoughts, Marvin turned to face her and asked, "Are you sure that you're making the right decision, Betty?"

She didn't have to ponder the question long and nodded, "I'm sure, Marvin." She knew he was faced with a huge life-changing decision to make—to stay with a woman who got pregnant by another man. Under those circumstances it was a hard pill to swallow, so she gave him all the time he needed and braced herself in the process. It seemed an eternity waiting for Marvin to respond. Finally he lifted his eyes up from the ground, looked her in the eyes, and said, "It looks like I'm going to be a father."

Feeling as if a tremendously burdensome weight had been lifted, she stretched out her arms for him to hug her, and he did. She kissed him hard and passionately, loving him even more. When they pulled away, Betty had a great epiphany.

"Marvin, when you pick me up tomorrow, let's just leave. Let's just leave everything in the apartment and fly to Atlanta tomorrow and never look back!" Marvin smiled as he saw the sparkle in his Betty's eyes, something he hadn't seen in quite awhile.

"You crazy, Betty" he guffawed. "How are we gonna do that, not pack up and leave just like that?"

"You already told me they approved your transfer. What else do we need?" Betty answered still excited.

"We don't even have a place to stay or know anyone down there," he rationalized, but Betty wasn't taking no for an answer. In the past, she was always able to convince him to do anything for her. He never told her no nor denied any request she asked of him.

"Baby, we could stay in a hotel until we find a place of our own. Between the two of us we have enough money to put a small down payment on a house, car, and furnishings." Betty pouted her face and shrugged. "Besides, we can start all over with a clean slate, and I could be the wife and give you everything you deserve if you'll have me." Marvin once again was moved by her words and fell into her arms and cried.

Betty could hardly sleep that night and was already showered and dressed by seven A.M. The night before, Marvin brought her some fresh clothing, toiletries, and one hundred dollars to pay the hospital's telephone and television fees. By eleven o'clock, she had been screened and processed and given her release papers and all her medicine and waited patiently for Marvin to arrive.

Three hours later, Marvin still hadn't arrived. She'd called the house over a dozen times within that time and received no answer and grew concerned.

By four o'clock, Betty decided to leave and simply take a cab from the hospital back to Harlem. Since it occurred during a change in shift, nobody noticed Betty slip past the hub of the unit desk area alone without the mandatory escort and onto the elevator.

The cab pulled up in front of her building, and she paid the driver for his services. She exited the cab unsteadily and walked slowly up the three flights in the tenement building. She still had hopeful thoughts and rationalized that Marvin may have overslept because he was working long hours lately, and the night before he did work an overnight shift.

When she finally arrived at her door, she stuck her keys inside and was ready to surprise him and smiled like a teen-ager, but as soon as she entered the apartment, her smile instantly turned into distress when she saw the room had been stripped totally bare of all furnishings. Her heart sank. She quickly ran toward her bedroom to see that it was also bare. Her mind didn't want to believe it as she swayed her head feeling as if she was ready to die as she trudged toward her closest where she had her entire life savings of nearly $60,000 all in shoe boxes and opened them.

To her heartbreak, nothing but a stack of bills, maybe a thousand dollars, was left. She fell back to the wall and slowly collapsed to the floor. She rocked back and forth, crossing her arms around both her shoulders trying to hold herself together and sat the rest of the night and cried her heart out as she thought about the uncertainties of her future alone.

Chapter 17

Broke, alone, and becoming more and more destitute and depressed, Betty was all cried out, far too numb. She came to the conclusion that she had no other choice but to move on and live with the hand that she was dealt.

First thing Betty did was make a deal with her landlord after receiving an eviction notice under her door. She explained and showed him proof about what happened to her and offered to pay two months of the four months' back rent for her apartment. He reluctantly agreed but warned her that the remaining two months would be due along with next month's rent or she would be evicted for sure. Betty humbly agreed, knowing she could surely earn that money, and more, if she went back to stripping. It registered to her that Marvin had planned all along to leave her and chose not to pay the rent while she was in the hospital. With the remaining money, she went to 125th Street to get a total makeover at the hair and nail salon, all of which she needed badly. Betty's goal was a lofty one: she figured that she could go back to work stripping before she began to show her maternity and earn enough money to hold her and the baby over till she figured out what to do next.

Because of her facial disfigurement, she remembered the popular geometrically shaped hairstyle that Salt-N-Pepa used to wear, where one side was short, and the other hung lengthwise over the other side of the face nearly down to the lower cheek. It was perfectly suited to hide her scars.

As soon as Betty stepped out of the smelly cab in front of The Kitty Kat Club, she felt a pit in the center of her stomach the size of a small cantaloupe. The palms of her hands began to perspire, and she had a sudden urge to throw up. She closed her eyes to block out the bad memories, taking slow and measured breaths. Then she opened her eyes, smoothed and patted her hand through her hair ensuring it was strategically still in place to hide her atrocious scars. Satisfied, she took one last breath and ambled toward the club entrance.

The rhythmic thumping sound filtered from the speakers when she arrived at her former place of employment. Betty was greeted with a grand reception by the other girls, though she was never friendly with any of them. They all heard about her grave misfortune. They complimented her on how well she looked, and she thanked them, knowing full well what they really meant—she was as thin as a seasoned crack addict. In addition to her mutilation, Betty lost over twenty pounds because she was fed liquid or geriatric food the vast majority of her time in the hospital. Betty was long considered the

uncrowned princess among the strippers because of her outrageously pretty face and well proportioned curves and cleavage.
But, in Betty's mind, she still had enough curves to perform
her stripping duties to get enough money to live on—she
was sure of it—she thought—but in reality, her breasts had
turned into saggy doorknobs and her ass into boney mush.

As she was greeted by all the girls, she received a tap on her
shoulder—it was Big Black, the evening bouncer, doorman,
and all-around club enforcer. Big Black was just as his name
entailed. He was six-foot-five, coal-black, and sloppily fat, but
had the power of ten men. He was a giant teddy bear under
normal circumstances, but when trouble arose in the club, or
if someone tried to get overly physical with one of the girls,
he turned into an unruly customer's worst nightmare and
made them regret the day they were born. He was the person
closest person to Betty out of everyone in the club, someone
she genuinely liked. Big Black reminded her so much of her
cousin Chubby, in nature and in looks.

Betty's eyes gleamed, and her huge smile flashed across her
face when she saw him. He approached and hugged her with
all the gentleness of a lamb. When they parted, he turned his
head, ashamed that a tear had fallen from his eye, and tried
to hide that fact from her, which did no good. Betty was so
smitten that she even became emotional and tried to wrap
her arms around him again, but was unsuccessful because of
his massive frame. Sure that tears were no longer around, Big
Black scanned the club as if he was searching for something
or someone. He stared menacingly at Betty and spoke in a
low whisper, "Betty, come with me over here."

Big Black looked over both shoulders before he continued. "I got something to tell you. Come with me over here." Betty followed him toward one of the booths off in the corner away from everyone, and they sat down. Big Black put his head down and spoke with remorse. "Betty, I'm so sorry to hear about what happened to you that night; that shit nearly killed me when I first heard about it." Betty nodded and patted his huge hand. Big Black scanned the club cautiously and again gritted his teeth. "I remember when you left with that motherfucker that night, so I know how that motherfucker look, and if I see that bitch-ass nigga again, I'm going to murk his ass for you, believe me." Betty wasn't about to change his mind and remained silent.

"Anyway," Big Black said, "I'm just happy you came out of that shit alive." Again, he looked over his shoulder and stared at Betty as if he was spooked, and revealed, "I'm going to give you the heads-up before you hear it from anyone else. Since that shit happened to you, police been in and out of this place, investigating the incident and been sniffing around asking everybody all kinds of questions." He looked over his broad shoulders again before he continued.

"But that wasn't the worst part. They started staking out outside and harassing our customers as soon as they entered their cars to drive off; they stopped them checking their system to see if they was driving drunk and had a reason to search them." Big Black shook his head. "They sent every agency in the city to inspect the place . . . the buildings department, fire department, department of health, consumer affairs, everybody—checking our permits and doing inspections and writing us up for the smallest thing and the fines was in the tens of thousands, and Tony got pissed, and he blames you for all those problems."

Betty couldn't believe her ears and asked with dire surprise, "How the fuck does Tony blame me? I was the one who almost died that night!"

Big Black agreed. "I know, Betty, that's how Tony is. He don't give a fuck about nobody or nothing but his money flow. I think he had to pay those two detectives off, because those fucks were coming around every day, until one day they just suddenly stopped, and that was the day Tony went around telling everybody your business."

Big Black looked deeply in Betty's eyes and emphasized, "*Detailed* information, Betty."

Betty got his point and was deflated by it. She looked Big Black in the eyes not wanting to believe it until he said, "Betty, we even knows about the baby inside of you. So, as a friend, this place is not a good place for you anymore."

All at once Betty lowered her head and ran her hair away from her eyes, not realizing she gave Big Black a bird's-eye view of her damaged face for the first time. He grimaced in heartfelt pity and couldn't stand to watch any longer. He felt even more horrible at that moment. He knew Betty must have withstood more pain and suffering than any human being, especially a woman. Judging from what he knew about her, it would only be the beginning and so he offered, "Betty, if you should need me for anything, you need to just holler at me and I got you, OK?" Betty tried to smile, but only managed a stiff nod. Big Black stood up and gave her a gentle hug.

"Oh," he said as an afterthought, "I forgot. House took up a collection for you when we first found out what happened to you, so just come back next week and pick it up, OK?" He smiled and walked toward the back and disappeared. Betty realized at that moment that the money was more like severance pay, hush money, because her boss Tony knew she was underage when he hired her at sixteen and she even gave him sex at the beginning, which he'd done to many of the girls. She knew everything about how he operated, from prostitution, drugs, and underage girls that danced, so instead of risking her as a liability, it was better to simply pay her off.

Big Black was only delivering a message from his boss Tony Nero to kindly tell her that her services were no longer needed at The Kitty Kat Club.

Chapter 18

Things soon began to fall apart fast. Betty became a recluse and drowned herself in painkillers the doctor prescribed for her, and alcohol, just to make it past the day. The nights were even worse; she grew alarmingly unstable from delusions and loneliness and barricaded herself inside her room with kitchen knives and her pistol, having delusions of Sebastian coming back to finish her off. She methodically painted all the mirrors in her apartment with lipstick because she loathed seeing her face any longer and covered all the windows with sheets and towels so no light would enter the apartment.

Soon, Betty's human skills became nil, resulting in animalistic behaviors. She wallowed in filth within the confines of her small bedroom by no longer showering and started using a bucket that she had by her bedside as a toilet to urinate and defecate in—the stench was appalling. She'd hear sporadic knocks at her door, but she never answered it under any circumstances, mostly from the landlord or detectives.

Betty barely had eaten since she was released from the hospital nearly two weeks earlier. She didn't care or think about eating so long as she popped her pills, nullifying any appetite, but within that time, the ninety-day supply of pain medication was already consumed and she began to grow painfully sick for the opiate-based pills and was forced to seek action so she went back to the hospital for a new supply.

By the time Betty arrived in the Bronx at the hospital her body was spent. She had already thrown up four times, keeling over like an elderly woman, sweating bullets. Sooty dark rings of weariness encircled her eyes as she lugged her deteriorating and desperately thin body toward the triage nurse's station. Everyone was in sickly haste to see a doctor in the crowded emergency room, and when it was her turn in line, she warily asked to see Dr. Jessup. The robotic nurse never bothered to even look away from her computer, only giving a protocol spiel to go to that specific department if she wanted to see a specific physician. Betty's vision was becoming blurred; she was inches from passing out, but, luckily for Betty, someone recognized her.

Molly, a petite nurse with sandy blond hair cut short and soft, with doelike eyes, was on her way out, having completed her normal overnight shift, and she immediately remembered Betty as the woman in the intensive care unit the day she first arrived and became the talk around the hospital. Molly was a floating nurse, who happened to have been assigned to the intensive care unit that day, and actually shed a tear and gave a prayer after she got a glimpse of the woman who was brought in savagely mutilated and butchered and near death on that fateful day of May 13.

Molly took immediate action and informed the triage staff who she was and to bypass the formalities. She took charge by escorting Betty directly into the emergency room hub of the hospital to a gurney and informed the head nurse and attending physicians of her dire conditions and the name of the doctor who had been treating her. Instantaneously, an army of medical personnel began treating her. They took Betty's blood pressure, vital signs, and administered an IV.

Once again, Betty escaped a certain death and was placed into the Intensive Care Unit because her vital signs were critical to the point where her fragile, unhealed kidney was infected. Unless treated, it would shut down in a matter of hours because of her severe dehydration and gravely low blood pressure.

Twenty-four hours had passed since Betty walked into the hospital under dire circumstances. She now woke up in a hospital bed. Dr. Jessup was already in the room standing at Betty's bedside reading her latest vitals. When he discovered that she had awakened, his grave face turned into a soft, jovial smile. "Good morning, Annabelle, how are you feeling this morning?"

Betty simply shrugged her shoulders; she had nothing to feel good about, and spewed her thoughts. "What the fuck I got good to feel about?"

Dr. Jessup accepted her curt response and realized she didn't have a good transition adapting to her bleak future since she had left the hospital and he surely understood why. Judging from how badly she had regressed since her departure, mentally and physically, and how unpleasant the room reeked of pungent human odor when he walked in, he knew her life and the baby inside of her were spiraling downward for the worse. Dr. Jessup decided to go beyond the typical doctor/patient relationship and pulled up a chair and sat down beside her to lend her a sympathetic ear.

"Annabelle, I'm going to be straight with you. The test shows that your kidney area has an infection which tells me you haven't been taking your medicine and that you are still pregnant, by just over three months, which is a miracle under the circumstances of your present conditions." Betty was unforgiving as she stared angrily at the ceiling without showing the least concern.

"In order for your baby to have a chance at life, you will have to take better care of yourself and be strong, because you have been very lucky thus far."

Betty flashed Dr. Jessup a bitter stare and disgorged her displeasure and raised her voice. "Lucky?" she bitterly questioned with steel eyes. "How the fuck have I been lucky, Doctor, huh? I got one fucking kidney and one foot in the grave if I even fall down the wrong way. I have a huge hideous scar down the side of my face with the word 'WHORE' permanently engraved on it."

Dr. Jessup tried to explain, "Plastic surgery will—" Betty heard it all before and cut him off.

"Will plastic surgery give me back my kidney? Will it fix my pussy, Doctor?" He could not offer her an answer, nor could he match her gaze and lowered his head. "I still can't bring myself to look at it, and nor will I ever have any feelings down there during sex for the rest of my life, and I'm not even twenty years old yet." Betty threw daggers with her eyes at the good doctor. "So, how am I lucky?"

Dr. Jessup remained silent. He wanted her to get the anger out and let her purge herself free of frustration. She tensed her jaw and turned away, and as expected, Betty's eyes began to soften and her shoulders collapsed.

She turned back toward him, no longer an ounce of defiance in her, and gloomily asked, "Who's going to want me, Dr. Jessup?" Her mouth began to quiver. She warily repeated, "Who's going to want a person like me?"

Dr. Jessup embraced her hand in his and offered hope. "It's a cruel and heinous world out there, Betty, and I've seen the after effect right here in this very hospital for years, and the one thing that I do know is that it happens and one must move on because life is never fair. What about your fiancé, the one who was here for you all those days?"

Betty's chin collapsed to her chest, and she cried uncontrollable tears. The distraught woman spent the last half hour bleeding her soul out to Dr. Marc Jessup, who listened intently to what her fiancé had done to her. After Betty purged her darkened soul, which she knew she needed to do, she wiped the remaining tears from her puffy eyes and saw no point explaining anything further just to open up more wounds. She was tired—tired of even living.

Three days later, Betty was released from the hospital and back on the street with another full supply of medication—after lying to Dr. Jessup that someone had stolen her pills. The timing couldn't have been worse when she arrived at her apartment door to see a City Marshall Seal Notice taped to her front door and the locks changed. In grave despair, Betty sighed loudly and gazed up toward the ceiling and shook her head, cursing God in the process. She had a morbid inkling to walk up to the roof and end everything by jumping off it right then and there.

But she dismissed the thought, because she was simply physically incapable of making the climb to the roof, already drained from the trek from the hospital in the Bronx to Harlem. The words of Dr. Jessup suddenly came to mind. She accepted life for what it was and things that she could not control, but being locked out of her only sanctuary was a heavy blow to absorb. She forced her tired and sickly body back toward the staircase and exited her apartment building, sure she would never return to it again.

After trudging a few blocks, Betty had to pause to catch her breath, so she leaned against the front of a neighborhood bodega plastered with beer and cigarette posters. It suddenly occurred to her that she hadn't a single place to go but one. So she made up her mind to go to the one place she always had as a sanctuary when things got too rough in her own home when she was younger. It was the one place where she was accepted with open arms because she was family—her mother's sister's house, Aunt Vera's house, also the mother of her cousins, Vonda and Chubby.

"Who is it?" was the sound Betty heard from behind apartment 4C after she knocked on it for over five minutes. It was clearly her aunt she thought, but never in her life had she heard her use that tone.

"It's me, Aunt Vera, Annabelle."

"Who?" Aunt Vera repeated, only this time louder.

"It's me, Annabelle, your niece, Sarah's daughter." Betty heard the fast lumbering sound of footsteps, then the sliding of the peephole on the door. Betty smiled and was truly excited to see her aunt, who she hadn't seen in nearly two years. Betty had lived with them for three years when her own mother, Vera's younger and only sibling from her mother, died from loneliness, constant heartbreak, and cirrhosis of the liver, when Betty was just fourteen. But when Betty turned seventeen, both her cousins Vonda and Chubby went to prison at nearly the same time. Shortly after that, Betty and her aunt Vera started not seeing eye to eye about her hanging out, all the boys and men that were calling the house, and her not going to school. Ultimately, she packed up and left once she got into the stripping business and hadn't been back since.

Betty repeated, "It's me, Auntie Vera, Annabelle." She heard the clicking of the door lock and seconds later, she stood starry-eyed with her mother's elder sister.

Vera Williams, forty-nine, heavily built, with a dark, round face, mother of six, five boys and one girl. She was twelve years her younger sister Sarah's senior when her family first moved and migrated up to Harlem from Charleston, South Carolina, when she was only sixteen. She was a very hard worker, who worked two or more jobs since she arrived in New York in order to provide for her children, but she had little time to devote to the guidance of them, leaving the boys to consume the streets and embrace criminal behavior, becoming petty thieves, drug dealers, kidnappers, and murderers. The five brothers were notorious, known throughout Harlem, as well as feared, but none were feared more than Chubby—the baby of the family. Vonda, however, the only girl, was always a straight-A student. Though her daughter Vonda was just as in-tuned with the streets, she attended and graduated from a prestigious Catholic high school in downtown Manhattan.

Vera knew all her sons were incorrigible and were cursed with their father's blood, who was also a brazen gangster and killer that ultimately died in the streets. Vera long accepted that fact and left it into God's hands to guide them and simply prayed for them every night. Vonda, her only girl, was the apple of her father's eye. Right before he died, when she was three years old, he brought home ill-gotten gains of over thirty thousand dollars after robbing an illegal numbers spot, and gave twenty thousand of the proceeds to his on-and-off again wife strictly toward his baby girl's future education. Under normal circumstances, Vera would never have accepted what she called "blood money" from her husband, which is the reason she worked two jobs to support her family. She only agreed because it made sense when he explained to her that Vonda was already at a disadvantage in society by being black and poor from Harlem. He argued she would need every advantage if she had hopes of making it out of the ghetto by going to college to have chance at life. Ironically, and as fate would have it, Vonda and her three best friends, Jessica, Lynn, and Tiny, were arrested for murder on the very night of their high school prom.

Aunt Vera looked at her niece with the same permanent unyielding mask that riddled her face since she last saw her. Ever since Betty could remember, her aunt Vera seemed older than she really was, and never the consummate conversationalist, but rather a no-nonsense, straight-to-the-point kind of person, which basically meant, abide by her rules or leave—period. She was neither overly religious, nor a nurturer; she just called it how she saw it and accepted life for what it was. She motioned Betty in without so much as a comforting smile or friendly greeting. Betty timidly leaned her back against the narrow hallway wall to allow her to relock the door and allowed her to pass to take the lead inside the apartment.

Vera led her into the kitchen, and she instantly smelled the familiar aroma of pan fried chicken that she ate many nights growing up. The apartment was exactly the way Betty last remembered it; comfortable, neat, and sparse. With the exception of new kitchen cabinets and a refrigerator, nothing changed. Betty stood obedient, still gripping her bags of medications when her aunt asked, with her back turned toward her as she poked and turned the chicken wings in the fryer, "You hungry?"

Betty's throat was so dry and brittle that her voice cracked when she attempted to answer. She cleared it. "Umm, no, not right now, Auntie, but I could use something to drink to take my medicine." Mechanically, her aunt walked toward the cabinet and removed a drinking glass and rinsed it out, then went over toward the refrigerator, pulled out a container of orange juice, and poured her a glass. She handed it to Betty and turned her attention back to the fryer without once looking at her.

Betty finally felt comfortable enough to sit down at the dining table, and as she began to open her medicine, her aunt inquired, "What's wrong with you? Are you sick?"

Betty had thought about what she would tell her aunt if she asked when she reached her block on 140th Street between Lenox and Seventh Avenue and still hadn't thought of a way to tell her. She cleared her throat again before she answered and said, "Yes, I just got out of the hospital a little while ago."

Aunt Vera finally turned to engage her and demanded, point-blank, "Annabelle, are you on that stuff?"

Betty quickly scoffed as if her life depended on it. "No, Auntie, I don't do any of those drugs; never have."

Aunt Vera gave her a reserved stare and questioned, "Girl, why do you look like you do and lost so much weight?" Before Betty could answer, her aunt continued and as if she could read her mind, she said in one quick burst, "Now, I put up with a lot of your cousins' shit when they got hooked on that stuff, and I refuse to put up with anymore of that lying and stealing. I didn't put up with it with my sons, and I won't put up with it from you, so if you want to stay here, don't bring none of that shit in my house. Now, get yourself set up in Vonda's room. Find some of her clothes that will fit you and take a shower because you smell, then come out and get yourself something to eat."

Betty was stung by the words, but thankful for not having to explain about what had happened to her. Aunt Vera added one final thing. "Since you just got outta the hospital, I'm giving you three days to rest; after that, you leave the house when I leave and start searching for a job until you get on your feet and find your own place."

Chapter 19

Ten days had passed, and true to her promise, Betty got up every single morning with her aunt, and they left the house together. Betty spent the first few days, at the suggestion of a social worker that interviewed her at the hospital, to apply for disability at the Social Security Office because of her permanent injuries that she assured her she qualified for, and HRA to apply for welfare and food stamps until her disability claim kicked in, which sometimes took over a year to get approved. When Betty had taken care of all her business, she'd simply spend the rest of the day gaining her strength back by usually walking around Central Park, that stretched from 110th Street all the way down to 59th Street from Eighth Avenue on the westside to Fifth Avenue on the east and back around. Not only did Betty feel invigorated by walking, she also found a sense of normalcy by getting away from all the hustle and bustle of Harlem and to be around a different race of people for a change.

By five o'clock, Betty would start returning back to her aunt's house to eat dinner and get some much-needed rest. Betty and Vera spoke sparingly, but she was at least happy to know that her cousin Chubby would be coming up for parole within a couple of months as well as Vonda about the same time, so she couldn't be happier. She was thankful that she kept both their commissaries filled the last two years while she was earning money, but regretted not visiting them, too ashamed to face them because she knew they heard that she was stripping and selling her body.

Many days she wanted to admit to her aunt what had happened to her and reveal her present condition, but she never had the nerve to. She still felt alone and scared, mainly at night as she lay in bed, and that's when ill-gotten and intrusive thoughts of death perforated and weighed heavily on her mind, and forced her to overmedicate on her pain medicine, just to get those depressing thoughts out of her head. Unwittingly, Betty's tolerance for the drug began to increase, never realizing she entered the grips of addiction to the opiate-based drug, and she would soon find out in the worst of ways.

Betty returned to The Kitty Kat Club on an impromptu meet to pick up the money she was promised after spending the entire morning and afternoon on follow-up appointments at the hospital. She was critically low on her pain medication already because instead of taking the prescribed one pill every six hours or when needed, she was taking four. She figured she could play the sympathy card and get the doctor to feel sorry for her like she did the last time, but this time was different, and the doctor explained that pills were a controlled substance, and it was against to law to give her more. Betty walked out of the club with ten one-hundred dollar bills stuffed in a white envelope. It was just after seven that evening, when she tried to hail a cab as the night began to sweep the city. She cursed when no cab was in sight in the near desolate Hunts Point section of the Bronx and decided to walk closer to a more populated area.

She walked until she passed the abandoned lots. Ugly graffiti smeared buildings all along 138th Street. Just as Betty got to Taylor Avenue and turned the corner, she spotted them immediately—Trina, Cocoa, and Diamond, the three girls she had been in a beef with and pulled a gun on over three months ago. Her reflexes made her reach for her purse to get her weapon, an impulse that she used many times before to ward off trouble, but this time would be different. She realized she wasn't carrying one. From their mannerisms, and at the pace that they were walking toward her, she knew they were looking for some payback. For the second time in Betty's short life, the first being in that motel room that fateful night, she wanted to run away.

"Bitch, what the fuck are you going to do now?" voiced one of the girls as they came within fifteen feet of her.

"Yeah, you ain't got no gun now, so let's fuck her up!" shouted another.

Betty knew the outcome wouldn't be a good one; she was still much too sickly to defend herself and braced herself for the worst. Just as they converged on her and were about to pounce, out of the shadows, their pimp Rico threatened loudly, "Bitches, take one more step, and I'm going to beat the dog shit out of all of you!"

As if they were well trained, they paused instantaneously in their tracks. Rico approached the group and stared at the three girls sinisterly as if they had committed a cardinal sin. "Did I tell any of you bitches you could cross the street?" Like a child caught with their hand in the cookie jar, they stood silent by his imposing presence and eyed the ground. This was a different Rico; his smooth demeanor had somehow changed Betty thought, even in the midst of discerning trouble. His eyes were glassy, his clothing were disheveled, and his normal smooth baby face was now shadowed with beard stubble.

"Why you trying to defend her, Rico?" the more defiant, shorter girl demanded. "That bitch pulled a gun out on us and took your money, and you ain't never dealt with her!"

Rico lurched forward with a hand waved in the air, causing her to wince, but he failed to follow through and strike her. "Bitch, the next time you try thinking for me will be your last time. Now take y'all dumb asses back across that street and get my money." He turned his full attention toward the shorter girl, Trina, who dared to question him and threatened, "Bitch, I'm gonna deal with you later. Now get the fuck back across the street, now!" he barked. The girls obediently complied.

Satisfied, Rico turned his attention to Betty and sniffed. He stood grilling her with crazed eyes, not saying a word until Betty grew uneasy—scared, in fact. He could simply cut her throat at that moment, she feared, easily and get away with it because not a single person was in the area to stop him from doing it. She lowered her head and meekly said, "I'm sorry for what happened that day."

She waited for a response, but instead, he said, "Rico."

Betty quickly corrected. "I'm sorry for what happened that day . . . Rico, but, I got money to square us." Rico nodded. Not giving him a reason to tempt him, Betty reached in her jeans, pulled out the white envelope, and turned her back so he couldn't see the large wad of cash. She quickly thumbed out two bills and stuffed the envelope back in her front pocket, turned around, and extended her hand to give it to him. He smugly looked at the money and took it, stuffing it into his pants pocket. He nodded his approval and turned on his charm.

"Good, girl, we squared."

Betty returned a smile and tried to walk around him, but he stopped her and asked, "You know, I heard about what happened to you, and that was tragic." Betty put her head down and nodded. Rico added, "You know, if you had been with me that would have never happened, so if—"

Betty stopped him midsentence by throwing up her hand and said, "Thanks, Rico, but I'm outta the business. This is not for me anymore. I was never supposed to be out here in the first place. I been through enough."

Rico nodded and said like a caring uncle, "I feel you. I always wondered myself why you was out here. We all deserve better, and I respect your decision. I'm actually happy to know you survived that shit, because what happened to you should never happen to no one." In spite of knowing who he was, Betty suddenly looked at him in a different light and smiled.

"Thanks again, Rico, that really means a lot to me. I'll see you around." Just as she tried to leave again, he took hold of her hand with his soft, girly hands, and said, "Let me walk you to a cab or something to make sure you get out of here safely so I don't have to worry if you get home this time."

Betty guffawed and said smiling from ear to ear, "No, I'm still a big girl and trust me, the cabstand is right around the corner, so I'll be OK, but thanks for your concern."

He smiled and gave her the same look that seduced hundreds of women in his lifetime, then he reached in his pocket and pulled out a pen, patted his person, and reached in his back pocket and pulled out a black wallet and a white card the read, "Boris Auto Repairs." He turned the card around and jotted down his beeper number and handed it to her. Betty was reluctant to take it, but he insisted. "Take it, Betty. It's not going to bite you."

Betty took the card out of courtesy, just so she could end the conversation and get home. He reminded her, "OK, you just remember, if you should need anything, and I mean *anything,* just beep me and I'll be right there to get you whatever you need. I got you covered, deal?"

Betty smiled and relented. "Yes, I'll do that."

Chapter 20

By the time Betty arrived back at her aunt Vera's apartment later that night, she felt good about the $800 dollars she had left, because she had enough to put down on a small studio apartment or kitchenette when her welfare kicked in, so she'd be ready to move in with no problem. But the only thing was her body began to feel as if it was rigid and in a viselike grip. She felt like she was coming down with a cold. She hurried up the stairs so she could take her pills that she hadn't taken in over ten hours.

When she got to her aunt's door she immediately heard loud voices, what sounded like arguing, coming from inside the apartment. Betty pounded on the door rapidly, concerned for her aunt's safety. "Aunt Vera, open the door. Aunt Vera!"

Suddenly, the door swung open. It was her aunt, who didn't even acknowledge her as she always did, and she went back to the person she was arguing with. Betty hurriedly locked the door and rushed quickly behind her to see who was there. It was one of her cousins, Victor.

Victor was the middle child in the family. He was dark skinned, tall and lanky, and had a mischievous look on his face that gave the impression that he was always scheming or up to something. Out of all her cousins, she rarely had a conversation with him because he was always in the street getting in some kind of trouble ever since he was little, or in a juvenile detention center as a teen mandated by the courts. Even his own sister never trusted him and warned Betty to never turn her back on him whenever he was home. He always reminded Betty of a weasel, because he was grimy—a thief. It was rumored that when Harlem had the huge blackout in the seventies, he stole a television from Bloomsteins Department Store on 125th Street, brought it home, and sold it to his mother, and the next day he stole it out of the apartment and resold it to their next-door neighbor.

When she saw him as she entered the kitchen, he smiled and said, "Cuzzo, what's good with you?"

Betty smiled and said, "Oh, what's up, Victor?" They gave each other a light embrace. Betty quickly tapped her front pocket slyly to ensure that the envelope of money remained in her pocket.

"Well, you know, them crackers tried to charge me with some shit I didn't do, had me on Riker's Island for like ninety days, but they ain't have enough evidence when they took it to grand jury, so they had to release me, know what I'm saying?"

"And if you keep up doing what you doing, and running

in them streets, it's going to be only a matter of time before the cops get you on something you can't get yourself out of, you watch. And don't be calling my phone expecting me to bail you out either. I'm sick of you and your brothers going in and out those prisons," shouted his mother.

Victor countered shrewdly and questioned, "Just the boys, Ma? I guess Vonda don't count, even though she sitting upstate in a prison cell right now, huh, Ma?"

His mother slapped him and spewed, "Vonda was just in the wrong place at the wrong time, so don't be comparing her to none of y'all. She graduated and was about to go to college, unlike you who was getting into trouble your whole life. So watch what you say in my house."

Victor knew it was pointless to argue with his mother because she was stuck in her ways, and he didn't want to risk getting on her bad side because he needed a temporary place to stay and so he changed the subject. "Yeah, whatever, Ma."

He turned his attention back to Betty and shrewdly asked, "So, Annabelle, I see you back staying here again. Why you look like shit? You smoking that crack, them jumbs?"

Betty stared at her cousin with malice, and it suddenly occurred to her why she hated him. He had a natural mean streak, a vengeful nasty one.

"Stop that, Victor," chided his mother. "That's your first cousin. You respect her. She just got out of the hospital; she been sick. I saw all her pills."

"You sure she ain't been in no rehab, Mama?" Victor laughed at his own words and waved his hands and said,

"Naw, cuzzo, I just messing with you. I'm sorry you got sick. If you need my help with anything, just let me know."

Betty looked at his face and smiled. It reminded her of a sneaky weasel. She knew she would have to sleep with all her money on her when she slept that night, and every other night, for that matter. She wiped her nose with her hand and sniffled, then excused herself and walked down the hall to her bedroom.

By the time she entered, her muscle aches had intensified, and she felt nauseated. She doubled her pace to her dresser drawer and ripped it open. Her hands began to tremble and shake violently as she fumbled to open the childproof narcotic medicine bottle. When she finally got it open, she threw caution to the wind and sucked a gross amount of pills down her throat all at once. She closed her eyes and strained until she swallowed all of them. She breathed lightly when she opened her eyes; the pains began to instantly lessen, and her body began to warm—when suddenly she felt a presence it the room—it was her cousin Victor staring from the doorway. "You must've really been sick."

He smiled cynically as he walked down the hall to his old room.

Chapter 21

Apartment hunting went well that day for Betty and she found a modest kitchenette apartment for rent in a brownstone located on 122nd Street between Lenox and Seventh Avenue for a meager fifty dollars a week. She'd be able to move in the following week. The only thing the landlord requested was an award letter from a public assistant, and a notarized letter from her present landlord—her Aunt Vera, so she didn't anticipate any problems; she even gave them a month's rent in advance, just to secure the kitchenette, and would give them another $200 for security once she moved in.

The rest of the afternoon was long, hard, and depressing while she waited hours inside the crowded HRA Office on 125th Street waiting for her number to be called to see her caseworker. Betty grew uncomfortable and edgy as she sat for hours on the hard mismatched chairs, listening to crying babies or older kids' mothers yelling at them because of rambunctious behavior. On top of all that, she felt like she was coming down with flu-like symptoms, a runny nose, muscle and back pains, and she felt nauseated, making things even worse. She thought it was her pregnancy and couldn't wait to get home.

Finally, four hours later, she received the letter that she needed, which took a total of eight minutes after she sat in the cubical with her caseworker.

It was already twenty after five when she got home. Her aunt Vera had already been home nearly an hour. Betty was simply happy she didn't need to walk around the city for hours like she normally did. Within a week, she would be in her own place and wouldn't have to be under her aunt's rules any longer, bringing a slight smile to her face.

Betty greeted her aunt with pleasantries, who, as usual, muttered something low and inaudible and went back inside the kitchen to continue cooking dinner. Betty, her stomach in knots, went straight to her room and closed the door behind her, then walked toward the dresser drawer to take some much-needed pain pills. When she opened the top drawer, she was stricken with total panic when she saw none of her medication was there. She began to throw the entire contents of the drawer on the floor, then pulled frantically on the other drawers repeating the same process to no avail.

Betty stopped long enough to process everything as her chest heaved in and out rapidly as her jaws grinded and her nose began to flare. As if she had an epiphany, Betty balled her fist and stomped hard toward the door and ripped it open. She growled at the top of her voice, "Victor!" and stepped in the hallway and looked in both directions. She leaned forward, opting to check his bedroom first, ripping the door open. His room was empty, and like a madman, she began searching his drawers on the hunt to retrieve what was rightly hers.

"What hell is going on, Annabelle?" screamed her aunt Vera, who stood at the bedroom door. Betty didn't miss a beat and pounced over to his closet. She began tossing and flipping its content on the floor too. Aunt Vera lunged her huge body toward her to wrestle her hand to prevent further destruction.

"Annabelle, what is wrong with you? Stop it!"

Betty was transfixed and determined to find her drugs and twisted and turned her hands to be released, but Aunt Vera was much too strong. Reality came back instantly when Aunt Vera slapped her viciously across her face, bringing her back to the present.

Vera shook her violently and shouted, "If you don't stop, Annabelle, you got to get out my house! I told you I'm not having no drama inside my house!"

Still in a rage, Betty cursed, "That dirty, thieving, mother-fucking Victor took my medication!"

"Watch your mouth, Annabelle. Don't forget who you're talking to," warned Aunt Vera, staring at her niece as if she had lost her mind. "Why in the world would Victor want to steal some damn medication from you, Annabelle?"

"My Oxycontin pills, Auntie Vera," Betty cried.

Aunt Vera scrunched her face and asked, "Oxy what?"

Betty's shoulders collapsed, and she crossed both arms

over them, and whimpered, "They were pain medication for my injuries. Victor saw me taking them last night, so he was the only one who knew where I had them."

"What would he want with any pain pills? Victor may be a thief, but he ain't never into no drugs."

Betty knew her pleas would be to no avail—they were already long gone, and she knew that the highly sought after Oxycontin pills were already sold. They went for as much as fifteen dollars a pill on the streets, and she had well over seventy left before Victor took them.

Vera looked at her frail niece and saw how broken and sickly she was and felt sorry for her and offered, "Can't you just go back to the hospital and get some more?"

Betty was hunched over with beads of sweat forming down her face and body. "No, I'm only allowed a certain amount a visit, because it's a controlled substance." Unconsciously, Betty parted her hair away from her face exposing her ugly pinkish scar for her aunt to see for the first time.

"Annabelle," she asked in shock, "what happened to your face?"

Betty was much too sick to explain and attempted to just leave, but her aunt stopped her. Betty tried to go around her, but failed when her aunt blocked her and physically grabbed her by her chin and parted her hair from the side of her face and stared at the hideous disfigurement in sheer horror and demanded to know, "Annabelle, what the hell happened to you?" Betty remained silent and broke free of her grip and trudged to her room and slammed the door behind her.

Seconds later, her aunt ripped opened the door and threatened, "Annabelle, you're not going to disrespect me in my own house, and if you are going to continue staying here, you are going to have to tell me what's going on and what happened to your face."

Betty was growing painfully sick by the second and could not hear her. She busied herself checking all her pants pockets in search of some pills that she may have overlooked when she came across a white business card with the name Rico written on the back of it.

"Annabelle!" her aunt snapped. "What happened to your face?" Betty turned to face her, knowing she had to tell her something so she could get out of the house quickly, and be able to come back as well.

"This girl cut me with a razor because she thought I was messing around with her man. That's why I was in the hospital and needed those pills for my pain because my face is still hurting."

Aunt Vera shook her head and ridiculed sadly, "You young people these days, always fighting over a man who ain't even thinking about you."

Aunt Vera went on chastising her until she could no longer take it. Betty interrupted her rant. "Auntie, I got to run to see somebody I know to borrow some pills because my face is really hurting. When I come back I'll tell you everything."

Aunt Vera's sullen red eyes stared at her. She shook her head and said, "OK, but when you come we going to have to talk about you getting your own place soon, because I'm not putting up with all this drama no more. I been through too much as it is."

Betty quickly put on a sweater, in spite of sweating badly; she felt cold chills as she flew out the door.

Betty called Rico at a pay phone on the corner of 140th Street and Lenox Avenue and told him to meet her on 142nd Street, so he wouldn't know exactly where she lived. She asked Rico if he had any connections with someone who sold some pain medication and and asked if he could he cop some pills for her if she would pay him. He said he could and took down the location on where to meet her.

After another fifteen minutes or so, he finally pulled up in his white, 1985 Lincoln Town Car. Her stomach churned so badly, she fought desperately to prevent herself from defecating right there. She had thrown up four times already in deep anticipation awaiting his arrival.

As Rico pulled up to the curb, Betty wiped the continuous snot and sweat that poured from her face before getting in. She hopped in the passenger seat, smiled weakly, and said "Thanks for meeting me, Rico; I owe you for this one."

Rico flashed his million-dollar smile and wooed, "Like, I told you, Sunshine, Rico always come through for his people." Rico then sat in silence purposely as he played one of his many mental games when he wanted to cop a whore for his stable. He needed to control Betty's mind, build her into believing he was Alpha and the Omega, and the only one who could protect and save her when she was in need. Rico already knew she was strung out; he'd been in the streets too long not to know the symptoms, and Betty had them written all over her face. He knew when a dope fiend needed their drug they would do anything to get it—anything—and knew Betty would be no different, so he would use this moment to his advantage. So he just sat there. Betty's skin felt as if it were on fire; she rocked her body back and forth. Every second she sat, her body felt as if it were being wrung like a mop. She no longer could prevent the sweat from pouring off her body, and it began to leak on his plush suede burgundy seats.

Rico stared at her and feigned concern. "You alright, Sunshine? You looking kind of peaked."

Betty smiled nervously and admitted, "Yeah, I kind of ran out of my medicine and can't get no more till tomorrow when I see my doctor to get my prescription filled, you know, cause of my injuries." She partially lied and put her head down feeling Rico's eyes read through her.

"I understand," he said with compassion. "That's the reason I dropped everything I was doing when you beeped me, just to get you what you wanted because I knew you needed it."

Despite her pain, Betty was smitten by his genuine concern for her and thanked him. "I really appreciate that, Rico."

They gazed into each other's eyes until Rico snapped her out of her trance by reaching in his shirt pocket for a couple of small cellophane bags and extended them out to her. Betty stared at the small bags with confusion, and muttered, "That's not what I asked you to get me, Rico. I asked you to get me some pills. That looks like heroin."

"I know," Rico admitted, "my pill connection don't come out till in the morning, and I knew by the way you sounded over the phone that you were sick and needed something now."

"But, Rico, I don't use heroin. I'm not a junkie."

"Listen, Betty, you told me you needed Oxycontin pills, right?" Betty nodded. "Well, heroin is opiate based, the same thing from which Oxycontin is made. It's just in pill form, and heroin is in powder. They are exactly the same thing. The only thing different about them is that the government don't get their cut from the money made off of heroin on the street, so that's the only reason they say it's illegal and give them the power to lock up black and Latino people." Rico saw that Betty was still skeptical and shrugged. "What are you afraid of? I sell this on the side, and I even take some every now and again when I need to relax. Do I look like a junkie?" Betty softened and shook her head.

Rico sat up and challenged, "I can see that you are in pain, and that makes me feel bad for you, but if you take a one-on-one up your nose right now, I promise you that your pain will go away in five seconds."

Betty looked in his eyes and saw how determined they were and at that moment she knew that she had nothing to lose. She simply had to try something to get rid of the pain. She relented by nodding her head.

Excited for her, he reached over to his glove compartment, opened it and retrieved a plastic straw that was cut in half, set it on his lap, and opened the tiny cellophane bag. He took the straw and scooped out an ample amount and snorted it up his nose loudly. He repeated the process in his other nostril and passed the bag and straw to her. Betty stared at Rico's smiling face, and it looked to her as if he had tasted a slice of ecstasy. She looked at the bag and straw in her hand and didn't hesitate. She mimicked his action and scooped out a small amount and snorted it up her nose. She sneezed. She looked at Rico who was smiling and who urged her to take another—she did. In seconds, she fell back into her seat as her body warmed and her pain subsided instantly. Rico smiled when he watched Betty's head and chin fall to her chest.

"Betty," Rico yelled, snapping Betty out of her soothing bliss, erecting her head to attention. Smiling widely, he asked, "So, how do you feel now?"

For the first time, Betty gave him a genuine smile. Rico nodded and said, "Good, I'm glad I could help you out." He then reached in his shirt pocket again and handed her the other bag and said, "Here, this will hold you over till you see your doctor tomorrow."

Betty took the bag in her hand and eagerly said, "Thanks, Rico, just tell me how much I owe you." She attempted to reach into the sweater she was wearing to retrieve her money, but he stopped her.

"No, Betty, I don't want your money. Like I said before, I came as a friend because you needed help, and where I'm from, we friends should always be there for each other, and we all need help sometimes." Any doubts that she had toward Rico at that moment had been removed, and suddenly she began to grow feelings for him—just like that.

Betty walked back to her aunt's house with an extra pep

in her step, feeling anew and jubilant. When she walked in the apartment, it was as if she was a totally different person her aunt observed when she entered the kitchen.

They sat in the living room, and Betty lied about everything, from what happened to her face and how she lost a kidney. She said that when the girl stabbed her she lost her kidney because of it. Betty couldn't bear to tell her how she really sustained her injuries because of shame. For reasons she could not explain, she also couldn't build up the nerve to tell her aunt she was fourteen weeks pregnant.

After they ate dinner together and talked some more, they went to their respective rooms and bid each other a good night. Aunt Vera assured her that she would take care of her son Victor and get him to return her medicine.

Later that evening, the drugs in her system began to wane as her body began to crave more heroin, so she went to her now secure stash in a tiny slit she made in her mattress. She pulled out the two small bags and quickly reopened the one that she had already used. It still had an ample amount of powder inside. She searched the room for something to scoop the drug out, then her eyes happened upon a book of matches. She tore the upper portion of the match cover off and creased the end diagonally, creating a pointed tip, scooped a portion of the powder from the bag and sniffed it heartily up both nostrils until it was empty. A quiet calm instantly surged through her body, relaxing every muscle and fiber in her body as her arms and head collapsed while she took a soothing ride on the white horse.

Hours later, when Betty opened her eyes, she saw two

daunting figures standing over her—Aunt Vera and her cousin Victor, who was smiling wickedly. Her heart sank to the pit of her stomach when she heard Victor say, "See, I told you, Ma, that she was on that stuff."

Betty looked around, and saw the heroin bags and torn off matches still beside her, then looked up at her aunt Vera, who was staring down at her with disgust.

"I told you, Ma, she was lying on me. You can't trust a dope fiend!" said her cousin.

"Annabelle, I done warned you when you first got here I wasn't going to allow no drugs in my house. Now, pack your stuff. You got to leave tonight."

For the remainder of the night, Betty sat in an all-night Soul Food restaurant called M&G's, located on Morningside Avenue and 125th. She sat at a table and ordered tap water and slices of apple pie till dawn, reflecting on how badly her life had changed in a few short months. With her were all her meager belongings in a pink Conway's bag, along with some underwear, shirts, jeans, and bras. But her immediate concern was getting some more heroin and a place to lay her head until she moved into her kitchenette the following week, so she decided once again to call on her newfound friend—Rico.

True to his word, Rico arrived at the restaurant like a knight in shining armor to meet her. He greeted her lovingly with a huge smile and a gentle hug, then sat down. A waitress arrived at their table, pen and pad in her hand, and asked him if he would like to place an order. Rico had little intentions of eating, but shrugged and looked at Betty and said, "Why not?" He asked Betty if she wanted to order something, but she declined, already full from eating apple pie all night, but she did request some tea. He made his order and turned his attention to Betty.

For the next hour and a half, Betty poured her heart out to Rico and explained to him everything that had happened to her from the beginning. Rico listened earnestly the whole time, never even batting an eyelash at her horrid confessions, making it easier for Betty as she saw the compassion in his eyes and felt the soft gentle touch of his hands whenever she came to the hard parts—she told him everything, down to the part about her pregnancy.

When it was over, there was an eerily long pause. Betty halfheartedly expected him to walk away while he still had the chance, but he stood up, walked to the adjacent seat next to her, and wrapped his arms around her. Betty, humbled, closed her eyes and buried her head in his chest and felt a warm, strong sensation within her soul—she felt loved. They pulled away, and Rico noticed Betty had an uncertain look on her face as she gazed out the window, then he asked, "Tell me what else is on your mind, Betty."

She stared at him briefly. "Why are you doing what you're doing for me? I mean, the one thing I've learned in my life is that no man is gonna do something for nothing for a woman; they always want something."

It didn't take long for Rico to answer and admit, "You're right, even a rank sucker knows that. To be honest, I felt sorry for you when I heard what happened when I saw Big Black and he laid the news on me." Betty didn't flinch because she already suspected he was the one spreading her business from the get-go. Rico continued. "I'm not going to lie. I, like everybody in the club, felt like you got what you deserved. But that day I saw you, and how different and weak you looked, I started feeling different." Rico put his head down. "It reminded me of what happened to my own mother, how she got used up by men and those streets to the point that they couldn't use her anymore, because she had nothing else to give, and she died."

Betty suddenly felt a kindred spirit within him; a connection she never ever found in a man—even Marvin, but she still felt uneasy about things and made it clear. "I know who you are, Rico, and I don't knock what you do, but I'm not getting back on those streets, if that's what you had in mind; I'm having a baby, Rico. I'm going to be a mother, and I can't afford to have it raised up like I was."

"As you should," Rico agreed, "but I sat here and listened to you, and it sounds to me that life's been shitting on you and that you could use a break. Now the only immediate problem you have right now is not having somewhere to crash until you get your place next week. I'm offering that you can stay with me, even pay me a piece of rent if that makes you happy, until your place is ready. All I'm saying is that it's your own decision. I'm just extending out to you an option, and you can make up your own mind." He saw that she was still unsure and finished with a request. "Can you trust me?" Betty was hypnotized by his unexpected concern and affection and nodded. "Show me your face."

Betty lowered her head in reluctance and muttered, "I can't do that. It's too ugly."

He placed his finger softly under her chin and lifted it gently so she could see his face. He assured her with a comforting smile and said, "Beauty is in the eye of the beholder." Betty saw the sincerity in his eyes and slowly pulled back her hair, not having the nerve to see his reaction, choosing to stare down at the table. Unexpectedly, she felt a soft, gentle kiss on her wounded and scarred face. She looked up and gave Rico a long stare, then heard him say, "You're beautiful." Betty sat there and melted. He gave her a long warm embrace. She desperately needed one.

The laws of human nature never fail and are never wrong; from human beings to the wildest of animals: The female species chooses her mate and will give her body, her mind, and her soul if she feels it in her heart. Betty would be no different. If she had any reservations about Rico before, they instantly vanished. From that moment on, she knew—she chose him.

Chapter 22

Betty arrived at her new home on 180th Street and Mohegan Avenue, just south of the Bronx Zoo. The neighborhood was mostly an outrageously poor and high-crime area with an equal mixture of blacks and Puerto Ricans. When Betty entered the ugly and dim graffiti-laden, five-story, prewar building which had "fire hazard" written all over it, she looked around and thought, even in her younger, bad years in Harlem, she was never subjected to such a depressing setting. Rico smiled and waved her on to follow him. She stiffly trailed him up the winding staircase that smelled strongly of disinfectant, dust, and decay. As she ascended, she heard what sounded like mass stomping and laughter on the upper levels.

When she got to the third floor, she saw children playing in the hallway, just as if they were in a park. Little girls jump roping, boys bouncing basketballs or playing catch. At the sight of Rico, all the children's eyes lit up like a Christmas tree and they said gleefully in unison, "Hi, Mr. Rico!"

Betty watched Rico greet them all by name. She smiled at the genuine love the children had for Rico, as he had for them. Just as Rico was about to reach in his pocket to give all the children a dollar as he always did, an apartment door swung open, and out came William Riley, who everyone called Mr. Bill.

He was, by profession, a retired corrections officer, but still very young, in his midforties. He stood six-foot-two and was powerfully built and could more than hold his own. Many people said Mr. Bill favored Mike Tyson in looks, by their warriorlike, fearsome eyes, and permanently flared nostrils, the kind of face that white people were taught to be afraid of. But Mr. Bill was a loving man that cared for his family, his community, and fought hard all his life trying to be a perfect example.

Though their building wasn't the most accommodating building in the neighborhood, it was by far the safest, thanks to Mr. Bill and his unwavering efforts to keep crime out of the building and as clean as possible by taking it upon himself to sweep and mop the entire building, and the tenants loved him for that. But he did have one flaw. He despised people that preyed of the weak and took advantage of people, drug dealers, women or child abusers. And one thing he hated above anything else was a pimp—and he hated the man known as Rico—and he hated him with a passion.

All the children swung their heads around at the daunting presence of Mr. Bill standing in front of his apartment door and froze in place. Betty watched the unknown man, sharklike, with dead sullen eyes that stared grimly and transfixed upon Rico. The silence was deafening until Mr. Bill finally spoke in a slow and deliberate manner, "Y'all kids go take a break and go inside your apartments for a little while. I'm about to sweep the building," never once losing eye contact with Rico as he spoke. The children obeyed his command without question and gathered up all their toys and accessories, and scampered up or down the stairs to their respective apartments.

Mr. Bill walked directly up to Rico's face and said through gritted teeth, "What did I tell you about talking to these kids and giving them money, pimp?"

Though Rico was grossly undersized in mass and weight as he stood face to face with Mr. Bill, they were equal in height and Rico was unfazed by his lurid presence and said smoothly, "Hey, my man, I'm just trying to look out for the kids. Nobody else seems to be looking out for them."

"They have their parents looking out for them, not you, pimp, and your slave money," spewed Mr. Bill.

Rico chuckled and rudely said, "Listen, Mister Policeman, you ain't their daddy and don't have the right to tell me who I give my money to. So, play that superhero shit to somebody who gives a fuck and stay outta my business."

Mr. Bill loathed the snake bastard from the day he moved in and at that moment wanted to snap his neck and could have easily done so if he had wanted to, but he knew the last thing he wanted was to have any witnesses around seeing him do it. "You know, one day it's gonna be just me and you, pimp, and trust me, it's not going to be pretty," Bill threatened.

Rico turned on his heels and proceeded up the stairs leaving Mr. Bill to watch his retreating back. "Yeah, whatever, Mister Policeman, but in the meantime, talk to my back!" he mocked. "Come on, baby," said Rico. Betty watched Mr. Bill's sullen hard eyes stare at her as he shook his head in pity at her.

Ironically, Rico's apartment, 4C, was one flight above his enemy Mr. Bill's, Betty noted. When Rico got to his door, he walked straight inside, not even using a key. As Betty stepped inside, she noticed they were directly in the living room—modest in size, with expensive black lamps, end tables, and with a conventional beige leather love seat and couch. Though the furnishings were sparse, it looked well-maintained and comfortable, with three bedrooms.

Seconds later, from out of one of the bedrooms, Trina, one of Rico's girls, the very one she had the most trouble with on the street, poked her head out and looked as if she had seen a ghost and immediately voiced her displeasure. "Uh-uh, Rico, what the fuck is this bitch doing here?"

"Shut your mouth, Trina. I don't have time for your shit right now. Go back into your room."

Trina wasn't having it and continued her verbiage of discontentment with Betty being inside her house. Hearing the ruckus, the other two girls in Rico's stable came rushing out of the other room to see what all the noise was about.

"Nah, Rico, I hope you not thinking she's going to stay

here," she quipped. "She got to go 'cause I'm not going to stay here if she—"

Before she could say another word, Rico was on her and grabbed her tightly by her throat. "Bitch, don't you ever tell me what the fuck I should do." His grip was so tight around her that Trina's eyes began to bulge as she fought for air. "Don't forget who you are talking to. I'm the one who tells you what to do, bitch. Don't ever forget that, you hear me?" The whites in Trina's eyes began to burst in red blots, and she agreed by nodding her head as if her life depended on it. He released her, and she immediately took in huge, rapid gasps of air.

"Now get the fuck back in your room and get ready to get on them streets." Rico kicked her in the rear end for good measure just as she scampered off. He gave the two other girls an evil leer to see if they had any opinions about whomever he brought home, but they opted to stay silent and retreated back into their room.

Betty stood in silence, feeling rather uncomfortable, but Rico assured her, "You don't need to worry. You can take your stuff into my room." He pointed to the door. "You'll be staying in there. I'll take the couch." Betty smiled uncomfortably, then nodded. Rico added one more thing. "I'll lay out a washcloth and a towel in the bathroom if you want to take a bath or shower."

He reached into his pocket and said, "Oh, yeah, here's some candy for you, but it's going to cost you this time." He handed her four glassine bags, and she quickly took them. "So, leave forty dollars on the dresser." Betty nodded again and was more than happy to, because she was already growing sick. She closed the door behind her, and Rico smiled cunningly; his plans were working perfectly.

Within a week's time, Betty had already gone through her savings by paying Rico one week of rent and consuming more and more heroin—just as Rico had planned. As the days went by, Trina, Cocoa, and Diamond grew increasingly disenfranchised and angry with Rico because they saw less and less of him. He was giving all his attention to Betty. Even though they all stayed in the very same household, Rico no longer came out to the strip like he had always done to watch their backs like he used to, up until when he brought Betty to the house. They were pissed. But, the final straw came when they woke up one morning and no longer saw Rico sleeping on the couch. Instead, he was in his room sleeping with their enemy.

Betty woke up in panic to loud pounding on the bedroom door. She quickly and nervously threw on a skimpy pair of shorts and a tank top to cover her nude body.

Just two nights prior, Betty had sex for the first time since she got out of the hospital, and she was scared to do so, because she still felt dirty about Rico seeing her mutilated vagina, on top of the fact that she didn't know if she had healed sufficiently. But, Rico was persistent and convinced her he would be gentle. Though it felt unusually different at the beginning, the passion and gentleness she received from Rico overwhelmed her. She never had a man perform such foreplay on her before—including Marvin, where the man took his time and gently romanced her neck, her back, her shoulders and her stomach, all over. When he made love to her, his soft hands explored every inch of her body, sending millions of titillating love sensations coursing through her in ways she never in her life felt before. Betty, her entire life, looked at sex as a job, simply waiting for the man to cum and accepted it for what it was, but it was different with Rico. He never pounded her; instead, he took his time, ever so slow, all the while whispering in her ear that he loved her, told her how beautiful she was and how he wanted to be with her forever. When they finished, hours later, he held her in his arms, something she never experienced nor allowed a man to do, and she felt safe and warm—for she was in love.

Betty had to shake Rico awake from his drugged-out state to address the pounding at the door. "Rico, somebody is knocking on the door. It sounds like the police, get up!"

Rico woke up instantly at the very mention of police, than looked toward the door, got out of the bed, and quickly walked over to his closet and pulled out a pistol. He then put his ear to the door and heard one of his girls say, "Rico, open the door." Rico frowned when he opened the door and saw his three girls standing with their arms on their hips.

"You bitches better have a good goddamn reason for knocking on my door like that!" he hissed.

Trina rolled her eyes and spoke with attitude. "You told us when we finished to bring you the money—well, we finished and here's your damn money." She showed him the wad of money in her palm. Rico realized she was right, but he had to show face.

"Bitch, you better check your ring tone before I come over there and put a foot in your ass," he warned. Trina twisted her mouth, sucked her teeth, and dismissed his threat as an idle one. Rico collected all their money one by one. He looked at it with dissatisfaction and questioned, "This shit looks real light. I know you bitches better not be holding out on me."

Defiantly, Trina voiced her displeasure once again and boldly said, "Yeah, whatever, Rico. If you were out there on your job, you would've saw that it was slow, instead of lying up all night with that li'l girl." Rico looked at her as if she was crazy as his fair skin began to turn red. Trina went on, "Big Mike even came up to us and told us that you been slipping lately and that we should—"

Before she could finish her sentence, Rico punched her so viciously that her eye swelled to the size of a small plum before her body reached the floor. He snapped and pounced on and punched the girl as if she was a man, refusing to stop his vicious assault as she pleaded for her life.

"I'm sorry, Rico, I'm sorry . . ." She began to gurgle as teeth broke and blood spewed from her mouth. But Rico could not hear her begging and continued to beat her unmercifully.

Cocoa and Diamond could no longer stand by and tearfully began to beg him to stop. They even jumped on his back and fought him to stop. Too strong for them, Rico flipped them off his shoulder and in the heat of the battle elbowed Diamond so brutally she flew into the lamp and end table, loudly smashing it into oblivion. Now Rico set his red, blazing eyes on Cocoa, who had the good sense to retrieve her switchblade from her purse.

Rico grimaced. "Bitch, you pull a knife out on me? You're fucking dead!"

Cocoa was shaken as her hand trembled. She nervously begged, "Rico, please, just stop beating on her. She's sorry."

Tasting blood in his mouth, he shook his head. "Nah, bitch, I'm gonna teach you a whore's place." Just as he went on the attack, Rico was lifted off his feet and slammed into the wall so ferociously, his skull indented the wall—it was Mr. Bill.

Mr. Bill's huge massive body and fists began raining down upon him so savagely, Rico's face was a crimson red and bloodied pulp as he sprawled across the floor unconscious. He stopped abruptly when he heard *click*. It was Betty standing over Mr. Bill with Rico's gun pointed four inches from his face.

"Get the fuck off of him!" Betty warned.

Mr. Bill snarled at her, "You're going to protect this woman-beating pimp?"

Betty didn't answer and continued to point the gun at him as he stood to his feet. The two girls helped their beaten friend to her feet when Cocoa fearfully pleaded, "Can you stay with us a few minutes until we get our things out of our room, mister?" Mr. Bill nodded. Within two minutes, Trina, Cocoa, and Diamond had their entire belongings in their hands and under their arms heading out the door. Betty, still with the gun in her hand, watched Mr. Bill stare at her with apathy. "Little girls like you only see in bloodsuckers like him what you lack most in your life—but will never find." He shook his head in disgust.

"You're only going to realize it when he sucks you dry and you have nothing else to give but your soul, then you will see that it was one big lie, and when that happens . . ."

Mr. Bill looked down at the bleeding and dazed pimp with a venomous glare, and then toward Betty and warned, "I'm going to pray that you survive without losing your mind or your life." Then he stomped out of the apartment in a huff. Betty's hands trembled as she slowly lowered the weapon. She didn't know whether it was from fear or the truth of his words.

Chapter 23

In less than two weeks, Rico's funds were all depleted. He realized in hindsight he had made a fatal miscalculation of his whores' worth and that he went too far. His judgment was clouded because of his drug usage and that he got too friendly with his new drug of choice—crack cocaine, which he hid secretly from all his girls.

Crack cocaine wasn't anything like the streets had ever seen before, even heroin. A heroin addict could consistently use the drug for months, even years, without any outward effect, but with a crack addict, it only took mere days to consume the mind, body, and soul—it had an immediate effect, and Rico would be no different.

Since he lost his three girls, who were now under the tutelage of another pimp he knew named Big Mike, it was nearly impossible to get them back with his wit and charm, something he used effectively on women and girls his entire life. Desperate times called for desperate measures in Rico's world. It was a matter of survival, and he still had one card up his sleeve—and that was his Betty.

Betty lay in bed or paced the room all day while Rico was gone, supposedly in search of some heroin. She was so sick. Her body dripped painfully cold sweat incessantly, and she shivered uncontrollably. Though never religious, Betty begged God to take away her pain and curled up in a tight knot on the bed.

Miraculously, Betty heard the front door slam. She rose to her feet and ran quickly from out of the bedroom like a jackrabbit—it was Rico. Desperate, Betty hopefully asked with glassy eyes revealing her dire straits, "Rico, did you cop?"

Rico was so flushed, he didn't even answer and rushed straight to the bed and pulled out his works to shoot it in his veins. His appearance had made a dramatic turn for the worse. He had been wearing the same dirty clothes for days, having sold all of his jewelry and nice threads, anything of value that he could get rid of in the apartment.

"I only made enough to get one bag," Rico angrily admitted.

Betty didn't care. All she cared about was sniffing some up her nose so the pain could go away. She shook violently as she waited for her share to be given to her, but when Rico poured most of the heroin in his spoon and laid the rest to the side, Betty hysterically complained, "Rico, what about me?"

Rico hardly paid her any mind and shrugged. "I was out all day trying to cop. I need this more than you."

Betty's eyes widened in mortal fear. "Rico, don't do this to me now. I'm sick just like you."

Rico snapped, "Bitch, all you doing is laying your ass around the house all day while I'm making shit happen. You better start getting your ass out on the streets and start making some money."

"I will, Rico," she pleaded frantically, "I just need a taste right now."

Rico turned around and looked at her teary face and offered, "OK, I'll give you some, but that ain't going to be enough to get you off by sniffing it. You got to mainline it if you want the pain gone."

Betty paused; she was reluctant to shoot it in her veins because she feared of being a hard-core heroin addict. Rico finished cooking the heroin and pooled it up into the syringe, then shrugged. "It's on you if you want to stay sick." He lifted the ready filled syringe in her face and said, "I'll let you get off first."

It didn't take Betty long to make up her mind. The powerful temptation for the drug was too hard to resist. She said, "Give it to me."

As seasons changed and the months went by, Betty's stomach grew, though she was unhealthily small. She hadn't once gone to the hospital for prenatal care, too afraid, too concerned and caught in the vicious cycle of drug addiction. The drugs made her numb, and she forgot her problems that were mounting by the day.

Soon, Betty and Rico's roles began to change. No longer was he able to take care of her, nor himself, as she assumed all the responsibility of the primary provider of the household. Since her public assistance kicked in, she used the money to pay the rent, the utilities, and food stamps to purchase food.

Whenever the money ran out after paying the bills and supplying Rico's out-of-control drug habit, she had to hit the streets and sell her body which eventually was every other day. Then one day everything changed when she felt the baby inside of her kick for the first time.

That single moment changed her, and she was determined to stop getting high and minimize her drug usage drastically when she went back to the hospital and received her pain medication. She sniffed only one bag a week until she weaned herself off the drug totally.

Rico was another story. In just a few short weeks, the constant drug use plagued and ravaged his body badly. He cried like a child, pleading with Betty to go out and get him some, and he would even slap her around when she wasn't quick to follow his orders. The first time he hit her, Betty planned to leave him, but each time he begged for her forgiveness and told her how much he loved her and would never lay a hand on her again. For the life of Betty, she couldn't leave him; she loved him and felt he was the only man who really knew her or would ever love her for who she was. Betty rationalized that she could somehow save him from himself and give him a chance the same way he gave her, until one night when everything would change.

Betty returned from a prenatal appointment at the hospital, and the doctor determined that her baby was doing well and she was twenty-two weeks pregnant. But her doctor detected the opiates in her blood work and wanted to wean her off the pain medication because it could pose a threat to the baby's growth and development and be harmful to the baby's overall health. Betty had no problem with complying. She was just happy to know the baby was still healthy despite what she had been through all those months. When she got home that evening, about six o'clock, she was on cloud nine and wanted to share the good news with Rico. When she walked in the apartment, she smelled the pungent odor of crack and cheap malt liquor looming in the air. Rico was sitting on the couch, still unshaven, in the same tattered, smelly clothes he had worn for days, watching television, smoking a Newport cigarette.

"Hey, baby, guess what?"

Rico wasn't in the best mood and continued watching the television. Still excited and wide-eyed, Betty explained, "The prenatal doctor said the baby is healthy and growing normal." Rico was still aloof and took a swig from his can of beer and remained silent as Betty awaited him to acknowledge her good fortune.

"Rico," Betty questioned, "did you hear what I said? You're happy for me?"

Rico stared at the television a little longer and answered coldly, "Maybe that's the reason the tricks don't want to pick you up, because they see that swollen belly of yours."

Betty was astonished. "Is that all you care about? How much money I'm not making out there to provide you with your dope and crack? Rico, I'm paying every single bill in this house, and that's the best you can say to me?" Rico didn't answer, making Betty grow angrier. "Well, you don't have to worry anymore, because I'm not going to be your supplier no longer. You gonna have to get another bitch to sell her ass because I'm through."

Rico realized he was wrong and said, "I'm sorry, baby. Come over here so I can make it up to you."

"Kiss my ass, Rico," Betty retorted before she walked in the bedroom and slammed the door behind her.

"Kiss your ass? You told me to kiss your ass?" Rico said in a rage. He vaulted off the couch and kicked in the door, all the while unbuckling his belt from his trousers. He charged at Betty like a raging bull, catching her by complete surprise and kicked her viciously in the side of her stomach into the vanity dresser. She fell hard to the floor. Betty let out an eerie shrill, so painful she flapped around the floor like a caught fish, gripping the side of her torso. That didn't stop Rico from waging war on her body with his belt. He beat her cruelly as she tried to crawl, protecting her stomach all the while.

Betty begged and pleaded for him to stop, but her cries fell on deaf ears. He was too deranged and beat her into submission until she was silent and curled up in a tight ball.

Chest heaving in and out heavily, Rico wiped the sweat from his brow, placed his hands on his hips, and sighed. "I'm, I'm sorry, baby, I'm so sorry." He pleaded yet again. Slowly he crouched down beside her and picked her up in his arms and gently laid her down on the bed and began taking off her clothes and started kissing her. Betty cried and fought to resist, but he grabbed both her arms above her head and kept whispering in her ear that he loved her. Within minutes he was inside of her, rendering her defenseless.

After Rico made love to Betty, she was stricken with pain from the beating, mainly from her stomach.

"I'm not feeling too well, Rico," Betty complained as she held tight to her stomach area. Having just finished shooting up, Rico was nodding peacefully. "Rico!" Betty yelled, snapping him out of his bliss.

"What, baby?" he asked in oblivion.

"I'm not feeling good. I think I might have to go to the hospital."

"Aww, baby, you just got a li'l monkey on your back." He reached onto the table next to the bed and handed her a half bag of heroin. "Just take a couple of hits and you'll be fine."

"I don't do that no more, Rico, you know that."

"Suit yourself," he said and eased back into a nod.

Betty looked at him angrily and tried to lie down, but moments later she popped back up, still feeling the nagging pain in her back and stomach. She eyed the bag of heroin on the table and shook her head, but the fight didn't last long and seconds later, she reached over and retrieved the cellophane bag, found a straw, and sniffed the contents up her nose.

Six hours later, Rico woke up dope sick and began begging Betty to go out and turn a trick to get some money to buy him some heroin. Betty initially told him she didn't want to do it. After receiving the good news from the hospital, she no longer wanted to jeopardize the baby's health. He continued to cry in pain. "Baby, help me. I love you, don't you love me? I took you in when you needed me most. I'm asking you to do the same for me. Please, baby, I'm about to die. I promise you this will be the last time."

Feeling sorry for him, Betty agreed, but assured him that it would be the last trick she turned. Hardly able to control his contentment, he kissed her deeply and said, "Thank you, baby. After this, I'm gonna get myself together and be ready to take care of our baby when it comes."

This was Betty's dream, to have a real family. She fell into Rico's arms and kissed him over and over. In her mind she believed she could save him from his path of destruction and have the baby and they would live happily ever after, but life is never a perfect one—and the only thing in life you can truly expect—is the unexpected. Betty would find that no different.

Twenty-five minutes later, Betty walked out of the apartment and ran into Mr. Bill. She couldn't look him in his face ever since she pulled the gun out on him weeks ago. Shamed, she put her head down ruefully and tried to walk quickly past, but he grabbed her gently by her arm and asked, stunned, "Girl, what happened to the side of your face?" Betty suddenly realized she still had her hair pinned to the back when she took a quick shower and forgot to lay it down because Rico was rushing her out so fast. Mr. Bill grimaced and demanded to know, "Did *he* do that to you?"

Betty answered, "No, this is old."

Mr. Bill looked her over from head to toe and said knowingly, "I guess those whip marks on your face and legs are old, too."

Betty couldn't answer and wrapped her arms over her belly, a habit she'd been doing since her stomach began to grow. Though she carried small, she still didn't want the tricks to see it, nor anyone else.

"You know you don't have to live like this," offered Mr. Bill. "If you think nobody sees that you're having a child and knows what you are doing, you are only fooling yourself."

Betty knew she was doing wrong and wanted nothing more than to reach her arms out for his protection, but her love for Rico was just too great and she just couldn't leave him. Seeing her reluctance, Mr. Bill made one last offer.

"Listen, if at any time you should need me for anything, I mean *anything,* and you need me to handle that piece of shit up there . . ." he pointed his thumb upward, "just knock right here on my door." Mr. Bill reached in his back pocket to retrieve his wallet and opened it. "And if you ever get tired of leading the life you living and you and that precious baby inside of you needs somewhere to go and away from that woman-abusing pimp, this is the name and an address to a place in Harlem that takes in young women like yourself and their children. She's my aunt, sweet lady named Ms. Geneva. Just tell her Mr. Bill sent you, and she'll put you right up till you get on your feet." He handed Betty the white card, and she read it. MS. GENEVA GRANT, 621 WEST 122ND STREET.

By the time Betty arrived on the strip, she could barely stand up straight or maintain her balance. Every car that slowed down to look at her merchandise would drive off because she simply looked too sickly for them to take a chance with, fearing she had some hideous disease or bad drug that caused her to sweat and hold her body as she did. Even the pimps who normally tried to win her over with their silver tongues stayed clear of her because she looked that bad.

After only an hour, Betty knew something was wrong when she felt her vagina area grow warm and moist, then blood began seeping down her skirt and legs. She immediately panicked and walked off the strip to find a pay phone. Her efforts were futile. She made it only half a block before she was knocked off her feet by an intensive pain to her abdomen, letting out a cry so loud everyone on the strip stopped what they were doing and looked at the girl everyone called Black Betty, lying helplessly in the middle of the street.

"*911* . . . Where's the emergency?"

"Hello, yeah, we need an ambulance out here right now!"

"Where's the emergency, ma'am?"

The panicked young girl looked around frantically for a street sign but could not find one. Though the girl worked the area for months, she never thought to take to memory the actual location. "Um, um . . . shit I don't know! It's Hunts Point, by, umm, by the strip club."

"Ma'am, we need a little more information than that. What's your name?"

"What difference does it make what my name is? We need an ambulance right now!"

"What is the address, ma'am?"

The girl grew impatient and spewed her anger. "Bitch, I told you I don't know . . . It's on Taylor Avenue, three blocks up from that strip club, The Kitty Kat! A girl is having a baby in the street right now!"

"Ma'am, it's important you stay calm. Is there anyone you can get an address from?"

The girl growled but complied. "Hold on." She dropped the pay phone, ran closer to her friends, and yelled, "Cocoa! Cocoa! What is the exact address here?"

The girl who was attending to Black Betty looked up and read the street sign above her head and yelled, "East 138th, between Taylor and Cliff."

Diamond rushed back to the pay phone and repeated the address to the operator, "138th between Taylor and Cliff. Hurry!"

She hung up the phone and huffed back over to where Betty lay in the desolate street. Trina and Cocoa tried to make her as comfortable as possible and assured her that help was on the way. A curious, motley crowd had already started to gather around watching the melee.

"Hold on, baby," the girl said over Betty's moans, "they said they be here in five minutes," she lied, "so just hold on."

Sweating profusely, Betty pleaded through gritted teeth, "Please help me . . . I'm sorry for what I did to you. I'll make it up to you . . . Just help me!"

The three girls cautiously assured her not to worry and that help was indeed on the way. "Don't worry, Betty," Trina said, "we just found out what happened to you in that motel, and we got your back. Just try to relax, OK?" Betty managed a faint smile and nodded as her breathing increased.

When the paramedics arrived, they cleared away the gawking crowd that had formed. Screaming in agony, the pregnant girl lay in the cesspool of her own mixture of birth liquid that had already burst forth, mixed with blood. The paramedics knew she would have to deliver in the street and removed her panties.

"She's crowning partner," said one paramedic. "We have to start delivery here."

"Aghhhhhh!" screamed Betty as sweat poured from every inch of her body. "This shit hurts . . . Take it out! Take it out!"

The paramedics cut the remaining portion of her denim minidress off and comforted her. "Everything is OK now. What's your name?"

Her breathing became labored. "Annabelle . . . Annabelle Blaise."

All three girls impulsively looked at each other.

The paramedics lifted her carefully and placed a clean sheet under her bottom as she lay spread-eagle near the curb in the street.

"OK, Annabelle, when I say push, I want you to give me a good push, OK?" Annabelle was breathing rapidly but managed to nod between pains. "OK, push!"

Annabelle followed orders and took a deep breath and pushed with all her might. It was if a group of banshees had circled the site as she screamed in shear pain that only motherhood can cause. Her voice grew hoarse, dry, and brittle.

"Oh my God . . . I can't take it. Get it out of me. Get it out of me," she pleaded. They struggled like this for more than five minutes when suddenly, with a volley of pushes, the head and birth matter spewed out.

"OK, Annabelle, you're doing fine. Now what I want you to do is give me one more push, just like you did, OK, Annabelle?"

Black Betty's eyes rolled to the back of her head, she felt as if she would pass out and just desperately wanted the pain to stop. She continued to pant rapidly and again nodded and took one final breath and pushed with all the strength she could muster when suddenly, silence fell on the group.

Then came the faint sound of a gurgle, followed by a faint cry of the child that came out of her. The paramedics looked at each other in disbelief before quickly wrapping the baby in a blanket, while the three girls held their hands over their mouths. The baby was so tiny it looked the size of a newborn kitten. Dazed and confused, Betty looked from face to face, and then asked in a terror-filled voice, "What wrong with my baby?"

Ironically, Betty and her newborn arrived at Mount Sinai Hospital just seventeen minutes later, the very hospital where she was treated for her trauma a short six months prior. Betty gave birth to her daughter three months premature. The baby was immediately placed in the prenatal intensive care unit.

Two days later, Betty's spirits were the lowest they had ever been, blaming herself for her baby's condition and praying each night for her to recover. Alone once again and just as she was about to break down and cry once more, in walked Trina, Cocoa, and Diamond, each holding pink balloons that read IT'S A GIRL! on them. They carried little teddy bears and bouquets of flowers as they slowly walked in and greeted her.

"Hey, Betty," each girl said. Betty was surprised, yet elated to see them and waved them in.

They were chatting and laughing it up as if they were lifetime girlfriends when in walked a woman in plainclothes, who smiled and greeted everyone. She introduced herself, and then she looked at her papers and said, "Annabelle Blaise?" Betty nodded. "I'm Ms. Bledsoe from the birth records department. I've come to get information regarding the birth father's name and find out whether he was there to sign the baby's birth certificate."

Betty grew uneasy and lowered her head. She never even thought about what to tell them, especially, what to say regarding the father. All the girls picked up on it and decided to save her from further shame and embarrassment, so Trina covered, "She's sorry, miss, but her child's father recently died in a car accident, so you can put down deceased."

The lady was saddened and when she looked at Betty she felt even worse. "I'm so sorry to hear that." The girls all nodded for Betty. She annotated the information on her records and moved on with a smile, then asked, "OK, Annabelle, what name did you choose for your daughter?"

Betty's shoulders collapsed. She didn't think of her daughter's name either. She was too worried because the doctors couldn't make any promises whether her daughter would make it, only telling her that statistically, a baby born three months premature had a fifty percent survival rate. She was distressed and blamed herself and began to cry.

Trina, Cocoa, and Diamond all consoled her by rubbing Betty's back and said comforting words. "Betty, it's going to be, okay," the three girls assured her.

Ms. Bledsoe, already behind schedule, heard them mention the name *"Betty"* and asked, "So, is her name going to be Betty?"

Trina smiled, looked at Betty, and tried to lift her spirits and joked, *"Fly Betty,* that's what they call girls down in D.C., where I'm from. It means a street and book smart pretty girl that can dress her ass off. A girl that no matter what is thrown her way, she stays on because she is a survivor." Betty wiped her eyes and thought about those words. Trina looked at Betty seriously. "And if the baby is anything like her mother, key word is 'survivor.'"

They all agreed, and Diamond cosigned. "Yeah, now that has a ring to it. That would be a perfect name for her, right, girls?" Both girls nodded.

Trina smiled and told Betty, "There's always room in the world for two Fly Betty's . . . What do you think, Annabelle?"

This brought a smile to Betty's face, and she agreed with a nod. "Fly Betty it is."

Betty was released from the hospital three days later with a clean bill of health. But the baby wasn't so lucky and had to remain in an incubator to assist her in breathing because she was still in critical condition; however, her chances of survival had increased a hundred percent. It killed Betty to have to leave the hospital without her, but she had no other choice. To make matters worse, they found heroin in her and the baby's blood work. Betty was informed that the baby would be placed under the Bureau of Children's Welfare once it became healthy, and the best thing she could do at that point was to enroll in a drug treatment facility and find a stable home.

Fresh out of the hospital and still depressed, Betty followed the hospital's advice and she used the card that Mr. Bill had given her and went to see his people in Harlem.

She was accepted immediately by the director, Ms. Geneva, but still felt guilty about having to leave Rico. Ms. Geneva gave her a bed date for the very next day, giving her time to gather her clothing and tie up any loose ends. She thought hard about the matter all the way back to the Bronx. She knew she had to do right by the baby and made up her mind to get her remaining clothes from Rico's apartment.

When she arrived at the apartment, it was a mess. She noticed the leather furniture was no longer in the living room and was sure he sold it. When she walked into the bedroom, it was equally filthy. She carefully stepped over mounds of clothes and drug paraphernalia thrown about on the floor. Rico was sprawled out unconscious on the bed, fully clothed, shoes and all.

Betty took off her jacket, a brand-new denim acid washed two piece given to her by the girls. Her original plan was to simply pack up and leave without him knowing, but when she saw him sleeping so innocently, her feelings for him took control. She slowly eased her body into the bed and wrapped her arms around him. Rico soon came out of his drug-induced stupor, wiped the drool from his mouth, and mumbled, "Betty, you came back."

Betty rubbed his silky black hair and said softly, "Yeah, baby, I'm not going anywhere." He continued in his dazed state and grunted, "Where you been? I thought you up and left me."

Betty smiled and answered, "I was in the hospital, Rico. I had the baby."

Rico drifted back to sleep.

Betty shook him, "Rico, did you hear what I said? I said I had the baby, a baby girl."

Rico turned on his side and grunted again. In a sleepy babble, he muttered unconsciously, "He gave you the baby. I never told him to have sex with you. I just paid him to . . ."

Confused, Betty's head bolted up and she inquired, "Who did you tell not to have sex with me?"

Rico kicked off his scuffled shoes and switched sides again, this time with his back to her. Betty asked again, "Rico, who did you tell not to have sex with me?"

As if he was getting annoyed, he answered, "The African . . . Sebastian."

It was as if she were hit in the face with a brick. Betty's jaw dropped agape; her heart began hammering in her chest. The dreaded name Sebastian echoed repeatedly in her head. She sat paralyzed—she couldn't move. It took her a few minutes to regain her equilibrium to process what she had just heard, then she stared at Rico grimly, who slept like a baby as he lay on his back.

Betty rose from the bed slowly and stepped lightly, very tentatively, out of the bedroom. As if she was sleepwalking, she entered the kitchen and opened the kitchen drawer and retrieved a huge butcher's knife, clutching it firmly in her hand.

BOOK 3

Betty and the Beast

$$Chapter\ 24$$

NEW YORK STATE MENTAL INSTITUTION
FOR THE CRIMINALLY INSANE . . .

After entering the secure state facility, Betty, Vonda, and Chubby waited inside the cafeteria-like room for Annabelle Blaise to enter. Traditionally, the inmates at the asylum rarely had family members visit them, and so it was not structured for them to have visitors, but because of Annabelle's history, having had Betty right before she was arrested, the chief psychiatrist and state officials saw the necessity that she develop a bond with her newborn. Betty was fortunate, indeed, to have bonded with her mother, though only on a monthly basis, over the course of twenty years.

When Annabelle arrived in the room, escorted by two state correctional officers, she wore the blue state-issued one-piece dress. Though Annabelle was still beautiful, despite her hideous scar, she had aged badly.

After they greeted each other, had their birthday meal and cake that they had brought Annabelle, Vonda and Chubby always gave mother and daughter the last half hour to themselves to bond privately.

"So, how are you feeling, Mommy?" Betty asked.

Her mother dismissed the question and got straight to the point as she did each time over the years. "It's not about me, Betty. What's going on with school and your personal life?"

Betty cleared her throat. "I finished all my curriculums one semester early with a 4.0 GPA and will graduate summa cum laude and start my Ph.D. in September." Betty half-expected her mother to give her some sort of praise, but her mother showed not even a hint of reaction. Her mother had been a stickler for perfection and pushed her to not settle for less.

With determined and stern eyes that bored through her, as if she could read her mind, her mother asked, "Who are you fucking with out there?"

Betty stammered, "What?"

"Betty, don't fuckin' play with me. You heard what I said. What nigga are you fuckin' with?"

"I'm not messing with anyone, Mommy. I'm just into my education." Betty held her breath, hoping she was convincing enough so she wouldn't be pressed on the subject.

Her mother nodded her head and relented. "That's good. I'm proud of you." Betty smiled. She loved to please her mother because she knew she was the only thing that gave her mother hope, the will to live, the sole reason she look forward to another day. So, she lived her whole life and did everything in her power to make her mom happy and to not disappoint her.

"Are you still a virgin?"

Betty blushed, caught off guard by the question. "Mommy," she guffawed, feeling embarrassed like a little girl. The mood was lightened, but her mother was serious and wanted to know.

"I just think it's important that a mother should know what's going in her baby's life."

Betty smiled and submitted. "If you need to know . . . Yes, I'm still a virgin."

At that moment they laughed like best friends. They were having the time of their lives when the correction officer walked over and told them it was time to wrap it up. With less than five minutes left on the visit, Annabelle handed her a notebook. "I redid, added, and made some important changes to the Blaise Diaries and want you to really study them." Betty's mother grew very serious and repeated, "Betty, I want you to really read it because I waited and added some things that you are going to need to know about certain men because . . ." Her mother began to get teary eyed and choked up.

"Mommy, what's wrong?" Betty asked, growing equally emotional. Barely able to continue, her mother said as the tears flowed freely, "You grew up so beautiful—perfect, and I just don't want any man coming along and ruining your life like they ruined mine."

As if they were one, Betty felt her mother's pain and assured her, "I'm all right, Mommy. Nothing is going to happen to me."

They embraced. The two correctional officers hovered nearby and said, "It's that time, Annabelle."

They pulled apart and wiped the tears from their eyes. Vonda and Chubby walked back over and gave her their farewells. Betty smiled and said, "Happy birthday, Mommy. I'll see you next month." Her mother nodded.

Just as she was about to be escorted out of the room, Annabelle looked over her shoulder and reminded her only child, "Always remember, Betty, *'If ever you become a fool for love, be prepared to become a fool for pain.'*"

After visiting Betty's mother at the institution, Vonda, Chubby, and Betty headed downtown to the westside of Manhattan, like they always used to do when Betty was growing up, to eat out at a nice restaurant. They all agreed to eat at a high-end steakhouse in the Meatpacking District. When they got off the Henry Hudson Highway exit at 59th Street, Chubby made the first left toward 11th Avenue. Betty was still in too much of a funk, hating each time leaving her mother behind and alone in such a depressing place.

As she gazed out the window caught up in her own thoughts, she noticed what looked like official cars by the way the front and taillights blinked in front of the very shop she had her tire fixed at just months earlier. To her surprise, she watched José, the man who fixed her car and befriended her, being led out in handcuffs by two federal officers. "Stop the car, Uncle Chubby!" Betty screamed.

When he came to a halt, Betty hopped out of the truck quickly and ran in the direction of the tire shop with her uncle following closely behind his niece, clueless of what was going on.

"José, what's going on?"

José looked in her direction with a distraught and defeated look on his face and simply lowered his head again.

"Stand back, lady," said one of the officers, who was short and very young, infuriating Betty by his callous attitude.

"That's my family," Betty lied. "I have the right to know where you are taking him."

The other officer, who was much older than his partner, defused a possibly volatile situation, one of many which he had seen over the years. He calmly explained, "We're with the Department of Immigration and Naturalization, and the gentleman here is not a United States citizen."

Betty knew from the conversation they had earlier that he was in a lot of trouble and was genuinely concerned for him as she watched them stuff him into the backseat of the police car and close the door.

"Is there anything I can do to help him, Officer?"

Sympathetic, the older officer reached in the inside of his shirt pocket and offered her his card. "The best thing you can do right now is get him a great immigration attorney, ma'am."

Betty stared at José through the window of the car as he hung his solemn, sad face down to his chest as they drove away. Betty, equally sad, turned to the one person she knew that could help with this problem—she looked up into her Uncle Chubby's eyes, and he simply said, "I got him."

Betty was physically drained by the time she finally arrived at her condo. Because of José and his immigration situation, the three of them opted to cancel their plans for dinner. Instead they met her Uncle Chubby's attorney, Mr. Kenneth Russo, a handsome, bold, smart, and brazen lawyer who was on the verge of becoming a lawyer legend, defending and winning every single case that he took to trial. Mr. Russo normally didn't deal with immigration cases, but as a favor to Chubby, who he genuinely liked, he didn't hesitate to represent José and meet them at the Federal Immigration Offices to set things in motion in hopes of getting him released.

After taking a much-needed hot bath, Betty fixed a modest chicken tossed salad, curled up on her living-room couch, and watched prerecorded episodes of *The Basketball Wives.* Just as the show was heating up, her cellphone rang—it was Fabian. Betty was so engrossed with the drama in the show she snatched up the phone and answered with quickness, "Fabian, I'll call you back in ten minutes."

"No, Betty, listen," Fabian said even quicker.

"Fabian, I'm watching *The Basketball Wives.* Evelyn Lozada is about to get it on with homegirl."

"Fuck them bitches. You got to get dressed and get down here."

"Get down where?" Betty frowned, too tired to even think about going out, but curious enough to inquire.

"At The Platinum Lounge in the Village," Fabian revealed excitedly.

"Nah, girl, only place I'm going tonight is my bed. I was out the whole day visiting my moms with my aunt and uncle, and I just got home a little over an hour ago. Hell, I'm tired."

In a calm, unapologetic tone, Fabian said, "OK, I guess I'll just have to say hello to Drake for you."

Betty froze and placed her salad to the side and asked, "What Drake, Fabian?"

"Bitch, what other Drake you know? YMCMB Drake!"

Betty stood to her feet. If there was one person on the planet that she had a crush on, it was Drake. She loved his look and his style—even his music.

"So, what kind of event is it?"

"It's his release party for his second album, and he kicking it off first, right here in New York, and it's going to be huge and everybody's going to be there—Baby, Slim, Lil Wayne, Nicki Minaj, Diddy, Busta Rhymes, Trey Songz . . . everybody, and it's by exclusive invitation only, and guess who got two passes to the VIP?"

"You got passes?"

Fabian was offended by her asking and sucked his teeth. "Bitch, have you forgot who I am?" he snapped.

"So, what time are we going?"

"Are you even *listening* to me? I said I was already down here, and it is already packed with people trying to get in. Just hang up the phone and get down here instead of creaming on yourself."

Betty glanced at her Cartier watch. It was ten to eleven.

"Call me when you are out in front and I'll come out to get you, OK?" added Fabian, but Betty was already off the phone and in the bathroom to take a quick shower.

RULE #10

This is where the average woman goes wrong. They give up the vagina far too soon, which means they are giving away their power. See, here's the trick. If your mission in life is to have anything you want—a man, money, fame or fortune—you got to have attitude. When it comes to wealthy men, never give it up to them, and if you do, you better have a vagina clause signed.

Your attitude and vagina are your ticket; it is everything. Even Beyoncé put a vagina clause on her box. How the hell do you think she got one of the richest entertainers in the business, Jay-Z? Only the smartest and strongest women figure this out—and they are not telling, because it's a lifestyle—it's reality.

There's also a few other characteristics women must have if they want to get what's coming to them and keep the advantage over men.

Ladies, you need to shut the fuck up and stop running your mouths when you just meet a man. When you give up too much information too soon about yourself or your past, it takes away from the intrigue, mystique, the romance. Men need to access and paint images in their minds of a woman. The also love a woman with a future, as well a surreptitious past. It keeps them guessing. The more you talk, the more you are rendering yourself mortal. Keep it casual. There's a time and a place for everything.

Chapter 25

When Betty arrived on Eighth Street in the West Village and in front of The Platinum Lounge, it looked like pandemonium. Two velvet ropes were set up on both ends of the club, but they were useless. The security and club staff members argued and stood in force, keeping the hundreds of partygoers at bay from entering the star-studded event despite them even having passes.

Cash Money Records was hands-down the biggest rap label since the golden days of Def Jam. It was founded by brothers Bryan "Birdman" Williams aka Baby and Ronald "Slim" Williams. They recently started a publishing company, Cash Money Content, and signed the top urban fiction authors in the business today—K'wan, Wahida Clark, husband and wife duo Ashley and JaQuavis, Treasure Blue, and the backlog titles of the great Iceberg Slim.

Betty sighed and took out her phone to call Fabian

and prayed that she didn't come all the way downtown for nothing.

Within minutes of calling him, Betty watched Fabian exit the club searching around for her. Betty, waiting patiently curbside, waved her hand to get his attention. Fabian spotted her and waved for her to come and turned his attention toward one of the security staff, a hulking man, who had to bend over to hear what he was saying. The man unhooked the velvet rope and waved her in, causing mass grumbles from the crowd of people standing in line.

As Betty walked through the ropes, she recognized the regular motley crew of girls that frequented nearly every major event in the city giving her the screw-face. Betty knew they despised her and tossed her long hair and let it bounce on her shoulders. Fabian, who never could stand any of them, rolled his eyes at them and took Betty by the hand and swung on his heels inside the club.

Betty and Fabian laughed and joked at their small victory. "Did you see all them bitches all up in your bone structure?"

Betty chuckled and said, "You think I didn't?"

Fabian gave Betty the once-over and cooed, "Ooh, girl, those heels are fierce! Jimmy Choo's?"

Betty gave Fabian a knowing look. "Girl, anything else would be uncivilized," she joked. They laughed all the way past yet another velvet rope and showed their exclusive passes, and were escorted inside the elevator to the rooftop portion of the lounge where the VIP section was.

When the elevator opened, they were welcomed by Drake's smooth voice emitting from the speakers, but when the lights hit them, they both went into Hollywood mode. Betty lowered her Prada shades, as did Fabian, and sashayed their way into the hub of the party and mixed and mingled with the young and filthy rich.

After two hours, the place was packed with wall-to-wall celebrities, and virtually every rapper from the East Coast, West Coast, and the South, sports professionals and music executives alike, all there to pay homage to Drake and YMCMB. And they spared no expense—open bar, nonstop hors d'oeuvres, and a huge neon blue-lit outdoor lounge area that gave a one-of-a-kind spectacular view of the city. Betty was shining that evening, as many male suitors, black and white, were smitten by her rare stunning looks and casual demeanor, offering her spots in their videos if she was interested in modeling or simply going to an after-party after the event.

Betty was poised, but humbly declined all of their invitations. She was only interested in meeting Drake, not there for business, but as a true fan—she loved his music, but he and the rest of Cash Money had yet to arrive.

Betty and Fabian sat in the outdoor lounge on the many plush chairs and sofas, having the time of their lives up until the moment they spotted Main Man—Betty's kind-of-sorta ex.

"Oh, Lord, guess who's coming this way?"

Fabian didn't even have to look and said, "Main Man?"

Betty nodded. Fabian looked over at Main Man, who was greeting and getting love from everybody, and looked like the true celebrity he was. Behind him were some of the very girls that he and Betty saw standing in the line waiting to get in only hours earlier, with his flunkies close by.

Though Betty hadn't heard from or seen him in months, she knew Main Man was still heated with her because he had a huge ego and wouldn't let things go that easily. This was the only downside of her business. She prayed that he lived by the universal players' code of the industry and sucked it up if he ever got played by a woman, but she doubted seriously that he would abide by the rules.

Just as she figured, when he spotted her, his smile turned into a scowl, and he tapped his man. They started walking toward her.

"What's up, you gold-digging bitch? You here looking to find another sucker to swindle for their money again?"

In unison, Betty and Fabian sprang to their feet. Betty's face twisted, and her eyes grew into a slant, and then she flew into a rage. "If you see a bitch slap a bitch, motherfucker, and see what happen?"

Main Man chuckled and looked behind him at the people he was with and joked, "Look at this, superhead and a faggot want to bring it to me. Ain't this a bitch?"

"No, *you* are the bitch, and if you keep talking to me and my friend like that, you're going to get your ass beat by this faggot—and you better believe, I did it before, so fuck with me."

Main Man grew serious, and he and his two boys stepped closer to Fabian and threatened, "Li'l faggot, if you ever come out your mouth like that again to me I swear to God I'll throw your li'l ass off this balcony."

FLY BETTY

Betty wasn't having it and stepped between all of them. "See, you and your fucking punk-ass friends rather jump somebody smaller than all of you. You wouldn't do that shit to one of them niggas in there." Betty pointed inside the inner room.

"Bitch, please, you think I'm worried about any of these niggas in here? I'm from Queensbridge, where any nigga can get it."

Caught up in the moment, Main Man didn't see the group of men who were standing in the shadows behind him, listening to every word he said. Just as he was about to commit to more verbal threats, out of the corner of her eye, Betty spotted a huge grim-faced man lurking directly behind Main Man, who sensed something afoul when he followed Betty and Fabian's eyes shift to the left of him. He turned, and instantly lost his machismo, causing his heart to get stuck in his throat.

"Oh shit, what's up, Scar?" he said in a much-lower octave and more respectful tone, extending out his hand to show him some love.

Wearing his typical outerwear, jeans, black hooded sweat-shirt, with his hands stuffed in the pockets, Scar stared harshly into his eyes, never acknowledging his extended hand. The situation began to grow even more dire when Main Man watched a mob of young thugs surround him.

"Yo," Scar said with a twisted face and tight jaw, "why you up in my people's face like that and talking to my wife like that?"

As if Main Man just found out he tested positive for a

deadly virus, he was overwhelmed by the news. "My, dude, I didn't know she was your people. My bad, fam—"

"Fuck all that," Scar sneered, "you been popping shit on your records and that pussy-ass Facebook and Twitter shit. I want to see if you want to clear that shit up to my face."

His entire crew had out their cellphones and were videoing the confrontation. Main Man was shaken—and began to stumble over his words. "Man, I was just talking shit. I didn't mean anything by it, I was—"

Before he could finish his plea, Scar squared off and punched him in the mouth. The two men who were with Main Man tried to aid him but were quickly subdued by Li'l Felony and Weeg, who shoved guns in their ribs.

Bent over and grimacing in pain, Main Man held his bleeding mouth and threw his other hand up to signal submission. "Man, you ain't got to be like that. We can sit down and chop it up and straighten this out."

Scar smashed him again with a brutal blow to the side of his head, and he fell instantly to the ground with a loud thud.

"Nigga, I told you I ain't into that talk shit, now get the fuck up!"

Scar's crew of young guns was growing rabid—they saw blood spilled and wanted in and to do what they did best— eat the weak. Just as they were about to pounce, security came running out into the open court in force.

They helped Main Man to his feet and in a calm, measured tone, one of them addressed Scar, who was standing over Main Man, obvious that he was the aggressor, and asked him to leave the premises. Defiant, Scar removed the hood from off his head and challenged them. "I'm not going nowhere—*you* put me out."

Though the security was massive and in force, half a dozen of them, they weren't stupid. They knew who Scar was, and they knew even more about his reputation of shooting up clubs. And when they saw the young, black, and dangerous mob circling them like hungry wolves, they instantly knew they had to reevaluate their tactics before things got out of hand—real fast.

In the standoff, security was able to breathe again when they saw Baby and Slim, the party's hosts, approach the melee.

Baby was smooth about this, and so was his brother Slim, even in the midst of natural-born killers. They were born and raised in hard streets of New Orleans, in a neighborhood that was unforgiving and where survival was by any means necessary. Poverty wasn't only a way of life; it was accepted in their paucity-ridden environment.

Baby flashed his million-dollar smile—literally—and looked at Scar and said softly, while he stuck his hand out toward him, "Mr. Scar, it's a pleasure to finally meet you."

Scar took his hand into his, and they gave each other a warm embrace. Slim smiled and stuck out his hand and repeated the same process. Baby looked at Main Man, and asked, "You OK, pa?"

With his head down, Main Man simply nodded, avoiding eye contact with him.

Baby didn't address anyone in particular but humbly let it be known, "That's great news, because we want to keep everything positive tonight so everyone can have a good time and get home safely, you feel me?"

On cue, several bar runners appeared with bottles and bottles of top-shelf champagne on trays. Like the true leader he was, Baby continued in his sincere and genuine voice and addressed Scar. "Drake just showed up and we are downstairs in the VVIP room, and it would be an honor to have you in our presence." He looked over at the bar runners setting up a table with champagne glasses and continued. "In the meantime, my staff is going to hold your people down with some bubbly, and it's an open bar if they want anything else while you are away."

Scar looked around at his people, all smiling as they popped champagne bottles and agreed with a nod. Baby smiled and turned to ask Main Man if he would like to attend, but he declined. He thanked him, claiming he had a prior engagement. Baby shook his hand and gave him a warm embrace.

It took quite a minute for Baby and Slim to actually leave because they were approached by Scar's entire crew, showing them much love and respect, as the brothers returned equal love and shook hands with each and every one of them. Finally, just as they were about to leave, Scar waved at Betty and Fabian to follow him—and they did.

Before they began to walk off, Main Man, nervous and fidgety, approached Betty, Fabian, and Scar. As if his lungs were collapsed and in a stuttering whisper, he timidly asked, "Um, yo, Scar, man, I, I hope we got that squashed. I ain't got no beef with you."

Scar looked into his pleading eyes, and then at Betty, who felt rather sorry for him and implored Scar with her eyes to let it go. Scar said simply, "Just watch what comes out of your mouth next time."

Main Man nodded graciously and walked away to leave the party before Scar changed his mind. Turning to his soldiers, Scar stared his cold, sullen eyes toward Li'l Felony, Weeg, and his crime partner, Diesel, and signaled with his head for them to follow him—they automatically knew what they had to do.

Inside the VVIP room downstairs, true to his word, Baby introduced Scar to some of the biggest figures in the entertainment industry. Scar's reputation preceded him, and each rapper that he met gave him total respect. This was the first time he ever attended an event of this magnitude because he was a loner and notoriously antisocial. Later, Baby, the true impresario he was, did what he did best, promoting, talking to the press, and being the gracious host, while Slim kicked it and shared his wisdom with the young Scar about the business end of the entertainment world; he also shared with him his personal experience.

"My brother, in this business, you have to learn to get along, in order to *get along*, if you can understand that. Me and my brother, as well as many others we know when we was coming up, was filled with uncertainties of our future, because on every corner all we saw was pain and disparity and that only the tough survived. But, through it all, we only had one thing that we could hold on to, and that was our dream, despite what many people told us and what our surroundings dictated. So, what I'm really trying to say is, live your dream, my brother, 'cause at the end of the day, it's just about you, family, and survival." Scar internalized his words of knowledge and absorbed a lot, and he really respected him for it, because it got him thinking and may have forced him to reevaluate things as he saw them.

By the end of the night, and because of Baby and Slim, they opened Scar's eyes to the benefits of coexisting with others so he could stay consistent and relevant in the fickle business of hip-hop and he met and mingled with people who he wouldn't have before.

Scar finally made time for Betty and sat down beside her in silence until Betty said, "So, you telling people I'm your wifey now?" Scar avoided eye contact and only grinned slyly.

"I guess you looked me up and know who I am now?"

Betty was sure to play her hand right and remained as detached as possible. "Yes, I know who you are now." That's all Betty said on the subject, not wanting to inflate his ego, but more importantly, not wanting to appear interested in his money, and changed the subject.

"What was that with you and Main Man? You can't keep assaulting people like that without consequences, you know. Plus, I'm getting tired of you coming to my rescue," Betty joked.

"Nah, it ain't had nothing to do with you this time—it was personal."

Betty nodded. "From what I read about you, you got something personal against everybody in the industry."

Scar just shrugged and stretched his arms out on the booth. "I just don't respect weak-ass, fake-ass niggas. That's why I don't fuck with nobody."

"But you seem cool with Baby and Slim."

Scar nodded and admitted, "Yeah, but they're an exception to the rule—they fuckin' smart. Them two cats walk it like they talk it and stayed true to who they was since they started and remained a family. I was following them since I was a youngin. When they first came out, New York was running this rap shit, but they didn't try to be like us and jump on New York's dick or our style. They said, 'Fuck it, I'm from the South, and this is who the fuck we are; take it or leave it.' You got to respect that, plus they are loyal to their own. Puffy and Russell are slime; them dude are not loyal and could care less than a fuck about their artists when they are not hot anymore—it's all about the fuckin' paper with them. Betty watched Scar's eyes come to life with passion.

"Look what happened to Bad Boy, Def Jam, Roc-a-Fella, and Death Row. They all gone and the only true hip-hop label left standing is Cash Money, and that shit speaks volumes. So, I could fucks with them. I rather fuck with people I could see than motherfuckers who be fakin' who they are not, like that punk-bitch Main Man."

Betty saw the passion all over his face; he respected loyalty and honesty, obvious traits that he lacked with people in his past and the prime reason why he was so guarded to this day. She took this assessment to memory, and precluded to never allow him to catch her in a lie, even if it meant telling him the truth. He was smarter than she thought. He seemed to only ask questions he already knew the answers to, and would constantly test her on things he knew were a fact about her.

"Is there any rapper you do respect?"

Scar shrugged. "But to answer your question, I fucks with Lil Wayne's music heavy, Maino, Fat Joe, Scarface, Jeezy, Cam, the whole YMCMB, and, of course, my niggas from Wagner, Boy Billions, King Freaky, Mix, and Big Chris— Bout That Bread Crew."

Betty smiled and shook her head. "All hard-core rappers, I see. It figures," she joked.

Scar jerked his head. "Nah, it's not just that."

"Then what is it?" asked Betty.

"Every one of them came up on them streets—they represent their hood and their projects above everything, giving hope to a nigga like me who came from the gutter." Scar looked at her and asked her the same question.

"What rappers you listen to?"

Betty frowned and shrugged her shoulder. "I'm not really that much into rap. The last rap album I remember downloading was Pink Friday by my girl Nicki Minaj."

Scar smirked. "It figures it would be a female rapper."

"What . . . Nicki is the shit. Us sisters got to stick together. There's not too many in the game as it is, so we got to represent. Plus, she on some next level shit, and her fashion and shoe game, ain't nobody fuckin' with her." Scar chuckled, he loved how Betty could switch up and show the street in her. He changed the subject.

"So, I see you and dude got some past history together. Was he your man or something?"

Betty answered casually, "Who, Main Man? He wasn't my man, if that's what you're driving at."

"You must have been something to him for him to spazz out on you like that."

"I'll admit, we used to kick it for a quick minute, but I wasn't feeling him like that and told him to move on."

"Um-hmm," Scar nodded, giving Betty a sarcastic, leery stare.

Betty felt the slight of his innuendo and took off the gloves. "Let me tell you something, Calvin, whatever I do is my business. I'm a grown woman, and if a dude offer me something I got a choice to take it or leave it. If he gets mad because I'm not giving up anything for it and decide not to be with him anymore, that's on them, and they just have to handle it."

Scar listened to Betty's rant with a slick grin, pissing Betty off even further. Betty checked her feelings and wasn't about to let him get to her. She knew his manipulation game was above average; probably perfecting it from being in and surviving prison all those years, and was about to flip the script and show him a little bit of hers. That's when she saw him coming toward them and he tapped Scar on his shoulder—it was Drake.

"Yo, Scar, it was a pleasure meeting you, my dude."

Scar stood to his feet to embrace his hand and reciprocated the same sentiments. Drake then flashed Betty a smile, exposing a perfect set of white teeth, and said, "It was a pleasure meeting you also Betty. Hope to see you both again soon."

Betty returned the smiled with seduction in her eyes and

a sensual bite on her glossed, robust bottom lip and in the sexiest voice she could conjure, she cooed, "Nice meeting you also, Drake. I hope to see you soon."

Scar stared at Betty in silence. Betty avoided his gaze and blew Drake a kiss for good measure and knew that would tug at his ego. Scar was pissed, but he held it in well.

All of a sudden, Fabian approached their table and sat down next to Betty with a huge smile across his face. "How you doing, girl?"

Betty forced a smile and answered, "I'm good." She looked at Scar, and out of courtesy, she officially introduced her best friend to Scar. "Scar, this is my friend Fabian; Fabian, Scar."

Fabian put on a wide smile and extended his delicate, well-manicured hand out toward Scar. Scar gave Fabian a cold, scornful look, and simply gave him a head check and said, "'Wassup?" choosing not to shake his hand and coldly turned away.

Fabian looked at Betty and gave her a "no-he-didn't" look. Just then, Scar's grimy partner Diesel came over to the table with two beautiful, blond, young white girls in tow. Diesel stared scornfully at both Betty and Fabian, then bent over and whispered in Scar's ear.

Scar turned and sized the two girls up and stared lustfully at them. He nodded in what appeared to Betty a sign of approval to Diesel. Scar then stood up and gave Betty a rare smile and asked, "So, when I'm going to see you again?" Betty could not believe his audaciousness and looked contemptuously at the perky white girls, then back at Scar and kindly said, "I don't think so."

Chapter 26

It was midmorning that Monday *at* Wagner's Senior Citizen Community Center when Betty saw Ms. Clara Mae's grandson, Scar, walk in alone. For reasons unknown to Betty, she found herself blushing like a teenager and continued helping one of the center members as if she hadn't noticed him.

Scar greeted his grandmother, and seconds later, she heard her name being called. Betty turned around and saw Ms. Clara Mae waving for her to come over. Betty rubbed the shoulder of the member she was aiding and promised her she would be back. With the sexiest walk she could muster, she tossed her long, flowing hair and sashayed over toward her. Betty remained professional and nodded at Scar despite her encounter with him the other night.

"Oh, Betty," said Ms. Clara Mae, "I need you to do me a huge favor. I just received a call from the Meals On Wheels program and they said their truck broke down and won't be delivering meals to our sick and shut-in elderly members in their apartments here in Wagner. There are about fifty or so senior citizens that rely on them for their lunch. We have limited supplies in the pantry and on such short notice, all we can supply them with is a few peanut butter and jelly sandwiches."

"That's terrible," Betty said sadly and quickly offered, "Is there anything I can do to help?"

Ms. Clara Mae patted her on the arm and said, "Thank you, Betty, I do need your help. I called Calvin up, and he offered to help out and go purchase some items, but he needs someone to drive him to the supermarket." Betty looked at Scar who had a sly grin splashed across his face as he feigned his attention elsewhere. She knew he had made the suggestion to drive him—she thought it was very clever.

"Yes, Ms. Clara," Betty said cordially. "I'd love to help in any way I can."

Ms. Clara Mae smiled heartily. "Good. You all have to leave right away because it's almost noon." She handed Betty the list of food to get, and they were on their way. Ms. Clara Mae added with a wink just as they were about to exit, "Oh, and Betty, after you finish, you can leave for the day. I'll cover for you."

RULE #11
You got to keep a man hot and cold . . . sweet one minute, and the bitchiest of bitchy the next; that will keep you interesting and hard to figure out.

They walked side by side toward her vehicle that was parked on 121st Street and Pleasant Avenue in total silence until Betty said jokingly, "If you think I don't know what you are doing, you're wrong."

Scar gave her a quick glance and tried his best to keep a straight face and answered coolly, shrugging his broad shoulders, "I don't know what you're talking about."

Betty twisted her mouth and cracked, "Yeah, OK. You keep believing that."

"What? Because I'm helping my grandmother out and need somebody to drive me you think I'm trying to get with you or something?"

Betty just smiled suspiciously at him.

"What? I'm not that vain or shallow," he added with another cunning grin. Betty burst out in laughter. These were the very words she said to him a week earlier when they first met. "Yeah," he nodded, "a brother got a dictionary, too." They laughed about it all the way to her vehicle, breaking the ominous ice between them from the night in the club.

Stopping at the red light, Betty asked, "I guess you had a ball with those white girls you left the club with. You don't seem so mean today."

"It was a'ight."

Betty stole a quick glance over at him. "So, sisters aren't good enough for you anymore?"

Scar pondered the question carefully and said, "Maybe."

Betty stared at him with surprise and chucked. "I don't believe you said that. You're just like the rest of them sorry black men. As soon as they make a little paper, those white girls shake their asses in front of you, and y'all get pussy whipped."

Scar chuckled and admitted, "It ain't got nothing to do with sex, it's about y'all attitude."

"Attitude?" snapped Betty. "What kind of dumb shit is that? Our attitude was never an issue when you were broke, why switch up now? I bet you them bitches weren't thinking about your sorry ass when you were locked the fuck up all those years."

Scar stared at Betty and shook his head. "See, that's my point. Ever since I first met you, you were nice and sweet, talking all proper and shit. Now look at you. It was all just a front, huh?"

Scar sat back lazily and added, "That's a typical sister who adjusts her attitude when it's convenient to the occasion to get what she wants. Find 'em, fuck 'em, and forget 'em. That's all I seen you pretty broads do since I started getting money, and it's always the black one that's doing it."

Betty was livid as she braked for a red traffic light. "Motherfucker, I don't want shit from you and haven't asked you or any other man to give me shit, which is why I do for my damn self." She pressed her foot on the gas, opting to get this over with as soon as possible.

Scar remained silent and instead scrolled through his smartphone and moments later said, "Oh shit." He looked at Betty. "Somebody put you on World Star Hip-Hop." He raised the sound up to the max, and then turned his phone toward her. Betty quickly pulled her car over as she watched and heard the voice. She squinted and sure enough, somebody had recorded the entire event at The Platinum Lounge Saturday night between her, Fabian, and Main Man, from start to finish.

"What's up, you gold-digging bitch? You here looking to find another sucker to swindle for their money again?"

"So, I guess Main Man isn't considered a man in your world, 'cause he sure sound like he gave you something."

Betty didn't want to watch any further and looked at Scar smirking mercilessly and knew exactly what he was doing and barked, "Fuck you, Calvin!" She drove off in a screech.

Betty drove into the inside parking lot at B.J.'s that was located in the mall on 116th Street to purchase the items, all in bulk, at the suggestion of Scar's grandmother. She was amazed at the sheer size of the place, because she had never been in the huge superstore before. The mall was fairly new, and she had not yet had the chance to patronize the place, nor had Scar.

Betty, like a typical woman, was astounded by the huge and discounted prices of the bulky items, and voiced her enthusiasm, "Man, I got to come back here. I never seen prices this low at my supermarket. Where have I been? I won't have to shop but every other month if I come here."

Scar smiled on the inside at her unbridled mind and enthusiasm from the normally reserved person he first met. He also was astounded by her way of not holding on to an attitude, recovering quickly right after the small disagreement in her car only moments ago. Scar saw in Betty a simple elegance by the way she spoke, acted, even the way she moved, and was equally turned on by her ability to switch up and get ghetto whenever she was threatened—in short, he was fascinated by her.

The two of them walked around the store for nearly an hour racking up on loads and loads of bread, huge jars of peanut butter and jelly, pounds of fruit, juices, and dry goods. When they finally finished, their cart had nearly exceeded capacity.

As they were waiting in line to pay for their items, Betty questioned Scar and asked, "Tell me why you really needed me to drive you to the supermarket."

Scar shrugged and finally said, "Because I don't have a driver's license."

"Then how do you get around?"

"My people drive me," he answered matter-of-factly.

Betty then asked point-blank, "Are you talking about your so-called manager, Diesel? I saw the Benz y'all got into after the party with them white girls. You must pay him well."

Scar flared his nostrils and looked coldly at her. "Why you worrying about what I do with my money and pay my people?"

Betty purposely wanted to piss Scar off for being an ass with her on their way to the supermarket, to give him a taste of his own head games he was playing. She just ignored him and smiled as she pushed the shopping cart forward.

When they got to the register and the cashier had rung up everything, it came to a total of $354.73. The cashier then asked for their membership card. Confused, Betty looked at

Scar, who looked as if the cashier was speaking a foreign language, so Betty asked her, "What is that?"

The cashier, a short, squat black woman in her late twenties, explained lazily as if well rehearsed and had said it a million times before, "You have to be a member to shop here."

Betty shrugged her shoulders and asked, "Well, how do you become a member?"

The cashier rolled her eyes and exhaled. "You have to purchase a membership card to get the discount."

Scar detested her type and snapped, "Bitch, do your job and save that stink-ass attitude of yours. Fuck the discount. I'll pay for it at regular price." His sharp tongue caught the girl off guard. When she looked at Scar's menacing scowl, she took two steps backward, suddenly regretting she angered him.

Stuttering over her words, the girl made more of a nervous plea than an explanation. "Sorry, umm, we . . . we don't do it that way. It's just one price, and you have to have a card to purchase food from the store."

Betty felt sorry for the girl and stepped in front of Scar and softly asked, "Well, can you tell us where to get the card at?"

The girl pointed to a counter and said more humbly this time, "You can purchase it over there. They charge an annual fee to become a member."

A young, rail-thin black guy wearing an button-up shirt with a name tag that read, "Asst. Mgr." came over when he heard there was some problem at register twelve and asked in a tone that was deeper and bigger than his body or age, "Is there some kind of problem I can help you with, sir?"

Scar, who was wearing a gray hooded sweatshirt, hood over his head as always, answered defiantly and grimly, "Why, do you want one?"

The manager, ready to do his usual job of defusing a possible volatile situation, being that the mall was in the middle of Spanish Harlem, saw this scenario many times before, followed protocol and said, "Sir, no need to . . ." Before he could finish his words, he stopped and studied the man's face and nearly lost his breath. "Oh shit, you're Scar the Hyena." A huge enlightened smile overcame his face. "Oh, man, I got all your mix *CD*s." He quickly caught himself as he saw the line of people behind them and snapped back into manager mode. "I'm sorry, sir, but, how can I be of some assistance to you?"

Scar wasn't the type to make a plea and remained silent.

The manager looked at his cashier for an answer, and she explained what was wrong. The manager frowned, waved his hand, then pushed her aside and stood at the register. He used his own store card to scan and smiled like a lad who made his father proud. "You straight, man. I used my store courtesy card. Just pay and you are all good."

Scar reached in the back pocket of his jeans and pulled out a huge stack of bills, all one hundreds—so much that they could not be folded. He peeled off six one hundred dollar bills and tossed them on the conveyor belt and told the girl to give the manager the change.

When Scar and Betty walked off, he stuck his fist out to the manager, and they tapped fists. When they got back to her truck, Betty popped the trunk and allowed Scar to load the goods in the back, jumped in her seat and started the ignition. When Scar opened the door to the passenger's seat, he noticed money placed on the seat. He bent over and picked up the money—it was three crisp one hundred dollar bills, then he stared at Betty with confusion and asked, "What's this?"

Betty nonchalantly answered, "It's my half for the groceries." Scar was totally caught off guard by the unexpected gesture and hopped inside the truck and extended the money back to her. Betty ignored it and said, "I don't want it. I told your grandmother I was going to help out, so that's my way of helping." Scar saw that Betty was serious and cared nothing about the money. It perplexed him.

As they pulled up on Second Avenue and 122nd Street in front of Wagner, she saw a huge crowd lined up for blocks, standing by two white vans with logos that read AMY RUTH'S SOUL FOOD RESTAURANT. In the crowd, she recognized a face that she never forgot, Scar's associate from Wagner, Weeg, who looked like he was the organizer, by the way he was handing out Styrofoam white takeout food, like the ones from a Chinese restaurant. Weeg was methodically writing building numbers and apartments on the top portion of the plate, and then handed it off to another person who filled them in a box according to the building when they walked up.

Weeg spotted Scar and gave him love with a handshake and embrace.

"So what you get?" Scar asked.

Weeg waved him over and showed him what was in the

Styrofoam containers. "We got fried chicken, candied yams, collard greens, and macaroni and cheese in this one, and cheeseburgers and french fries, with lettuce, tomatoes, and onions on the side."

Scar nodded his approval and looked at the vans. "I see you called Amy Ruth's."

"Hell, yeah," Weeg smiled. "If our people gonna eat something for free, it might as well taste good."

Scar agreed and asked, "So, how much food did you get?"

"My dude, Carl, he's the owner, and he hooked me up on short notice and made it happen, and even cut the price in half on every order. It came to like, six a plate, and I ordered five hundred. We might as well make the whole projects happy."

"You paid for it yet?"

Weeg nodded. "Came to like only three stacks."

Scar reached in his back pocket and thumbed out forty one hundred dollar bills, and then handed them to Weeg.

"That's your three and another stack to give to the two drivers to split, a'ight?"

Weeg nodded and walked over, counting out a thousand dollars, and waved toward the two men who dropped what they were doing immediately when they saw the money.

"This is a gratuity from my man over there. His name is Scar."

The man's hands trembled as he accepted it.

"Y'all split that between the two of you."

They nodded graciously and said to Weeg and Scar, "Thank you, Mr. Scar."

Betty then watched Scar whisper something to Weeg again. Weeg turned around to some boys who were milling around, and who snapped quickly to his call. "Yo, unload that stuff out of the truck and take it to Ms. Clara in the community center." In seconds, everything was removed and going to the center.

Betty watched and heard everything and was more impressed with Scar's giving nature. He was literally feeding the entire projects. She knew he had no intentions of letting those elderly tenants eat only sandwiches and planned for the food to be brought all along. That was only a ploy for him to try to get with her.

When Scar approached Betty, she was amazed he knew exactly what she was thinking when he said, "Picture me feeding old people peanut butter and jelly sandwiches."

He leaned on her truck and rubbed his stomach and said, "Damn, all that good-smelling food is making me hungry." He looked at his phone for the time as he continued. "Since you are already off and it is lunch time, how about you treat me to something to eat?" For the first time since she met him, Scar looked her directly in the eyes, and she saw a subtle softness in them and thought they were beautiful.

She smiled, and said, "OK, where you want to eat at?"

RULE #12

You must train a man so you can reap the rewards. Whenever he gives you something, you have be able to turn on the light switch and make him feel like it's the greatest gift in the world and thank him with a wide array of exuberant kisses and hugs. He will never forget your reaction and it becomes addictive without him even knowing it, and he will always want to get that feeling again, that high again. Play sad and distant a lot, and when he asks you those two words, "What's wrong?" you got him.

For example, always sigh and say, "Nothing." He knows that the only way to snap you out of that depressive mode and to get his boo back is to buy or give you something special—trained!

Chapter 27

The sun was sweltering and beating down on the afternoon revelers at Pier 51, South Street Seaport. Betty and Scar had eaten fresh lobsters with sides of calamari and ice-cold lemonade and freshly brewed iced tea. Betty was actually having a fantastic time, listening and laughing at the stories Scar was telling her about encounters he had during his lifetime and people he met, adding his own twist to it. Their conversation was based consistently on Scar and his journey into the music industry and Scar dogging everyone who he deemed fake or phony. Betty listened to every word with keen interest, simply to train him to purge his soul to her.

"I just don't get some of these fake-ass rappin' niggas. They speak on shit they never done before, how they were hustlers, how they busted their guns when they was on the block, how they did bids and slammin' niggas' bodies with the ox. But, see what they do when you catch them by themselves and bring it to them. They pussy," he spewed with extreme displeasure.

Betty laughed but questioned, "Why are you so worried about them, Calvin? Maybe they just embellishing the lifestyle to sell records because that's what the fans want."

Scar stared at her and asked, "Write that big word that you just used down, the word with the 'I,' imbell something."

Betty quickly corrected him. "That's embellishing, and it's spelled with an 'e,' and it means to add fictional details, to make it shine."

"Yeah, that's them, for sure. But to answer your question, it fucks me up when I hear these niggas fakin' their struggle on records, about how they lived when they were growing up, knowing damn well they had a good mother and father who gave them anything they wanted, clothes, food, nice house, nice school, when dudes like me ain't never had none of that shit.

"I experienced more hell and saw more things through these eyes, and no matter how much I try, I'm not trying to sound like I'm innocent, because just as much shit people did to me, I did just as much damage to others, and still can't get it out of my head. These niggas been reaping millions rapping about shit people like me really been through. But, real cats, who really took bullets, got real bodies, and did some real heinous shit, have to live with that, reliving it over and over in their sleep, waking up in a cold sweat."

Scar shook his head and admitted, "You would never hear real dudes who did real things glorify that shit! We are fucked up mentally for the rest of our lives and will never be fixed, never going to be normal. So I'm on a mission to weed these niggas outta the game and be their worst nightmare—their fuckin' Antichrist!" Scar sneered and nodded as if he was confirming his dutiful mission in life. "Both my parents were junkies, and I saw everything that comes with that lifestyle and will die young just like them, so I accept my fate in life."

Betty began to see exactly why he was the way he was and respected him for his honesty. Her studies showed that people like Scar were in desperate need to share their dreams, triumphs, and failures, and she wanted to fill that void—she saw her angle in, so she immediately began to formulate a plan in her mind, because he seemed genetically compelled to make his life parallel to his parents' destructive past.

After they ate lunch, they took a gingerly walk along the pier and watched the tugboats and ships splash through the murky East River water in silence. Betty pondered how dark and morbidly similar both their childhoods were. She wanted so badly to tell him about her past, but stuck to her monologue to gain his trust. But something was nagging at her mind and she needed to know.

"Calvin, can I ask you something personal?"

Scar shrugged and said, "Go ahead. But if I answer it I have to ask you something personal, too." Betty thought about it and saw no harm.

"OK, bet," she agreed. "You mentioned that you were going to die at a young age like your parents, correct?"

Scar shrugged again. "Yeah. I never saw it any other way, so?"

Betty nodded, but was careful to choose the right words,

"So, is that the reason you give away and spend money on other people more than you do on yourself?"

Scar flashed a heated discerning look, one she had never seen before. It was more like a fear of being exposed than anger. Scar could not answer and remained silent. Finally, he looked at her and said, "Can you take me somewhere?"

"Sure, where you want to go?"

"Jersey."

It was about a fifty minute drive to New Jersey and Scar gave Betty the directions all the way. When they finally pulled off the exit ramp, it didn't take Betty long to realize the neighborhood she was in was exclusive and privy to the wealthy. Minutes later, Scar told her to make a right—she did, and went into an area dotted with mansions.

Betty looked around at the beautiful scenery and homes and asked, "Who do you know out here?"

"Nobody," answered Scar. Betty grew confused and glanced toward Scar who was still gazing out the window until he said, "Slow down and pull over to the right." She slowed, and he said, "Pull over here."

Betty pulled over to the curb and stopped in front of a huge, neat property with a sprawling green grass lawn which had a "For Sale" sign stuck in the front. Scar exited the vehicle, and Betty followed suit, walking over to where he stood, admiring the magnificent vastness of the property. It was a gorgeous, spectacular sight to behold, incomparable to and seemingly light-years away from Harlem.

Betty parted her hair from out of her eyes and watched Scar who still stood in silence as he continued taking in the breathtaking, panoramic landscape. She glanced at the "For Sale" sign and quietly asked, "Are you thinking about buying this?" He snapped out of his moody, trancelike state, focusing his eyes on hers, then suddenly walked over to the sale sign and uprooted it and tossed it aside.

To Betty's surprise, she watched him continue his efforts across the lawn and toward the Italian-marbled circular driveway and fish into his pocket and pull out a set of keys. Scar stuck his keys inside the fifteen-foot double white oak doors and opened them. He looked toward Betty, who still stood at the foot of the lawn, and waved her over.

Scar extended his arm for her to enter first. Slowly she peeked in and was overwhelmed when she entered. The foyer looked like a grand lobby in a French hotel, with huge authentic, turn-of-the-century winding staircases on both ends of the home. Betty was in awe of the sheer size of it. When he turned on the switch, the all-white marble flooring glistened blindingly from the rows of crystal chandeliers that sparkled overhead, illuminating the entire room.

"Is this your house, Calvin?"

He nodded, almost proudly. Betty crept inside, and for the first time she noticed that it had no furnishings whatsoever.

"Let me show you upstairs."

Scar showed Betty bedroom after bedroom—six total— each one as empty as the next, so she asked, "Did you just purchase this place?"

"Nah, I had it for like six months now."

Betty stopped in her tracks and repeated, "Six months? And you haven't furnished your house, yet?"

He shrugged and said, "Something like that, but I did furnish the most important room." He tossed her a cunning, nasty smirk.

Betty read his thought and said, "Yeah, I bet."

He said, "C'mon, let me show you."

Scar led her back downstairs, past the spacious kitchen, dining room, and gargantuan living-room area toward the back. When he got to the first door, he opened it and Betty couldn't believe her eyes. It was obvious to her that this was the main bedroom, which was bigger than the size of her two-bedroom condominium combined. It was totally furnished, and it was apparent that he didn't spare any expense. The bed alone was the hugest she'd ever seen, and the bathroom had a sauna, Jacuzzi, and vanity mirrors that nearly stretched the width of the entire enormous bathroom itself. Betty nodded and halfheartedly joked, "Yep, this definitely is furnished and is definitely you. It looks like you can fit a whole harem of white girls on that bed if you want, huh?"

"Funny, but this isn't my bedroom."

Betty frowned and said, "It's not?"

He shook his head and walked her toward another room located on the other side of the living room. He opened the door, and she looked in. She was bemused; it was just as large as the one he had just shown her, but was ridiculously sparse and underfurnished, with simply a large television on the wall, with white cables hanging precariously to the floor, connected to a PlayStation and DVD player. It also had a king-sized mattress, frameless and no frills. The mattress lay sloppily on the floor. Scar saw her questioning face and said, "The bedroom you just saw is my grandmother's."

He looked around the room they were standing in and said proudly, "This one here is mine, and I never bring anyone here, out of respect if my grandma ever comes over."

Betty was blown away by his thoughtful humbleness, yet saddened at the same time by his meagerness. She looked around at his DVD collection. It consisted of all animated cartoon shows, such as *Family Guy, The Boondocks, King of the Hill,* and *The Cleveland Show.* Betty suddenly saw that he was nothing more than a child in a man's body. Every time when she thought she had him pegged or figured out, he revealed a different side of him, throwing her for a loop.

"Plus," he continued, "I don't like anyone knowing where I lay my head at."

"Then why did you bring me here?" Betty questioned, almost honored.

Scar put his head down and eyed the floor like a child and uncomfortably answered, "I don't really know. Maybe it's because I need your help."

Betty was totally caught off guard by his answer and asked, "What do you need my help with, Calvin?"

He continued eyeing the floor, unable to face her, and said, "I don't know." He finally looked at her and admitted, "Anything." He lowered his head again and shyly added, "Everything."

"Calvin, I'm willing to help you, but you got to be specific with what you want me to help you with." Betty watched him lift his head toward the ceiling, knowing it was a struggle to reach out for help.

"I been in a lot of institutions in my life and saw many of those, you know, shrinks." She watched him choose his words cautiously by him straining for the right expression to say. "I never really let them in, but they be all saying the same thing, that if I don't open up with somebody, I'm always going to have problems and will likely be miserable and alone for the rest of my life. So, what I guess I'm driving at is, I want you to, you know, I guess, be like my doctor." Betty thought that it was an honorable gesture, but she had to be honest.

"Calvin, that's very sweet of you to think of me that highly, but I'm not a professional yet, and wouldn't want to do you a disservice because I still haven't met my credentials. There are many, many people who can help you much better than I can."

For the first time he looked her in her eyes and said, "I know that, but many wouldn't understand me better than you, because we from the same place. You grew up just like me; you told me yourself."

"I know, Calvin, but I just wouldn't feel comfortable doing it because of ethical reasons."

Scar grew silent, then quickly offered, "Then why don't you be my life coach?"

Betty chuckled, "Your life coach?"

"Yeah, why not? You said that's what you do to earn a living. Let me hire you to be mine."

Betty thought about it for a second, and then shook her head. "No, Calvin, I don't think that would work out."

"Why not?"

Betty threw her hands up and said, "Because, me and you are in two different worlds. I'm going one direction, and you are going another." Betty shook her head. "It just wouldn't work."

Scar was disappointed and said, "A'ight."

As they were about to leave, Scar paused in his tracks and recited, *"A life coach is when you mentor, consult, and counsel certain people, in my case, mostly professionals, and address specific personal issues they may have in their life, personal or professional, by examining what is going on right now, discovering what their obstacles or challenges might be, and help them choose a course of action to make their life be what that want it to be."*

Scar turned to face her and said despondently, "Those are your words, and I'm that certain person you mentioned."

Betty was moved, as well as impressed, and asked, "You remember everything I said that night?" Scar nodded. Betty was suddenly engulfed with mass confusion—she was at a loss for words. His words seemingly pierced her soul, rendering her defenseless. It was a new emotion she felt—she didn't feel in control and hated herself for it.

RULE #13

I must say, this is probably the hardest rule to follow, so listen very closely. I don't care if this guy has a Denzel Washington face, a Tyson Beckford body, and is hung like a quarter horse. You must never, ever—under any circumstances—say those three fatal words—I love you.

Like I said earlier, a man's nature is to conquer. If he doesn't have a mountain to climb what's the use? The minute you tell him you love him, it's pretty much broken the spell; you've given up your power, and it's all downhill after that, and he will be on the hunt for the next one, looking for another more challenging task to overcome, and that, my dear, is where I come in.

Though women are smarter than men, women's Kryptonite always has, and will always be, a need to be loved. And the gateway to that is through her heart and through touch.

Chapter 28

"*Bitch, where you at? I been trying* to reach you all day," said Fabian excitedly over the phone. He didn't wait for a response and continued. "Did you know that we are on World Star Hip-Hop?"

"Yeah, I saw it," Betty said, totally unenthusiastically.

"Girl, I don't know why you sounding like you ain't interested, but I received over a hundred calls today, and everybody said I was fierce and I'm going to be a star."

Betty put him on speaker because she knew that Fabian was long-winded, and she busied herself by unpolishing her nails.

"Oh, did you hear about what happened to that motherfucker that same night?"

This caught Betty's attention, so she picked up the phone and took it off speaker and placed it toward her ear. "Who are you talking about?"

"Bitch, you haven't been watching the news or been on Twitter? Main Man."

Oblivious, Betty frowned and asked, "Why? What happened to him?"

"Girl, somebody robbed his punk ass when he left the party and beat his ass like a runaway slave. When the police arrived, they found him stripped buck-naked and bleeding in the street."

Betty was speechless. She rushed toward her laptop and Googled his name, and sure enough, he was trending news.

"So, where you been all day?"

Betty was reading the article intently and answered, "I was with Calvin today."

"Calvin?"

"I mean, Scar," Betty corrected.

Fabian frowned at the mention of his name, and then sucked his teeth loudly. "I thought you said you won't be messing with him anymore, Betty."

Betty cringed; she slipped up because she was too busy reading the article about Main Man, never wanting to reveal it to Fabian to save herself from having to explain herself.

"No, he just came by to see his grandmother at the center, and she sent us to do some food shopping at B.J.'s for the senior citizens."

"Uh-huh, and I guess that took you *all day*."

Betty didn't answer him and tried to switch the subject. "So, how did we look on the video?"

Fabian wasn't a fool and lashed out, "Don't even try changing the subject, Betty. You seen how he dissed me by not shaking my hand. He don't like gay people. Him or that ugly-ass gargoyle friend he was with. He even dissed you by bringing them white bitches over to the table while he was talking to you."

Betty shook her head. She wasn't in the mood to get into it with him and said, "Fabian, I don't want to talk about it. Just let the shit go, OK?"

"OK, but I'm telling you, them niggas are trouble and up to no good. No amount of money is worth getting involved with them, and if you ask me, they were the ones who did that shit to Main Man."

Late the following afternoon, Betty had just gotten off from work at the community center when her cellphone rang. "Hello?"

"Tootie Too." It was her Uncle Chubby. "Where you at?"

Betty smiled at the sound of his voice and joyfully answered, "Hey, Uncle, I'm just getting off from my internship over here at Wagner Projects. What's up?"

"I'm in front of Chase Bank on 135th Street and Eighth. I got something for you. I'll see you in about fifteen minutes." Before Betty could respond, her uncle hung up the phone.

Betty parked her truck inside her building's garage and walked toward Eighth Avenue to meet Chubby at Chase Bank, which was only at the next corner from where she lived. When Betty got to the corner and in front of Chase, she didn't see her uncle's vehicle.

"Tootie Too!" Betty heard over her shoulder.

She turned and saw her uncle with what appeared to be a can of beverage in his hand, exiting the corner deli. She watched his behemoth body lumber across the street in brazen disregard for traffic, with his eyes totally transfixed on her. When he came upon her, he picked up and squeezed her gently. Chubby had no kids, and Betty was the absolute joy of his life, and each time he saw her, he'd greet her as if it was, in fact, his last. Chubby practically raised her, along with his sister Vonda, and Betty was never in need for anything her entire life, which is the very reason for her vast inclination for expensive sophistication for clothing and the finer things in life. One would never know from the meager way Chubby lived, still living with his mother Vera, and driving the same car that he had for over fifteen years, with not an ounce of jewelry, but he had more money than he would ever need in two lifetimes, with dozens of rental properties and businesses all over Harlem and the Bronx. He'd spend most of his day casually driving around the city collecting rent and depositing money in the bank.

Chubby was a gangster from the old school and ran with all Harlem legends from the late seventies and eighties—all killers. If he wasn't out taking care of his business, he'd be with his longtime friend and barber, Denny Moe, who owned Denny Moe's Barbershop located right down the block located between 134th and 133rd Street and Eighth Avenue. Denny Moe was also a Harlem legend and held the title as Harlem's premier barber to the celebrities.

Chubby and Denny had known each other for years. Denny was one of the few people Chubby truly respected because of his honorable and giving nature. Since the eighties, Denny has taken an interest in his community, hosting many neighborhood events and causes for kids, such as summer block parties, sports teams, scholarships, summer camps, voter's registration drive, AIDS Awareness, and the list goes on and on, doing it from the heart, doing it all for free. In fact, it was Denny who taught Chubby, through his action, the importance of taking care of your own—your community—and Chubby had been doing it ever since. Chubby brought Betty with him to the shop many times when she was growing up, and Denny gave her five dollars each time he saw her. Even to this very day, she still calls him Uncle Denny.

"What's up, Unc?" Betty asked, smiling from ear to ear.

"I need you to walk with me over to Denny's shop. I got my car parked in front; I want to give you something."

Betty sighed on the inside, because she knew that he was going to give her some more money or something expensive. Though she appreciated her uncle providing for her, she no longer liked receiving anything from him since she was now a grown woman, wanting to earn things on her own. Betty's pace quickened to keep up with him because he seemed so excited.

"Uncle Chubby," Betty said, "you don't have to keep giving me things. I told you I was OK."

Chubby continued as if he hadn't heard her and asked, "You should see what I got you. You gonna love this shit." Betty shook her head and chuckled, knowing her uncle was never going to change. Nearly in front of his Pathfinder, she was about to make one final plea when she saw a man exit from out of the vehicle behind his—it was José from the tire shop smiling widely.

Chubby had his lawyer, Mr. Russo, who he had retained for the past three years, to work José's case. Mr. Russo took over after Chubby's longtime attorney, Mr. Greenberg, passed away. Mr. Greenberg had had a twenty-five-year relationship with Chubby, getting him out of more than his fair share of trouble. Mr. Russo was Greenberg's protégé and proved to be a chip off his former mentor's block. He was so effective, not only was José Caledonia not deported, he also applied and received political asylum to become a United States citizen. José was so overwhelmingly thankful, he invited both Betty and Chubby to his home in Washington Heights to celebrate with his family.

When they arrived at his home, in addition to meeting his wife and children, José introduced her to his extended family, well over forty of them, who awaited his homecoming and showered Chubby and Betty with heartfelt tears and praise.

Later that evening, José had a quiet moment alone with his savior and told her, "Ms. Betty, I cannot tell you how . . ."

José was so choked up he could hardly express himself. Betty rubbed his shoulders and told him, "José, you and your family have shown me enough thanks. I'm just so happy that I could help."

José shook his head. "No, it's much deeper than that. You owed me nothing, yet you came to my rescue, even hired me a lawyer at your own expense, and got me out of jail, and I'm even about to become a U.S. citizen after being on the run for over thirty years." He could no longer hold back his tears. "We are now familia. I am forever in debt to you, and if you should ever need me for anything . . ."

Betty looked in his watery, sincere eyes.

". . . I mean, anything . . . I'm at your disposal even if it means giving up my life."

Betty could tell he really meant it.

RULE #14

If men think pimpin' ain't easy, let them try being a woman. Appearances early in any relationship are the most important, I mean critical, thing. The minute a man sees you differently from the time you met him, things go downhill steadily. Take, for instance, you both are still fairly new in the relationship and not fully committed yet. But you stay with him overnight or away somewhere knocking boots all weekend. He will see how you really look in the morning, and, ladies, you know what I mean. Once he sees the real version of you, your stock has declined in his eyes, so I suggest either never spending the night with him or leave before he wakes up. It's your job to maintain character and poise at all times and never let him catch you slipping. It's a hard job, but the payoffs are incredible.

Chapter 29

It was a perfect, blue-skied Saturday afternoon when Betty met with Scar on 81st Street and Central Park West at the Museum of Natural History. This was officially their first planned meeting together and for Betty to discuss her services and expectations from him. When Betty pulled up in front of the museum, she saw that Scar had already arrived and was sitting on the steps waiting for her. She honked her horn to let him know she had arrived and drove off to find parking.

It took Betty twenty-five minutes to find parking. She was about to explain what happened, but he waved her off with a half smile and said, "Hard to find parking, right?" Betty nodded. Scar noticed she didn't wear her usual bright smile, so he asked, "You OK?"

Betty looked at him uneasily and said, "I want to ask you something, Calvin, and I hope you will tell me the truth."

He looked at her with a stern face and answered, "Yeah, go ahead and ask me."

"Did you have anything to do with Main Man getting put in the hospital?"

Scar looked at her as if he was offended. "Why the fuck would I do that when I already did something worse and exposed his punk ass for the world to see? What could be worse than that?"

It made sense to Betty, and she nodded with a smile.

Scar smiled back and extended his hand out to her and said with a beaming smirk, "C'mon, let's go see some dinosaurs."

They walked and talked for hours, switching between admiring the displays, serious conversations, to having laughs. If Betty was puzzled about Scar before, she had a much-clearer picture on him now.

They finally sat down inside the food court and snacked on frankfurters, french fries, and diet cokes. After they consumed their food, Betty grew real serious and stated, "OK, Calvin, here it is. Many of your present issues stem directly from your childhood, and it's definitely not going to be an overnight process of change, and it's going to take some really hard work and a lot of honesty involved to do so." She looked for a reaction—he showed none.

"From what I see, you had a miserable, lonely childhood filled with uncertainties, neglect, and pain. Life was hard for you, cruel, but that cannot be a reason to be on a suicidal path of destruction. You had no control and were not responsible for your past, but you are definitely responsible for your future, because you are now an adult and have basic control over that. You will have to be able to face your fears, and your greatest fear is within you, and the only way to remove those fears is to admit to them. My only question to you, Calvin, is . . . what is your greatest fear?"

Scar looked at her stoically and shook his head as if he didn't get the question. "I don't fear nothing."

Betty lifted her head up, searching for a better way to put it, and said, "OK, put it like this. Have you ever seen a car stuck on a highway and the driver has the hood up?" He nodded. "Well, tell me, why does he have the hood up, Calvin?"

As if it was obvious, he answered, "Because something is wrong with the car, and he is checking the engine."

Betty's eyes lit up, and she said emphatically, "Exactly. It is obvious to everyone that passes him by that something is wrong with his car, because no one would simply stop on the highway to check their engine if there wasn't something wrong with it." She looked directly into Scar's eyes. "Calvin, something is broken in you, and it needs to be fixed, or you will forever be stalled unless you admit to your fears." Betty lectured Scar on a philosophical level for almost an hour, and then she spoke on reality. "My mother once told me a quote by an author named Treasure Blue. He happens to be from Harlem also, and he said, 'If your true enemies don't get you, your false friends will.'" Scar knew this was coming and began to grow uncomfortable.

"Do you understand what he's trying to say, Calvin?"

Scar scratched his brow and answered, "I guess he's saying that a friend can be just as bad as your enemies."

Betty nodded, and said, "That's exactly what he means, Calvin. From what I've been seeing, all those people that you have around can only hurt you in the end. They don't have the talent or future that you have and have absolutely nothing to look forward to but prison or death, and if something ever happens, it will be you that will lose the most. You are much better than them, Calvin."

"What makes you think that I'm any different from them?"

Betty quickly said, "Because otherwise, you wouldn't be sitting here with me seeking help, Calvin. Let's be honest. You are slowly beginning to see people for who they are since you got money. The same people who otherwise would've never paid you any mind if you had nothing to offer them. Don't tell me you don't see it, Calvin."

"Yeah, but my man been with me since we was in prison and held me down way before all this rap shit."

"Who are you talking about? Diesel? C'mon, Calvin, I'm sure you two been through a lot of shit together, and I get it. But I'm sure he reaped the reward a thousand times over since you got paid, so that about makes y'all even. He's a grown-ass man, and you can't take care of another man for the rest of his life. The person you are today is not who you will be tomorrow. Everybody changes, and so will you."

By the time they exited the museum, they both were surprised that time had flown by so quickly; the sun had already begun to set. They walked to Betty's truck in silence. Scar was heavy inside his own thoughts as Betty's words reverberated in his head, when he suddenly asked, "What are you doing for the rest of the night?"

Betty looked at him suspiciously and said, "Now, Calvin, I already told you that I'm not looking for anything other than being your life coach."

Scar quickly said, "Nah, it's nothing like that. I just want to know if you want to come to a show I have at B.B. King tonight."

"You've got a show at B.B. King on 42nd Street?" she asked surprised.

"Yeah, why you say it like that?" he chuckled.

Betty shrugged her shoulder and admitted, "I don't know. I guess I never looked at you as the kind of rapper that would perform at that type of venue."

He understood and nodded. "Have you ever heard any of my music?"

Betty was honest and shook her head.

"So, are you down to come out?"

Betty looked him up and down and asked, "What are you going to be wearing?"

Scar looked at her as if she were an alien. "I'm wearing the clothes I got on, why?"

Betty gave him a frown and asked, "Can I ask you a question?"

Scar was hesitant to answer, but he said, "Depends on what you ask and how you say it," he joked.

"Why do you always wear hooded sweatshirts all the time?"

Scar turned away from her. "Why you think?"

"Because you are hiding your scar, that's why."

Scar grew silent and rigid.

"You know, my mother got a big scar on the side of her face also. She got it when she was nineteen years old," Betty said.

Scar suddenly stared at her. "So is that the reason you feel sorry for me?" he halfheartedly joked.

"No, and I don't feel sorry for you."

They arrived at her truck and Betty said, "OK, I'll come with you, but you got to let me buy you something."

He stared at her for a moment and relented. "What's wrong with the clothes I'm wearing now? They are brand-new, and this is my style: Timberlands, jeans, and hoodie."

"Calvin, there's nothing wrong with switching up every now and then. There's a lot of stuff you would look good in. You cannot keep being resistant or afraid of change."

Betty watched Scar pause, and she knew she hit a nerve in him; she wanted to make him think and sniped, "Remember, if nothing changes, nothing changes."

Betty and Scar returned from shopping and made it back uptown to Harlem just after eight o'clock that evening. Betty paid for everything, further solidifying her trust factor with him. Since Scar's show wasn't until eleven that evening, Betty thought it would be a great idea for him to get a quick haircut, and she knew exactly where to take him—Denny Moe's barbershop.

When Betty and Scar walked in the shop, it was engulfed with wall-to-wall customers awaiting fresh cuts. Scar looked at Betty and said, "I'm not going to have enough time to get a cut, go back to the eastside, shower and change and make the show." Undeterred, Betty turned around and spotted Denny Moe at the second chair on the left in the front of the shop just as he finished cutting someone's hair, so she approached him.

Denny Moe was famously known for his skillful hands and flawless touch—and everybody in Harlem, from normal to notorious, knew him. Though only in his midforties, he had over thirty years of experience as a barber, starting his journey in the eighties at the small, yet notable Superstar Barbershop on 124th, just off of Manhattan Avenue, that was frequented by the biggest names in hip-hop and R&B at that time—Teddy Riley, Aaron Hall, Bobby Brown, just to name a few.

When he spotted Betty, his normally concentrated, determined face turned into a gleeful, abundant smile.

"Betty, I haven't seen you in a minute. How you been?"

Betty fell into his arms as he gave her a warm embrace.

He pulled away and complimented her, "Wow, you are really looking good."

"Thanks, Uncle Denny, I'm doing well. I'll be graduating early, so I'll be attending Columbia University this September," she said, genuinely happy to see him.

"That's fantastic, Betty, I'm proud of you. I knew you could do it." He hugged her again for her vast accomplishments.

"So, what brings you by this time of night?" he asked.

Betty turned around and looked at Scar, who busied himself staring at the pictures, awards, and framed newspaper and magazine clippings that hung all over the walls.

"The guy over there in the gray hooded sweater is a client of mine who has an important event to attend tonight, and he is kind of pressed for time and wondering if you can do him a favor and give him a quick cut."

"You sure he's *just* a client? Don't make me have to call Chubby up. You know how he feels about these dudes trying to get close to you," Denny joked.

Betty smiled and shook her head and denied, "No, it's not like that. You know I would tell you if I was seeing somebody."

"Who is he?" Denny inquired.

Betty waved for him to come over. She smiled when he arrived and said, "Calvin, I want you to meet my uncle Denny."

Scar immediately corrected her and muttered, "My name is Scar."

Denny looked him in the face and vaguely recognized him, but noticed Scar shy away from his eyes. He smiled and said respectfully, "It's a pleasure meeting you, Mr. Scar," and stuck out his hand to greet him. Scar pulled his hand from out of his sweater and shook it. Betty forgot how antisocial Scar was around people he didn't know and recovered.

"Do you think you can squeeze us in somewhere?"

Denny winced, looking around the packed shop and told her truthfully, "I got about five or six people waiting and seven more on standby."

Betty frowned and looked around, knowing he was right.

Seeing the disappointment in his niece's eyes he said, "Let me see if I can talk to them and see if they don't mind letting him go ahead of them."

Denny caught the attention of five of the waiting customers, and they walked over. He humbly asked them, "Listen, my man here has a show in a couple of hours and needs a quick cut done. Do any of you mind if he goes ahead of you so I can get him out of here?"

Because of the high respect they had for Denny, they didn't hesitate to tell him it wasn't a problem.

Less than forty minutes later, Scar stepped out of Denny's chair looking totally different from the person who walked in. For the first time, Betty realized how handsome he really was, even in spite of the hideous scar along the side of his face. She was moved. Scar himself could not hide his admiration and couldn't take his eyes off the mirror on the wall and admitted to Denny, "This shit is tight, Doc. I thank you."

"I'm glad you like it, sir. Come back and see me anytime."

Scar nodded and reached inside his back pocket while asking Denny to bring over the five brothers who he went ahead of. Denny called them over, and they surrounded his chair. Scar pulled his thick stack of money and one by one handed each of them a hundred dollar bill for their trouble. They excitedly thanked him. Scar turned toward Denny Moe, then looked around at the pictures and certificates on his workstation and said, "I see you do a lot of things for the community."

"Yes, I give back as much as I can because it's a very rewarding feeling to give to my people who cannot pay you back and see children smile at a block party, receive a gift at Christmas or go away for camp for part of the summer, going places they would never have seen otherwise. I love Harlem, and if we don't take care of our own people and our children, then who will?"

Scar agreed by nodding his head. "I tell you what." Scar handed him the remaining stack of money in his hand, well over five thousand dollars. He reached inside his front pocket and pulled out another equally large stack and handed it to him also. "Take that and put it toward whatever you see fit."

Denny was grateful and stuck out his palm and gave him a powerful shake.

"On behalf of me and the children, we really appreciate your contribution." Scar nodded and walked away.

Betty smiled at her uncle and hugged him again. "Thanks, Uncle Denny."

He looked at the enormous wad of money in his hand and said, "No, I should be thanking you." Denny watched Scar exit the shop and grew serious. "Betty, how long have you known your friend?"

"Not long. Why do you ask?"

"I don't know; he just reminds me of someone," said Denny with a strained look.

"Well, you may have seen him on television— he's a rapper." Betty turned toward the front exits and saw that he was still outside and continued. "He goes by the name of Scar the Hyena."

Denny Moe squinted as he stared at Scar who stood outside the shop's front window.

"Yeah, I heard about him . . . they were talking about him in the shop this week, something about him whipping on that other rapper Main Man's ass at a Cash Money party."

He turned toward the window again and asked, "That's him?" Betty nodded, careful not to reveal that the fight partly had to do with her and she was right in the middle of it.

Denny Moe shrugged. "Well, maybe that's where I remember him from, but I'm not knocking you or nothing, but you family and I have to ask what you're doing with a dude like that."

Betty sighed and smiled. "Uncle Denny, it's nothing like that. I work with his grandmother and it's more like business if anything."

Denny was never the kind to get involved in anyone's personal life, but like Chubby, he was protective and concerned because he knew Betty since she was a baby. He let it go and gave her a kiss on her cheek and wished her luck as she exited the shop.

Denny Moe stared uneasily at both his niece and the man named Scar as they stood talking outside his shop window.

RULE #15

Many of you may think this is small, but this rule is one of the biggest. Cellphones. When a man calls you, take a few hours to call or text him back. Think about it, do you think you can get ahold of a powerful person like Barack Obama, Oprah, or Bill Gates with just one phone call? No, you can't. The reason why is that their time is important, and a man should always see you as just that. He has to know your time is valuable to answer him back immediately. He will then start treating you and your time accordingly.

Chapter 30

Night had long fallen and time was ticking dangerously close to his first major appearance. Scar checked the time on his phone. "So, you gonna drop me off on the Eastside, and then meet me downtown?"

Betty glanced at her watch and realized he was running far too late to take him to his grandmother's apartment, to shower, change clothes, and still make it before eleven, so she suggested, "I don't think you're going to have time to change and everything if you go to your grandmother's house, Calvin."

Scar shrugged and said, "I ain't got much of a choice now, do I? I had to get new clothes and a cut first, remember?"

Betty knew he was being facetious, but ignored it and said, "Listen, I'm going to let you shower and change at my house. I only live one block away, and we can drive downtown together and save us some time." Betty watched Scar's face turn into a sly grin.

"Don't even think about it, buddy," she jokingly warned.

"That's cool, but, I ain't got a change of underwear . . ."

Betty didn't think of that but smiled when she saw, right next door to Denny Moe's shop, one of those African stores that sold T-shirts and accessories.

Scar was definitely impressed with her pricey condominium. He knew that it was in the high $300,000 range and became even more intrigued by her clandestine way of living. Betty could tell he was impressed as she watched his eyes dart around her spacious apartment in awe. It was supplied with fine neocontemporary Italian furnishings, high ceilings, and had a vast and impressive view of the downtown Manhattan skyline that illuminated at night.

Betty gave him fresh towels and a washcloth and showed him the direction to the bathroom and the room where he could change in. She opted not to take a shower or change clothing, something she never would conceive of doing under normal circumstances if she was going out to an event, but due to time constrictions, she made an exception to the rule. And she simply didn't feel comfortable with a man in her home to do so anyway.

Inside her master bedroom, Betty touched up her face when her cellphone rang—it was Fabian.

"What's up, Fabian?"

"Hey, girl, I'm on my way up. I'm getting on the elevator now," Fabian informed her casually and hung up.

Betty panicked. She flew out of her bedroom, hoping to catch him before he got off the elevator, but failed when she heard him ring the front doorbell. When she opened the door he barged in, something he'd done for the past couple of years, and greeted her with a hug and kiss. Taking off his jacket while walking past her, he voiced his displeasure.

"Girl, I'm tired. I had a bitch doing inventory tonight. I think I'm going to stay here tonight instead of going home to Brooklyn. Did you tape everything?" Fabian's mouth was running a mile a minute when he noticed the look on her face and questioned her. "What's wrong with you?"

Just then, Fabian heard one of her room doors down the hallway open and close. When he turned his head, out came Scar, walking stiffly in his newly styled outfit as he scoffed, "Yo, you got me looking like one of these R&B, Trey Songz-type niggas . . ."

Fabian's face went flush at the sight of him and then bedeviled Betty with his eyes. Betty awkwardly announced to him, "Oh, Fabian, you remember Calvin, right? I was just letting him change clothes here for a show he's running late for tonight."

There was a long, uncomfortable silence until Betty asked Fabian, "What are you doing here? I didn't know you were going to stop by." Fabian rolled his eyes with disdain as his voice dripped with sarcasm.

"I guess you forgot you asked me to come over to watch *The Basketball Wives* with you tonight, but I see you must have been too busy to remember."

Betty grimaced. "Oh, that's right. I'm so sorry, Fabian."

"So, I guess that means I came all the way uptown for nothing. It looks like you changed plans."

Betty knew he was pissed and warily admitted, "Yeah, I

promised to take him downtown to a show he has tonight." As an afterthought, Betty quickly offered, "Why don't you come with us? We're going to B.B. King on Times Square." Betty looked urgently at Scar, who stood silent the entire time and asked, "Calvin, you don't mind if Fabian rolls with us, do you?" Scar remained silent and poker-faced until she repeated, "Calvin, do you mind?"

"Whatever, man," Scar said grudgingly and disinterested. Betty looked at Fabian bright-eyed.

"So, do you want to go?"

In a slow, deliberate voice, Fabian rolled his eyes and answered, "No, I don't think so." Betty knew his feelings were hurt and felt it was all her fault and begged, "Come on, Fabian, come with us. When we come back, we could still watch the show. It'll be fun."

"That's OK, Betty," he dismissed as he put his jacket back on and stomped quickly toward the door. "I'll just see you when you are not busy slumming around with your white girl-loving roughneck."

"What you say, li'l faggot? Speak up," snapped Scar as he approached him.

Betty waved her hands in the air to control the situation and hastily ordered for harmony. "No, we are not going to have this up in my apartment." She looked at both Fabian and Scar and chided, "Now, Fabian, you were wrong for talking to my guest like that."

Fabian rolled his head back. "Guest?" he said. "Betty, I'm your best friend, and you're gonna let him call me a faggot and address me first over a nigga you just met?"

"No, Fabian, right is right. He didn't disrespect you; you did."

"So, calling me a faggot ain't disrespect, Betty?" Betty shook her head and was too confused to answer. Her silence was Fabian's cue to leave. He stomped toward the front door and swung it open. Just before he walked away, he turned and reminded her, "If your true enemies don't get you, your false friends will. You remember when you taught me that, Betty?" Betty never saw Fabian that hurt or angry before and felt horrible and wanted to make a final plea, but he slammed the door behind him before she could utter a word.

Betty and Scar drove downtown to Times Square in silence with Betty growing more remorseful by the second. Fabian was her best and only friend, and she felt horrible about the situation and her lapse of memory for forgetting that he was coming over. She reasoned that if she just gave Fabian time to cool off, she would make a heartfelt appeal for forgiveness and would more than make it up to him.

Inside B.B. King, the venue was sold out and overwhelmingly packed. Betty was astounded by the amount of vast and diverse fans, white, black, and Asian, young and old, which came out in droves to see a rapper who hadn't even a single out, much less an album. It appeared that the incident with Main Man had gone ultraviral, receiving over eight million views on YouTube within a week's time, and his stock went up tremendously, which was the reason his record label rushed to get him out into the public's eye to capitalize on his notoriety. Betty recalled an episode she watched on VH1, on the life of 50 Cent, how he gained unbelievable recognition when he put out a single "How to Rob," brazenly rapping about how he would rob all the top industry professionals and entertainers, pissing off some of the people he named, like Jay-Z, who made a response on one of his records, solidifying him in. But, when he got shot nine times, almost losing his life, it catapulted him into legendary status, and he reaped millions in the process.

It suddenly occurred to her that the reason all of Scar's people had out their camera phones recording the incident was nothing more than a calculated, premeditated plot to garner a huge buzz to his name, giving him millions of dollars worth of priceless free publicity.

Scar got Betty the perfect table with a perfect view near the performance stage, and she was to receive complimentary drinks, she was told, the entire night. Since she rarely drank alcohol, she ordered diet sodas. The place was packed with standing room only. It took nearly an hour after she sat down for him to actually come on stage, but when he did, the audience gave him a colossal round of applause. They clapped and stomped so vigorously that Betty thought the house would fall down. Scar went right into his performance, being backed by a live band.

After his first two songs, Betty was highly impressed and knew immediately she had underestimated his talent. Though the content and the subject were hard-core and explicit, she was in awe by his poetic lyrics, detailed storytelling ability and delivery, as were the majority of the fans that gave him standing ovations. He reminded her of Tupac meets Biggie Smalls, she thought.

After another song, Scar finally spoke and addressed the audience. "I never have been much for words, but I just want to thank y'all for coming out and showing a brother some love." The crowd thanked him back with more thunderous applause as he continued.

"I'm not the kinda of nigga to be on some celebrity shit because I know where I come from, I know where I been, and I don't take this shit for granted. I'm saying all that to say that I'm from the fucking gutter and saw too much shit in my lifetime to ever be on some new shit. I did just as much damage to people as they did to me, so I'm not claiming innocence. I wasn't shit and couldn't trust anyone, even myself. I'm fucked up like that."

The crowd yelled out their support for him.

"But through it all, the only person I could ever trust in my life was my grandmother—and I love that sweet woman." The crowd clapped even louder as he continued. "Someone special has entered into my life recently, teaching me that I'm not the garbage I thought I was like everyone told me I was. So, ladies and gentlemen, I wrote this song on my way down here from Harlem and want to dedicate it to a good friend and that person who is here with me today."

Betty began to recall that she was with him all day and never saw him write anything down when unexpectedly, a spotlight shined on her and her table. Betty was speechless and totally embarrassed, and tried in vain to maintain her composure as they clapped.

"I call this one, 'Fly Betty.'"

Scar approached the band for his impromptu set, and they

all nodded. From the moment he started, Betty realized that he had, in fact, written the song off the top of his head. By the time he finished, he rapped and explained about the first time he encountered her on the train, right up to the part about the incident with her best friend in her apartment, using all the words that she ever used and taught him in the lyrics. Betty nearly swooned in total admiration for Scar and his unforeseen genius.

After the show was over and he left the stage, Betty blushed proudly and could hardly wait to see him and congratulate him on the success of his first show. As she watched the venue clear out, she knew it would be a number of minutes before he came back out to meet her and decided to use the ladies' room.

When Betty came out of the stall, she noticed four black girls looming around, all staring at her with evil vigilance. She thought it was strange that they would loiter around a near-empty bathroom. When Betty went to the sink to wash her hands, she knew they weren't there to powder their noses.

By nature, Betty prepared her defense by opening up her purse as she placed it on the sink top, reaching in and pulling her ever ready blade to the surface of her bag, just in case she needed quick access. Then she pulled out her lipstick to throw them off and set it down on the sink counter. She started washing her hands, and it was then that she heard the first girl speak.

"You know, these bitches these days think that they can fuck with somebody's man and think that there won't be any consequence. They should learn to stay in their lane instead of coming out of pocket."

Betty remained calm and poised, not allowing them to see any reaction, but the woman grew bolder. "What was that bullshit song that nigga was singing, 'Bum Betty'?" They all laughed.

Betty took a quick glance at her through the mirror, as well as taking a mental note on their positions, then thought it was pointless to even address them and decided to just leave. She rationalized that the girl was probably one of Scar's old girlfriends who was jealous when they saw the spotlight on her. As Betty was going for a napkin dispenser on the wall, the girl who was speaking stepped in front of her.

"Yeah, you know I'm talking to you." The girl had wicked, keen eyes and was older, in her late twenties. She was equal in stature, maybe an inch or two more than Betty, but the same slender figure. She was supremely gorgeous, with expensive tastes in clothing that rivaled even Betty's. Betty eased her hand into her bag and gripped her knife, prepared for anything.

With a twisted face of displeasure the girl continued. "Usually, I would just beat a bitch like you down on sight, but since you don't know who the fuck I am, I'm going to give you a pass, little girl."

Betty remained calm, despite the verbal abuse as the woman continued. "But, I'm telling you this one last time, if I ever see you in my husband's face again, on YouTube or anywhere else, you're not going to be so lucky. You best believe that shit!" The girl put one hand on her hip, and the other she pointed in Betty's face. "Tell that motherfucker that

I ain't going nowhere until I get my money, and if he even think about trying to not give me mines, tell him I know everything he knows and I got proof." The girl turned on her heels and stormed out of the bathroom, with her three friends eying Betty with malice as they walked out behind her.

Betty let out a huge breath and placed her hands on the sink for support. She wasn't so much upset at the girl's idle threat, but all she could think of was her revealing that Scar was her husband.

When Betty regained her bearings, she sauntered out of the bathroom boiling over in anger and scanned the venue looking for Scar. When she finally saw him, he was surrounded by reporters and cameramen, with the inclusion of Diesel and the very two white females she saw in the Cash Money party before. Betty loomed irately on the side because she only wanted the instant satisfaction of cursing him out and telling him to his face that she would not have any more future dealings with him.

When the fanfare finally let up, Scar spotted her and ambled over to her. He immediately read the dissatisfaction on her face and quickly asked, "What's wrong?" Just as she was about to let him have it, another volley of cameramen caught his attention by calling his name and snapping photos. The last thing Betty wanted was being in another compromising picture with Scar and turned away. When they finished, he turned his attention back to Betty, but again, was interrupted when Diesel walked up and stared directly into Betty's face. "So, what's up, Scar? You ready?"

"Hold up, let me finish talking to my people."

"Your people? I got all the people you need right over there," Diesel snarled, looking Betty directly in the eyes as he spoke.

Scar caught the friction and said, "Yo, back up, man, and give me a minute."

Diesel turned his cold, sullen eyes on Scar, but Scar stared him down. Then Diesel glared at Betty, took two deliberate steps backward, and clasped his hands. Scar was about to check him, but Betty relented and said, "Scar, I'm just going to go home, but I'll talk to you tomorrow." Scar stared at her for a brief moment and said, "OK, I'll call you tomorrow." Betty walked away quickly and exited the building.

Betty could hardly think straight as she waited for the parking attendant to bring her car out of the garage. She floored her truck and headed west toward Twelfth Avenue to take the Westside Highway to the 125th Street exit as quickly as she could. For the life of her, she could not figure out why she was so angry. She easily could have just let it go and wash her hands of everything like she'd done so many times before with other men, but this time was different and it awakened feelings within her that she never felt before—she allowed Scar to get inside her head and was growing attached to him and hated herself for it.

Lost in thought, just as she passed the 96th Street exit, she saw the bright headlights of a car coming up fast behind her, almost blinding her. She maintained speed, squinting in the rear and side mirrors, hoping they would just pass her, but grew concerned when they stayed directly behind her.

Now, what seemed like only inches in the rear of her. Betty panicked when she felt the first knock on her bumper and floored the accelerator, picking up speed. Doing sixty-five, she looked in the rear mirror again, which, this time, totally blinded her. Her neck snapped back when she felt another bump and spun the wheel violently to the right, sending her truck careening out of control. She hit the brakes, causing the truck to spin, tires screeching and burning, doing two and a half rotating circles before slamming into the guard rail.

Chapter 31

Chubby arrived in no less than seventeen minutes after she made the call to where his niece sat shaken and near delirious on the side of the highway. He rushed to her truck and swung the door open with reckless abandonment of the traffic. In a panicked frenzy, he asked her, "Are you OK, Tootie? Are you hurt?" Betty was still distraught and shaken up, but managed to nod. Once he found out she was OK, he asked her what happened.

"Somebody ran me off the road," she shrilled in a terror-laden voice.

Chubby was on the warpath and out for blood. All he wanted to know was whether she got a look at the car that had done this to her or its license plate. Betty explained that she didn't because of the glaring headlights that blinded her and how it happened so fast.

"Motherfuckers!" Chubby spewed, clearly wanting to put

his hands on something or someone. "Let me call 911 to get you to the hospital."

Betty waved him off. "No, Uncle Chubby, I just want to go home."

Chubby looked in his niece's innocent eyes and began to soften. They reminded him of the many nights he had to lull her back to sleep when she missed her mother when she was younger.

"I got you, Tootie Too. Just leave your truck here, and I'll take you home. I'll call somebody to pick up the truck on my way back."

"It's OK, Uncle Chubby. I called José, and he has a tow truck and is already on his way to take it back to his shop."

In perfect timing, both Betty and Chubby turned around when they saw the headlights of a truck pulling up behind them—it was José. He, too, rushed over to her truck, concern and anger written on his face. José looked at the carnage done to the driver's side of the truck and the deployed air bags.

"Mami, my God, are you OK?"

With her hands over her eyes, Betty shivered uneasily in her seat. Chubby barked, "She's OK, just a little shook up after a bastard tried to run her off the road and almost killed her." José heaved a sigh of relief and uttered something in Spanish.

Chubby bowed his head helplessly as the cars zoomed past. In despair, he looked at his niece and said to José, "Listen, thanks for coming out. I'm gonna get her out of here and get her home."

José bobbed his head quickly. "Yes, and don't worry about

nothing. I'll tow it back to my shop and take care of everything. You just go home and get some rest." Chubby nodded, and they both embraced. He turned to Betty and tenderly assisted her out of her truck as she exited it stiffly.

Back at home, Betty tried in vain to contact Fabian, but each time it went to voicemail. It took nearly an act of Congress for Betty to convince her Uncle Chubby that she was well enough to be by herself. He finally agreed, only after she lied that her best friend Fabian was on his way to stay with her, ensuring that she wouldn't be alone for long. He agreed and promised that he would, in fact, be back first thing in the morning and left.

When Betty closed the door, she folded her arms as flashes of her near fatal car crash flashed before her eyes. She gritted her teeth as she thought back to the incident she had with the girl only a few hours before in B.B. King's bathroom and treaded heavily toward her kitchen counter to retrieve her cellphone to call Scar.

She called him at least a dozen times, crying and cursing him out each time. She couldn't sleep until she got to the bottom of this matter here and now, growing angrier and angrier with each passing minute waiting for him to call back.

Betty awoke to pounding on her door. She batted her eyes and realized she had fallen asleep on her living-room sofa. She reached for her phone and saw a blank screen, and saw that the battery had died. She smiled because she knew it was Fabian and limped to the door and opened it, ready to fall into his arms to pour her heart out, but was surprised when she saw Scar standing there.

Betty turned her back on him and walked away, leaving Scar totally baffled, so he asked, "What's wrong . . . what happened?" he asked with urgency.

Betty turned around and tossed him daggers with her eyes and bitterly spewed, "What's wrong is that your fucking wife tried to run me off the road and tried to fucking kill me."

Scar was stunned. "What?" he stammered, more dazed than confused.

"What my ass. You heard me. Your fucking wife tried to kill me tonight." Scar heard her loud and clear that time and eyed the ceiling in mortification.

"Do you have a wife, Calvin?"

Scar could not answer and could not face her. By his reaction, he confirmed to Betty that it was, in fact, the truth, making her grow even more irate.

"Why didn't you tell me you had a crazy-ass wife, Calvin?"

"Just tell me everything that happened."

Annoyed, Betty shouted again, "What part of *your wife tried to kill me* don't you get?"

"I'm talking about telling me everything she said and all that happened."

Betty was shaking in anger and closed her eyes to try to calm herself.

"C'mon, sit down," Scar said in the sweetest and gentlest tone she heard since she met him. He walked her over toward her sofa and sat her down. Then he followed suit and sat next to her.

Betty went on and explained everything to him from the

very beginning, starting with when she entered the bathroom, to the accident, and who brought her home.

She described Scar's wife to the tee, from how she spoke, how she looked, and everything she said. Scar exhaled noisily while scratching his head and nodded, like his past was coming back to haunt him, and then just came out with it.

"Yes, I am married, and yes, that was my wife. Her name is Porsche." He put his head down and continued. "I met her years ago, in Brooklyn on Fulton Street. Her father was a big cat that had half of Brooklyn on lock on the heroin and cocaine tip and so she had mad loot and crazy connect."

Scar frowned, suddenly looking older than he was. "To make a long story short, we hooked up and she became my girl. She was like four years older than me. In addition to hitting me off with drugs to bump Uptown, I started working for her father.

"She was holding me down every time I went in and out of prison, and when I was up north, we decided to get married while I was in prison just so we could, you know, do our business."

Scar shrugged and said, "Soon after we got married, not even two months afterward, the letters, the visits and packages stopped. I ain't heard from her in three years; that was, until I signed that deal and started appearing on television, the she suddenly pops up." Scar finally looked her in the eyes, feeling miserable.

Betty looked as if she was trying to process it all, staring blankly at a spot on her wall. She finally spoke. "So now she's trying to get back with you?"

"She tried, but I ain't going to play sucker for nobody. She left me hanging for all those years when I was fucked up. Now her gold-digging ass wanna suddenly come back with her hand out thinking I owe her something. I told the bitch to get the fuck out of my face. Being the evil bitch that she is, she starts threatening me with divorce and saying she's going to get half. Then she started harassing my grandmother. That's when I bought the house. I wanted to move my grandmother out of the projects so she would be safe, because I didn't know what my wife would do, but my Nana didn't want to move. That's why I got my man, Weeg, to be my eyes in the projects when I'm not there. This chick is really that crazy and evil."

It all began to make sense to Betty, but she still had a question that demanded an answer.

"What did she mean by she knows everything about you and she's got proof, Calvin?"

Scar shook his head and stated "Nah, I don't want to get you involved."

Betty quickly snapped, "Calvin, this bitch tried to kill me tonight, and I ain't going to just sit idly by and let her do it. So tell me what I got myself into or I'm leaving you alone."

Scar was reluctant, but knew he had to come to her correctly with the truth. "Like I told you, her father was a big nigga out there in Brooklyn, and when you in that kind of business, necessities were needed to keep things running smoothly, and he used me from time to time."

"What do you mean . . ." Betty stopped suddenly when

she looked into his brooding eyes and knew that it hinted that he killed people.

"I was young and didn't know nothing but wildin' and tearing shit down. Little did I know, her father was just as evil and detailed evidence just in case he needed to use it against us if somebody ever turned on him. He's dead now; he got killed a few years ago, but they were real close and he told her everything, gave her everything, including dirt on me."

"Calvin, why don't you just give her what she wants?" Betty asked, hoping it made sense.

"You think I didn't try? I gave her damn near half a million dollars already and she still wants more," Scar freely admitted. "If she was a dude, I know how to handle it, but I don't know what to do when it's a female. I was taught not to put my hands on them from my Nana. I always could just walk away, but . . ." He shook his head sadly. "That's when I got tired of it and stop giving her shit."

Knowingly, Betty said, "She's extorting you."

Sadly, Scar whispered, "Yes."

Betty realized this was Scar's first time not in control and he appeared helpless. She felt sorry for him and had a sudden need to protect him.

"I'm sorry I brought all this drama around you, Betty. That was never my intent. I never been with a girl like you before and you got me thinking about things I never knew before and I'm just finding myself gravitating toward you and I can't explain it."

Betty was truly touched. Instinctively, she scooted closer to him and put her hands into his.

To lighten the moment, Scar asked, "Did you at least like the song I wrote for you?"

Betty gazed in his eyes and admitted, "It was beautiful."

Scar grew serious. "Betty, I swear on my grandmother, I will die before I ever let anyone so much as lay a hand on you again."

Before Betty knew it, they were kissing passionately. She felt a sudden vulnerability, submissive, in fact, and laid her head on his powerful shoulders. He hugged her back and comforted her in his arms. Never in Betty's short life had she ever felt so safe, so warm, as she snuggled blissfully with her head on his chest. When they pulled away, within inches of each other, they gazed lustily into each other's eyes and slowly kissed. The passion was soft, as Scar rubbed his rough hands all over her body, sending spine-tingling sensations, something she never felt before, course throughout her body.

The moistness between her legs began to drench her panties, causing her to feel instant guilt because she wanted it touched. The passion overcame her, and suddenly she found her breasts and nipples harden and her body nude. Scar picked her up as if she was a rag doll as she wrapped her legs around him. They licked and kissed each other like rabid animals. Scar lay her down on the plush Berber carpeting and slowly pecked and kissed her neck while rubbing her breasts simultaneously, causing her juices to explode all over her carpet. As he licked her lower and lower, she could no longer contain herself, and began bucking her hips, anticipating his tongue to sate her wet flowing vagina. With one peck, one kiss, on her neatly manicured pussy hairs, she found herself, again, exploding like a waterfall until her body shook and trembled beyond her control. As if Betty was in another stratosphere, she lay back while he gave her all of his tongue, as it darted in and out of her like a jackrabbit, until she begged, pleaded, and beseeched him to put his penis inside of her, but her pleas fell on deaf ears as he continued to magnify his oral duties.

Just when Betty could no longer take it anymore, Scar rose to his knees and grabbed her and pulled her closer and massaged his hardened, saluting penis. For the first time in Betty's life, she saw a penis up close and personal as she looked at his. She gasped at the size of it, as it had the girth of her wrist and its length matched her wrist to her elbow. Just as she was about to admit her innocence and virginity, Scar had the head of his penis inside of her, causing her to gasp aloud.

"Scar, I don't think I can take all that, I'm a virgin . . ." He stuck his tongue down her throat and used his hips and penetrated her slow.

"I got you, baby, I got you," he repeated. "I'm never going to let nothing happen to you, and I'm never going to let you go," Scar whispered earnestly in her ear while he inched, at a snail's pace, inside of her. Tears streamed from her eyes because of the pain and his sincerity, but with each stroke, the pain began to ebb, her legs were less constricted, until finally, she took in all of him. Betty wrapped her arms around him tightly, matching his rhythm perfectly in unbelievable bliss that she would have never imagined.

With each dynamic stroke, Scar whispered in her ear, "Do you love me?"

Betty could only babble incoherently, until after continued pleas for an answer, continued strokes and a hard grind,
Scar finally got his answer when Betty screamed out at the top
of her lungs at the apex of a mind-blowing extreme orgasm,
"I love you, baby, I love you so much!"

Two hours later, Betty, once again, awakened to the sound
of frantic pounding at her door. She and Scar, still on the
floor, unfurled their arms from around each other and scram-
bled to their feet. Totally nude, Betty panicked when she suddenly remembered her Uncle Chubby promised he'd come
back and check on her. She turned hysterically toward Scar,
her eyes twice as big as normal, and pleaded, "Calvin, that's
my uncle. You've got to stay in the bedroom until he leaves.
He can't see you here."

Scar slowly put on his clothes, his ego too strong to be
hiding from a man. Betty knew what he was thinking and
pleaded, "Baby, please do me a favor out of respect. He was
the one who raised me like a father." Her desperate solemn
eyes beamed for a positive response, then watched him force
the fakest smile, which was more than enough for her. Betty
wiped the haze from her eyes and scurried quickly to put on
her clothes, stuffing her thongs behind the couch, and gave
herself a once-over. She looked down the hall to ensure Scar
was out of sight, then looked over toward the door, giving her
clothes another once-over before she opened the door. She
was mortified when she saw that it wasn't her Uncle Chubby,
but, instead, her best friend Fabian again.

Despite their earlier disagreement, Fabian hadn't an inkling of reservation and rushed in with genuine fear and concern plastered across his face. "Betty, are you OK? Are you alright?"

She could not answer; she could only gaze at him in complete silence when he asked again. "Betty, you said someone tried to run you off the road. What happened?"

Betty's face began to crumble, a look he'd never seen on her face since he met her, as he gasped in panic, "Come on, Betty, now, tell me what happened. You're scaring me."

Eager to support his one and only true friend, Fabian took her into his arms to soothe her, when out from the periphery of his eye, he saw Scar lurking. He stared back at Fabian contemptuously. Fabian pulled away from Betty and stared at her with defiant sorrow, not an ounce of fight left in him, and nodded, "So, I see you got a new shoulder to lean on now, huh, Betty?"

Betty didn't even have to turn around. She knew he was referring to Scar, and pleaded, "No, Fabian, it's not what you think. Just come in for one minute and let me talk to you."

Fabian wasn't convinced and quickly rebuked, "I don't want to be anywhere near him, Betty, so if you want me to come in, tell him that he's going to have to leave." Fabian eyed Scar, and then folded his arms awaiting Betty's decision as if he was daring her to make the wrong choice so he could walk out.

Well in earshot of the conversation, Scar saved Betty from having to make a choice and said, "You don't have to go through all that, Betty. You been through enough."

Scar gathered his belongings off the living-room table, then approached Betty and hunched over and gave her a supportive, strong hug as he rubbed her back. He took her hands into his and assured her, "You don't have nothing to worry about, because I'm going to take care of that."

Out of spite, Scar took the brazen lead and kissed her on the lips. Betty was caught totally off guard and was very embarrassed. "I'll call you later and see if you need me for anything."

Betty nodded quickly and uneasily parted her hair from her flushed face. Scar scowled grimly at Fabian as he exited the apartment, but Fabian in no way shied away and matched his gaze, refusing to back down. As soon as Scar exited the apartment, Fabian took hold of the door and slammed it shut for emphasis.

"Fabian," yelled Betty, "why are you acting like this?"

Fabian pursed his lips and rolled his eyes, astonished. "Why am *I* acting like this?" he repeated. "Because you putting that Chia Pet-looking motherfucker over me, that's why. Don't act like you don't think I don't know what's going on, Betty." Fabian didn't give her a chance to retort. "You are getting caught up with all the lights, money, bullshit YouTube and World Star Hip-Hop shit, and you becoming just like them other trash bag bitches that you be talking about in the clubs."

"Fuck you, Fabian!" Betty said point-blank.

Fabian grimaced and asked, "Fuck me? No, that's what that bastard who just left was trying to do to you . . ." Fabian was about to make his point again when he noticed Betty turned away from him and lowered her head. He stopped and observed her, and then it suddenly became clear as day, and he looked away from her in disgust. Betty knew Fabian could see right through her and simply could not look at him because she knew she broke two of her golden rules in one night.

Fabian felt no need to go on with the conversation any longer and said with all the sarcasm he could conjure, "Since Mister Good-Dick seems to be turning you out on your own game, maybe you be smart enough not to break your final rule.

"Until then, Ms. Blaise, only call me when his ninety days run out!" he turned on his heels and scampered out of her apartment with the gait of a satisfied whore.

Chapter 32

Over the next three weeks, Scar and Betty became insep-
arable, spending nearly every waking hour together. Scar's
career had taken off drastically, and he received approval from
his parole officer that allowed him to leave the state of New
York, so he traveled all over the United States, with Betty
right there by his side.

Betty received word from Mrs. Cathi Miller, her supervi-
sor at the community center, that she had fulfilled her obligations with flying colors and signed her papers of completion
for her credits, and told her to enjoy the rest of her summer.
Unknown to Betty, Scar had given Mrs. Miller a thick yellow envelope filled with cash, one hundred thousand dollars,
telling her it was a donation to the community center.

"I want to just thank you for investing your time in my
community and doing so much for the people," Scar humbly
said. "My grandma told me about you, and how you could've

gotten a job anywhere, but you chose to stay here all these years. She also told me about your eye condition, so if it means anything, and no disrespect, there's something extra inside for you. Half is for the community center, and the other half for you."

Mrs. Miller was taken aback and shook her head to resist, but Scar was prepared to explain. "Maybe you can use it for your condition, or you can use it toward your two boys, Danny and Dwayne's future. But whatever you do with it, you surely deserve that and more. My neighborhood thanks you."

Mrs. Miller was fighting back tears. She was, in fact, legally blind from glaucoma since she was twelve years old but that didn't stop her at all from getting her degree and raising two wonderful young men in the process. She fell into Scar's arms and thanked him with a loving, sincere hug. Just as he was about to walk away, he added, "Oh, just one more thing. Would you mind if I stole that intern of yours for the next few weeks as my assistant? I think her name is Betty."

Ms. Miller stared at his blank face, then at the thick robust envelope, and then recovered like the true professional she was and flashed a bright smile. "I don't see a problem with that, sir. In fact, let's just call this a lateral transfer of services. I'll take care of everything."

Over these three weeks, Fabian and Betty hadn't spoken to each other once, which was extremely rare. Betty rationalized that she just would let time heal their relationship.

Another person who wasn't particularly happy with their newfound relationship was Diesel, who came along with Scar early on, but suddenly stopped, for reasons unknown to her. She did, however, hear them squabble a number of times on the road, and Betty knew it was about her, but remained silent and let them work it out until finally he no longer came around.

Betty started preparing Scar for interviews, photoshoots, and more importantly, dress techniques. That was the biggest fight he had with Betty, but Betty eventually had her way and he dressed accordingly, and it worked.

When they weren't together and Betty was back home in the East, she now spent most of her time at Scar's mansion interior decorating the entire house. He gave her unlimited control over it. Betty felt a pureness about the arrangement, purposeful, in fact, and was sure to prove to him every dime of his money was spent accordingly.

When Scar did return home, they were like two children together, laughing, joking, and playing tricks on each other, and then at night, every night, they made long and passionate love together, leaving Betty totally mesmerized and blinded by love, which felt uncomfortable to her at the beginning, but before long, she became submissive to allowing love to embrace her.

Then one morning, her cellphone rang, making a familiar and eerie alert as it awakened her. She picked it up from off of the endtable as she rubbed her eyes and looked at the text message that simply read, 90 DAYZ. She knew exactly what it meant and looked over at Scar, who was sleeping peacefully next to her and smiled. She looked at the message once more and pressed DELETE, then rolled back under the covers while wrapping her arms around her man.

Life couldn't have been better for Betty, and the world suddenly couldn't have been so complete. It was a feeling which she was unfamiliar with and never could trust, but Betty threw caution to the wind and simply rolled with it. She was on a natural high and never wanted to get off. But like all good things, they always come to an end.

BOOK 4

The Reckoning

Chapter 33

ONE MONTH LATER . . .

Scar's whirlwind fame had yet to let up. He was now the most sought-after entertainer in the music industry, making regular appearances on MTV, BET, VH1. Every imaginable late-night talk show raved over his music, life, and compelling bad boy past and the money, and glory poured in at a rapid rate.

Since Betty had only five months to prepare and take the Examination for Professional Practice in Psychology (EPPP), which was the objective exam required in all jurisdictions of practicing psychologists, she needed all the time she could to ensure she passed the exam.

Meanwhile, Scar's record company hired him a top artist

management agency to take over full time, and he was now on the road twenty-eight days out of the month. He and Betty rarely saw each other any longer, other than on late-night Skype video conferences. Though Betty missed him, she understood his career and accepted the estrangement as a temporary one, but suddenly, she saw her life correlating to the very things she saw herself judging when she watched shows like *The Basketball Wives* and *Love & Hip Hop,* which was so ironic to her. She even grew so bored that she meticulously rearranged Scar's huge mansion more times than she could count, until everything was perfect.

Betty then thought it was time she confront her BFF, Fabian, because she really missed him and needed him dearly back in her life. She decided to make it up to him by taking him on an all-out shopping excursion and dinner to the most expensive restaurant in the city, but each time she called him, it went straight to voicemail. Since he wasn't picking up, she decided to leave him a heartfelt apology, which she did, leaving out the part about her and Scar being a couple now. Betty hung up and simply would wait until he called her back.

Later that night, Betty studied till her eyes grew red. Finally, she closed up her huge study books, took a long, hot bath, and prepared to go back to her apartment in the morning and stay there until Scar came home from his current tour. She also looked forward to checking up on her future grandmother-in-law, who she honestly missed and hadn't seen in over a month.

The Glove
Gay Night Club in the Village

The thumping techno music was so loud, Fabian, who was sitting on a deluxe plush sofa in the middle of the club with some friends, did not notice his missed calls and saw that the last one was from Betty. He smiled and was just about to return the call when he heard a shrill voice excitedly calling him.

"Fabian!" It was Pebbles, his longtime Spanish homegirl from Wagner Projects. Pebbles was a booster by trade, and Fabian was her best customer, making her rich, and making him the finest dresser in the club scene. Fabian was just as excited and jumped up and screamed just as loud. They ran to each other and embraced as if they hadn't seen each other in ten years, though it had only been eighteen months since she was arrested for credit card fraud. Then they pulled apart and complimented each other on how well each looked.

"When you got out?" Fabian asked with unbridled enthusiasm.

"I got out just last week, Mami," Pebbles said in a thick, Rosie Perez accent. "Look at you. I see you still the flyest bitch in Harlem. Let me find out you got some rich nigga taking care of you," she joked, causing him to blush widely. Fabian introduced Pebbles to all his friends, then excused himself and escorted her into the VIP to show her the time of her life.

The two friends drank, talked, and laughed for two hours when he suddenly remembered. "Oh, I need you to tell me about one of them niggas you probably grew up with in Wagner."

Pebbles took a sip from her drink and asked nonchalantly, "What's his name?"

"An ugly motherfucker named Calvin, but they call him Scar, and he's now that big rapper."

Pebbles nearly choked on her drink at the mention of his name, and her eyes grew wide as she was suddenly stricken with fear. She rambled off, "Calvin . . . from 2370 on the third floor, old Ms. Clara's grandson Calvin?"

Fabian nodded, taken aback by her reaction.

"Psycho-set-it-off-Calvin, the one who was married to that crazy bitch from Brooklyn?"

Fabian sat dumbfounded as he recalled all the messages Betty left on his cellphone that night about Scar having a wife and somebody trying to kill her.

"Yeah, I think so," he responded cautiously.

Pebbles shook her head rapidly. "No, something ain't right here. Explain everything to me."

Fabian started from the very beginning for twenty minutes. After he was finished, Pebbles became the embodiment of a wealth of information, shocking Fabian with each new revelation. Fabian finally had heard what he needed and pulled out his cellphone and quickly called Betty, but it rang until it went straight to voicemail.

Fabian was always the worrying type and wore it on his sleeve, causing Pebbles to offer, "Fabian, you want me to help you, cause you know you are my people and I'm down for whatever, whatever. Fuck parole; I'm not scared of none of those bitches."

Fabian barely heard her. He was too concerned for his

best friend's life and had to take immediate action and tried calling again, and still no answer. He gritted his teeth, then turned to Pebbles and said, "Listen, Pebbles, thanks for letting me know, but I . . . I got to head uptown and check my homegirl." They embraced.

Pebbles offered one last time, "Yo, you make sure you call me if you need my help, Papi."

Fabian tried to nod, but he knew deep down that he would need much more help than that, he was sure of it, and immediately left the VIP, walking into the massive crowd maneuvering around them when his eyes, in fear and determination, suddenly lit on Diesel.

Betty walked into her bedroom wrapped in a large, beige towel with a matching smaller one tied around her hair feeling clean and refreshed. She picked up her phone and saw she had missed two calls and had two messages, one with an unknown number and the other with Fabian's name and number. She smiled widely and fell back into the huge, overly soft king-sized bed and scooted up on the many pillows and snuggled back with glee while she listened to her messages.

"Listen, bitch, I done warned you the first fuckin' time to stay away from Scar, so I guess you thought this was a game, but I can show you better than I can tell you. You just fucked yourself!"

Betty was stunned and knew immediately that it was Scar's wife, Hollywood Gene, and was baffled how she had obtained her number. She snapped out of her momentary alarm when she heard her next message. It was Fabian. She listened to his message. He sounded distraught and had a sense of urgency in his voice requesting her to call him back immediately. She did.

Fabian felt the vibration and saw the glow on his phone come alive as he made his way through the open dance floor of the club and knew instantly. "Betty!" Fabian tried earnestly to decipher what she was saying, but he couldn't hear because of the earsplitting music pulsating from the surrounding speakers. "Betty, Betty . . ." Fabian yelled while holding a finger in his other ear, "I'm in a club. I can't hear you. I'll call you back once I'm outside. Pick up your phone."

Fabian reached outside and the circle of the excited crowd that swamped the entrance waiting to get in was just as deafening. He pushed his way through and quickened his pace to give him some distance from the loud crowd and turned down a desolate street and hit the call button. After the second ring, Betty picked up and expressed her happiness that he called. He shook his head and yelled, "Betty, you got to be quiet and listen to me. It's about Scar and that girl he calls his wife. They are—" Betty sighed and cut him off.

"Listen, Fabian, I'm not in the mood to rehash this beef you got with Calvin. I called you to tell you that I miss our friendship and want to make it up to you."

"Betty, would you just fucking listen! I got something real important you need to hear!" The phone went silent on the other end, and he took in a breath when he knew he had her full attention and continued. "Scar ain't who you think he is . . . He is—"

Before Fabian could get the rest of the words out of his mouth, Betty heard a faint scream, and what appeared to be the sound of Fabian's phone dropping on concrete.

"Hello? Fabian, are you still there . . . hello?" Betty repeated it over and over again until she finally hung up after ten minutes of appeals. She called back over and over, but it went straight to voicemail. Betty decided to wait for him to call back, but he never did. Later she fell asleep, still clasping her cellphone in her hand.

Betty awoke that morning, perplexed about why Fabian still wasn't picking up her phone calls. She decided it was time to head back to the city and confront him face to face at his job, but first she would stop at her home and change her clothes and check her apartment.

When Betty walked into the lobby of her building, she instantly grew uneasy seeing the building manager, doorman, and two white men that she immediately took for law enforcement all staring at her upon her entrance. Betty watched her building manager nod to one of the white men, who approached her, wearing permanently fixed stress marks on his forehead. He tried to put on a smile, but he was unsuccessful. "Ms. Blaise?"

Betty cautiously looked at each man before answering and responded, "Yes, how can I help you?"

"My name is Detective Alexander, and that's my partner Detective Ludwig." His partner remained silent; grim faced, and simply nodded.

Betty confused them when she asked in an articulate and a measured tone, "Nice to meet you, Detective Alexander, Detective Ludwig, but do you mind if I see some credentials?" They didn't hesitate to produce their IDs and badges, though they did feel a slight sting to their egos. Both detectives extended their wallets out clearly until she was satisfied by nodding. "OK, Detective, how can I help you?"

"Do you know a person named Fabian Vanderbilt?"

Betty suddenly felt nauseous at hearing his name, and the first thing to come to mind was the years of store embezzlement they did with the clothing and that it had come back to haunt her. She remained composed, however, and decided to play it by ear, but if they had a warrant to look in her apartment, she knew she would be going to jail. "Yes, he is a friend of mine."

Suddenly, his partner chimed in and asked, "When was the last time you spoke to Mr. Vanderbilt, ma'am?"

A feeling of dread overcame her with all the questioning so she got to the point. "Detective, please forgive me if I appear curt, but can you tell me what this is about?"

Both detectives tossed each other a knowing look, and Detective Alexander came out and said it. "Well, Mr. Vanderbilt was found murdered in the East Village last night and your phone number shows that you were the last person he spoke to."

Betty grew light-headed, and the lobby began to spin. The last thing she heard before she passed out was someone yell, "Call 911."

Chapter 34

After Betty awoke and was treated at Harlem Hospital for shock, she cried uncontrollably the entire time, not wanting to believe what was happening. The detectives waited and allowed her enough time to gather her composure so they could gain some much-needed information pertaining to the case. It was apparent that Fabian was a victim of robbery. His throat had been slit, and he bled to death instantly. Betty was so distraught that she could not stop from shaking. Her doctor had to give her medicine to calm her down. She answered every question for the detectives truthfully, down to the part about them having a fallout and said that they hadn't spoken to each other until that very night. During the process, she left several messages for Scar, who was scheduled for an appearance at the House of Blues in Las Vegas, Nevada, and who had a ton of interviews, but he had yet to call her back.

The hospital staff and treating physician pleaded for Betty to stay overnight, but, she refused and simply wanted to go home to cry out her pain. The detectives left their cards and assured her that they would work around the clock to find Fabian's killer and wished her adieu.

Just as she dressed in her own clothing and was to exit the emergency room, she heard a loud ruckus as one of the double doors burst open.

"Sir, you cannot go back there. Call security!" yelled a short Asian nurse. It was Scar, and he was on a rampage, fuming as his eyes darted rapidly around the emergency room, ripping curtains open in haste in search of his woman, Betty. The detectives, who were right behind Betty, gripped their weapons when they saw the brutish looking huge man approaching them.

"Calvin!" yelled Betty, who suddenly grew weaker when she saw him.

Like a scene out of the movie *The Bodyguard,* Scar rushed toward Betty, and she collapsed in his arms. He scooped her off her feet to carry her out of the hospital. Just as he was about to walk away, a squadron of hospital police, guns drawn and all, ordered Scar to put her down and put his hands on top of his head.

On cue, both Detective Alexander and Ludwig produced their badges and ordered the officers to put their weapons away. They then escorted both Scar and Betty out of the hospital together.

Scar comforted Betty the remainder of the night, even giving her a bath and carrying her to bed. He held her tightly until she fell asleep, still shivering and having nightmares. He never once pressured her to recount everything that happened.

By morning, Betty was well enough to go over the horrible events that occurred within the last twenty-four hours. This time around Betty barely shed a tear. Scar listened intently, offering her support by rubbing her back and stroking her hair to soothe her. Betty found out that when he finally got the message that she was in the hospital and what happened, he immediately chartered a private jet, getting him back to New York as soon as possible.

Chapter 35

Scar didn't want to leave Betty, but she insisted that she was okay. He still had some major appearances to make and she would've felt guilty and selfish if he stayed home with her since she was out of danger. She had to beg him to go and catch his flight. Betty in no way wanted to be a burden or clingy, something she'd never been her entire life. He relented and assured her that he would be back in two days when everything was over.

That afternoon, Betty turned off the television and grew lonely. She called Scar to see if he arrived back in Las Vegas all right, but it went straight to voicemail. She chose not to leave a message. She scrolled through her phone and came across her Aunt Vonda's number and decided this was a good moment to give her a call.

Aunt Vonda was shocked and concerned for her niece's present state of mind, and promised she would come right over as soon as she got back uptown from her job.

Two hours later Betty's doorbell rang. Relieved, she rushed toward the door to open it. When Betty did, she was greeted with a powerful blow to her face with a baseball bat. Scar's wife—Hollywood Gene—stood there.

Instant pain overtook Betty as her lean body sprawled across the hardwood floor. Her body went cold. The pain was unbearable. She struggled to see, but saw only black and white flashes of stars.

Hollywood Gene stood audaciously over her as if she was savoring the moment, dangling the bat precariously at her side. She chuckled a dry, maniacal laugh. "Bitch, what the fuck did I tell you? You thought this was a fucking game? You thought I was playing?" The more Hollywood Gene spoke, the more bitter she became. She took a firm grip of the bat and delivered another brutal blow to Betty's body, this time on her shoulder blades, causing her body to flatten again and writhe in intense pain.

Hollywood Gene continued her verbal assault, but Betty could not hear a thing. On her knees, dazed and breathing rapidly, she crammed all her focus on one thing at that moment, and that was to live or die. So with total concentration, and lack of vision, Betty conjured up all her remaining strength. Used her hearing to hone in on her attacker, sure she had only one last chance of survival, and sprang toward her as if her life depended on it, which it sure did. Catching Hollywood Gene off guard, Betty tackled her midsection to the ground. The two women were fighting, grappling, scratching, and pounding each other ferociously for control of the bat. Betty fought valiantly, but Hollywood Gene proved to be far stronger when she used her razor-like fingernails, gouging deeply into Betty's eye sockets. Betty shrieked from intense pain, rendering her helpless and defenseless. Fear once again overcame her when she felt the wooden bat slip from her sweaty palms. Hollywood Gene loomed over her, circling her wounded prey as her chest heaved heavily, wiping the hair and sweat from her demented eyes.

"See, bitch, you done fucked up now." Hollywood Gene gave Betty one last deathly stare, took a firmer grip around the bat and gritted her teeth and said, "Now say good-bye to everything you love, bitch." Hollywood Gene raised the deadly weapon high in the air, and Betty braced herself for the worst and covered her head with both her arms expecting a mighty blow to her head that would end it all—when she suddenly heard a deafening yell and commotion.

Betty removed her arms just in time to see her Aunt Vonda become a black streak of lightning, catching Hollywood Gene totally off balance. The momentum sent them both flying, with Hollywood Gene slamming headfirst into the solid kitchen counter. The snapping of her neck was sickening as it echoed off the apartment walls. As her body lay flat on her stomach, her head now in a grotesque, twisted position with her dead eyes staring up at the ceiling, Vonda, who was from the old school and was overwhelmed with blind rage and seething anger, quickly retrieved the bat from off the floor and commenced viciously beating Hollywood Gene's lifeless body all over, oblivious to overkill and leaving nothing to chance, resorting back to prison behavior.

Betty stumbled to her feet and made her way over to stop her aunt's assault.

"Auntie, stop!"

Vonda was in such a rabid frenzy, Betty had to grab hold of the bat. "It's over Auntie. She's dead already. She's dead."

It took a few moments for Vonda to process it all as her bulging flaming eyes stared deeply into her niece's. Finally, reality overcame her. Betty let her aunt go when she was sure she was stable, and watched her aunt stare down upon her victim—and the bloody mess on the floor, the wall, and the appliances. Vonda dropped the bat wayside and immediately tossed her head in her niece's direction and angrily questioned.

"What the hell is going on, Betty?"

Still in shock, Betty just shook her head while rubbing the wound on the side of her head and tried to explain, but at that moment she was physically and mentally incapable of uttering a word. Vonda looked at her crumbling and battered niece and grew compassionate. She hugged her.

Vonda walked Betty into the living room and sat her down, building her confidence until she was able to talk. As Betty tearfully explained everything from the beginning, Vonda sat in silence until after she finished. Then she stood up and retrieved her bag from off the floor and searched for her cellphone and assured her, "Don't worry, I'm going to call your Uncle Chubby. He will have his lawyer tell us what we need to do."

Vonda began dialing his number when Betty suddenly yelled out, "No, Auntie, don't call Uncle Chubby yet!" Her terror-laden tone immediately stopped Vonda, who tried to make sense of it.

"Betty, we have a dead body in your kitchen, and we have to know what to do before the police get here."

Betty closed her eyes, at her wit's end and lifted her hand as if she wanted to tell her otherwise. "Just give me a second to think."

Vonda rolled her eyes in frustration, but allowed her niece to gather her thoughts. Betty paced the floor in deep concentration when she suddenly stated, "You can't be involved in this, Auntie, if we are going to get out of this, and plus, you've got too much to lose."

Vonda shook her head and repeated, "Baby girl, just let me call your Uncle Chubby and we'll be fine."

"Auntie, think . . ." Betty spewed, "if you make a call to Chubby, which is traceable, it can be construed as premeditation, or a conspiracy because they will then track his call which will be directly to his lawyer. In court, that will raise questions about why we didn't call the police first, opening doors to too many doubts. You already have a past charge for murder, and it would jeopardize both of our futures."

Betty stared sternly into her aunt's eyes and challenged, "Are you willing to gamble on a grand jury like you did over twenty years ago?" Vonda was bitten by the truth. Her niece was right. Slowly, she sat down on her sofa and allowed her niece to take the lead without any questions. As if Betty came to a conclusion, she swerved her head toward the dead body and rushed toward it and picked up the bat. Vonda watched in horror as her niece raised the bat and began pounding

Hollywood Gene's face without mercy. Betty then retrieved a dish towel and walked hastily over to where her aunt sat and ordered her to stand up. When Vonda did, Betty began wiping away the splats of blood she had on her face and clothing without saying a word.

When Betty saw her aunt's questioning eyes, she revealed, "I can't have you part of her death. The way the blood is splattered on you will tell CSI that you hit the body. I don't want you part of that. I'm going to own it." Betty gave her aunt the once-over, sure that no blood splats were visible. She then wiped the bat down for fingerprints and gripped the bat all over, then walked over to Hollywood Gene's body, and cuffed her fingerprints all over the bat as well.

When Betty stood up, she scanned the crime scene to ensure everything was in order. Satisfied, she gave her aunt the rundown and what to tell the authorities when they arrived. They rehearsed it one final time, and then she ordered her aunt to make the call. Vonda placed two phone calls, one to 911, and then the other to her younger brother, Chubby.

Chapter 36

Almost seven hours after the incident occurred, Betty, Vonda, Chubby, and their lawyer walked out of the 32nd precinct tight-lipped in deep thought. The statement that they gave was consistent with the time, Betty's injuries, and motives.

> On or about 2:15 P.M., my doorbell rang. I was expecting my aunt Vonda Williams, who I spoke to on my cellphone earlier, who was to stop by to visit me at my apartment at 625 W. 135th Street. When I answered the door, I fully expected it to be my aunt, but to my surprise, and horror, I was hit with a blunt weapon to my face. Dazed and confused, I found myself on the floor in pain. As I regained my equilibrium, I heard a familiar voice of the person I met before that threatened me over a

month ago at B.B. King's on 42nd Street in Times Square where I was a guest of my boyfriend Calvin McGriff, who was performing that night.

At the end of the show, I headed to the ladies' room and it was then that I was confronted by the victim, who was with three other females that surrounded me. The victim then identified herself as my boyfriend's wife. At the time I was unaware that he was married. She clearly threatened me that if I continued seeing him, that I would, in fact, suffer the consequences. After that, she showed up at my condominium, unannounced, uninvited, with a deadly weapon, which she used on my person, several times. In fear of my life, I defended myself, as within my rights, and finally gained the upper hand after I took the weapon away her. She fell in my kitchen. Her head hit the counter. I commenced to subdue her by inflicting the very bodily harm that she had done to me earlier on her person.

After I was sure she was no longer a threat, I retreated to my hallway, screaming for help, and it was then that I saw my aunt getting off the elevator. She calmed me down from the hysteria I was experiencing, and after doing that, she then called the police.

Signed Betty Blaise

The four of them walked toward Eighth Avenue having a final discussion when a shiny black Range Rover, already parked, honked its horn. The party strained their eyes to see the occupant inside, when they suddenly heard Betty's name being called. "Betty . . ."

Betty walked closer while hunching over and to her surprise, it was Scar sitting in the driver's seat.

"Is that the motherfucker she's fuckin' with that started all this shit?" Chubby scowled, his eyes focused directly on the truck.

Arms folded, Vonda nodded her head, "Yeah, I think so. He don't even have the common courtesy to get out of his car to meet her family."

"Fuck that . . ." Chubby cursed, "this nigga gonna have to answer some fuckin' questions."

Vonda grabbed him by his huge arms and reasoned, "No, Chubby. Not here, not in front of the precinct . . ." Vonda knew her brother. She knew he lacked people skills when he was angry, and even more so if it regarded family—especially his precious Betty.

Mr. Russo, wearing a three thousand dollar, blue pin-stripped suit, knew Chubby's history very well and decided it was time to leave to prevent any possible conflicts of interest in case his volatile client committed a criminal act. He gave him the very advice his mentor, Mr. Greenberg, Chubby's former and longtime lawyer, used to give him. "Chubby!" yelled the normally smooth and reserved jurist.

"Putting a future opponent on your radar always gives them the upper hand . . ."

Chubby stared at his lawyer and instantly became calm. Over the past three years, Mr. Russo has opened Chubby's eyes to many things about life, philosophy, and books. He taught Chubby how to think before he reacted, and it actually made him a better person, a calmer person, to the point where he hadn't committed a violent act or murder in well over five years.

In his deep, husky voice, Chubby finished his statement from memory and concluded, "Hence, giving away your greatest weapon . . . the element of surprise. *The Art of War.*"

Mr. Russo smiled and nodded. He looked at his gold Rolex watch and said, "You got it, but I think I'd better get moving. I have a late bail hearing with a client at the Bookings in Queens, so I'll talk to you all later." He embraced both Chubby and Vonda and hailed a cab. His luck, a rare Yellow Cab, slowed. He opened the door and yelled, "Tell your niece to call me Monday to meet in my office." He waved, jumped inside the cab, and was gone.

Vonda and Chubby turned their attention back to Betty, who was still curbside having a conversation through the passenger-side window with Scar.

"Betty, are you okay?" Vonda called to her.

Betty turned, "Yes, Auntie, I'm okay. Give me a second."

Still agitated, Chubby said to his sister, "Let me go before I put my hands on young dude. I'll be at the store on the corner." Vonda nodded her head, more than happy he was leaving.

Betty turned her attention back to Scar. "I think you should come meet my family, Calvin."

Scar quickly declined. "Nah, not right now." He glanced out the window. "They don't look none too happy to meet me for the first time right now."

Betty agreed and said, "Okay, just give me a minute so I can say good-bye." Scar nodded. She took a deep breath and braced herself; sure she was going to have to do some explaining, especially to her uncle.

Betty was relieved when she turned and saw he was already gone. "Auntie . . . where did Uncle Chubby go?"

Vonda quickly snapped, "You should be thankful he left, 'cause we both ain't too happy right now. Look, Betty, there's something wrong with a man who can't even be courteous enough to even get out of his car to meet your people after everything that happened today with his wife." Vonda fumed, "He put your life and mine in jeopardy, and I don't trust him." Betty felt horrible and lowered her head, knowing she was right. Vonda never saw Betty so vulnerable and offered her some advice. "Listen, Betty, you are a good girl with a bright, bright future ahead of you and have come too far to have someone come along and take that away from you. You know your mother, as well as me and your uncle want better for you. You've sacrificed too much to throw that away." Her aunt's words stung, and Betty felt even worse.

Vonda relented and asked, "I don't want you staying in your apartment alone tonight, and so are you coming with me?" Betty turned and looked at Scar's vehicle and answered, "I'm not sure. I'm just going to explain to him everything that happened, but I'll call you and let you know what I decide to do." Though Vonda felt uneasy about it she simply had no choice but to let it go.

"Just be careful, Betty."

Betty sat with Scar in the car over the next hour and repeated in detail the nightmare. Scar remained silent the entire time. When Betty finished, he still sat for several minutes before he spoke.

"So, that means you gave them my name?"

Betty was taken aback. "What the fuck do you mean did I give them your name, Calvin? You damn right I did because that's *your* fucking wife," she spat in disgust. "Did you even *hear* anything I said?" She pointed to the thick white gauze taped above her eyes and spewed, "That bitch came to kill me. Look at my damn face."

Scar explained, "No, Betty, it's nothing like that. Of course I heard everything you said. I'm just trying to process everything so I'll know what to say to Po-Po when they come looking for me."

Betty was further flabbergasted. "Why should they have to come looking for you, Calvin? They right in there . . ." Betty pointed at the precinct through the window.

"I'm not going to talk to them without my lawyer present, you know that, Betty." Betty turned away from him and rolled her eyes. Scar put his head down and admitted, "I just feel so bad about what happened, and it's fuckin' me up to think what would have happened to you if your aunt wasn't there to stop her because I know just how evil Gene was. I . . . I mean . . ." Scar began to grow so emotional, his voice began to crack. "I finally found someone that I love and don't know what I would do if something had happened . . ." Scar became too overwhelmed to continue and got choked up. He turned away. To her surprise, Betty knew he was shedding tears. She grew emotional as well. If Betty had any doubt, this single moment confirmed how deeply in love he was with her. She gently put her hand on his chin and pulled it toward her. Ashamed, he resisted at first, until finally, they looked in each other's watery eyes.

Before Betty knew what was happening, the words just flowed from her lips and she said, "I love you, Calvin."

Scar tried his best to wipe away the tears and reciprocated the sentiments. "I love you too, Betty." They kissed, and Betty felt their worlds realign. Scar pulled away, and his penetrating watery eyes grew cold and sharp. "From now on I'm never going to leave your side. If I have to go out of town, you are gonna be right there next to me, you understand?"

For the first time in Betty's short lifetime, she felt totally safe, totally secure. Without a thought, Betty put her whole life behind her and answered, "Yes, I understand, Calvin."

BOOK 5

The Finale

Chapter 37

As promised, Scar had Betty by his side every step of the way as they grew even closer. Betty officially moved into his mansion and brought everything she needed to accommodate herself, including her vast wardrobe, all her cosmetics and sleepwear, giving her no reason to go back to the crime scene, her home in Harlem. It was like a fairy tale to Betty. Scar pampered her with his lavish lifestyle, giving her a Platinum American Express Card that had unlimited spending privileges with her name embossed on the card.

For the first time, Betty actually felt guilty for all the spending she was doing, but Scar assured her not to worry and that he wanted to do it, which made him happy. In spite of it all, Betty never spent over five thousand dollars at a time, when she could've spent in the tens of thousands. But Betty became overwhelmed when he made her his general power of attorney, which gives her sweeping authority as an agent to act as principal in virtually any and all matters with regard to all of Scar's personal property.

Betty felt honored that he could trust her like that, because she literally had access to all his money at her fingertips. He constantly told Betty that he didn't like anything in his name because the government would seize it for his past crimes. Prior to Betty handling his affairs, he used his grandmother, but she hated having to spend her day away from the center to help him handle his affairs.

Each night and most mornings, he made deep passionate love to her, and she became totally intoxicated with him. They even talked about getting married next year after they got the news that she was officially cleared of all charges in Scar's wife's death. It was ruled a justifiable homicide.

Within months, Betty began to compromise her future plans and decided to put her education on hold. She became fully involved in building Scar's career and with the release of his very first album. Finally, Scar's scheduled tours slowed down, and he was able to stay in their own home more often instead of living out of hotels and their suitcases.

Betty was shaken by the past events, including the still unsolved murder of her best friend Fabian, so Scar bought Betty a small caliber weapon, a .25 automatic, for her safety. She grew up around guns from being around her Uncle Chubby, who took her to upstate New York many times, where she learned how to protect herself, so she wasn't afraid to use one like most girls. She simply kept it in her purse and forgot about it.

Betty stayed in contact through periodic calls with the

detectives working Fabian's case, and the pain from his death still haunted her. Even though she paid for his entire funeral services and his family thanked her for being a good friend, she couldn't help but feel guilty because of everything that happened in their friendship before he died.

Betty also felt and harbored guilt, because she found herself ducking her aunt and uncle's calls, putting a strain between them, and she felt horrible knowing one day she'd have to tell them the reason she put her education on hold—to support Scar's career. She knew they wouldn't understand, but she rationalized that she would make it up to them once she enrolled back in school.

Scar devoted every waking hour to completing his first album. Since he had a state-of-the-art recording studio built in the basement of his mansion with keyboards, computers, mixing boards, and a soundproof recording booth, he rarely left the house, spending up to eighteen hours a day hard at work.

One day while he was mixing one of the songs he created at his complex workstation, Betty smiled as the melodic smooth sound wafted and thumped through the expensive speakers.

"Sounds good," Betty yelled over the loud music.

Scar turned. "What?"

Betty repeated even louder, "I said it sounds great." Scar hit the control button, and the music came to a sudden cease.

"I said that the music sounds great," Betty said with glee.

Scar smiled sheepishly. "For real, you like it?"

She nodded her head. "Yes, it sounds dope," Betty joked. "You did that?" Scar nodded proudly. Betty was highly impressed. She knew little about music, but she knew quality sounds when she heard them.

"So, are you going to make all the music for your whole album yourself?" Betty asked curiously. Scar shrugged and answered, "Majority of it, why you ask?"

Betty was hesitant but said, "Because . . ."

"Because what?"

She shrugged her shoulder and said, "Well, I just finished watching a VH1 Behind The Music marathon yesterday, and all them other big-name rappers be getting those big-time producers like Timbaland and Pharrell to do it for them."

Scar didn't seem impressed. "So, what that got to do with me? You tryin' to say my tracks are wack?" he joked.

Betty goofily chuckled. "No, I'm not saying that. I'm just wondering why you wouldn't want them to make the tracks for you. I mean, this is your first debut album, and so shouldn't you want to ensure that it's the best?" She was being honest.

Scar showed no reaction and only stared at her, then said, "Let me explain something to you, Betty." He said in a calm, measured tone, "Ever since I could remember, I always knew I wanted to rap. I thought about music all day, went to sleep with music and woke up to it. It was, and still is, my only true friend, the only thing that I ever loved, besides my nana, and now you . . ."

Betty blushed like a schoolgirl.

He continued. "I wanted it so badly that I got to the point where I no longer had to write my shit down. I took it to memory and got thousands of songs that I keep all up in here." Scar pointed to his head.

"I know exactly what I want and how I want it to sound, and no producer could give me that."

Betty stared deeply at him, amazed at how when she thought she had him figured out, he'd thrown her a curve and say things so profound. Scar broke the silence and joked, "Besides, Timbaland and Pharrell charge hundreds of thousands of dollars for a beat."

Betty's facial muscles dropped, and her mouth flew agape. "Shut the hell up! Are you serious, Calvin?"

"Hell fucking yeah. Those niggas got it better than fucking rappers, because a rapper still got to sell albums to make money. They get their stacks straight-up front; they can't lose."

Betty was still confused and asked, "But your record company gave you money up front . . ." She chuckled and waved her hand around the expensive, state-of-the-art studio, "You got the biggest contract of any unsigned rapper in history. They talk about you on television all the time, and plus, you got me handling your banking business. You don't look broke to me."

Scar agreed with her assessment and shook his head, then stated, "True, but don't believe everything you hear on television or on the internet, because it's not like that."

Scar saw Betty was still confused. He explained, "A lot of entertainers can say they snagged, let's say, a million-dollar deal, but the truth is they really didn't, because it is based off of record sale bonuses, incentives if they make number one on Billboard or the Grammy Awards, a certain amount of downloads on iTunes, and shit like that, but in reality, if they don't reach a certain criteria and fall below that, they may get only two hundred and fifty thousand, and that's *before* the IRS even taxes that ass for half, so, they only really seeing a hundred stacks, if that. So when they blow that li'l piece of change, they won't see another red cent until the record company recoups every last dime."

Dumbfounded, Betty asked, "What about their shows? I deposited many checks from your shows and appearances, and never saw one less than fifty thousand."

"True, but I'm on the come up and can get that now, but no telling how long that will last. As they say, 'A rapper is only hot as their last album.' Besides, that ain't where the real money is at anyway."

Betty frowned, "It's not?"

"Hell no, the real, real money is in publishing, the mechanical rights."

Betty shook her head, clueless to what he was talking about.

Scar sighed. "Whoever makes the beats, does the production, writes hook, the bridge, writes the lyrics to the song and it's a hit, it can earn the person millions through public performances when that song is sung or played, recorded or live, on radio and television, as well as through other media such as the internet and live concerts. You eating off all of that."

This piqued Betty's attention. "You mean, every time a song is played on the radio, they have to pay you?"

Scar grinned cunningly and nodded his head and said, "Yep."

Betty nodded and smiled, "So, that's the reason you've producing all your songs?"

"You are finally catching on. All I need is one hit record and that can buy me a whole island if I wanted it," Scar admitted. "Why you think Berry Gordy from Motown still receives crazy millions a year even though he no longer owns Motown? Because that nigga still owns the rights to the songs, so he will never go broke cause they still play that old-school shit all over the world."

Betty thought about it and was definitely impressed. "But how do you know who's playing your songs? That would be impossible to track yourself."

"C'mon, Betty, you supposed to be up on this shit . . . BMI, ASCAP, SESAC . . ." Betty threw up her hands, still clueless.

"For you to be so smart, you sure are dumb," Scar said as he continued. "You suppose to be my backbone, and you should be knowing the game to protect my interest, Miss Summa Cum Laude," Scar teased.

"Fuck you, Calvin . . ." Betty said, smiling. "How the hell am I supposed to know all that technical stuff?"

Scar turned in his swivel chair and picked up a thick well-worn book from the side of the control boards and handed it to her. She accepted the book and read the cover, *All You Need To Know About The Music Industry* by Donald Passman.

"Now, if you read that book from cover to cover and learn this music game, we can be like Berry Gordy on an island somewhere never having to worry about money for the rest of our life."

Betty stared at the book in her hand with curiosity.

"And the first thing you need to brush up on is the royalties section, because I need you to fill out the paperwork so I can assign my ownership rights over to my granny. Okay? Now if you don't mind, I got a deadline to make."

Betty nodded and walked upstairs. She buried her head into the book for the remainder of the night.

Chapter 38

Life could not have been better for Betty and Scar. She became totally enmeshed in every aspect of his business affairs, handling everything from booking his events, scheduling his itinerary, to dealing directly with his lawyer, accountant, and record company. She also became the good wife and had dinner, bath, and sexual treats waiting for him when he arrived back at the mansion.

Then one day, out of the blue, things suddenly changed. Betty would call Scar whenever he was in the city visiting his grandmother or out of town performing, and he no longer picked up his phone as he once did. When he did come home, always in the wee hours of the morning, if that at all, they would argue and become distant.

Their lovemaking totally ceased. It had gotten to the point that they now slept in different rooms, and she no longer saw him anymore. Betty's head told her to leave and quit while she was ahead, but her heart stopped her cold, unable to leave him.

Then one morning, Betty grew frustrated and called up a cab and went to the city to visit the one person who knew her man best, Ms. Clara Mae—Nana.

Betty stopped off at her apartment building first to get her truck from the garage. She refused to go up to her apartment alone and went straight to Wagner Projects.

Clara Mae was so happy to see Betty, she placed her hand over her mouth and rejoiced in her presence. She quickly rushed her and hugged her tightly.

The two of them chatted like lifelong friends. Clara Mae saw the occasion befitting a full meal of fried chicken, red rice, fried cabbage, and cornbread. Betty didn't want her to go to so much trouble, but she insisted.

After dinner, it was already nighttime, just after eight, when they started doing the dishes. Betty put off questioning her about her grandson, unsure of what to ask, but she knew in her heart that she would have to, so she decided to make her inquiries after they finished.

DENNY MOE'S BARBERSHOP
9 P.M.

"No, fuck what you heard. The hardest killers to ever come out Harlem was Nicky Barnes, them Black Murder Inc. nig- gas, and Sweepers boys from Manhattan Avenue, Preacher and Alpo," said one middle-aged man that dressed signature old-school Harlem style, all-white Uptowns, a white oversized tee, beige cargo shorts, and a blue Yankee hat.

One of the barbers around the same age grimaced, "Get the fuck out of here with that bullshit! Alpo was a fucking snitch, and he don't get no points in Harlem for that shit."

Another man who was getting his hair cut by Denny Moe interjected, "So was Nicky Barnes. That nigga ratted too. And them Black Murder Inc. niggas was murder for hire, so they don't count. They wasn't a single person, they were crew."

Harlem had deep, complex fable tales of the Harlem underworld in every generation. Once a person reached a certain status in the drug and murder game, he gained legendary status of mythical proportions, being talked about and mulled over for years.

The first man with the white Nikes agreed. "Yeah, y'all right," he admitted, "they went out like bitches, but I know one for damn sure, a dude you can't deny. This ninja put more bodies in the cemetery than cancer. He turned off more ninjas' lights than Con Edison, and he *still* walking around Harlem to this very day."

The fifteen or so barbers, customers, and loiterers were all up in arms to hear the loud man's next choice of selections of elite Harlem killers. He smiled, knowing he had everyone's attention, and purposely let his words linger to build anticipation.

One of the barbers with a chair in the middle broke the silence and ordered, "Who, nigga? Spit it out."

Mischievously, the man turned his focus to the shop owner, Denny Moe, and said, "Denny's man."

With caution, the beer-bellied man stood up, looked around the entire shop before he continued, and said, "Black Chubbs."

Everyone looked at Denny Moe, and then turned their heads away, no longer wanting any part of the debate.

Denny Moe had the consummate poker face, never the one to wear his emotions on his sleeve, and simply continued cutting his customer's hair with precision. When he finished, he thanked his client humbly with a pound and hug, and finally turned his shrewd, sullen eyes to the loud-mouthed man and asked him to walk to the back with him. Moments later, they both walked from out of the back, but this time the loud-mouthed man was in deep apologetic mode, humbly telling Denny how sorry he was. Being the gentleman he was, Denny Moe simply told him, "No need to apologize any further. Just let it go." The man nodded and made a beeline for the door and exited the shop.

Everyone in the shop knew the man had violated an unwritten rule, because everyone in Harlem knew never to talk in detail about anyone in the underworld—truth or fiction, because Denny Moe had clientele in his shop from every walk of life, including government and city employees—like the police.

The barber who cut hair right next to Denny's chair shook his head when Denny got back to his station and said to ease the tension, "I think they are all wrong." He smirked. "Remember that young ninja a few years ago? I forgot his name."

The barber shook his head, "Man, I remember he had them drug ninjas on Eastside shook for a couple of years by robbing them."

He chuckled again. "It got to the point where they just gave that shit up to him on sight. He was on some Omar Little shit from the *Wire*."

Denny Moe, with another customer in his chair, asked curiously, "So, what happened to him?"

"Man, I heard he moved to Brooklyn for a while, but came back and just picked up where he left off and by now, them young boys had took over and wasn't having that shit and blazed him with bullets."

The man shrugged. "You know him too, because you used to cut his hair when we were at Level's. You was his barber. You remember, kinda light skin and fuckin' ugly. He looked like a cross between a wolf and a hyena."

Denny Moe suddenly paused and questioned, "What did you say?"

The man chuckled and repeated, "The nigga looked like a wolf and a hyena. You got to remember him. He had a small bald patch in the back of his head from being shot before. You remember him?"

Denny turned as if he finally remembered and quickly asked, "Where you said he from on the Eastside?"

The man was surprised by his boss's reaction and said, "He was from Wagner Projects."

Denny Moe cut off his clippers and put them down, then picked up his cellphone and headed out of the shop.

As Clara Mae and Betty sat in the living room having tea, Betty still hadn't come to grips with what to say, so she finally spoke from her heart and coyly admitted, "Ms. Clara Mae, I'm not sure if you are aware of this, but me and your grandson have been dating and living together for about three months now."

Ms. Clara Mae's face became radiant and aglow at the joyous news and looked up toward the ceiling and thanked God by praising Him. Amen.

Betty was so happy she took kindly to the news. In fact, she was overwhelmed. Clara Mae leaned forward, and they hugged as she wiped a tear from her eyes.

Smiling widely, Clara Mae took Betty's hands into hers and patted them and said, "I pray to God every night that he would find a good person like you and give up that lifestyle he was in."

Betty's smile faded. "Yes, I love him," she admitted. "In the beginning, things were wonderful, like a fairy tale, but one day he suddenly turned into a different person. He stopped taking my calls, staying out all night, and he won't tell me what's wrong."

Suddenly Betty's cellphone began to vibrate. She looked at the number. It was her Uncle Chubby. She ignored it and continued talking to Clara Mae. "Anyway, he just stopped talking to me, leaving me in his house in New Jersey for days by myself." Betty shook her head as her eyes began to well up. "And he won't tell me why."

Clara Mae gave her some comfort by patting her hands to let her know she had her support. Betty inhaled deeply and sighed. "I've even been helping him learn to read better, so maybe he can go back to school and get his GED or something, so those people he's with don't try to cheat him."

Clara Mae finally spoke. She appeared confused and gave her a slight chuckle. "Betty, I think you are mistaken. Dalvin can read very well. Why would he need a GED, when he already has a diploma?" Betty was taken aback and was utterly confused. She shook her head and frowned.

"Dalvin? Who is Dalvin?"

"Dear, Dalvin is my grandson, the one we are talking about now. He got everybody calling him by that Scar mess; I think I'm the only one who still calls him that."

Betty frowned, "I thought his name was Calvin."

Clara Mae's face turned blank and saddened. "Calvin is his twin brother." She shook her head and continued. "Calvin was just born bad. As long as I can remember he kept himself in some kind of trouble. He and Dalvin were like night and day. Dalvin was always into the books; Calvin was getting into trouble in the streets. At thirteen, Calvin came to live with me after his mother could no longer control him, and Dalvin stayed up in the Bronx with his mother, my daughter." Clara Mae sighed, and continued. "I did everything I could to handle that boy, but he just had the devil in him and wouldn't let him go." The elderly woman grew sad. "It was only a matter of time before them streets caught up with him, and they shot him down like a dog. They didn't kill him, but they done paralyzed him for good."

Betty could not process what she just heard and jumped to her feet while shaking her head. Seeing her confusion, Clara

Mae told Betty to give her a minute and left the room. She came out seconds later. "See, this was Calvin and Dalvin when they were about five years old."

She handed the eight-by-ten color photograph to Betty, whose mouth fell to the floor. They were identical twins. But what Clara Mae showed her next made her head spin.

"See," the older woman said to Betty as she extended her other hand and smiled. "This here is my most prized possession."

Betty, still flabbergasted, took in her hand what appeared to be a diploma. When she opened it, it nearly stopped her heart. It was a degree from Fordham University for a doctorate of psychology. Betty could no longer take it and began to grow dizzy, as if the air was being sucked out of her lungs. She had to get out of the apartment. "Ms. Clara Mae, I have to go. I'm sorry, but I have to leave."

Betty stumbled awkwardly toward the front door, fumbling with the locks, all the while Clara Mae asking her what was wrong, but she could not hear her. Betty finally got the door open and flew down the stairs and out into the evening air, breathing heavily.

Chapter 39

When Betty made it to her car, she jumped in and locked all the doors and cried her heart out. She pounded the steering wheel over and over again, cursing herself for being so stupid.

"Get it together, Betty, get it together," she repeated to herself over and over. Her cellphone was vibrating nonstop since she left Clara Mae's apartment, and in frustration, she reached in her purse to see who it was. Fifteen missed calls, all from Chubby. She couldn't possibly answer in the condition she was in and threw the phone on the passenger seat. Betty closed her eyes and let her cognitive thinking take over. Twenty minutes later, she opened her eyes, looked at her watch, and then picked up her smartphone and began searching. Betty knew Scar had an appearance that night, because she was the one who kept his phone updated, months in advance for him.

Bingo. Club Milli, on the west side of 57th Street.

Betty waited silently, parked directly across the street and out of sight, in front of a crowded Club Milli. She reached into the glove compartment to retrieve the note that her mother had given her when she saw her last. She stared at the cover that read *The New Blaise Diaries* and decided to read it for the very first time. She opened it and began flipping through the pages until she landed on the final page where her mother had written in big bold letters,

FINAL LESSON:
"A WOMAN CAN FAKE AN ORGASM, BUT A MAN CAN FAKE AN ENTIRE RELATIONSHIP."

Her mother's words hit her like a ton of bricks as her brain began to scramble, when just then, she was snapped out of her confusion when her cellphone rang. It was Uncle Chubby, and she answered it.

Three hours later, her patience finally paid off, when, exactly at 2 A.M., some familiar faces appeared—Scar, Diesel, and in tow, two exceptionally young, blonde, white girls, and about a dozen of Scar's young hardheads poured out of the club. Security unclipped the velvet rope, allowing them all to exit. A few of the onlookers tried to engage in conversation with Scar or get a picture, but they were all kept away by Scar's force.

Moments later, the very Range Rover Scar had been driving pulled up to the curb, and Scar's homie, Weeg jumped out and Diesel jumped in the driver's seat, with the young blondes following suit, getting in the rear. Scar embraced his partner Weeg and reached in his pocket and handed him a stack of cash, then embraced him once again and hopped in the passenger seat and they took off east, down 57th Street.

When Betty was sure they weren't riding in a convoy, she eased from the curb and started following them, ensuring she kept a good distance behind so she couldn't be seen. She didn't have to travel too long, because they stopped and parked on 59th Street and Central Park South at the pricey Trump Hotel.

Betty watched them all exit the vehicle. A parking attendant quickly ran toward the driver's-side door and Diesel chucked him the keys and slipped him a twenty dollar bill.

Betty watched their every move until they entered the hotel. Then she looked at her watch. It was 2:35 A.M. She let some more time pass. As she settled back in her seat, she reached over for her purse and searched inside for some gum. As she searched, she felt something heavy and cold; it was the .25 automatic that Scar had given her. She had forgotten she even had it.

After one hour and twenty minutes of waiting, she decided it was now time to catch him red-handed. She grabbed her purse and saw the .25 still sitting on the seat. Her first reaction was to put it in the glove compartment, but she changed her mind and put it into her purse and locked the doors.

The hotel lobby looked like a grand castle; no expenses were spared. Betty decided to put on her game face and walked the walk like she owned it and went up to the check-in counter and was greeted majestically.

"Welcome to Trump Hotel. Do you have a reservation?"

Betty smiled. "I'm not sure; my husband's flight was delayed and I don't know if he checked in yet. But, don't worry. I'll figure that out later. I'm too tired to wait for him as it is. I have an early flight tomorrow. Just give me a suite and leave him a message that I checked in." Betty reached in her bag and pulled out her purse that carried her many credit cards.

She handed the reservationist a Visa card and smiled. After the clerk punched in the computer, she said, "Ma'am, the only suites we have available are $2,700 a night."

Betty didn't flinch and smiled, "That will be good."

The clerk became sympathetic and reluctantly offered, "Mrs. Blaise, you mention that you don't even know if your husband has checked in yet. Wouldn't it be easier if I checked to see if he has already arrived before you spend another $3,000 for a suite?"

The poor girl fell right into her hands, Betty thought, as she smiled and thanked her.

"What is your husband's name?"

Poised, and taking a huge chance, Betty said, "Mr. Dalvin McGriff."

It seemed like forever as the girl punched his name into the computer, when suddenly, she smiled and said enthusiastically, "Yes, he checked in over an hour ago. He's in suite 706."

Betty didn't even have to ask for a key as the clerk had the key card already printed out and handed it to her. Betty smiled and followed the woman's finger over to the elevator.

When Betty got off on the seventh floor, the entire floor was totally quiet and empty. She looked at the room directions on the wall and followed the instructions. As she stealthily walked toward the room, she clandestinely reached her hand inside her purse, because she knew the cameras would be recording. When she arrived at suite 706, she suddenly began to tremble and shake. She took in a deep breath and slid the key card in the slot. Slowly, she turned down the door handle and crept inside very, very slowly. She heard sounds coming from the open suite area, which had connecting bedroom doors, one on the left and the other on the right. Gun in hand, she gripped it tightly and chose to try the room on the right first. She slowly turned the metal knob, careful not to make a sound and catch him in the act. She could already hear one of the girl's moans and grunting. When she peeked inside, luckily, the desk lamp was still on and she could see everything.

The white girl was in sexual bliss, hands squarely on the head of the person under the white sheets who ferociously was eating her out with reckless abandonment. The girl was in such a zone, she never even noticed Betty, who now was standing beside her. When the young girl finally opened her eyes, she jumped in fear. Betty quickly placed her finger toward her lips, signaling to her to remain silent, while pointing the weapon directly at her face—she did. Betty took a tight grip of the sheet and pulled it backward with all her might.

Horrified, Betty couldn't believe her eyes—it was the other white girl between the first one's legs.

The two extremely young white girls, no older than eighteen years old, shrieked, and begged for their lives. "Please don't hurt us."

One of the girls said, "I'm only sixteen."

Betty blinked twice, never expecting to see what she saw. As she stared into the two frightened girls' pleading eyes, the silence was deafening—until she heard, just in the adjacent room, what sounded like more grunting and squeals. Betty turned her attention back to the two young girls and whispered, "Get your shit and get out!" and gestured for them to gather their clothes.

As the girls raced around the room gathering their clothing, Betty threatened, "You were never here, right?"

Both girls nodded as if their lives depended on it. Betty waved the gun in the direction of the door and watched them tiptoe and stumble out of the suite door. She then set her sights on the other room's door and approached it, where the grunting, howling, and moans grew louder. A million uncertainties swirled around in her mind at that moment. Betty closed her eyes, sweat trickling down her brow; she took one last breath and pushed open the door.

What she saw next made her grow nauseated, causing her head to spin. Diesel was mounted behind Scar pounding his penis rapidly into his ass. As Betty pointed the weapon in their direction, her knees began to buckle, the room began to spin, and she began to stumble. The last thing Betty remembered just before she passed out was pulling the trigger of the .25 automatic in rapid succession, the smell of gunpowder, and the agonizing screams.

Two weeks later . . .

Bellevue Hospital Mental Ward

Scar got off the elevator on the fifth floor carrying a bouquet of red roses in one hand, and his other arm in a cast and sling. It was visiting hour, and it would be his first time seeing her since the shooting. Betty, apparently, was now in a near vegetative state, unresponsive—she'd snapped.

He casually checked in with the nurse at the desk and asked, "Ma'am, I'm looking for room 524 . . . Betty Blaise." The small Filipino nurse pointed him in the right direction, and he thanked her. He proceeded down the hall and stopped in front of room 524 and peeked in.

Scar strolled slowly inside and gazed at Betty, dressed in a yellow top and bottom patient garb with a flimsy blue robe hung awkwardly off her shoulders. Betty sat stiffly in a cheap plastic chair, gazing blankly and stoically out the window, with long, thick saliva dripping down the side of her mouth.

Scar smiled and grew relaxed. He placed the roses on her bed and sat down. He looked around the sparse room and noticed it looked more like a rubber room, with no identifiable items in the room that could be used to harm her or others. He stood up and walked over toward where she sat and studied her face.

He casually began snapping his fingers and waving an open hand in front of her eyes and said, "Betty . . . Betty. Are you in there?"

Betty didn't even blink. Scar circled around her as if he was inspecting her, and then abruptly yelled, "Boo!" behind her, hoping to get a reaction—but she didn't flinch. He now seemed even more relaxed and began pacing the room.

"Betty, Betty, Betty . . ." Scar said, shaking his head. "Look what the hell you got yourself into." He stopped directly in front of her. "Now look at you." He continued to pace the floor. "I talked to my grandma, and she told me she showed you the pictures and I guess you found out about my twin Calvin."

He paused as if he was gathering his thoughts and continued. "I did the right thing my entire life, while my brother got all the shine, all the attention, he got everything, and I didn't get shit but a pat on the head. He ran faster than me, played sports better than me, got better grades and never even had to study," Scar ranted. "Me and this motherfucker was identical twins. You couldn't tell us apart, and he was just as ugly as me, but he got all the attention; all the girls picked him."

Scar wore a preposterous frown. "Can you believe that shit? It was as if I was fucking invisible." He gazed at the ceiling as if he was reminiscent of the past. He chuckled. "I guess he just had that *'je ne sais quoi,'* that swagger. But you know what? That's when it all hit me. It wasn't about how you look, it's all about attitude." He shook his head as if he was reaffirming it to himself.

"Anyway, there was one thing I was better than him at, and that was rapping." Scar smiled as he thought back. "See, I knew more words than my brother, and rap is all about words, and that wound up being my one trump card over ole Calvin." Scar smiled wickedly at his small victory.

"Then at about thirteen years old, that's when everybody realized what I already knew, when I was caught sucking another boy's dick in the project staircase." He turned on his heels hoping to get a reaction from Betty, but she never flinched and he continued. "Yeah, had the whole Webster Projects talking about how I like boy-pussy, how I was a faggot. My brother hated me for that when he found out. After all, we were twins, so they didn't know which one of us was the cocksucker. He felt a need to fight any and everybody that looked at him funny. He never talked to me after that and became a neighborhood nightmare by fighting for my sins, so I guess I'm partly the reason he turned out so bad." Scar shrugged. "He shot this older guy when he was fifteen. That was about the time he went on the run and went down in Harlem with our grandmother."

He lowered his head down, and his tone turned feminine. "So in the end he got a bullet and I got a degree." He looked at Betty and admitted, "Oh, just like you, I studied psychology and was actually working my clinical residency at Harlem Hospital's Psychiatric Ward, but I grew bored and thank God I got assaulted by a schizophrenic patient."

Scar gazed at Betty and chuckled. "You ever wondered how I got this scar on the side of my face?"

Scar snorted as he giggled like a shy schoolgirl. He lowered his voice and admitted, "He was placed in my unit on a seventy-two-hour hold, and this man was fine. I just had to suck his dick. Since I was the treating physician, I prescribed him a higher dose of Risperidone. That shit will knock out an elephant, so I thought. So I snuck into his hospital bed, closed the shades, and went to town on that big dick." Scar beamed. "But I got too greedy and went back for seconds an hour later, and while I was sucking it again, he snapped out of it and pulled out a razor he must've had hidden and sliced me across the face."

He sighed and continued. "When they arrested him, the cops and staff didn't believe him. Shit, who's going to believe a schizo, right? I was on paid medical leave after that and decided to really try to be a rapper, but I was homo and people would have exposed me, plus, I had no background. So when my brother got shot and paralyzed, that was my opportunity to get in the game. My brother was known; he was a stone-cold killer so you couldn't question his gangster, and my skills took care of the rest. Everything was perfect, except for one thing—that bitch Hollywood Gene, my brother's wife, and she was the only person in the world who knew the truth about me. That I was homo, that I was impersonating my own brother."

He turned to Betty and admitted, "That was the secret that she had on me. Can you believe this dirty cold bitch wanted a million dollars to keep it a secret, and I was going to give it to her, but didn't trust her, so that's when I found your black ass."

Scar stared at her with a sly grin and explained. "See, I needed someone to be the sacrificial lamb, and when you came along, a gold digger like you, you became a perfect fit; smart, educated, and greedy, and you fell for it because my money was blinding you.

"You assumed I was a typical, uneducated, dunce of a

rapper. I knew only a bitch can take down a bitch, and I started feeding Gene information that it was you that was preventing me from giving her the million; even gave her your address, so you wind up killing two birds with one stone for me.

"You probably saved me millions, plus killed the bitch for me, so I don't have to worry if she sells my secrets to the tabloids for millions more. Smart, right?" Scar's face turned sour. "But I have to admit, the worst part about all this was when I had to fuck your pussy, girl." He frowned with disgust. "That was the worst of it, because I don't like no vagina."

Scar began to grow bored and rubbed his bad arm. "Oh, don't worry about being charged for the shooting. We blamed it on those white girls. The police won't find them, because they are only little girls and from wealthy families. Me and my lover Diesel put all the blame on them and got the Po-Po looking for twenty-five-year-old women, and we got shot when they tried to rob us, and you happened to be at the wrong place at the wrong time."

Scar chuckled. "You were a good shot though. Broke my wrist bone with the first bullet, and caught my man Diesel in his shoulder, but we a'ight." Scar ended with a smug sigh. "Oh, well, I got some interviews to do at some radio stations to talk about me getting shot." He smiled. "You shooting me was the best thing that ever happened to me. It boosted my gangster to legendary status."

As Scar walked toward the door, he added one final thing. "Oh, by the way, I don't know if you hear me or not, but don't even think about opening your mouth, because even if you are faking, which I think you are, don't forget you told me how Hollywood Gene REALLY got killed. So, if you want to involve your dear sweet Aunt Vonda in murder and conspiracy, try opening your mouth. I'll have your whole family locked up and I got the money to do it. And just remember, I'm still a licensed psychiatrist, and I'm much smarter than you."

Scar walked gingerly out of the hospital with a broad smile on his face and an extra pep in his step. Diesel pulled up in front of the hospital and Scar jumped in. He was so happy that he no longer had any loose ends to worry about. He leaned over and gave his longtime lover a passionate kiss and then said, "Let's go home, baby." He grinned as he looked out of the window at the horizon and thought, *I can finally live the good life as Scar the Hyena.*

Suddenly, Betty's face began to twitch, the saliva ceased to drip, and a small laugh escaped her mouth that slowly began to grow louder and more sinister. Her laugh grew into a crescendo, drawing the attention of the hospital staff. It was as if Betty was going mad. The orderlies rushed into her room and shifted Betty from her chair into a restraint chair. The head nurse finally got there with a full dose of Thorazine to administer to her. Just as they topped the syringe with the medicine, they all heard a loud *BOOM!*

So powerful was the blast that it shook the entire hospital. Everyone panicked, sure that it was a terrorist attack on the city, and ran for cover, but Betty knew better as she continued laughing all the while and peering out the window. In the distance she saw black smoke pouring from a burning black Range Rover.

Betty edged even closer toward the window. In the hospital's parking lot stood her Uncle Chubby, Auntie Vonda, and her good old friend José, waving to her.

Epilogue

Seventy-two hours after the mysterious car explosion that caused the instant death of the two male occupants, Scar and his longtime lover Diesel, Vonda, Chubby, and José escorted Betty out of the hospital's entrance. She was released from Bellevue Hospital with a clean bill of health. The fiery car explosion was quickly contained with minimum damage to the surroundings, caused by a faulty gas tank, so the authorities thought, burning alive both men and ending their lives in horrible deaths. They never had a chance.

Once again, Betty took care of and paid for the expenses of someone's funeral, comforting Ms. Clara Mae through the trying time of the death of her grandson.

Thanks to Denny Moe, Chubby's longtime friend from the barbershop, he realized that the man who was dating Betty wasn't who he appeared to be. Because of his fellow barber it finally hit Denny, that he had been the barber for the original Wagner Project terrorist, the man who looked like a cross between a wolf and a hyena, who had an ugly patch on his head. The man that Betty brought to the barbershop that night and whose hair he cut didn't have any patch on his head. He gave Chubby the heads-up of this bogus fuckery.

When Chubby finally reached Betty the night of the shooting while she sat in her truck staking out Scar at the club he informed her of what Denny Moe had told him. This information coupled with the information she had received from Clara Mae finally all made sense to her. She was being deceived all along and knew then and there what exactly had to be done. She told her uncle to contact two people that would set her next plans into action—his lawyer Mr. Russo and her old friend José the mechanic.

Over the next two weeks, Betty remained at her Aunt Vonda's apartment, preparing, calculating, and anticipating the release of Scar's debut album. The news of his untimely death was sensational, and he quickly reached James Dean and Tupac Shakur status. When Scar's album was released posthumously, he became the first rapper ever to have the highest grossing first week sales at 2.6 million albums, a record previously held only by rapper Eminem. His album *To Thy Self Be True* went on eventually to sell more than twenty million albums worldwide, the biggest-selling album in hip-hop history.

Betty Blaise had every right to be a part of Scar's success. She had an invested interest in the album. When Scar handed her the book, *All You Need To Know About The Music Industry* by Donald Passman, she had devoured the contents and realized that Scar was right about one thing when he said, *"Whoever makes the beats, does the production, writes the hook, the bridge, the lyrics to the song and it's a hit, it can earn that person millions."* She understood that person would be set for life. Betty took those words literally, and since she had power of attorney over Scar's business affairs, he never noticed that at the very last minute, after he had signed the papers from his record company, that Betty had assigned herself the sole ownership of the album's publishing rights. She went on to reap millions, ensuring that she would be wealthy for the rest of her life.

Several months later, Betty went on to receive the news she had been waiting for—the police had finally found and apprehended the killer of her best friend Fabian—it was her old boyfriend Main Man. He ultimately confessed to the murder. He tried to justify it by citing the night at the Cash Money party when he was virally embarrassed all over the world, which ruined his entire career. In addition to his statement, he copped to the fact that he was also the one who tried to run Betty off the road the night of Scar's B.B. King performance after stalking her for weeks. His motives were hatred and jealousy.

Posthumously, after the glory of Scar's demise, with over thirty million dollars in her bank account, compliments of the massive success of Scar's one album, Betty, in spite of the money, achieved her lifelong dream of becoming a doctor. She was now a licensed and practicing psychiatrist at the very place that Scar once practiced—Harlem Hospital's Mental Division. Even over the years, Betty did the right thing and ensured that Scar's grandmother and Scar's paralyzed twin brother, would be taken care of for life.

Since Betty long changed and manipulated Scar's paperwork, and will, she was the executrix of Scar's estate. She sold his mansion in New Jersey for two million dollars and endowed it all to Scar's grandmother. Soon after, and not surprising to Betty, Ms. Clara Mae donated all the money to the Wagner Project Senior Citizens Community Center. She still lives in the projects and spends her days at the community center and her nights taking care of her last and only grandson, the real Calvin McGriff.

Two years to the day that Betty was released from the mental hospital, Vonda, Chubby, Mr. Russo, and Betty waited in the reception area of the New York State Mental Institution for the Criminally Insane. They waited for nearly two hours in nervous anticipation when they finally heard the buzzing of the blue security controlled doors, and out walked a frail, middle-aged woman, carrying a simple and plain long brown bag with all the meager contents she had in the world.

At the sight of her mother, Betty was so overwhelmed she became frozen, hands over her mouth, tears streaming down her face, and keeling over. The day she had dreamed about as long as she could remember was finally happening—her mother—Annabelle Blaise—the original Fly Betty—was finally released, tasting freedom for the first time in twenty-five years.

Later that night Betty took out The Blaise Diaries, opened to a blank page and for the first time put to paper her own rules.

Betty's Five Rules To Any Relationship:

1. *Never love a man who doesn't love you back.*
2. *Never give a man who won't give back.*
3. *Never try to keep a man who doesn't want to stay.*
4. *Never cry over a man who won't cry over you.*
5. *And the most important—Every man GOT to know, from the very beginning, that if they should ever disrespect or violate you for ANY reason, they MUST know you would not hesitate to leave them without looking back.*

She paused before scribbling down a new rule.

6. *Final Rule—If you can't beat them . . . STEAL FROM THEM!*

About the Author

TREASURE E. BLUE is the Essence Magazine Best Selling Author of *Harlem Girl Lost, Get It Girls, A Street Girl Named Desire, Keyshia & Clyde* and a contributor to several anthologies. A former fire inspector with the New York City Fire Department, he is also winner of the Black Issue Book Reviews Urban Lit Book of the Year and a starred Kirkus Review recipient. Mr. Blue currently resides in North Carolina after living most of his life in Harlem, New York. He is a puolic speaker that shows today's youth the dangers of drug addiction and the importance of literacy.

Other Works by TREASURE BLUE

Novels
Get It Girls: A Harlem Girl Lost Novel
Harlem Girl Lost
Keyshia and Clyde
A Street Girl Named Desire

eShorts
Little Bad Girl 1
Little Bad Girl 2

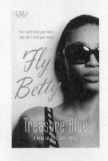
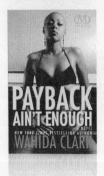
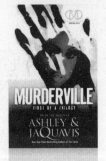

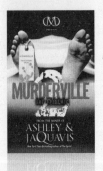